FREE FALL

AN M/M BODYGUARD ROMANCE

KATHRYN NOLAN

That's What She Said Publishing, Inc.

Copyright © 2024 Kathryn Nolan

All Rights Reserved

This is a work of fiction. Names, characters, places, and incidents either are the products of the author's imagination or are used fictitiously. Any resemblance to actual persons, living or dead, businesses, companies, events, or locales is entirely coincidental.

Editing: Faith N. Erline
and Jessica Snyder
Cover Design: Kari March Designs
Cover Photo: © Shutterstock

ISBN: 979-8-88643-947-2 (ebook)
ISBN: 979-8-88643-948-9 (paperback)

052924

This book is dedicated to Luke and Elijah—the heroes of this story. As I was leading them on their own journeys of self-discovery and liberation, they were leading me on my own.

NOTE FROM THE AUTHOR

Writing Luke and Elijah's love story was pure joy, from start to finish. Thank you for reading. It means so much to me! FREE FALL takes place in a fictionalized version of the Hamptons, on Long Island, in a town that I invented called Cape Avalon. While there are a few real-life landmarks, most of the location has been fictionalized and invented for the purposes of the story.

Luke and Elijah are both survivors of different kinds of abuse in their childhoods, and it's a theme that is discussed in the story. Their experiences occur off the page, are in the past and are not gratuitous.

If this is a topic that you're sensitive to, please be aware.

1

LUKE

The darkened windows of my father's estate glared down at me, as if they could smell last night's gin through my pores and disapproved. Even the stone gargoyles appeared especially smug amid the morning fog rolling in off the ocean.

I gave them a mocking salute before shoving open the heavy front door.

Once inside, my reluctant footsteps echoed up into the vaulted ceilings. The decor was a garish combination of old money meets Gothic revival: Victorian antiques, moody war paintings, splashes of gold and granite. Gauzy light flickered from the tarnished wall sconces, barely illuminating the double staircases curving up and away from me on either side like a pair of parentheses, closing me in.

On my eleventh birthday, I'd ridden backward down the left banister, flying off much too fast and crashing into a vase. It shattered instantly and I landed on top of the spiky porcelain pieces, promptly breaking my collarbone. My punishment had been waxing those banisters for the next three months—no easy feat with my right arm in a sling.

I turned toward the east wing just as sunlight sliced through the fog, catching me in the eyes. I winced and dropped my sunglasses back down. Going out with Harriet last night had been a mistake. She'd wrangled a babysitter at the last minute, then spent the evening trying to get me to flirt with the various hot people crowding the Shipwreck.

I didn't usually require much convincing, but my heart wasn't in it. Instead, I'd downed a series of gin and tonics that grew stronger as the night wore on. In the end, it was Harriet who left with the phone number of the pretty bartender.

Meanwhile, I felt like liquid fucking *death* and was about to subject myself to the mercurial whims of my family.

Portraits hung on the long hallway leading to the library. Most were of my father posing with various dignitaries—politicians and tech billionaires and celebrities, all flocking to the Hamptons for the beachfront privacy Lincoln Beaumont could guarantee with his luxury properties. There were a dozen more pictures of him with my current stepmother, Celine. A handful with my older brother, Preston, including one at his graduation from Wharton.

And at the very end, covered in a film of dust, was a photograph of my mother standing on the beach behind the estate, beaming as she held me as a baby.

I pressed my fingers to my lips, then touched her face. Took a deep breath and turned toward the mahogany doors. My brother shoved them open at the same moment, looking startled to see me and then pissed. Taking me by the arm, he dragged me a few feet away.

"Why are you wearing sunglasses inside?" he hissed. "You look ridiculous."

I flipped them up into my hair and grinned. "And a *good morning* to you too."

He sniffed. Frowned. "Drunk, really? At your own father's will reading?"

"Give me an ounce of credit. I'm not drunk. I'm severely hungover." I waved back at the library. "No one in there cares if I'm here anyway."

Preston examined me from head to toe, like I was a pesky mosquito daring to fly in his presence. He was the spitting image of Dad, right down to the permanent furrow in his brow. His skin was much paler than mine, which I assumed came from spending every hour of his day in an office. We shared the same mop of wavy black hair, but my blue eyes were our mother's, through and through.

He pulled a stray piece of lint from the blazer I'd tossed on as an afterthought. "After I take over the company, I expect you to quit that surfing job and join me here."

I arched an eyebrow. "Yeah, that's gonna be a big, fat, no thanks from me."

"You can't turn your back on your obligations, Lucas. You have *always*—"

"Good seein' you, bro." I brushed past him, clapping him on the shoulder. "Love our little chats."

Inside, the library had been rearranged to pull in extra chairs, a long table full of food and a minibar. I made my way toward the bucket of ice, filling a glass while I scanned the room. Orderly shelves of books climbed from the floor to the ceiling, and large windows opened out to the beach, where cattails waved in the breeze. A small team of my father's lawyers stood ramrod straight at the very front.

I recognized one of them—an extremely cute woman named Courtney who I'd once spent a passionate weekend with a few years back. Her cheeks flushed when she caught me staring. I sent her a wink and the ends of her lips twitched as she fought a smile.

Celine, my stepmother, posed gracefully in the front row, dabbing at her eyes with tissue. Those same eyes kept darting to a large envelope on the table, which I assumed was the will. The same will every single person in this room was hopeful would contain a massive payout just for them. I'd only dragged myself here because the lawyers had begged me to. Dad had likely left me something vaguely dismissive. The oldest shoes in his closet, maybe, or the loose change from his pockets.

My father's protection agents were stationed at each of the doors, their postures rigid, expressions inscrutable. Every person with money in town had at least one bodyguard, and it wasn't odd to see them trailing some up-and-coming movie star while they strolled the beach. But the amount of protection he'd employed was over the top and always had been.

Their cool assessment made my skin itch, brought back too many memories of them catching me when I'd snuck out past curfew. Or attempted to raid the high-end liquor stored in this very library. They'd made it clear from Day One they were here to serve my father, which included pretending not to notice his more monstrous behaviors.

My phone buzzed with a text from Harriet. *I know today will make you wanna bungee-back-flip off a bridge, or whatever it is you do for fun. Please know that I love you more than chocolate chip pancakes. He can't hurt you anymore, Luke. And for that, I'm grateful.*

A raw tightness had been coiling in my chest since the funeral, only a few days ago. I tapped my finger against the screen, re-reading her words. Then sent, *I'm glad he can't hurt you anymore either, sis. Love you more than hot fudge sundaes.*

I moved to the back of the room, hoping to slink into a chair and remain unnoticed. But I was intercepted by

Kenneth Bromley, the president of The Beaumont Group's board and my father's closest friend. He rose from his seat, his cheeks ruddy and his bald head shining. He was a short white man with a booming voice and a fondness for cigars. Not a fondness for me, however. After my mother died, Kenneth liked to swoop in with what he believed was the extra parental support Preston and I needed. It wasn't loving *or* supportive. It wasn't even particularly *nice*.

His eyes narrowed with disdain as he took me in, cataloging every wrinkle and loose thread. "I'm shocked to see you gracing us with your presence, Lucas," he said. "You look a mess."

I shrugged a shoulder. "Guess I'm just full of surprises today."

He huffed. "I didn't get a chance to tell you at the service how pleased Lincoln would have been to see the hundreds of people who came to pay their respects. There was even a line waiting out the church door and halfway down the block. You don't see things like that anymore."

Kenneth shook his head with a satisfied smile. "It just goes to show the power of his impact. Your father was a titan of industry, the most innovative businessman I've ever known. Cape Avalon owes him everything. Your brother will have big shoes to fill when he takes over."

"He sure will," I managed, raising my glass in response, then turning to the back. There was an empty chair, close to an open window. I inhaled the scent of late summer sun, saltwater, the last traces of morning fog. Outside, the waves were a sparkling cobalt blue.

Calmed by the view, I sprawled in my seat and pressed the glass of ice to my pounding forehead. One of the lawyers at the front of the room stepped forward, clearing his throat. Gregory Miller had served as the family's legal counsel since before I was born. He was a thin Black man with salt-and-pepper hair and a serious countenance. The sun glinted off the silver letter opener as he unsealed the will.

The room fell silent.

"Thank you for being here today for the reading of the last will and testament of Lincoln Branson Beaumont," he said. "Public will readings are quite unconventional these days, but Mr. Beaumont insisted it must be done. I will begin with personal financial holdings and assets, followed by those of his business, The Beaumont Group."

I eyed my brother, sitting piously in the front row. Gregory began reading and the air filled with a tangible anticipation. Dad had left large charitable donations for the Metropolitan Museum of Art, where he'd served on the board, and to Harvard's endowment. Locally, he'd given gifts to the Cape Avalon Historical Society, the performing arts center and a nearby food pantry.

The estate we were sitting in was left to Celine. The penthouse in New York and the cabin in Vail, as well as the private jet, the helicopter, and the luxury cars parked in the garage, went to my brother. My right knee shook with each item mentioned. I tried not to think about Harriet and my nieces, the jagged pain on her face when she first revealed what my father had done to her and her mother.

Gregory paused before his next announcement. A few hushed whispers quieted. In the silence came the clinking of ice against glass, the crashing of the waves outside.

"And finally," he continued, "I leave the entirety of the Beaumont Group to my son"—Preston rose from his chair—"Lucas Emerson Beaumont."

A rush of shocked and furious sounds followed the announcement. The entire room turned as one, gaping at me like a bunch of enraged owls. As if I'd been the one to kill my father and not the heart attack he'd had on the treadmill. Preston was already moving toward me, lips curled in a snarl.

Warily, I pushed to stand. "Uh...what was that again?"

"TBG was left to you," Gregory said.

Stunned, I offered the room my most charming smile. "Well...holy fucking shit."

2

LUKE

Preston paced back and forth like an angry bull, his suit jacket flaring open with each spin. Every other minute, he stopped to slam his hand onto the desk and yell, "This is *not* happening to me."

I was draped on the couch in my father's office with an actual ice pack on my forehead, wincing at my brother's blurred motion.

"*Preston.*" I sighed. "Will you please, for the love of god, *stop shouting*."

Another slap of his hand. "This is *not* happening to me."

"For fuck's sake," I whispered, sitting up and tossing the ice pack on the seat next to me. Preston whirled past once, twice, a third time. Behind him, Gregory stood next to the desk with an organized selection of documents in front of him. My father's last will and testament, which Gregory told us had been changed just three months before his death.

I shoved my fingers through my hair before focusing on our family's lawyer. Gregory appeared nonplussed by my brother's antics, although I had to imagine he'd seen worse over the years. I sent him a sympathetic smile and he nodded in response.

Preston halted midstep and pointed a finger at my head. "*You* did this, didn't you? Convinced Dad to change his will, to steal what had always been *promised* to me?"

"How in the hell would I have done that?" I asked.

"Charm him, like you do everyone else."

I dropped my elbows to my knees. "We're talking about the same dad here, right? Narcissistic asshole who took great pleasure in making us miserable when we were kids?"

He turned away from me. "It's poor manners to speak ill of the dead."

"Preston," I said, softening my voice. "Dad and I haven't had a real conversation in five, maybe six years? When would I have been using my powers of persuasion to change his mind? I don't even want the company."

TBG was in the business of luxury property development and had satellite offices all across the country, with the biggest in New York City. But Dad had been born in the town of East Hampton, here in the village of Cape Avalon, and had conducted business from the estate for the last decade.

Building swanky condos for the coastal elite wasn't exactly my area of expertise *or* my passion. Nor was continuing a legacy I didn't believe in.

"What did you say?" Preston asked.

"I don't want it. I've never wanted it."

He turned to Gregory, jerking his chin my way. "Does that matter at all? Luke doesn't want it and I've been prepped for this role my entire life."

Gregory's gaze slid my way. I shrugged. "I know this stuff is *legally binding* or whatever, but what's a guy gotta do to get out of this situation? The quicker, the better."

"You would say that," Preston muttered.

I quirked an eyebrow. "So you *want* me to inherit the company?"

My brother's face went red. "There must be a way out, Gregory. What do we do?"

The other man's lips pressed into a thin line. "You've inherited a corporation, Lucas. As the owner, your father was the majority shareholder, shares that you now own."

"Can I sell it then?"

"You *wouldn't*," Preston said with a growl.

"You could," Gregory replied. "But TBG's outstanding debts would need to be paid first and they're substantial. You'd be left with practically nothing. And I should mention that your father arranged for there to be consequences in the event of your noncompliance. He expressed concern that you would attempt to, in his words, shirk your responsibilities."

I tried to catch my brother's eye. These were the exact kinds of sibling rivalry mind games our father excelled at, pitting us against each other to win the table scraps of his affection. But Preston ignored me, and I was reminded yet again of our diminishing solidarity. How quickly he abandoned me as soon as Dad knighted him as the firstborn and presumed savior of our family. An heir-in-training.

What the fuck had he been *thinking*, leaving it all to me?

"What kind of consequences?" I asked.

Gregory cocked his head. "You don't inherit your trust."

My stomach pitched to the floor. We were set to inherit at the age of thirty—three years away for me, one for Preston.

"Yeah, that's not gonna work," I drawled. "I need that money."

"That's all this ever was to you," Preston said, pacing

again. "Partying your way through the South Shore. Biding your time until you can fuck off with your millions."

My fingers flexed, curling into fists. Some arguments, this one in particular, were never worth it. And some secrets were too important to tell.

"If you sell the company, Lucas, you don't inherit your trust," Gregory continued, ignoring my brother. "Given the finances, your trust is worth considerably more than what would be left after a sale. If a sale is even possible at this point."

I released a jagged breath. "What you're saying is, Dad saddled me with a sinking fucking ship?"

"That's one way to describe it," Gregory said. "But Preston, failure to comply affects you as well. Your father made it clear that in the event of his death, Lucas was to inherit and your position at the company would be terminated."

My brother's face turned an alarming shade of red. "I beg your pardon?"

Our lawyer slid the documents across the desk with a single finger. "He allowed two weeks for you to find a suitable replacement. If you try to evade this mandate, you forfeit your trust as well."

Preston snatched up the will. Then sent me a glare that scorched my skin. My hands rose like he was a dangerous animal. "Preston, I'm so—"

"*You did this*," he hissed.

"*Dad* did this," I snapped. "Don't come for me when you know this kind of shit was his favorite brand of emotional torture. I'm as shocked as you are."

But he didn't respond. Simply whirled out of the room with a barely concealed snarl of frustration. When I finally turned back to Gregory, he wore a mild expression with something almost like compassion in his eyes.

"You, Lucas Beaumont, are now the owner and CEO of TBG," he said softly.

He didn't even have to say the next part.

And there was nothing I could do about it.

3

ELIJAH

The married man on the lounger across from mine was having an affair.

Not with the woman next to him. They wore matching rings, so she was almost definitely his wife. But he'd been on my radar for the entire week, ever since I'd landed on this balmy Caribbean island.

I studied him from behind my aviators as pleasant waitstaff floated by, offering frothy drinks I was supposed to be enjoying. Every single one of his work calls took place out in the open, so loud they were practically performative. But when his wife was distracted or off to the bathroom, he texted with the fury of a man with a secret. All while wearing an expression I knew well—a smug superiority, the look of a man who believes he's getting away with it.

My father had looked like that.

The couple departed the beach after lunch, leaving me alone and without distraction. I tried to relax into the lounge chair, acutely aware of my rigid spine, the ache in my jaw. My gaze wouldn't settle, constantly scanning the never-changing aquamarine ocean surrounded by palm trees and pink umbrellas. Soft music and bursts of conversation blended with the gentle sound of the waves.

The scene was idyllic. Tranquil. Still, plenty of places for danger to lurk. It was easy to assume danger craved darkness, but I knew it could thrive in the light, ingratiating itself like a consummate host.

So when my phone rang, I didn't flinch. Just picked it up. "Knight speaking."

"It's Foster," my director said. "I'm sorry to interrupt your vacation."

I was already standing and on the move. "It's not a problem."

"It's your first one in years and I had to force you to take it."

"*Forced* is a strong word, sir," I countered. "You issued strongly worded advice and I was smart enough to listen."

"And you're enjoying yourself?" he asked.

I punched the button for the elevator and stretched my fingers, sore from where I'd clenched them. "Yes, sir. What's the problem?"

My boss hesitated. "Lincoln Beaumont passed away a week ago, on the same day you flew out for your vacation. He had a heart attack on his treadmill. Ripley was on duty and performed chest compressions but he was dead by the time paramedics arrived."

Something behind my sternum flinched at the news. Shock, but not grief. I'd been Lincoln Beaumont's lead protection agent for five years. He was courteous to me but cold. Ruthless in his business endeavors, though I hadn't met a CEO who wasn't. Still, I'd been this man's shadow and couldn't quite comprehend that he was gone.

"I'm sorry to hear it." I cleared my throat. "Why didn't you alert me? I would have flown back immediately."

"That's exactly why," Foster said. "There wasn't anything you could do about it and I'd prefer you well-rested before you step in as director and your chances of taking a vacation are even lower. Besides, it's looking like his death was natural. No foul play involved."

My eyes narrowed. "They're sure of that?"

"As sure as they can be until the autopsy report is released. But given his age and history of heart problems, his doctor thinks it was nothing more than a heart attack."

I was somewhat relieved to hear that, but it didn't answer the many questions I had about who'd been threatening him before he died. We'd caught a tail more than a few times. He'd received menacing voicemails and emails. And his office had been broken into twice. It was one of the many reasons I'd resisted the timing of this mandated vacation for as long as I could.

"You haven't heard the worst of it," Foster continued. "They unsealed his will yesterday and it was revealed that the younger son, Lucas, would be inheriting the company."

The elevator doors slid open and I strode through them, finding my hotel room and pushing inside. "That's a mistake. It was always intended for Preston to take over."

"No mistake. Per Ridley, yesterday's reading came as a major surprise to everyone there."

I hauled my suitcase onto the bed and flipped it open. The news wasn't sitting right with me. I'd never met the younger Beaumont. From what I'd observed, he and his father had no relationship whatsoever. And from what I saw in the local tabloids, Lucas was a rich party boy who lived off his family's money and had never held down a real job.

Lincoln leaving it to Lucas didn't make any fucking sense.

Foster sighed. "Elijah, I know you're not due to return for a few more days, but I'd consider it a great favor if you could fly back and meet with Lucas as soon as possible. Lincoln was set to renew our contract by the end of next week, but we'd been embroiled in negotiations with his lawyers. He was unhappy with us, saw the new threats as our failure—which wasn't a great launching pad for the increased contract rates I'd requested."

An icy guilt twisted in my gut. Every single breach of our security systems was a failure.

My failure.

"The value of the Beaumont contract cannot be overstated. I need you to meet with him and convince him to sign. Lincoln was already wavering and his son's motives are a mystery."

"I'm already packing, sir," I said, laying a neatly folded shirt in my suitcase. "He'll need to get up to speed on his father's recent threats and mounting concerns. My impression is that Lucas Beaumont is walking into this job without any background information whatsoever."

"Thank you, Knight," he replied. "There's a reason why you're taking over for me when I retire."

He ended the call and I proceeded to pack as quickly as possible. Mentally checking off the list of things I needed to do next relaxed my spine faster than any tranquil vista could. There were plane tickets to book, a team I needed to check in with, Lucas's file to study.

My promotion to director of Regent Executive Security Specialists was all but guaranteed, making me the youngest person to assume the role in the company's history.

That didn't mean this next part would be easy. The exact opposite, in fact. Rich party boy or not, Lucas's safety would remain my highest priority.

I'd convince him to sign that contract.

And then I'd guarantee I never failed again.

4

ELIJAH

One day later I was back in Cape Avalon, parked in front of Lucas's home.

It was typical for a cottage in the Hamptons—small, though extremely expensive given its location right on the beach. It was ranch-style, pale yellow siding with blue shutters and large windows. A hammock was strung between two trees in the front yard and a sandy surfboard leaned up against the garage.

From reading his file this morning, I knew that Lucas was twenty-seven, a decade younger than me, and a graduate of NYU. Contrary to the tabloids, he did, in fact, have a job. Had been an instructor at a local water sports company since high school, teaching people how to do things like surf and wakeboard. In the offseason, he worked full time at the South Shore Bookshop on Main Street.

And he'd invited me to meet here, at his house, instead of the offices at his father's estate.

I stepped out of the black sedan and rebuttoned my suit jacket. Ripley wasn't posted outside and no other protection agents were in the immediate area. Concerned, I knocked at the front door and listened for signs of life inside. There came the sound of loud, upbeat music—but no answer. No answer after the second, third and fourth knocks either. Given the threatening letter that had arrived at the estate this morning, I was about to use my shoulder to break down the door.

But then it swung open to reveal Lucas Beaumont wearing swim trunks and running a towel through his wet hair.

Shirtless.

I'd studied the picture clipped to his file and knew he had black, wavy hair like his father and blue eyes like his mother. The file didn't mention how carelessly the curls fell across his forehead. Or his deceptively long lashes. And the lopsided grin he offered me was all charm.

A dozen alarm bells went off in my head.

"You're my dad's bodyguard Elijah, yeah? Come on in," he said, kicking the door shut behind us and moving through a sitting room filled with morning light and built-in bookshelves. I scanned the open area—teal rugs, a few paperbacks stacked up on a coffee table, a lighter next to a half-finished joint. The room led directly to a kitchen with barstools pulled up to a counter and a large bowl of fruit next to a blender.

Beyond that were wall-to-wall windows and a glass door, revealing a stone path that led directly to the ocean.

Lucas tossed the towel across a chair and grabbed a short-sleeved button-up. I ignored the rippling of his back muscles as he shrugged it over his broad shoulders. "Sorry I'm a bit late," he said. "The surf was heavy this morning and I had to get out there. You surf too?"

"Absolutely not. Mr. Beaumont, I'm—"

"You want coffee? Water? Not to brag, but I make a mean smoothie."

I shook my head. "No. Thank you. Mr. Beaumont, I'm—"

"Luke."

My brows knit together. "I'm sorry?"

He sprawled on a large white chair, hooking an ankle over his knee. His shirt was unbuttoned and he tapped the center of his chest. "I'm Luke. Sometimes Lucas, depending on my mood. But definitely *not* Mr. Beaumont."

I hesitated. "Luke. I'm sorry for your loss. Your father was a wonderful person to work for."

Frustration—or maybe pain—rippled across his face so fast I wondered if I imagined it. Then he cleared his throat. "So I've been told."

An awkward pause lingered following his words. Scanning the room again, I said, "Where's your bodyguard? He was due here hours ago and you should have someone with you at all times, especially given your father's...of *your* current security risks."

His face brightened. "Oh, you mean Ripley? Super nice guy, but I sent him home. He put up a fight but I pulled the *technically I'm your boss* card and he left."

"He just...left you," I said flatly.

That charming smile reappeared. "I can tell you're pissed, so please don't yell at him, okay? It was my call. If you're mad at anyone, be mad at me."

I reined in the spiky edges of my irritation. Smoothed a hand down my tie. "Mr. Beaumont—"

"Luke."

"*Luke*," I said, more forcefully than I intended. "Per the contract your father had in place, you're to have round-the-clock protection."

He stood and moved closer to me, bringing the scent of

saltwater and sunscreen. "I looked into your company, Elijah. TBG's contract with Regent Executive Security Specialists ends next week."

"I'm here to walk you through re-signing it," I said with a nod. "It's merely paperwork at this point. Shouldn't take us more than a few minutes."

He spun on his heel and sauntered back toward the kitchen. "Dude, that shit is *expensive*."

"You can't pay too high a price to protect a person's life."

Luke poured himself a cup of coffee, then studied me from across the room. I held his gaze, ignoring the sweep of his eyes along the lines of my suit. "Let me ask you a question. You were by my father's side for five years, correct?"

"Yes, sir."

Another smile appeared, this one lazy. Wicked. The back of my neck went hot. "Calling me *sir* won't be necessary. But to my point, how many times was my father's life actually at risk?"

"In the months before your father died, the volume of hate mail and death threats he received increased. So much so that we involved local law enforcement."

"But were any of those threats successful?" he asked.

"No, they were not. Thankfully."

"Then why do I need your protection?"

I arched an eyebrow. "They weren't successful because he had me. *Sir*."

His low, raspy chuckle filled the space between us. "My father was an arrogant narcissist who believed he was the center of the world. He received death threats because he was a dick. Contrary to what my family has probably told you, I'm *not* a dick. And for however long my head bears this goddamn crown, I won't have some babysitter in a bespoke suit following me around, telling me what I can and cannot do."

A muscle in my jaw ticked. "You're deeply misunderstanding the relationship between a protection agent and their client. My team and I are not your *babysitters.* We're here to analyze threats, to protect you and your assets. You just inherited a billion-dollar company, Luke. That makes you a high-value target."

Luke closed the distance between us, so slowly that the air in the room seemed to rise in temperature. A few drops of water still clung to his tangled curls. "I lived my life just fine before you got here, Elijah."

I held my tongue. He'd lived *just fine* because of his family's significant wealth while my own scraped by with nothing.

"And I mean that literally," he continued. "Preston always had bodyguards but I never did."

I blinked, wrenched from my thoughts. I'd overseen his father's extensive team but someone else was in charge of the family members. "You've had no surveillance? Why not?"

Luke caught my eye. "My father protected what was valuable to him."

He brushed past me and opened the front door. "Anyway, thanks for coming all the way out here, especially since this meeting could have totally been an email. I'm not re-upping your contract. Nice to meet you, though."

Total shock had me stepping outside before I realized it. The Beaumont family was our most lucrative contract—and Foster's directive on this had been clear. A loss like this would be financially devastating to the company. I wasn't about to let it happen.

Couldn't let it happen, not if I wanted to keep that promotion.

Luke moved to shut the door, but I grabbed the side of it, keeping it open. His eyes widened, and some primitive part of me liked that I had a couple inches on him. Liked that he had to look up, just a little, to meet my gaze.

"I cannot *begin* to describe the mistake that you're making," I said gravely. "A letter arrived at your father's office early this morning. With *your* name on it, implying that you have information they want and they'll stop at nothing until they get it. Whether this letter is connected to these other recent threats, I don't know. What I *do* know is that this is the absolute worst time to be rid of the people meant to keep you safe."

His throat bobbed, forehead briefly creased. But then he plastered on another disarming smile. "I appreciate your concern. I really do. If it makes you feel any better, as soon as I figure out some legal loophole, I'm outta here. But I'm sure Preston would hire you back in a heartbeat."

I flattened my palm against the door frame. "Luke, you need to listen—"

"I'll see ya around, Elijah," he said cheerfully.

Then slammed the door in my face.

5

LUKE

I curled my toes in the cool sand and watched my coworkers mimic how to stand up on a surfboard for a small cluster of late-season tourists. Well, former coworkers now, at least until I figured out how to escape the situation I found myself in. I'd worked as an instructor for Cape Avalon Water Sports nearly ten years now. My winters were spent at the South Shore Bookshop, where a decent chunk of my paycheck went to purchasing new thrillers and used paperbacks.

But it was just easier this way, taking a leave of absence from both until I could wrangle my life back to normal.

My bosses had been stunned at the news, but I'd mustered up my cheeriest smile, even as a rising tide of dread filled my body. The dread of being back in that office, back in that house, surrounded by people who believed my father had been a genius. Tasked with running a company I knew nothing about and had absolutely no interest in.

The sharp, panicky fear I got whenever I found myself ensnared in Dad's many mind games. And this one—

Surprise! I left my legacy to the son I despise!—was the most fucked-up one yet.

A set of waves curved into beautiful barrels, shimmering beneath the mid-September sun. This was the beginning of every local's favorite time of year—when the beaches emptied, the crowds thinned, the streets quieted. I watched a surfer dip low beneath one of those barrels and felt a harsh yank behind my sternum. It was pure yearning, to be back in the ocean where I belonged, where I'd always belonged.

Weather-permitting, my mother had started every morning with a brisk swim in the ocean on the beach behind the estate. She'd taught me the ocean was an escape, a liberation from whatever plagued us on land. And I'd sought that liberation in as many ways as I could—in cages, surrounded by sharks. On Jet Skis and speedboats and wakeboards.

Mom had been dead for years by the time I came out to my father, foolishly walking into his office and declaring, as proudly as I could, that I was bisexual. Foolish because I'd expected compassion, or at the very least curiosity, from a man who'd shown me neither. He hadn't even looked up from the file he'd been reading. Simply said, "I don't care what the hell you call yourself, Lucas, as long as you marry a woman."

After, I'd done what my mother taught me—sought out the sea. I'd surfed till well past dark, crying rage-y, teenaged tears through most of it.

"*Uncle Luke!*" a tiny voice to the left of me shrieked.

That was the only warning I got before my nieces barreled into me on the sand, knocking me off my feet. I opened my eyes, squinting into the sun, and found my half sister, Harriet, beaming down at me.

Laughing, I rose onto my elbows while Lizzie and Rory scrambled close for a hug, looping their small arms around my neck. "Now isn't this the best kind of surprise."

Harriet kicked off her shoes and joined me on the beach, reaching over to tickle Lizzie until she squealed. Rory was already examining a buried seashell. They were four and two, respectively, and looked just like their mother.

"You'd mentioned coming by here to hand in your notice and we happened to be in the area," Harriet said, nudging her shoulder against mine. "We thought Uncle Luke could use a hug."

Lizzie snuggled in closer to me, placing her tiny palm against my chin.

"You thought correctly." I turned to look at Harriet. Her long, hot pink hair was in a high bun and her colorful tattoos danced up both bare arms. "Thanks, sis. It's appreciated."

She scrunched up her nose. "You still owe me details from the will reading. Given that you're quitting today, I'm guessing something's up."

"Technically, you still owe *me* details about the cute bartender from Thursday night."

"Oh, you mean Kat?" She gave a shrug. "We've been texting."

My eyebrows shot up. "*And?*"

"*And*...she's beautiful and funny and totally down to date a single mom. I'm seeing her this weekend."

Rory toddled over and presented me with the seashell she'd found. "Of course she's down to date you," I said. "Want me to babysit? I can order pizza and we can watch *Encanto* for the eleventh time. I'll cry all the way through it, also for the eleventh time."

Harriet wrapped me in a bear hug that almost toppled me over again. "We're so lucky to have you, Luke."

I held on to her for longer than usual, finally realizing how much I'd needed my sister. We'd first met when I was eighteen and she was sixteen, after she'd found me on social media and sent a message: *I know this sounds totally random but I think you're my half brother? Would you ever want to get coffee and talk about it?*

The Beaumonts held a kind of celebrity status in the Hamptons, so it wasn't the first time I'd received messages from complete strangers claiming to know secrets about my family. About my father. I'd known the truth of him by then. Knew that he'd been cheating on my mother, even during the year before she died.

So when Harriet sent a blurry picture of my dad, sixteen years younger, posing with her mom at some boozy-looking boat party, a sick curiosity had me replying, *I'd love to meet up.*

Harriet became the sibling and best friend I'd always wanted, connected by our shared queerness, our mutual disdain for our dad, our persistent loneliness. Dad had a years-long affair with Lois, Harriet's mom. When he found out Lois was pregnant, he abandoned her, refusing any contact and ignoring her many requests for him to meet his daughter.

And he provided not a single cent in financial support. Lois had only been able to afford to live in the famously wealthy Hamptons because she worked for a family in Southampton that allowed her and Harriet to stay in one of the small guest houses on the estate. My sister was keenly aware of my family's exorbitant affluence while her mother barely had enough money to pay bills each month.

After living in upstate New York for a few years, Harriet

had moved back into that same guest house with her daughters to take care of Lois, who'd been diagnosed with early-onset Alzheimer's. And while the family she'd worked for was sympathetic to what Lois was going through, Harriet worried they'd lose their housing soon.

"Something bad happened at the reading, didn't it?" Harriet asked softly, pulling back to study my face.

I blew out a long breath. "Dad left TBG to me. Left it to me with a whole bunch of weird and manipulative strings attached if I don't do as ordered. The board is pissed at Dad, but also at me, mostly just for existing. Preston's plotting my grisly murder as we speak."

Her mouth dropped open. "Holy shit, holy shit, holy shit."

"That's what I said."

"But *why*?" she asked.

"Who knows?" I raked a hand through my hair. "He used to do stuff like this to me and Preston all the time, but on a smaller scale. Apparently he made this change three months ago, which I had absolutely nothing to do with. Not that anyone believes me."

She made a sympathetic sound, and I flashed her a grin. "I'll be okay, I promise. I took your earlier advice and booked a bungee jump appointment starting in"—I glanced at my watch—"twenty minutes. A little bit of adrenaline-soaked euphoria will clear my head and help me figure out how to get out of this mess."

Harriet chewed on her bottom lip, reaching across me to brush sand from Rory's hair. Rory stuck her tongue out, dropped another shell into my palm, then sprinted back toward the makeshift sandcastle she was building.

"Maybe...maybe this isn't the worst thing," she said softly. "What if you made TBG better? Developed something other than luxury housing and fancy shopping malls? You know what it's like for us right now. The family Mom used to work for is well within their rights to ask us to leave that guest house at any moment. And there isn't anywhere I can afford here on a single parent's salary."

I grabbed her hand and squeezed. "I'd never let anything bad happen to you. You know that, right?"

She squeezed back. "I do, and I love you for it. But not everyone has a rich brother providing a safety net. There's a way to fix things around here and *you* could be a part of that. If anyone could do it, it'd be you."

I sent her a look. "You're sweet to suggest it, but I don't want it, Harry. Not one piece of it. It's all wrapped up in continuing Lincoln Beaumont's legacy, which you and I know is complete bullshit. I won't do it."

Understanding dawned on her face. "What are the weird and manipulative strings attached?"

I paused. "Failure to comply means I don't inherit my trust fund. Which is not an option."

"Oh, Luke." She winced. "Please...please don't do anything on my behalf. I'm being completely serious here. This is just another way for Lincoln to control you from the grave. We can find another way. We can."

I was already shaking my head. "We're in this together, sis. I'm gonna find a way out *and* keep the trust. There's gotta be a loophole; I just haven't found it yet." I pressed my chin into Lizzie's soft curls. "Everything goes to you and your daughters. That's still my plan."

Harriet and her mother had struggled their entire lives. And now my sister was back home, providing long-term care to Lois while astronomical medical bills piled up around her. And Harriet's ex-husband paid little in child support. As per Beaumont family tradition, I'd received a large sum of money upon graduating from college, with the expectation I'd use it to secure a business degree before coming back to work at TBG.

I'd done neither—I'd bought my house instead and given most of the remainder to Harriet and my nieces.

My trust fund was the final thing tying me to that family. Once Rory's and Lizzie's futures were secure, I could say goodbye to the Beaumonts for good.

My sister slowly pushed to stand, ruffling my hair before calling Rory back. "We should let you go make that bungee appointment. But I want you to know...I think you're making a mistake. Walk away from all of it, Luke. You already do so much for us, have already *paid* for so much. We love you regardless, and I know...I *know* what being back at that house is like for you. The trust isn't worth it."

I swallowed past a knot in my throat. "If I walk away, he wins. And I can't let that happen, Harry. Besides, that trust fund is *your* money. Money he rightfully owed to your mother, money he owed to your childhood. I'll be fine; you don't have to worry about me."

Her shoulders slumped in response, but then her eyes sharpened toward a point past my shoulder. "Um...an extremely handsome man in a suit is staring at you, Luke."

Curious, I followed her gaze to find Elijah Knight standing in front of a sedan with one hand clasped around the other wrist, stone-faced.

"Fuck me, that's my dad's bodyguard. Technically, *my* bodyguard, though I fired him yesterday."

"*Luke*," my sister warned.

I rose to my feet, handing her a sleepy Lizzie. "I don't need twenty-four seven protection. It's over the top."

She pinned me with a glare. "We're tabling this discussion since I quite like you alive and not kidnapped." Then she cocked her head, examining Elijah again. "Though I can see why you wouldn't want *that man*, specifically, shadowing you all day."

"Because he looks like he believes having fun should be punishable in a court of law?"

Harriet snorted. "No, because he's absurdly hot."

I stole a glance at the man in question. The sheer force of Elijah Knight's good looks hadn't been lost on me yesterday.

"Really? I hadn't noticed," I said airily, dropping a kiss on her cheek. "Thanks again for the surprise, sis. I needed it."

She hefted Lizzie onto her shoulder and I swept a giggling Rory up in a fast hug before she ran to catch Harriet's hand. "This conversation isn't over. Neither of them." A pause, then she called back, "Love you more than summer sunrises!"

"Love you more than winter sunsets," I said with a grin.

I waited until they were safely in their car before turning toward Elijah, acutely aware of his focus on me. This bodyguard was all coiled and brooding danger in a bespoke suit. Big and broad shouldered, with strong brows over his dark eyes. Eyes that clocked my every movement as I sauntered up to him.

The sun highlighted the shades of auburn in his brown hair and the very beginnings of gray at his temples. This close, it was obvious his nose had been broken before. And a web of scarring traced the curve of his right cheekbone.

Elijah had a jawline that could cut glass. Clean-shaven and subtly flexing with what I assumed was irritation.

"Are you following me?" I asked, slipping on my sunglasses.

"Our contract is still in place for another week," he replied. "I'm fully prepared to demonstrate the value of what we can provide for you. Respectful, elite, *discreet* protection that ensures your safety without impinging upon your daily life."

I cracked a smile. "So that's a yes on the following?"

His jaw flexed again. "I'm aware of your location at all times, Luke."

I glanced at my watch, noting the time. "I walked here, so was gonna call a cab, but I do need to be somewhere."

"Where?" he asked, opening the back passenger-side door.

"The Harbor Adventure Park. I've got a bungee jump appointment that starts in ten minutes."

Elijah stilled. "You have an appointment to...bungee jump?"

"Yep." I rubbed my palms together. "Is there a problem?"

His response was an arrogantly arched eyebrow. "I'll have you there with a minute to spare."

"That's a bold claim," I said, sliding into the dim interior.

He didn't waste time. We were moving the second I latched my seat belt, his large hands sure and confident on the wheel as he turned down a back road.

A glass partition started to rise between the front and back seats.

"What the hell is happening?" I asked.

"This is a high-security vehicle. That's protective glass. Bullet proof."

I scoffed. "You're telling me that if a bullet flies through that windshield, it'll ricochet off the glass and hit you instead?"

"There are risks to this job," he replied. "That is one of them."

"Dude, we don't know each other well enough for you to take a bullet for me. I'm literally in the process of *firing you.*"

His fingers clenched, just slightly, on the wheel. "I take my job seriously. Now, may I raise the glass?"

"You may not," I said mildly. "This shit makes me uncomfortable. If I *had* security, I wouldn't treat them like... like weird, silent robots here to do my bidding."

Silence. Then, "I imagine your family had staff who worked for you when you were growing up?"

My face flushed. *Staff* was an understatement. We had nannies and personal chefs and gardeners. A myriad of assistants at my father's beck and call. At my beck and call, by default.

"We did," I said reluctantly. "Doesn't mean I liked it then either."

His eyes briefly met mine in the rearview mirror and the flash of skepticism there only deepened my blush.

I cleared my throat. "You must have been close to my father, right? You worked with him for five years."

I could see the park in the distance. Elijah was smoothly passing slower cars, though I would bet he still managed to stay below the speed limit.

"That's not the nature of the relationship we have with clients," he said. "It's professional. Most don't converse with us either. In fact, silence is often preferred."

I tipped forward in my seat. "You shadow a guy every single day...and you're not friends?"

"Of course not."

"Friend*ly*?"

"No."

Elijah turned into the parking lot, coasting to a smooth stop. The jump platform rose up before us and I could just make out the bungee team huddled in the center. Dual bursts of fear and anticipation zipped down my spine so quickly I got lightheaded.

With perfect posture, Elijah rounded the front of the car to open my door. I unfolded from my seat and checked my watch.

"Nine minutes, eleven seconds. Not too bad."

Another modest lift of that eyebrow. "It was eight minutes and fifty-eight seconds. Your watch is off, *sir*."

A different kind of thrill zipped along my spine, and I wondered what it would feel like to have such a focused man by my side, intent on studying my every movement.

Wondered what, if anything, ever made Elijah Knight lose that finely honed control.

6

ELIJAH

I didn't like this one bit.

Now that I was staring up at the platform, uneasiness shuddered through me. There were too many risks, too many variables, too many *people*.

Let alone the danger of the act itself.

"Have you ever bungee jumped before?" Luke asked, his teeth bright white beneath the sun as he smiled at me. As if this was a delightful way to spend a Monday morning instead of what it really was.

A death trap waiting to happen.

I was walking a narrow line between what I'd do to convince Luke to keep our contract...and wantonly putting his life at risk. If our contract wasn't already on thin ice, I would have barred him from doing something as *reckless* as throwing himself into thin air with nothing but a rope tied to his feet.

"I'll take your icy silence for a no," Luke said, raking a hand through his hair. "Unless you're considering doing a buddy jump with me?"

I pinned him with a look. "I'm assuming it's pointless for me to remark on the inherent dangers of this?"

"I take risks like this all the time, Elijah. It's kinda my thing. Or didn't you see that in my file?"

Then he spun on his heel, heading toward a tall, narrow building that connected directly to the platform above us. Past the parking lot, the adventure park had other activities like giant swings, zip lines, large climbing walls.

"I'm aware of your proclivities," I called after him. "If there's anything else you'll be doing, any parties or..."

He paused midstep. "What parties?"

"Social events require protection, though I'll stress that we're trained to be discreet."

A flicker of disappointment crossed his face. "Don't believe everything you read in the tabloids. Or *anything* my father might have said."

He turned and started jogging toward the building's glass doors. I flexed my hands once before following after him, scanning every person, vehicle and object for signs of a threat. Inside, Luke greeted a staff member warmly and then we stepped inside an elevator with the words Next Stop: Adventure! painted in yellow.

The arrival of that letter yesterday weighed heavily on me. No return address, no other information, just a single scrawled message: *I know you have the flash drive. Give it back or you won't like what I do next.* And written in big block letters on the front: FOR LUCAS BEAUMONT.

Lincoln had had an entire lifetime to court his enemies—enemies that now appeared to be targeting his son. Yet here was Luke, smiling in the sunshine as if his safety was a given and not something fragile, to be protected at all costs.

I'd worked with plenty of people like Luke over the course of my career. People like my father, really—their hubris only matched by their carelessness, their own happiness and comfort prioritized over everyone else's.

My father certainly hadn't cared. What were the needs of his children over his own?

The elevator doors peeled open, revealing a wide platform filled with loud, pulsing music. Directly in front of us was boat-filled Wallops Harbor and, farther in the distance, I could see the very top of Laurel Lighthouse. The adventure company was entirely new to me. The best I could do in the moment was shoot a text to the other members of my team, asking for quick background checks and any other issues I should be aware of.

It was sloppy and shortsighted at best. But I was the one who'd made the hasty decision to force my way into Luke's day.

My client was speaking in a low voice to the dark-haired man and blond woman who worked there. They exchanged friendly hugs. Luke said something that had them all laughing. Then he reached behind his head and yanked off his T-shirt, tossing it to the ground. His skin was deeply tanned, and his shoulders rippled as he held his arms wide, stepping easily into a harness that fit snugly around his waist.

The employees moved in one seamless line, clipping rings, tightening carabiners, checking the rope. It was fast, faster than I'd anticipated, and the slightly patronizing look on Luke's face had me grinding my teeth.

I won't have some babysitter in a bespoke suit following me around, telling me what I can and cannot do.

"It's not too late to join me," he said. "I promise it's more fun than it looks."

"For the record, I refuse to endorse this behavior."

"Your concern has been duly noted," he drawled, just as the employees swooped back in. They hoisted him by the arms and placed him carefully at the edge of the bridge. A slight breeze kicked up, ruffling Luke's hair. I noted every single place where his safety was secured—the double knots, the extra rope, the clips.

A countdown began, people shouting *Five...Four...Three...*

Luke sent me a wink. And he fell off the bridge.

Backward.

My stomach lurched violently. It took every ounce of willpower not to rush to the edge and yell after him. Maybe thrill-seeking was the prerogative of people like Lucas Beaumont. No fears of late bills or low bank accounts, seeking that zap of adrenaline to feel alive amid their soft privilege.

From down below, I heard a joyous *whoop*. Gears locked in place, the rope pulled tight. The staff worked effortlessly around me as I stayed planted in the middle of the bridge, my pulse thrumming beneath my skin.

Someone lightly touched my elbow and said, "Don't worry; he's coming up now."

I turned to see a trio of people gathered at the other edge, moving as one to haul Luke up with an ease that shocked me. A single word floated up in my brain as I examined my client for any signs of hidden injury.

Ecstasy.

Luke was ecstatic, but that description felt unprofessional. He stood entirely still as he was unwound and unhooked. Head tipped back, eyes closed, throat exposed. I glued my gaze to the center of his collarbone, ignoring the heaving of his chest.

When he opened his eyes, they locked on mine through the buzzing crush of people and activity. They blazed bright blue, full of life. A lopsided grin appeared on his face and my stomach lurched again.

"Did ya miss me?" he asked.

I shifted on my feet. "I remain unconvinced that this is a wise use of your time."

Luke laughed as if I'd been making a joke, then made boisterous small talk with the staff while he tugged on his shirt and snapped a few pictures. There was an ease here, a familiarity, that told me how often he was here. It was concerning, to say the least, because the last thing a protection agent needed was high-risk scenarios that made it *easier* for a client to get hurt—or worse.

I followed him back down in the elevator and out to the parking lot, noting his body's looseness, the smile that wouldn't dim.

When he caught me looking, he cocked a thumb back toward the platform. "I'm not joking when I say you *need* to try it."

"And I'm not joking when I promise you I would never."

"You can't say *never*," he said. "You might end up wanting to someday."

"I won't."

"You could though."

My jaw ticked. "Lucas."

He raised his palms. "Okay, okay. I'm sorry. You're not into it. But I do highly recommend it as a way to clear your head when you're stressed. Like if your dad, who openly mocked and despised you, dies and leaves you his company as some kind of cosmic punishment."

I frowned at that and Luke must have sensed my unease, because he halted next to me. Slid his sunglasses back on and relaxed into an easy grin. "Forget I said anything. I'm always too chatty after a jump."

An awkward silence hung between us. Finally, I said, "You do this often then."

"Just one of my many proclivities." He shrugged. "Skydiving, rock climbing, whitewater rafting. The greater the risk, the greater the reward."

"The risk to your life, you mean."

"Exactly," he said. "Yet another reason why it won't work having a bodyguard. Though I did appreciate the ride out here."

I narrowed my eyes with irritation. "It's not only foolish to be so irresponsible, it's *absurd.* You wouldn't bungee jump with half a rope. So why take on a job that comes with a giant target on your back and be so cavalier about your own safety?"

I expected anger in return. Instead, Luke's smile only widened. "Finish out your contract this week, Elijah. That's fine by me. I'll ensure everyone on your team gets paid and then some. But I don't want the trappings of my father's lifestyle."

Maybe it was the arrogant grin, the way the sun burst around him like he was some kind of king. His jaunty body language, bringing up a host of bad memories. Because I opened my mouth and only fury came out.

"That's a ridiculous fucking thing to do," I snapped.

His smile faltered. "Excuse me?"

"It's ridiculous," I repeated. "Risking your life for no reason just because personal security might inconvenience you in the *slightest.*"

Luke's cheeks flushed red, though his eyes flashed with barely concealed frustration. "Damn, don't hold back on my account, Elijah. You wanna share any other misinformed opinions about me while you're at it?"

I took a step closer, watched him crane his neck to maintain eye contact. "You're about to fire a group of highly trained security specialists just to be petty. There are plenty of people in this world who would do anything to feel the kind of safety my team can guarantee."

"'Just to be *petty*,'" he drawled. "That's a cute interpretation. But you don't know what you're talking about."

I tipped my head. "You're right. I don't know what it was like to grow up in a mansion with a private jet at my disposal. Nor have I had the distinct privilege of inheriting a billion-dollar company without having to do a goddamn thing." I lowered my voice, watched his nostrils flare. "Perhaps I'm misinformed. *Sir*."

A heavy silence landed after my words. Regret curdled in my gut immediately. It was my own fault. I had never, *not once*, spoken with such frankness to a client, and if Foster were here, I'd be fired within the hour.

Pure pain flashed across Luke's face—so intense, I reared back.

"You don't know what it was like growing up with that man," he said harshly. "He taught me that my safety was *never* guaranteed."

An explosion rocked the parking lot.

I threw Luke to the ground and covered his body with mine, wrapping my hand around the back of his head as a wall of vicious heat passed over us. A surge of adrenaline wiped my mind clean of thoughts. My ears rang as a dozen car alarms went off at the same time. I reared up on my knees, searching for the source of the blast. The air was hazy, smoke-filled. Sirens rang out in the distance.

And fifty feet away, a car blazed with fire.

My car.

Luke struggled beneath me. I had him pinned to the ground with my knees bracketing his hips. When he tried to raise his head, I pressed him back gently.

"Do not move," I ground out. "You could be injured."

"What the *fuck*?" Luke said weakly. "Elijah, I think that's...that's your *car*."

I was already dialing 911. As I barked out the situation and the address, I searched Luke's body for signs of injury. His blue eyes caught mine, halting my inspection. They were a whirlpool of emotion—fear, shock, disorientation. The vulnerability there tugged at something primal, deep in my brain.

I wrenched my gaze away. There was no blood, no head wound I could see, only a few scrapes and some dirt. Then I realized where my hand had landed...in the center of his chest, with the distinct thump of his heart thrashing beneath it.

For *fuck's sake*, I was still straddling him.

I forced myself to move into a crouch by his side before I could fully register the corded muscle of his thighs. When the 911 call ended, I shot off a message to Foster. The back of my suit was growing hotter by the second, warmed by the blaze fifty feet away, bursting out of the car we'd been moments from stepping into.

Would have stepped into, if we hadn't been bickering in the parking lot.

"Elijah, I can stand up—"

"Do. Not. Move," I snapped, with my palm back on his chest again. "The ambulance will be here shortly."

"I didn't hit my head, thanks to you," he continued. "At least, I don't *think* I did. Maybe a little? Wait, no...no, I didn't."

Flashing lights appeared in the distance and relief coursed through my body. "This completely inept medical assessment is exactly why you'll do as I say."

His lips twitched. "Do you think *now* is the best time to insult me?"

"I'm not insulting you, I'm merely—"

"Dude, you just called me *inept.*"

My hand flexed against his chest, my fingertips digging softly into his T-shirt. Luke raised a single eyebrow. I snatched my hand back and stood so I could wave down the ambulance. "I was criticizing your assessment. I did not criticize *you.*"

"You did earlier," he shot back. "Pre-car bomb."

I avoided eye contact. "I'm sorry about that. Truly. I was out of line and unprofessional. If you feel compelled to report me to my supervisor for misconduct, I would understand completely."

"Report you? No, Elijah, I..." He tried to prop himself up on his elbows and I almost snarled at him. It must have shown on my face, because he sank back to the ground with a penitent look. "I'm no car expert or anything, but they don't usually *explode*, correct?"

"Correct."

An ambulance rolled to a stop in front of us, followed by a handful of police cars and a black sedan driven by Ripley. Just before they swarmed, Luke flicked his gaze up and asked, "So who the hell did my dad piss off?"

7

LUKE

I was out of the taxi and stalking up the front walk of the estate before the car came to a full stop, Elijah hot on my heels.

The twin gargoyles glared down at us as we reached the front door, but I didn't have time to glare back at them. I'd waited long enough back at the parking lot, through a paramedic examination and then a witness statement for the police.

Both had taken much too long. With the exception of a few stray bruises, I was uninjured, thanks to Elijah's quick instincts. And I had little information to report, given I'd been bungee jumping when the bomb was likely planted beneath the car. Elijah had straight-up refused the paramedics, then had what appeared to be an extremely tense phone call. He was saying something to me now, but I ignored him.

Couldn't ignore Preston, however, prowling down the hallway outside Dad's office with a pinched look on his face.

"Please tell me I did not just receive a call about someone trying to *blow you up*," he said.

I forced a cheery smile. "And I'm fine, thank you."

He narrowed his gaze, first at me and then to Elijah, hovering close. "You've had this job for three days and you've already angered somebody? How lovely."

"This one's on Dad, not me. Elijah told me that he'd been getting more death threats than usual right before he died."

Preston's face darkened. "He...he *what*?"

My eyebrows shot up in genuine surprise. "You didn't know? I thought Dad told you everything."

"He does...um, he did," Preston said, clearing his throat. "It must have slipped his mind. There was a lot going on. Still is, starting with the unfortunate fact that Dad's assistant, Adrian, quit ten days ago and we currently have no one in place to manage your schedule and your meetings. Also, the Sunrise Village project continues to be absolutely *fucked*. We need to figure something out as soon as possible. Regardless of my termination, I still want to further Dad's legacy instead of burning it to the ground."

"Little soon, don't you think?" I clicked my tongue. "I was literally almost burned to the ground an hour ago."

Preston gave a mirthless laugh. "Will you take something seriously, Lucas? For once in your life?"

It was a direct hit—and much too close to what Elijah had said to me moments before the car bomb went off. *Nor have I had the distinct privilege of inheriting a billion-dollar company without having to do a goddamn thing.*

But before I could answer, Elijah's hand shot out, stopping Preston from following us into the office. "I'm sorry, Mr. Beaumont. Luke requires a few minutes of peace and quiet to recover from the attack made on his life. Please wait outside."

Then he slammed the door in my brother's face.

Call it a side effect of the explosion, but watching Elijah slam the door on Preston was the biggest turn-on of my entire life. Though that wasn't counting what happened at the parking lot—Elijah pinning me to the ground with ease. Using his broad body to cover my own.

Which was *possibly* a messed-up thing to say. The man was trying to save my life, not seduce me. But I was obsessed with the heavy weight of his palm on my chest, shoving me down. The taut lines of his throat, his knees straddling my hips.

Elijah caught my eye and held out a glass of water, ostensibly mistaking my daydreaming for a trauma response. "Luke? You've had a shock. You should sit."

"Sit?"

He indicated the luxurious couch behind me. The cushions were a bold red, and a series of paintings from the Baroque era hung on the wall behind it. They were oversized, highly detailed, depicting various bloody hunting scenes. Dead boars, supine foxes, victorious men on horseback.

As a kid, I'd hated those paintings. There was a reason I'd become a vegetarian.

Shuddering, I stayed standing and accepted the water. "Thank you, Elijah."

"It's nothing."

I shook my head. "Not for the water. For protecting me from a fiery bomb blast. You didn't have to do that."

He pressed his lips together. "Technically, I'm paid to do that."

"Right, yes," I said quickly. "If we didn't have a contract, you would have let the bomb take me out, huh?"

He ignored my joke, his gaze sliding to the floor. "I

should have been watching the parking lot more closely. This is on me, Luke."

That snapped me out of it. I brushed past him and made my way to my father's gigantic desk. Started pulling out drawers, riffling through the papers that had been left there.

"You were right, Elijah. About everything."

"I'm sorry?"

I glanced up with a grin. "What was it you were telling me a couple days ago? Some letter addressed to me, asking about a flash drive?"

With a short nod, Elijah closed the distance between us and pulled out his phone to show me a picture of it. The message was scrawled on plain white paper.

I know you have the flash drive. Give it back or you won't like what I do next.

I tapped the screen. "See, it's just like you said. Someone was coming after him and now they're coming for me. This flash drive they're asking about, that tells me that Dad had secrets. Was *keeping* secrets, possibly dangerous ones. And that's the kind of information I can use."

Elijah eyed me narrowly. "I'm afraid I don't follow."

"I need a way out of this," I said, indicating the room around us. "If Dad hadn't put so many restrictions on things, Preston would already be here, kicking me out. And I'd be overjoyed to leave. So the only way I can think to challenge the will is by forcing open a loophole. Find this flash drive or find the person behind it, and figure out who he was screwing over. If I can dig up some dirt on him, dirt that carries *weight*, then I'll use that to threaten the board, to threaten the lawyers, with going public. The last thing they'll want is anything tarnishing Lincoln Beaumont's sterling reputation, destroying his legacy here in Cape Avalon."

My father was a monster who hid in plain sight, who

gathered up accolades and achievements while terrorizing Preston and me behind closed doors. And his behavior had only grown worse after our mother died when I was ten.

We were reminders of his loss, and grief, like every other emotion, was nothing more than *weakness* dressed up in finer clothing.

If he was going to harness me to his ill-gotten legacy, *I* was going to ensure the world knew exactly what kind of person he really was. But I needed something big, something dramatic, to move the board to action. In the rare moments when I felt safe enough to share my experiences growing up, I either wasn't believed or was completely dismissed.

The sparkling sheen of his privilege and wealth protected him in more ways than I could count—especially in the rooms that mattered and to the people with influence.

Elijah opened his mouth to speak, then snapped it shut. I watched him struggle, probably more comfortable with being a silent presence in the background.

I tipped my head to the side. "You have something to say."

His jaw tightened. "It's not important."

"We *did* just survive a car bombing together. Just say it, Elijah. You should know by now that I don't give a shit about whatever rules you're supposed to be following."

"Yes, that's been made very apparent to me."

"And...?"

"The car bomb was a clear escalation," he explained. "Whoever did it wanted to harm you—or at the very least *intimidate* you. Before your father died, the frequency of death threats and harassment had increased. We were tailed, multiple times. This very office was broken into.

Twice. Though Lincoln didn't believe they succeeded in taking anything."

I jerked my chin at the photo on his phone. "Maybe they were searching for this mystery flash drive the letter referenced?"

Elijah hesitated. "Maybe. But to be clear, none of this means your father was the instigator. These people could be seeking revenge for something pointless, a transgression they invented. In fact, that's the more likely reason. Lincoln was famous and wealthy. He worked with celebrities and politicians. That's enough to attract this kind of unwanted attention. I've done this job long enough to recognize the pattern."

He paused, his gaze sweeping the room. When it finally landed back on me, he said, "I was your father's lead protection agent for five years. Don't you think I would have known if he was engaging in something nefarious?"

A thousand light bulbs blazed to life in my brain. "That's right," I said slowly. "You were by his side nonstop. Probably traveled to meetings and dinners that were never recorded in his planner. Because he trusted you." I snapped my fingers. "You could help me, Elijah. We could do this together."

"Your father trusted me because I was bound by confidentiality. It's what he paid for."

I propped my hands on my hips. "Yeah, well...he's dead. I'm here, totally fucking alive, and asking for your help."

Elijah rolled his eyes to the ceiling. "Luke. I *am* here to help. An entire team of people is here to help. As your bodyguards. I'm contractually obligated to keep you alive every day that you're in my care. But *do not ask me* to go on some wild goose chase to dig up secrets your father probably didn't have."

I tapped the picture on his phone again. "Does this letter really read as a potential wild goose chase to you?"

He tipped forward, lowering his voice. "The letter is concerning to me and my team because of the intent. It doesn't mean its claims are true. In my experience, the *why* of these things matters less than understanding if they have the means to carry out acts of violence. Let law enforcement handle the *why*. That's their job. We're here to prevent the violence from happening."

I studied Elijah for a long moment—the sharp line of his shoulders, his rigid posture, not a single hair out of place even after a car bomb.

The man was too honorable for his own good. But I didn't want this job. I wanted *revenge*.

Rounding the desk, I stepped closer to Elijah. "But you are aware of *some* of his secrets. You know about Harriet, right?'

He didn't even blink. "We're aware of your father's blood relations. All of them. Just as I'm aware she was with you this morning when I picked you up."

"Did his file indicate what he did to her? What he did to her mother?"

"Having an affair isn't a crime, Luke," he said softly. "Even if some of us find it abhorrent."

I didn't have to guess who *some of us* was. "You already know one of his secrets, and it's a big one. All I'm asking is for you to help me go from there. Attempt to track down who's behind all of this. What do you think?"

His dark eyes hardened. "I *think* what you're asking of me is not only well beyond my job description, it's morally dubious at best."

I cracked a grin. "Life's more fun in the gray area, Elijah."

"No. It's not," he said simply.

He stared at me and I fought like hell to hold it. I had another card up my sleeve, but I wasn't looking forward to using it. Finally, I said, "I'll cancel your contract."

Irritation blazed across his face. "What did you say?"

I twisted at the waist and grabbed the contract I'd seen on top of a pile of papers at the edge of the desk. "Help me do this or I'll fire you and every one of your coworkers."

There was a heavy beat of silence and then his upper lip curled back in a snarl. "Backing me into a corner isn't the best way to start a working relationship that relies on trust. Yes, your father could be ruthless. I didn't expect you to be as well."

The words hit their intended target but I barreled through the discomfort. "Call it what you like, but I need something from you, and you need something from me."

"I *need you* to let me do my damn job. You've already had one attempt made on your life. Another will come. If I lose this contract, I'll lose my job. Same goes if I let you die on my watch."

"You don't want me to die? That's so sweet."

"*Lucas,*" he growled, and all the hair on the back of my neck stood up.

We stood like that—in a total stand-off—until I gave in, pinching the bridge of my nose with a sigh. "Let me ask you this. If you found out your client was doing evil shit, what would you do about it? And I'm not asking what your job *says* you should do. I'm asking what you, Elijah Knight, would do."

Elijah dropped my gaze to stare out the window.

"He hurt me," I said, hoping my voice sounded steady. "He hurt Preston. He hurt people that I love deeply, people I would do anything for. I know I just came at you with this wild idea, but you have to believe I'm doing this for the right reasons."

His throat worked on a swallow, and he released a controlled but furious breath through his nose. When he turned back to face me, his scowl was extremely...*murder-y*. He snatched the contract from my hand and slammed it onto the desk.

"Sign the new contract with my company first and you've got a deal."

"Happily," I said with a shrug, then signed with a flourish.

Elijah scanned my signature before holding it just out of my reach. "You will follow every one of my instructions for your own safety. Do you understand? You will give me advanced warning of where you're going so my team can assess it. You will inform me of the people in your life so I can research them. You will refrain from—"

My stomach dropped. "Please don't say it—"

"Yes, I *will* say it, because I'm the expert here and you're not," he said sternly. "You will refrain from any of your usual hobbies, including those that put your life at greater risk. And before you ask, I'll tell you why. Whoever did this today was serious. They fit my car with an explosive that could have killed us both. Throwing yourself out of airplanes just gives them an easier way to kill you."

I bristled at the implication that I didn't value my own life enough to take the requisite safety precautions. Quite the opposite. Thrill-seeking, for me, was about the preciousness of life. About grabbing onto every opportunity I could, like squeezing every last drop of juice from a lemon.

"Fine," I said, irked at the spark of victory in his expression. "But let me see this thing again."

My eyes glazed over at the legal jargon I probably should

have read before signing so confidently. But I homed in on the last paragraph on the third page. Pointing to it, I said, "What does this mean exactly? *No fraternization between agents and their clients, past or present.* I can't like...buy you a beer?"

He frowned. "Why would you do that?"

"Because you had a bad day?"

"Whether I had a good day or a bad one doesn't matter," he said. "Every single thing that doesn't serve to protect you is a distraction."

Elijah Knight was the fucking *distraction*. This close, he smelled crisp, like the coastal storms that sent wind rippling down the beach. And his tie was so impeccably knotted it looked unreal, though I could easily picture his long fingers folding the fabric *just* right.

The adrenaline still coursing beneath my skin had me feeling extra reckless. Had me imagining my hand closing around that tie and slowly, *slowly*, tugging him forward.

I wondered what, if anything, unraveled this man.

Wondered if he'd ever consider unraveling me.

"We're not friends then?" I asked, just to watch the muscle in his jaw twitch.

"If we became friends, my boss would have grounds to fire me immediately," he said. "Blurred boundaries and unprofessional behavior lead to mistakes we cannot afford. There's no room for error when lives are on the line."

That hadn't stopped him from speaking his mind earlier.

You're about to fire a group of highly trained security specialists just to be petty.

It was embarrassing how easily he'd seen through my bullshit. Maybe blurring those lines with Elijah was more dangerous than I thought.

I opened my mouth to respond but was cut off by the

high whine of metal, the creaking of wood, the soft tinkling of glass from the chandelier above our heads. It pulled my attention up, so I didn't see Elijah reach for me. But he did, hooking an arm around my waist and shoving me behind his body. I stumbled as he moved us both backward, but he caught a handful of my shirt and kept me upright.

Then we watched that very same chandelier crash to the floor exactly where we'd been standing. I covered my head as glass flew outright, showering the room with tiny shards. As I carefully blinked my eyes open, I realized Elijah had taken the brunt of it. In the sudden hush, I could hear people running down the hall, raised voices and shouts.

Panting, I said, "Holy shit, are you okay?"

My bodyguard brushed glass from his shoulders with a single eyebrow raised. "That's why you don't want me distracted."

8

ELIJAH

My alarm clock shrieked just after dawn. Yet I'd been awake for hours, thinking about falling chandeliers and fiery car bombs.

I swung my legs over the bed and sat up, rolling out an ache in my right shoulder. Adrenaline had been slow to leave my body last night. When it did, stress dreams lingered in its wake. Dreams of Luke, sliding into the car mere seconds before the explosion. Of Luke, smiling up at me while a chandelier hurtled toward his head. In both, I moved as if my limbs were trapped in quicksand, clumsy and slow and never reaching him in time.

A contractor had been dispatched immediately to clean up the mess from the chandelier. The thousands of glass shards had sparkled in the waning light, showing up in the oddest places: crushed into the carpet, a dusting on Luke's shoes, some in my hair. The contractor blamed the accident on an old mounting plate straining at the wood, which had gotten damp from an undetected leak.

"This was one hell of an unlucky accident," he'd said, carting away the shattered materials. Luke had agreed.

But I didn't believe in unlucky accidents.

After a quick cold shower and a cup of coffee, I dressed facing my apartment's floor-length mirror. Behind me, at the small kitchen table, my laptop chirped with a reminder for my virtual meeting with Foster in a few minutes. I finished buttoning my white shirt and draped a black tie around my neck. *A perfectly knotted tie will drive a woman wild*, my father once told me, under the auspices of helping me learn what he believed was a crucial skill.

He wielded fancy clothing and an expensive vocabulary like a precisely sharpened blade, charming women back to our house even as my mother worked the night shift to pay rent.

It can't be messy, he used to say. *Never sloppy. The tie must be exquisite. A work of art. You're telling the world that you, too, are a work of art. A person to be respected.*

The sun filtered in through the half-open curtains, highlighting the scarred lines on my cheekbone. I sniffed once. Cinched the tie tight, perfectly centered.

Not for art, but for purpose.

My father had already left when I came out as gay—not that it would have mattered if he'd stuck around. Handing over something as personal as my queerness would have been a mistake. All that luxurious clothing couldn't fully hide the ugliness of who he really was. Mercurial, moody, his temper on a hair-fine trigger, set off by any number of things. Once it was, however, he swerved from charming to furious, blaming anyone in his radius for whatever misfortune he believed had befallen him.

Finally satisfied, I pulled on my jacket and sat in the chair facing my laptop, gripping my mug of coffee so my fingers wouldn't fidget.

Foster joined the call ten seconds later. "Good morning, Knight."

"Sir," I said with a nod.

"Before we get to updates, I've gotta say I'm sorry again for pulling you from your vacation. And I really appreciate you stepping up like this."

"Nine days off was plenty," I said. "I'm feeling refreshed, all things considered."

Foster and I were cut from the same cloth, which was why he'd forced me on the vacation in the first place. I hadn't even given a thought to where I wanted to go. Simply found an island with affordable airfare and showed up, bags in hand, with absolutely nothing to do.

With all that unstructured time, it was far too easy for my thoughts to wander, for my old worries to crop up. I could scrutinize cheating spouses for only so long before a high whine would start up in my brain, sending my fingers curling into fists.

But being near seemingly happy people didn't help either. On the fourth day, my lounger had been close to a couple just a few years older than I was. Two men, one in navy blue trunks and the other in a rainbow-colored Speedo, so boisterously in love I could feel the entire beach getting drawn into their orbit.

Their affection was easy, practically careless. A kiss on the cheek, a ruffling of hair, the casual twining of their fingers as they read books and chatted.

It made my chest ache with a feeling I couldn't name.

"It sounds like everything's all set with the new contract and the new Beaumont, yes?" Foster asked, redrawing my focus.

My hand flexed around the mug. "Lucas Beaumont signed all documents, retaining the same number of protection agents as well as honoring the new rate you'd originally requested."

Foster looked relieved. "That's tremendous news. Well done. Any other issues I need to be aware of?"

I need something from you, and you need something from me.

"None whatsoever," I lied. The first time I'd done so to a supervisor, evidenced by the twisting knots in my stomach.

But my behavior yesterday was unprofessional, bordering on dangerous. Snapping at Luke. Letting him get under my skin. Allowing him to manipulate me into helping him tarnish his father's legacy.

I'd agreed for the right reasons—because Luke was my client and protecting him was the priority. Because the loss of this contract would be devastating to the company I was loyal to. And because the man in front of me had wished it to be done.

So it was done.

Except Luke was a fool if he thought I'd actually let him drag me along on this ill-advised quest. A quest that would turn up nothing, since Lincoln's secrets were no more scandalous than the average CEO's, even with that strange letter we'd received.

Luke would drop this ridiculous revenge plot as soon as something more interesting came along. I'd never met a person with that much privilege who could resist total power when it came calling for them.

"And what is Lucas like so far?" Foster asked, breaking into my thoughts.

My gut twisted tighter.

"He's impulsive," I said. "Reckless. Seems to have a complete disregard for his own safety."

Foster nodded at something off-screen, accepting a file he then tossed onto his desk. "The letter he received is concerning to me. I'd assumed these ongoing threats were directed at Lincoln Beaumont specifically. If they're continuing, unabated, it points to something bigger. A hatred for the entire company perhaps."

"It certainly puts everyone at higher risk," I admitted. "Ripley will be covering Luke's night shifts while I'm on days. The rest of the team will be assigned the estate, as well as mapping out driving routes and researching any public events or guests. As of right now, TBG's satellite offices, including the main one in Manhattan, haven't been hit with anything. They've been thrown into chaos with Lincoln's passing, but nothing dangerous."

Foster closed the file he'd been reading and flicked his gaze back to mine. "And I've got nothing to report from local law enforcement yet, though given the high value of this client, they're taking it seriously." He paused, then said, "I'm glad you weren't hurt."

The images from my nightmare came back to me—the horror when I realized Luke was behind the wheel of the car. His lopsided grin, so trusting, so amiable. The words I tried to scream at him. *You should have been more afraid.*

"I feel very lucky, sir," I replied. "Thank you for your concern."

"Maybe the timing of my retirement is for the best then. One more month and then you won't be in the field risking your life anymore. Are you sure you'll be fine with riding a desk and sitting through meetings all day?"

I thought about my mom, about my brother and my nephews. Remembered all the things I'd promised them. All the things they deserved—safety, security, stability.

"I'll be more than fine. As long as you are, sir."

He gave a small smile. "There's only one person I want filling that role, and that's you."

I cast my gaze to the side, humbled by the minor praise. "Thank you. That's nice to hear."

After we hung up, I set my empty mug in the sink and drove the short distance from my apartment in East Hampton to Luke's house in Cape Avalon. That stretch of the island was narrow, with the Atlantic Ocean shimmering on one side, the bay on the other.

After doing this same drive for five years, I hardly noticed the coastal scenery that drew wealthy New Yorkers every summer. Yet the temporary nature of this work couldn't be helped. It was true that my apartment was more hotel room than home, that my sense of community here was nonexistent. But it served a greater purpose—the protection of our clients—allowing me to blend into the background without bias.

Everything else was a distraction. And that included my new client's disarming smile and playful flirting.

I arrived at Luke's to relieve Ripley from his shift a few minutes early. He was stationed by the front door while a second agent, Sylvester, stayed parked in a car down the road.

Ripley was a new hire, young with a shock of red hair so bright he was easy to spot in a crowd. It only made the freckles on his face stand out darker on his pale skin—skin that flushed as soon as I approached. I hadn't been happy that he'd left Luke's detail simply because Luke had demanded it.

He'd been fidgety around me ever since.

"How did last night go?" I asked, rebuttoning my jacket. "Any issues?"

"None, uh...none at all," Ripley replied. "It was pretty quiet. The client had dinner at home, then I escorted him to a bar down the street, where he stayed for a few hours with a group of friends. Their backgrounds checked out."

I glanced in that direction. "Which bar? And was he inebriated?"

"The Shipwreck, sir. And no, he wasn't. I did keep a close eye on the bartender to make sure the drinks weren't tampered with."

I nodded. "He didn't happen to share today's agenda with you, did he?"

Ripley shook his head and I cursed under my breath. When I'd driven Luke home last night, after the chandelier fiasco, he'd promised to share his meeting calendar with my team, so we could start the tedious process of checking people's backgrounds and ensuring driving routes were safe, among other things.

This is part of our deal, I'd reminded him.

He'd given me a mocking salute and drawled, *Aye, aye, captain,* as if he had not a care in the world.

Now, an alarm clock blared through one of the open side windows, drawing my immediate attention.

"Is he up yet or still asleep?" I asked.

"Asleep, as far as we know," Ripley said. "No one's gone in or out."

The alarm persisted for another thirty seconds, prickling the skin at the back of my neck. Luke seemed the type to hit snooze about a dozen times—not leave it blaring nonstop.

I unlocked his front door and cracked it open. "Lucas?" I called out, listening for movement.

Nothing—just the alarm.

I pushed inside and followed the sound, Ripley close behind me. We passed his couch, where a paperback sat open next to a blanket. Passed his kitchen with a few pots filling the sink, a half-full cup of coffee on the counter. His surfboard was still where he'd left it the other day.

The alarm continued.

I followed it, down a long hallway toward what I assumed was his bedroom, dread pooling in my stomach. At the door, I knocked again, louder this time.

"Luke," I said. "Luke, can you hear me? It's Elijah."

I didn't think, just acted. Shoved the door open and braced myself for whatever it was I might find in there.

Which was the alarm clock, still shrieking. An open window, the sage-green curtain fluttering in the morning breeze.

And Luke's bed, completely empty.

9

LUKE

My feet pounded on the sand as I ran down the long stretch of beach leading back to my house.

The ocean was rough this morning, whitecapped and angry beneath a cloudy sky. Behind me, the Laurel Lighthouse stood tall at the end of the cape, candy-striped and blinking. To my right were the weathered, beachfront homes of Cape Avalon's oldest families, back when this part of East Hampton was a bohemian refuge, attracting artists and writers seeking a creative respite from New York City.

Scattered between the smaller bungalows were the mansions of the coastal elite, squeezed onto every last bit of space available. They towered above the older homes, with heated swimming pools, rooftop decks, and garages filled with gleaming sports cars.

These houses were occupied less than half the year, while the locals hunkered down for the winter, when the wind whipped knife-sharp through the sand.

Not that I could begrudge the summer people. I earned my living by teaching their kids and out-of-town guests how to windsurf and Jet Ski. But Cape Avalon's bohemian scene still thrived in protected pockets. Like at the Shipwreck, a dive-like gay bar that had been running a popular drag show every Thursday night for the past thirty-five years. The vibe was part queer oasis, part literary hideaway, with a smattering of surly locals warming barstools on the weekend.

The bookstore I worked at in the offseason held poetry readings there, with attendees huddled close in a drafty room steeped with secret queer history. Of broke writers and whiskey-stained manuscripts, charged glances and stolen intimacies.

I'd been there just last night, eager to join friends and get out of my house. Get out of my fucking *head*. In a single day, I'd bungee jumped off a bridge, been almost exploded by a car bomb and then narrowly missed being crushed to death by an antique chandelier.

Plus, I couldn't stop obsessing over my extremely serious bodyguard pinning me to the ground with his body to keep me safe. Couldn't stop obsessing over his perfectly straight tie. The strength in his grip. The gravelly restraint in his voice when he'd said, *You will follow every one of my instructions for your own safety. Do you understand?*

So really, I wasn't that surprised when I jogged closer to my house and felt the distinct weight of Elijah's attention, clocking me as I came to a stop on the sand. I stacked my hands on top of my head and took a moment to catch my breath. And when I tipped my head back down, he was standing right in front of me.

Furious, I would guess. Though he disguised it well—hands clasped, sunglasses hiding his eyes, not a hair out of place.

"Mornin'," I panted, lifting the end of my shirt to wipe

the sweat from my face. "Why do I get the feeling I'm in trouble?"

Ripley reddened. "You weren't in your bed, Mr. Beaumont."

"It's Luke," I corrected, then shot a grin toward Elijah. "Also, warn a guy before you traipse into his bedroom, will ya? Someone could have been sleeping over."

Elijah's eyebrow lifted slightly. "And was there someone?"

"Not this time. But it's been known to happen quite a bit."

His expression hardened. "Then you'll have to notify your security team in advance."

I raked a hand through my hair and brushed past them, heading toward the house. "Sounds romantic. I'm sure my future partners will appreciate being subjected to a thorough background check by you."

"Do you think this is a joke?" Elijah asked, his voice dangerously soft. I halted midstep, spun around. Ripley must have fled because only Elijah remained, standing completely still, his expression stoic.

"Excuse me?" I asked.

He closed the distance between us until the tips of his shoes almost brushed mine. "We had a deal yesterday. Part of that deal involved you obeying my instructions."

I crossed my arms and leaned back against the wall. "I remember our deal. And I don't see how I'm disobeying you. I went for a *run*, Elijah. On the beach where I live, with neighbors I've known for a good portion of my life. I don't think Dan and Tina two doors down are gonna finally take this opportunity to murder me in broad daylight, do you?"

"That depends. Do they have motive?"

"Oh sure," I said with a laugh. "'I'm so sorry, your honor.

But Luke Beaumont was simply much too charming and much, much too handsome. He had to go.'"

This close, I could have sworn the ends of Elijah's lips twitched, ever so slightly.

"We'll use that scenario then," he continued. "Your neighbors murder you in a fit of rage over your good looks and sparkling personality—"

"Why, *thank you*."

"—and as they do so, you're suddenly without the highly trained person literally paid to prevent such a thing from happening."

I opened my mouth to argue. Snapped it shut. With an eye roll, I passed through the opened screen door into the kitchen. "I didn't think it was a big deal, okay?" I called back, grabbing a coffee mug. "Do you actually expect Ripley to run alongside me on the beach?"

Elijah appeared next to the counter, sunglasses now tucked into his pocket. There wasn't a single nick on his clean-shaven jaw whereas I now had two days' worth of dark scruff.

"He would have done just that," he said. "It's what we're trained to do."

I poured a cup of coffee. Flashed him a smirk. "Would you run with me if I asked?"

"Absolutely."

I leaned forward, lowering my voice. "But what if I'm faster than you, Elijah?"

"You're not faster than me. And the point still stands. If you believed you weren't breaking the rules, you wouldn't have climbed out a window like a teenager breaking curfew." A muscle bunched in his jaw. "Anything could have happened to you. Nothing would have stopped the person who planted that bomb from attacking you on a deserted beach in the early morning. Violence isn't selective when it comes to location, friendly neighbors or not."

Elijah's gaze drilled into mine, so intensely that a blush climbed up my neck. I took a long sip of coffee, attempting to regain the upper hand.

"You *really* don't want me to get hurt, huh?"

"Luke, I'm being serious here," he said sharply.

"So am I. I told you I didn't want a babysitter. It's not my vibe, dude."

He tipped his head. "And yet you signed a contract yesterday that suggested otherwise."

"That's right," I said cheerfully, snapping my fingers. "I signed it after you agreed to help me dig up some scandalous shit on my dad. Which you're still going to do, right?"

A pause. "Yes. Right."

I held his gaze. "Really? 'Cause you've got the honor of a medieval knight. If you referred to me as *my liege*, I'd be less fucking surprised."

"Honor is a problematic virtue to you?" he asked mildly.

"It's certainly not as much fun as some of the other virtues."

"Ah, yes," he said. "Patience, chastity and humility. Three virtues you embody well."

Then he paused.

A slow grin slid up one side of my face. "You were about to say *my liege*, weren't you?"

"I was not."

I shook my head with a laugh, strolling toward the hallway. "Feel free to make jokes in my presence. Unless you think that blurs too many professional boundaries." I reached behind my head, yanking off my shirt. "I'm gonna take a quick shower before I head in. Help yourself to coffee, OJ, water, bagels, doughnuts..."

"Thanks, but I'm not hungry."

I glanced up from untying my swim trunks. The lines of his throat tightened but his face stayed passive. "Bodyguards are allowed to eat though, yeah?"

"Correct."

"But are you allowed to...*enjoy it*?" I whispered.

Elijah glanced at his watch, ignoring me. "If you had an itinerary for today, I'm guessing you're already behind."

"I'm a surf instructor in the summer and a bookseller in the winter. I don't really do itineraries," I called back, kicking the bathroom door shut and twisting on the shower. Wondering what his company's protocol said about the appropriate distance to keep when clients were bathing.

Wondering if Elijah was right outside.

Hot water streamed through my hair, loosening the tight muscles between my shoulder blades. I lathered shampoo, reminding myself that he was *not* fantasizing about me in this shower. He was probably coordinating the fastest route to the estate to ensure optimal safety. Or scrutinizing my disorganized bookshelf. Running a single finger along the hearth and staring at the dust streak left behind like it was a personal affront.

I, however, was thinking about Elijah running.

More specifically, running next to me. On the beach. Preferably shirtless, with a heaving chest and heavy breathing. Hair slightly disheveled. Sweat beading in the hollow of his throat. My cock twitched at the image. Twitched again when I pictured running my tongue up the cords of his neck, tasting salt.

Listening to whatever strangled sounds of pleasure he'd surely try to hide.

I cranked the water temperature to freezing and let a jittery burst of cold shock me back to earth. Once out, I wrapped a towel around my waist and pulled open the bathroom door. Steam billowed into the hallway, where I could just make out the very edge of Elijah's jacketed shoulder and the side of his right hand.

I opened my cabinet mirror and grabbed my razor and shaving cream. "Any news on who tried to blow us up yesterday? And if it has anything to do with that letter about the flash drive?"

"Nothing to report," he replied. "Given the violent nature of what happened, the local police have assigned my team an officer liaison, which means we'll be kept updated on any leads. But nothing's shaken out yet."

I smoothed shaving cream along my jaw and beard line. Wiped the mirror clean of steam and caught a quick glimpse of Elijah's profile. He turned away quickly. "What, uh..." I cleared my throat. "What other threats did he receive when you worked with my dad?"

"Most were one-off events, individuals targeting your father for his wealth and visibility," Elijah said. "They weren't made public and didn't result in anything dangerous."

I dragged the razor down the left side of my face, following my cheek. Water still dripped from my hair and onto my shoulders.

"He had a positive reputation throughout the Hamptons, so public threats and demonstrations were rare," he added. "Your brother will probably fill you in more on the Sunrise Village project, which Lincoln was working on before he died. There's a massive protest there right now, trying to block TBG from building."

The name Sunrise Village tickled the back of my brain. Preston had mentioned it yesterday, described it as "absolutely fucked" but I'd been distracted by everything else going on. The village was considered a Cape Avalon touchstone, a collection of seaside cottages turned into a beloved artist's retreat. I hadn't realized TBG was involved with it.

But knowing my father, it probably wasn't for good reasons.

"His building sites have been protested before by environmental groups," Elijah continued, "some more dramatically than others." His feet shifted in the hallway but I didn't look that direction. "Most of his public disagreements were with members of city council over building permits. Or disgruntled employees, trying to sue him."

I snorted, knocking excess shaving cream into the sink. "You mean Lincoln Beaumont was a horrible person to work for? Never could have guessed." I peered over my shoulder, trying to catch his eye. "Elijah?"

"Yes?"

"How did he treat you?"

The hesitation was barely there, but I sensed it. "Your father was always courteous to his protection agents."

You don't have to lie, I almost said, but he spoke before I could.

"He had a stalker once, right before I came on board."

My hand froze, midmotion. "Sorry, *what*?"

"Some B-list celebrity who believed your father had ruined the condo he paid him to build. He was obsessed with your dad. The guy ended up being pretty dangerous in the end. He used to wait outside the estate, try to get into the offices in New York. He followed your stepmother into a store once, scared her pretty badly. Until recently, that was the most nervous I'd ever seen your dad about his own safety."

I rinsed the razor and started on the right side of my face. "You told me there'd been an increase in threats in the months before he died. I'm assuming that's why he was nervous?"

There was movement in the hallway. Elijah's phone was buzzing, and whatever he read there had him lifting his walkie to his mouth and murmuring something I couldn't catch. After a few moments, he replied, "I believe that's why. He was...very agitated, almost paranoid. So much so that I was worried his stalker had returned and he hadn't told us. But I've seen no indication of that. You really weren't made aware that any of this was happening?"

"I, uh...no. No, I wasn't aware," I said with a shrug. "Lincoln and I weren't speaking when he died. Though apparently he didn't tell Preston any of this either."

"I'm sorry to hear that."

"Don't be," I said sharply. As sharp as the feelings trying to force their way through my body. A therapist might have called it regret. I knew what it really was—longing for a relationship that had never been and now never would be.

"Was your stepmother speaking to you?" Elijah asked.

"Celine? No way. She's perfectly nice, but it's not... It was never..." I paused, dragging the razor along my jawline. "I don't know why I'm telling you this. You've read our files, you know what happened to my mother."

Elijah didn't press and I didn't expand. I raised my chin, moving the razor down the side of my neck. Then cursed at a bite of pain.

"Luke?"

I winced at my neck in the mirror, where a decently sized cut was starting to bleed through the shaving cream. "It's nothing. I just cut myself." Opening the cabinet, I reached for a few cotton balls and a small first aid kit. Blood trickled down the front of my throat, more than I expected.

"Never mind about the cut. It's more of a 'slight stabbing' situation."

"May I come in?" Elijah asked gruffly.

I glanced down at my low-slung towel and bare feet, the room partially filled with steam, and almost cracked a joke about this situation looking suspiciously like one of those "blurred boundaries" mentioned in his contract. But then his broad shoulders and stern gaze appeared in the doorway.

"Sure…why not?" I sputtered.

He was all efficiency as he prowled forward, those dark eyes narrowing to the wound. Without looking away, he grabbed a cotton ball from the counter. Hooked two fingers beneath my chin and tilted my face up before firmly pressing cotton to the cut. I hissed in a breath.

"Does that hurt?" he asked.

"I can take it. Just wasn't aware that first aid would be part of your responsibilities."

He exhaled. I felt it like a caress along my skin. "Ensuring that you don't bleed out on your bathroom floor *is* my responsibility."

"In that case, thank you. I promise I'm not usually this much of a mess," I replied, hoping that the lie in my voice wasn't too obvious.

I heard the rustle of the first aid kit being opened.

"I'm going to bandage this now," he said, fingers leaving my chin. I sucked in a breath at Elijah's nearness, at my own vulnerability. He emanated a disciplined and dangerous control in that suit, his movements utilitarian while I fought a full-body tremble.

With a single snap of his fingers, I would have followed his every command. Happily.

"I know..." I swallowed hard. "I know what you must think of me."

He tossed the packaging into the trash. "That would imply I think of you. I do not."

"Ouch."

He finally shot me a look. "I think about your safety, Luke, as I should. Per the boundaries of my position and my own professional philosophies."

I cocked an eyebrow. "Which are?"

"Your safety above all else."

I propped my hip against the sink. "And were you thinking about my safety when you essentially called me a spoiled brat yesterday?"

"I didn't..." He stopped. Shook his head. "I was out of line as well as wrong. I'm sorry, Luke. Truly."

"*I'll say* you were wrong. We didn't even have a private jet." I shrugged, caught his eye. "We had a private helicopter."

He blinked. "And?"

I cracked a smile. "That was a joke, Elijah. I make a lot of them and you should feel free to laugh. Not that I'm *commanding* you as your boss. I'm simply encouraging you to express yourself. Especially if you find me funny."

His face remained impassive. "Duly noted. I look forward to the day."

"Fuck me," I said with a laugh. "Okay, I get it. You don't like my jokes."

He moved smoothly out of the bathroom and I ached to call him back in.

"When are you heading into the office today?" he asked.

Sensing defeat, I turned back to the sink and rinsed off the rest of the shaving cream. Patted my cheeks with after-shave. Reminded myself that flirting with my bodyguard was an inherently bad idea regardless of how intriguing he was.

"I'll be heading in as soon as I'm done here," I called over my shoulder.

"And when will you be sending me the itinerary information I requested?"

I draped a towel over my head and rubbed my hair dry. "Uh...also as soon as I'm done here?"

His silence was damning, and I wasn't sure why I cared so much about his approval. The faster I found the information I was looking for, the faster I could get back to my old life without Elijah "Fun Is My Archnemesis" Knight trailing me everywhere.

But then I walked out of the bathroom and found him standing in front of a picture of me with my nieces. When he saw me looking, he dropped his gaze and checked his watch instead.

"Those are my nieces, Lizzie and Rory," I said. "They've got me wrapped around their little fingers, if it's not obvious."

His reply was a short nod.

"Do you...have any?" I asked.

Elijah cleared his throat. "Yes. Three nephews."

"Do you see them often?"

"Couple times a year. Sometimes less."

"Well, that sucks," I said. "I'm sure they miss you."

His shoulders tensed. "They understand what my job entails and the sacrifices I make."

Guilt flickered through me at those words. I sighed, rubbing the back of my neck. "Elijah, I'm sorry about this morning. I was being a jackass. I'll only go running with you from now on."

"Thank you."

"From here on out, it's gonna be patience, humility and um...what was the third virtue again?"

A slight arch of his eyebrow. "Chastity."

I snorted. "Okay, just patience and humility."

"An improvement, then."

I cocked my head. "For the record, you've made like three jokes this morning alone."

"I wouldn't dream of it," he said—though I swore he was fighting a smile beneath that stony exterior.

I'm gonna crack this man wide open, I thought.

It was my worst idea yet.

10

ELIJAH

We were back at Lincoln Beaumont's estate.

I stood in the hallway, in front of the door to his office, while Luke tore the room apart. Searching for a flash drive full of secrets that probably didn't exist.

At least, that's what it sounded like he was doing—shifting boxes, pulling open drawers, cursing under his breath after muffled crashing sounds. His father had never played music in the five years I worked for him. But now the sounds of upbeat reggae filtered into the hallway, with Luke singing along.

I flexed both hands slowly, loosening the tension in my joints. Updates from the other protection agents circling the property came in over my earpiece while I scanned the oceanfront view from the windows. This part of the estate functioned as TBG's local offices when Lincoln stayed here. Which, when I was with him, was more often than not.

The hallway opened into a sitting area, decorated in dark wood paneling like the rest of the house. A large brick hearth dominated one wall with an oil portrait painting of

Lincoln and his wife, Celine, hanging above. To my left was the empty desk where his assistant Adrian had sat until recently. Four other doors led to meeting rooms and administrative offices.

The Beaumont family's private stretch of beach was visible through the large windows. Beneath Luke's music was the hushed sound of the ocean and passing sea gulls.

The staff who worked the estate operated here in near-perfect silence, cleaning and cooking around the people who used these offices and the family members who lived here. Providing a seamless array of constant food and gleaming floors, ensuring TBG's clients enjoyed an ambience of high-end luxury. The staff and I exchanged quick nods of understanding whenever our eyes met, used to people treating us like a spare piece of furniture, as ordinary as the wallpaper.

I was comfortable with the odd intimacy of my career by now. I'd escorted clients on their romantic vacations, to five-star hotel rooms and Michelin-starred restaurants. Over the years, I'd overheard their heated arguments, their most personal stories.

Their many fears and secrets.

"It's really fucking weird, the way you're facing away from me," Luke called out from inside the room. "A killer could break in through this window and murder me before you even noticed."

I gave him my profile. "There are agents outside for that exact reason."

"Are they as good as you are?"

"Yes. Or they wouldn't be there," I said. "What is *actually* weird is your continued need for conversation. Some of us are working."

I heard Luke approach me. Could smell the sandalwood aftershave he'd applied this morning, right after I'd stanched the blood from his cut. His skin had been warm from the shower, his pulse rapid beneath my fingers.

As if I made him nervous.

He popped his head out from the door. "Can you come inside so I can ask you some questions?"

"About what, exactly?"

He lowered his voice. "The stuff you promised to help me with yesterday. Right before a chandelier almost crushed us to death."

I slid my eyes back to the wall. "I'm needed out here. We're set up this way for a reason."

Luke sighed and went back inside. I released a breath, stretched my neck from side to side. It was barely noon and I was rapidly approaching my personal limit for unprofessional behavior. It was true that I'd been furious with Luke this morning—his cavalier attitude about his own safety, how quickly he'd assumed the rules didn't apply to him.

Probably because they never had.

Yet those frustrations weren't an excuse for storming into that bathroom to help him with a *minor cut* he'd given himself while shaving. A cut I'd only known about because I'd stationed myself directly outside the bathroom door, where I could hear him showering.

Concerns for his safety aside, I didn't need to be that close, that curious, that *interested*.

But somewhere in the middle of that shower, I'd heard something...the softest groan. Luke was naked beneath the shower spray. Groaning. The sound was as low and raspy as his voice, stripped of his usual charm and swagger.

And I never should have heard it.

Never should have stood close to him when he was

draped in just a towel, with drops of water in his chest hair and heat radiating from his skin. I'd kept my gaze trained and clinical and swore to myself I wouldn't do it again.

Couldn't do it again.

There came a crackling in my ear. Then, "Client is opening office window."

At the same time, I heard Luke opening the window and I turned toward it on instinct. Watched him hinge forward and wave.

"Hey, Sylvester," he called down. "Can you come up here real quick?"

"*Lucas*," I hissed, stepping into the office. "What the hell are you doing?"

He turned, flashing an arrogant smile. "Making sure we're protected while you're in here with me. My safety's the priority, yeah?"

Sylvester appeared ten seconds later, slightly out of breath. "Sir?"

Irritation zipped up my spine, made worse by Luke's smug expression. But I kept my cool and said, "Sorry for the change, Sylvester. Mr. Beaumont and I need to speak about the recent threats his father faced. Do you mind keeping an eye on things out here while we do it?"

He nodded. "Not a problem."

Then I turned, shut the door, and shot a glare at my aggravating client.

"We're back to *Mr. Beaumont* again?" Luke asked. "Or is that just because you're pissed at me?"

I stalked across the room and didn't miss the way his eyes darted up and down my body. "Is it your goal to make my job *absolutely impossible* for the entire length of our time together?"

Luke stood from where he'd been perched on the end of

the table. "My *goal* is to figure out my father's secret dastardly deeds. A goal you agreed to help me with yesterday so that I would reinstate your contract."

Guilt had me eyeing the door, where Sylvester stood outside. "Yes, and?"

"And I can feel you not wanting to help me."

"That's because I don't want to help you," I snapped. "And you broke our agreement this morning, the first chance you got."

His cheeks flushed. "I apologized for that. And it won't happen again. I've got too much information to dig through." He indicated the office, which had gone from tidy and elegant to pure chaos. "So far, nothing I've looked at has been labeled 'Warning: Flash drives filled with potentially dangerous secrets inside.'"

"Generally speaking, that's not how dangerous secrets work."

"Which is why I'd love to speak to the person who stood next to him for five years," Luke said. "That person being you, Elijah."

He crossed the room, brushing past me, and fell backward onto the black leather couch beneath the bay window. Kicked his legs up and leveled me with a smirk. "What were his days like?"

I dropped my gaze to the floor. "Busy."

"Busy how?"

I hedged, my fingers curling into fists. Reminded myself that keeping the Beaumont contract was vital and Luke would surely lose interest in a matter of days. "When he was here, in Cape Avalon, he took meetings in this office a lot. Went to on-site visits to different properties. Met with board members and clients. Stayed here working late sometimes. Nothing out of the ordinary."

Luke nodded. "Were you in some of these meetings?"

"No," I admitted. "Your father is...was...extremely private."

Luke raised his arms and settled the back of his head against his palms. "Who do you think I should meet with first? Who's known him long enough to know his secrets?"

"I honestly don't know."

He studied me, a smile playing on his lips. "In all that time, there wasn't a single person you thought was suspicious?"

"That's a long time to remember."

"And I bet you'd describe your memory as *perfect*."

I ground my molars. "I'll think about it."

He cocked his head to the side. "Didn't Preston mention that Dad had an assistant who just quit? Adrian something? Maybe he has some information he wouldn't mind sharing on his former boss."

"Lincoln had many assistants," I said. "Some only stayed a few months. Adrian wasn't here long."

"But he quit right before my dad died," Luke mused. "Interesting. Very interesting." He sat up on the couch, swinging his feet back to the carpet. "Can I ask you a question about what you said earlier? About needing to know the names of who I was sleeping with?"

I cleared my throat. "Something you'd like to share?"

"If I went on a date, would you or another bodyguard be there, like...with me?"

"Discreetly. But yes."

"Because so many of your clients are murdered on dates?" he asked, then snapped his fingers. "Wait, let me guess. Arsenic in their drink."

"Unless you're dating someone and haven't revealed that information to us, there isn't a need to discuss this now.

We can always reassess when, or if, you're next asked on a date."

Luke whistled under his breath. "*If* I'm asked on a date?"

I didn't reply but held his gaze. Luke hooked his arm around the back of the couch and his T-shirt stretched across his broad chest. "And the same goes if I'm bringing someone home for the night, correct?"

I wouldn't think about it. Wouldn't think about Luke at a bar, looking just like this. Knowing he could crook his finger and have every person in there crawling toward him. Begging for one taste, one kiss, one night.

"That's correct," I managed to say.

Luke nodded but didn't surrender my gaze. He had it trapped with a predator's skill, forcing me back into that bathroom, with my hand on his throat and drops of water clinging to his long eyelashes. *I know what you must think of me.*

"This is good to know, as it happens more often than you think," he said.

I lifted my chin in response. "Then I'll ensure the background check is thorough."

His expression shifted, growing serious. "Does that mean your company knew about my dad's affairs?"

What had he said, back at his house? *You've read our files. You know what happened to my mother.* I'd almost responded with, *I know. It happened to my mother too.*

I paused. Watched a twinge of sadness darken Luke's face. "We did know about the affairs. Do you believe that to be relevant to the missing flash drive?"

He turned his head away. "I believe every aspect of my father's shitty behavior to be relevant. We know people have killed for less."

"Why would they come after you though?" I asked before I could help myself.

"That's a good point," he said, eyes flicking back to me. "I knew there was a reason I was keeping you around, Elijah. And not only for your first aid abilities and sparkling conversational skills."

"I'm paid for one and not for the other."

He brightened. "Does that mean every conversation we've had has been out of the kindness of your own heart?"

"Every conversation we've had has been because you're badgering your bodyguard with questions...*sir*."

A devilish grin tugged at his lips, like we were in the middle of a game he just realized he won. But then came a knock at the door, Sylvester's head peeking in. He opened his mouth to speak but Preston was already barging through.

"*Fuck me*," Luke swore under his breath. Raising his voice, he said, "Get out of here, bro. I'm not in the mood and I'm clearly busy."

Preston regarded the mess of boxes with a haughty air of disapproval. "What is all of this?"

"I'm redecorating. What do you think?"

His focus lit back on Luke. "And what are you wearing? We strictly adhere to business attire in these offices."

Luke plucked at his navy blue board shorts. "This is business attire for me."

"Where are Dad's paintings? The one's from over the couch?"

I'd noticed their absence as well—three scenes depicting a hunt, vibrantly colored and so detailed they were almost gruesome.

Luke raked his hands through his dark hair. "I took them down, dumped them in one of the hall closets. Didn't you always hate those things too? You told me that the dead boar gave you nightmares."

"They're thematic." Preston scoffed.

Luke snorted. "Animal murder isn't a theme I vibe with. I'm a *vegetarian,* remember?"

Preston's eyes narrowed. "*Power* was the theme of those paintings. Something you'd know if you hadn't fucked off in every single one of your art history classes at NYU."

Luke's response was a wistful smile. "I was only fucking off because I was too busy hooking up with a hot TA named Jeremy. That man taught me everything I know about art."

I shifted on my feet, attempting to control my body's reaction to his words. I knew Luke was queer—it was buried in his file somewhere, plus he was anything *but* subtle. I'd registered his flirting with me as a sign of his boredom, a halfhearted interest in a shiny, new plaything. He certainly wasn't the first wealthy client to flirt with the help and he wouldn't be the last.

But there was a difference, knowing it for sure.

"I so love hearing all the ways you've shirked your responsibilities, Lucas," Preston replied.

Luke's jaw flexed but his tone stayed light. "Did you swing by just to ask me what and where various things are? I actually *am* busy."

Preston's attention shifted my way. "I need to speak with you about a few items. It's urgent. And private."

Luke followed his brother's gaze, then shook his head. "Elijah stays in the room. Haven't you heard someone's out to kill me?" He pointed his pen at the ceiling, where the chandelier had hung. "And this house is a fucking death trap."

His brother looked bemused. "You believe I'm a threat now?"

Luke tossed me a grin. "What's your professional opinion, Elijah? And before you answer, I'll have you know that Preston used to cheat during snowball fights by hitting me in the face."

I flinched in sympathy and Luke caught it, looking delighted. But before he could say anything, Preston sank down in the maroon armchair by the fireplace, dropping a file onto the coffee table with a sigh. He peered around at the disorganized mess and pinched the bridge of his nose.

"You need an assistant. I shudder to picture your inbox right now. Kenneth's fielding calls for you nonstop, if you'd like to thank him at some point."

"I'll do no such thing," Luke said archly. "Why would I thank a man who took great pleasure in belittling us when we were teenagers?"

"He was providing mentorship and guidance, something we sorely needed in the wake of Mom's death. Something you especially needed, if you recall."

Luke pulled a frown. "Sadly, I don't recall."

Preston's eyes flashed with irritation. "When it comes to hiring Adrian's replacement, I can pull together some candidates but you have to promise to actually interview them."

"Why did Adrian quit by the way?" Luke asked. "Did you ever meet him? Would you use words like 'shady' or 'quasi-dangerous' to describe him?"

Preston huffed out a dry laugh. "Adrian is exceptionally qualified and Dad didn't realize what he had, as usual. Adrian left because Dad ran him out of here. You know how he could be."

An uncomfortable silence stretched between the two siblings. Luke swallowed a few times. "I do. I do know how he could be."

Preston examined his nails with a bored expression that

looked forced. "It doesn't matter. As soon as I found out that you somehow convinced Dad to fire me, I hired Adrian to work with me at my own real estate company. It helps to have a plan B if you're ever betrayed."

"Dude, for the last time, I would never do that—"

"Can we talk about Sunrise Village now, please?" Preston said over Luke's objections. "It was the last project Dad worked on before he died. We're now so far behind schedule it's laughable, and you need to fix it. The press is starting to turn negative and we don't need the extra scrutiny right now."

Luke leaned back against the bookshelf, hooking one ankle over the other. "Is that because this project of Dad's is mildly to moderately evil?"

"Of course not."

"But why was Dad interested in building there? It's an artist collective. The bookstore works with some of their writers in residency."

"TBG purchased the buildings and the land from the owners," Preston said. "The cottages are being torn down for new luxury condos. Building permits have already been approved and we've got construction lined up. But the artists won't leave even though they were served eviction notices sixty days ago. They've chained themselves to the buildings and they're protesting every day."

"*Oooooh*," Luke said. "We're doing something illegal."

"It's perfectly legal."

"Unethical then?"

Preston's lips thinned. "Luckily for us, illegal and unethical are not the same things." He held out the file. "Handle it."

Luke laughed. "How? And why?"

"The protesters want to speak with the head of the

company. That's you now. If Dad were here, he'd smooth things over. Offer them whatever they wanted to get them to shut the hell up. Use that infamous Lucas Beaumont charm to do just that. And do it today. We're hemorrhaging money with every second that passes. Don't even get me started on what it took to get these permits. Senator Wallace will personally murder us herself if we delay a second longer."

He stood and crossed the room, slapping Luke in the chest with the file. "Do you think you can handle doing one single thing for your family?"

I saw the effort it took for Luke to remain unfazed at those words, made even more obvious at his lack of snappy comeback. His brother was halfway out the door when Luke finally said, "Did you really not know about the threats Dad was receiving?"

Preston hesitated. "I really didn't know. He was obviously hiding things from me. He didn't tell me I'd been removed from the will and summarily fired, either."

"He didn't remove you," Luke argued. "You inherited all of his shit plus *two houses*. Dad loved you, clearly, even with all this bullshit about losing your job. But we'll never know why he did this to us. We never understood his decisions."

The sibling anguish hovering between the two of them was deeply entrenched at this point. I almost averted my eyes, but then I froze, struck by the longing on Luke's face and the pain on Preston's.

"You wouldn't understand what it was like, working with him so closely," his brother said quietly. "Even at his most critical, even at his most dismissive, I still thought he believed in me."

"Then help me to understand," Luke replied. "He's not here anymore to drive us apart."

"What's the point?" Preston said, his spine rigid. "You didn't care then, Luke, so why start now?"

An awkward hush followed his exit from the room. I stared down at my hands, thinking about my promotion, the ardent trust Foster had placed in me. The extremely clear policies I was breaking by even entertaining helping Luke in this way. We didn't turn on our clients, didn't relinquish the many secrets of their lives, didn't participate in any activity that distracted us from the goal. Protection, above all else.

Not tempting the danger that lurked in the shadows.

When I glanced up, Luke was staring down at the open file, his mouth set in a flat line.

But his fingers trembled slightly, where they gripped the pages.

"Clarita Reyes-Castillo and Ethel Walker," I said.

Luke looked up. "What?"

"You asked me..." I paused. "You asked me who I thought you should talk to, and I think it's Clarita and Ethel."

"Those names sound familiar, why?"

"They were your father's former business partners, when he first started as a real estate agent. They're married, local to the area, and run a popular real estate practice. They might have been privy to his secrets when he was younger."

Guilt sat heavy as a stone in my belly. Luke wasn't the only person in my life I'd sworn to protect and I could feel the threads of that promise unraveling with every line that I blurred. But it was just this one time, just this one bit of information.

It wouldn't happen again.

Luke nodded, the ghost of a smile on his lips. "Thank you. That's very helpful."

I didn't reply.

He held up the file and cocked his head. "Can you drive me to meet with the protesters? I'll call the organizers on the way."

My eyebrows flew up. "That's no problem. I'll have two agents ride ahead and sweep the area."

"Great," he said, his grin slowly widening. "I think a clue just fell into our lap. Think any of these protesters are angry enough to set off a car bomb?"

11

LUKE

It was pure chaos at Sunrise Village.

Camera crews were parked haphazardly on the street. A crowd marched out front, holding signs that said TBG Can't Bulldoze Our Home and TBG Destroys Communities!

A dozen people had chained themselves to the front gate, making it impossible for the stalled construction crew to do much of anything. The three leaders of this movement were waiting for me in the community clubhouse, but the tension radiating from Elijah's shoulders had me wondering if he would even allow me to exit the vehicle.

Maybe I'd just have to make a break for it. And maybe he'd throw his big body over mine again, tackling me to the ground. Growl something into my ear like, *Is it your goal to make my job absolutely impossible for the entire length of our time together?*

It wasn't my goal. Not really. But it sure was fucking fun. And I was desperate to dredge up anything to replace the red-hot embarrassment crawling through my veins after what had happened between me and Preston in the office.

I so love hearing all the ways you've shirked your responsibilities, Lucas.

Elijah was a professional. Surely he'd witnessed family squabbles and awkward arguments before. Surely he'd witnessed them between my own father and brother even. But it was painfully uncomfortable, knowing he'd seen me and Preston sniping at each other.

Knowing that Elijah now understood that my family considered me to be worthless.

Outside, a news anchor interviewed one of the people chained to the front gate, where they sat surrounded by an array of coastal wildflowers, their pink and yellow petals waving in the breeze coming off the ocean. The village was a collection of fifty sky blue cottages that sat a block away from the beach. Built in the early 1900s, they'd quickly become known for their colorful residents and bohemian artist retreats. Novelists and poets, painters and photographers flocked to the cottages, especially in the summer, and it wasn't rare to find writers scribbling away in journals by the sand.

This wasn't the first time the village had been at the center of a protest or a cultural movement. But it was the first time their very existence had been in danger. The cottages had been passed down through a local family for generations and they'd never considered selling before, not when so many in the community believed this to be one of the last bastions of the "old" Cape Avalon. The one less swayed by wealth and celebrity and more concerned with being an artistic refuge.

Most of the file Preston had given me was beyond my understanding, although one name had stood out—Senator Rosamund Wallace. According to my brother, she was prepared to murder us in cold blood if these new luxury condos didn't get built. She was a popular state senator, heavily favored to run in the upcoming presidential election. But she had been born and raised here, had even been a two-term mayor.

I had no idea she'd been helping TBG grease bureaucratic wheels this entire time.

Elijah scanned the crowd with barely concealed irritation. "I don't like this. Too many variables. Too many people with close access to you, as well as the car."

I raked a hand through my hair and dropped the other onto the door handle. "This is my chance to talk to people who clearly hated my dad. I can see what they know, poke around at what they're hiding. Maybe we'll even get a confession out of them."

Elijah's eyes appeared in the rearview mirror. "You're not a detective, Luke. If you're their potential target, now they can carry out their threats in person."

"But you've got extra agents monitoring the situation," I pointed out. "And I'm heading into this meeting with *the* Elijah Knight. Aren't you the best in the business?"

"Flattering me won't change my mind."

I grinned. "It's not flattery if it's the truth." Then I opened the car door and stepped out into the crowd, which was even louder and more raucous than I realized. I caught the tail end of Elijah swearing—"For *fuck's sake,* Lucas"—then he was barreling around the car toward me. Which meant I was too distracted by the stern set of his mouth to notice someone had thrown a full can of soda directly at my head.

I ducked and it missed, smacking the car door and leaving a dime-sized dent. The crowd of protesters roared. Elijah was there a half second later, shoving me behind his back.

"What did I just *say?*" he hissed.

"Maybe they meant for me to catch it," I said, trying not to stare at the way his hair curled, just slightly, at the nape of his neck. "Maybe it was more of a friendly 'hey, you look thirsty' kind of throw."

"I swear to *god,* you are going to be the death of—"

"Whoa, whoa, hold it," yelled a voice from the crowd. "No more projectiles. It's not who we think it is."

Elijah stilled, though his left hand still gripped a handful of my shirt.

"Who do you think I am?" I yelled back, peeking around Elijah's shoulder. I saw who it was and sagged with relief. Attempted to move away from the glowering boulder of a man blocking me from the crowd, but his fingers only tightened where they gripped me.

"Elijah, stop, it's—" I wiggled again, but no luck. "It's *Steve.*"

"That means nothing to me," he snapped.

A bearded man in head-to-toe tie-dye waved, an apologetic smile splitting his face. "Sorry, Luke. We thought you were Preston for a sec."

"You thought I was my *brother*? That's fucked up, Steve. I trusted you." To Elijah, I said, "We used to work together before he retired. He ran the Jet Ski tours. He follows Phish on tour, feeds a lot of the stray cats that live near the beach."

"He almost killed you with a soda can."

"The keyword there being *almost.* Steve wouldn't hurt a fly."

My bodyguard muttered something under his breath that I didn't catch. Another person from his team joined us and the two of them escorted me through the crowd and to the meeting spot.

Steve yelled, "Sorry again, Luke!" and a few of the locals

flashed me sympathetic smiles. Though more of them jeered and scowled, sending a tendril of unease up my spine. I'd spent the past six years avoiding my father as best I could. Now I was stuck representing him.

And there was possibly someone here angry enough at whatever he'd done to plant a bomb in a car.

"Wait," Elijah commanded when we got to the clubhouse. The other agent went inside, did some kind of inspection, then nodded us through. I squared my shoulders, plastered on my friendliest smile and strode in to meet the organizers. The room was small and sunny and my focus immediately landed on the three people seated around a worn coffee table.

My smile widened. "Lucas Beaumont," I said, extending a hand. "Thanks for having me out here."

An older white man with silver hair tied back in a bun stood and took my hand. "Clarence Craven. Former village resident and photographer, one of the co-leads of this demonstration. Happened to be on-site today, usually I'm helping virtually from my place in Rodanthe Hills." His voice was gruff, his attention darting everywhere except my face.

"Great to meet you," I replied, turning to the tall woman next to me and shaking her hand. Her black hair was streaked with gray and there were deep lines around her dark eyes.

"Lovely to meet you, Lucas. My name is Mía Estrada, local poet and current resident of Sunrise Village. Also a co-lead."

When the woman next to her stood to greet me, I was stunned with recognition. "You're Nora Jackson."

She beamed a dazzling smile my way, taking my hand in

a strong grip. "I am, indeed. I'm also a co-lead, though I no longer live here. It's a pleasure, Lucas. I've heard a lot about you."

Nora Jackson was a Cape Avalon celebrity—a beloved thriller author who wrote her most famous murder mystery, *Death on the Dunes*, while living in one of the cottages here. That same book had been turned into a celebrated TV series, most of it filmed throughout the South Shore and bringing flocks of her fans every year to visit. She was a short Black woman with dark-brown skin, square-rimmed tortoiseshell glasses and chin-length curls.

"I work at the bookstore on Main Street in the winter," I explained. "You did a reading there, years ago. Total packed house. You very kindly signed my collection of your books."

She pressed a hand to her chest as we all took our seats. "I remember that reading; it was a favorite of mine. As is that bookstore." Her face softened. "Lucas, we're so sorry for your loss. I knew your father; it's one of the reasons I offered to help when Mía reached out to me. I was hoping our... friendship, for lack of a better word, might help us find common ground. But it's been months and we've still got people chained to the fence, so that shows you how well that strategy worked."

My eyebrows shot high. "You knew Lincoln?"

She and Mía shared a glance. "We first met when I needed insight on property development and real estate while writing *Mayhem at Montauk Point*. He was fascinating to speak with."

My thoughts scattered with the slew of words I'd never, not once, associated with the man who used to lock me in my bedroom every time I cried. Words like "friendship" and "common ground" and "fascinating."

"His ego must have loved that. I'm guessing he talked your ear off?"

"And then some, which ultimately worked in my favor. I'd been having a hard time envisioning the antagonist in the story."

"Percy, right?" I asked. "It's been awhile since I read it but he was a shady politician or something?"

With a nod, she said, "Percy, the shady city councilmember. Lincoln was the inspiration."

I dropped my elbows to my knees. "You're telling me that my father was the villain in *Mayhem at Montauk Point*?"

"I couldn't have crafted a better character if I tried. Lincoln had no shame. He was arrogant, entitled. Paranoid. But the mistake I made in all of this was foolishly assuming our tenuous connection was enough for me to talk him out of this project." Nora's smile faltered and she reached for my wrist. "Look, here I am, speaking ill of the dead. I'm so sorry. How rude of me."

I waved it off. "It's not rude—it's accurate. This is a small town. His reputation wasn't some kind of secret. He was loathed and beloved in equal measure, depending on who you were and what he thought he could get from you. We didn't have a relationship. And hadn't spoken in six years, so I'm not entirely sure what I can do to help you all. Until today, I had no idea this was going on."

"The artists who live here were given sixty days to get out and some have no place else to go," Mía said. "This is a community, a cultural and historical institution that your father decided to bulldoze for the money."

Clarence was fidgeting with his coffee mug, right knee shaking. "Not the first time Lincoln Beaumont's done something like this in Cape Avalon," he said with a grunt. "There's a clear pattern of prioritizing the rich over everyone else. It's why we're putting up such a big fight. Dead or alive, your dad can't bully this place out of existence. Can't bully *us* out of existence."

He dropped his mug down too sharply on the table, spilling a small amount. While he and Mía mopped up the liquid, Nora turned and caught my eye.

"You can stop all of this, Lucas," she said. "That's why we're meeting with you."

I whistled under my breath. "I wish I could. I've always supported the village—it *is* an institution. But I was given this gig a few days ago, and according to my brother, all the protests are doing is delaying a done deal. TBG's losing money by the second. No way the board and investors back down now. As soon as you get out of the way, the crews will break ground."

Mía's jaw set. "Then we won't get out of the way."

Guilt shivered through me, but I pushed past it. I needed *out* of this job and *back* to the life I'd carved out for myself. A life I'd fought for. And that meant figuring out what my father was hiding and exposing him for the monster that he was—not just the bastard responsible for turning this town into a summer playground for the wealthy. He'd done that out in the light whenever he wanted, collecting accolades along the way.

I wanted to know what he did in the dark.

I lowered my voice and went for a big swing. "I know the three of you are behind the threats my father was receiving before he died. I'm not mad about it, really. I get it—this is a horrible situation you're in. Though the car bomb was a *bit* intense. But it doesn't matter, because if you knew something about him, if you were blackmailing him—"

"If we were *what?*" Mía said, eyes wide.

Behind me, Elijah cleared his throat. Loudly. I cast him a sideways glance and he gave a minuscule shake of his head.

"Are you talking about that bomb out at the adventure park?" Nora asked. "You think the three of us are...trying to *kill* you?"

Heat suffused my cheeks as I looked between their genuinely confused faces. "Maybe not *kill*. Severely injure, perhaps?"

Mía started to laugh, and then Nora joined her. Even Clarence gave a soft chuckle.

"We're a bunch of artists," Mía said. "You really think we're capable of something like that?"

My gaze lit on Nora, who was still grinning. "Maybe the person who's written the most kidnapping scenes has a trick or two up her sleeve."

Nora only laughed harder at this, patting my hand like I was a precocious child at the park. "I'm flattered. But everything that we want to say to you, to your company, to those construction crews out there? We're saying it *out loud*. In public, in front of as many cameras as we can. We've got no use for secret threats or blackmail."

I felt, more than saw, Elijah's frustration with me. It had me fidgeting in my seat, attempting to regain the threads of an idea that seemed brilliant at the time. "Let me explain better. Someone is...was...pissed at my dad." Twisting at the waist, I took in Elijah's flared nostrils. "Do you want to tell them what you've been up against recently?"

His eyebrows winged up, like he was surprised I'd asked. But then he said, "Mr. Beaumont's security team was handling an increase in death threats prior to his passing. Calls, voicemails, letters. At least one person tailing him in public a few times, his office broken into. Most notably, a bomb was detonated beneath our vehicle yesterday."

I shrugged my shoulders. "Angry protesters. Angry threats. I thought I was putting two and two together. That maybe a group of you had something on him, something you were using as leverage to halt construction."

Nora crossed one leg over the other, her gaze steady from behind her glasses. "Whatever we might have on your father is information that's out in the open and always has been. He was rich and privileged; what did he have to hide? He was always protected, always adored by those with the most wealth and influence. I thought getting to know him better might unlock some vulnerability in him, some secret softness."

I dropped my eyes to the floor, already anticipating what she'd say next. When my mother finally died, succumbing to the cancer they'd diagnosed only a year earlier, I cried so hard that I threw up. Spent an entire week throwing up, in fact, sleeping curled up in Preston's bed and refusing to eat, though my brother did try to persuade me with my favorite foods.

My father's punishment for this was one of his favorites —the silent treatment. He used to pretend I didn't exist so thoroughly that I started to believe it.

"Finding vulnerability in him would have been impossible," I said. "He had no softness."

"No, he didn't," Nora said quietly.

Clarence coughed into his hand, cheeks red and fingers drumming on his knee. His jittery nerves were apparent enough in this small room that I wondered if Elijah was noticing too.

"I'm sorry to be rude, but there's no fucking way it's one of us," he said. "We're risking our careers and our reputations to be out here every day. Why would we try and harm Lincoln and risk going to jail even more than we already are? It's not the point. Half this town wants us to shut the hell up and move on. As if Cape Avalon is just a place for tech billionaires to enjoy a better ocean view."

Mía nodded at her co-organizer. "Clarence is right. Not all of us are protected from the law like the Beaumonts are. Getting involved in anything violent only hurts our message, distracts from the real issue at heart."

I sat back in the chair and dragged a tired hand down my face. "You're right, you're right. And I'm really sorry for accusing you. I didn't think of it that way. I'm just..."

I bit my tongue before the truth spilled from my lips. *I'm just overwhelmed and confused and wanted this to be easy.*

"Did you ever consider the responsibility you have, taking over this company?" Nora asked. "Maybe these threats would stop if you took TBG in another direction. A positive direction, one that benefited this community instead of what it's been doing for decades. Stripping Cape Avalon of all that makes it unique and wonderful."

Knots twisted in my stomach. Elijah's words came back to me then, jostling for my attention. *I don't know what it was like to grow up in a mansion with a private jet on hand. Nor have I had the distinct privilege of having a billion-dollar company handed to me without having to do a goddamn thing.*

Memories of my father made my skin crawl. So stepping into his shoes, taking on this role—even *if* it was to change things—felt even worse. A creepy-crawling feeling that had me breaking out in a cold sweat and wanting to run away, as fast and as far as I was able.

Elijah wasn't wrong about how lucky I was, how privileged this entire situation was. Didn't mean I wanted to do anything about the billion-dollar company handed to me by a narcissistic madman. Anything other than get rid of it.

"If I could change the trajectory of this project, I would,"

I said. "Right now, the power's in your hands. Maybe, if enough time passes and TBG loses too much money, they'll finally listen to you."

"We'll be out here every day until they do," Mía said. "But you have power too, Lucas. Maybe, if enough time passes, you'll do something about it."

12

ELIJAH

Three days later, Sylvester and I were escorting Luke and Kenneth Bromley, TBG's board president, to the Cape Avalon Historical Society's annual garden party.

I rode along in the passenger seat, keeping a careful eye on our surroundings. Things had been quiet, all things considered. While the protests at Sunset Village raged on, Luke had been holed up in his father's office, digging through old files and searching for flash drives while I avoided his questions with every last ounce of professionalism in my body.

Avoided them while trying to forget my recent string of sleepless nights. Nights where I replayed, over and over, how close that soda can had come to hitting Luke square in the head.

A fucking *soda can* had me tossing and turning like some kind of amateur. I'd been shot at before. Had foiled kidnapping attempts and multiple bombs.

And yet I couldn't unsee it. Couldn't unsee the way he'd looked at me right before—cocky grin, the smooth unfolding of his body from the car, the sound the can made when it left a dent. The way I'd grabbed him by the shirt and shoved him behind me had been more personal instinct than professional. Our mission was always *get low* then *get them back in the car.*

Not grab onto them with no intention of letting go.

Behind me, Kenneth was informing Luke of Lincoln's relationship with the Historical Society, who would be there, who he needed to greet.

"Your father would be appalled at what you're wearing," Kenneth chided. "The invitation specifically said black tie."

"You don't like me in burgundy?" Luke asked cheerfully.

"I'd like you in a *tie*."

Luke clicked his tongue. "My chest refuses to be constrained. I've always preferred an open-air situation."

I heard the mirth in Luke's voice. Could picture his smile—the slow reveal of teeth, his eyes crinkling at the sides. He wore a bespoke burgundy suit and a white shirt underneath, unbuttoned to the center of his chest, exposing a swath of tan skin. When I'd held the passenger-side door open for him earlier this evening, the covert wink he'd sent me had set heat traveling in a slow wave along my spine.

Which was almost assuredly due to my recent sleeplessness.

Kenneth grumbled noisily, rapping his ring against the windowpane. "Is it any wonder why no one takes you seriously, Lucas? You act as if being a disgrace to this family is a good thing."

"It isn't?" he said tightly. "I had no idea."

"Listen to me," Kenneth continued. "You *must* speak with Senator Wallace tonight. She's already furious about the complications at Sunrise Village—"

My phone vibrated in my pocket, tearing my concentration away from Kenneth's lectures to the urgent text I'd just received from Ripley. *Sent this to Foster*, the message read. *Figured you'd want to see it too. No letter this time, email instead. It came through a server overseas so can't be traced. Same server as the other six.*

My fingers tightened around the screen. The message was simple. *You know what I want. Give it back.*

And the picture attached was taken from the parking lot where the car bomb had exploded, capturing the smoke-filled chaos a minute after it detonated. In the photo, Luke's on the ground, propped up by a single elbow. I'm straddling his waist, my palm flat on his chest, the scowl on my face desperate at the edges.

The intimacy of our position poked at a primal possessiveness I had no business feeling. Of fantasies about my client I worked hard to keep fleeting.

Fucking *Foster* had seen this?

"What is it?" Sylvester muttered.

I slipped my phone back in my pocket. "I'll tell you later."

"Another threat?"

I nodded, my mind racing as we curved slowly up the driveway to a bright white mansion where party guests mingled beneath a large black tent sparkling with lights. The setting sun cast long, peachy shadows across the manicured grass and I was keenly aware of all that could hide there. Sending paparazzi-style photos to your victim sent a specific message. One that said, *I'm watching you. I'm two steps ahead. I know everywhere you go, because I'm there too.*

The car bomb was already a dramatic escalation tactic. This one was quieter, more subtle. In many ways, more dangerous. Someone had tailed us from Luke's house to the park that day, set a car bomb, taken our picture...and I'd missed it entirely. Was apparently too busy getting into an unprofessional argument with my client to do my actual job.

"Stay alert while you're watching the perimeter," I murmured. "We're being watched."

"Yes, sir," he answered, turning to speak to the valet station. Event staff wore all black with white gloves, bobbing between the wealthy patrons like seagulls on the breeze. My father believed life was different in the Hamptons. *They're classier up there,* he used to tell my brother and me. *They've got style. They've got gravitas. A man can live like a king in a place like that.* He'd wanted a life like this one, like the one Luke had—soft, cultured, opulent.

He'd flirted and seduced his way into events like this one while Mom worked third shift and I burned grilled cheese sandwiches on the stove for Christopher and me. This dream of his was only one of many. A whim, like so many others. Like fatherhood, even. But after years of working up here, I knew it to be no different from anyplace else. Just had a nicer sheen to it.

Sylvester negotiated the key exchange with the valet while I stepped out into the balmy night air, buttoning my jacket with one hand while opening the back door with the other. Kenneth stepped out with a barely concealed scowl, which quickly became a polite smile as he waved to a few guests.

Luke was next, bringing his scent of saltwater and sunscreen. He tried to get my attention but I ignored it, slamming the door and giving quick instructions to Sylvester.

I followed Kenneth and Luke into the party, comforted by the fact that we'd done our due diligence with the location and the guest list, a task made easier by the fact that I was one of twenty personal security guards in attendance.

I wondered if any of them had demanded to be let into their client's bathroom to treat a minor cut from a razor. Had felt the delicate thump of his pulse beneath their fingers while inches away from the vulnerable tilt of his throat.

A dozen people approached Luke to give their regards or comment on the sudden passing of his father. His smile came easily but there was a blankness to his expression. A fatigue in his movements as soon as the spotlight shifted away from him. With every lull in conversation his eyes sought mine, and I kept scanning the party to avoid them.

The air suddenly shifted—voices hushing, the flash of a few phone cameras. A team of security guards moved through the crowd with the grace of a battering ram. When they parted, Senator Rosamund Wallace stood there, striding up to Luke with her hand outstretched. The state senator—and former Cape Avalon mayor—was a pale-skinned woman in her sixties, her gray hair pulled back into a low bun, dressed in a black pant suit.

Luke was midsip of his gin and tonic when she finally reached him.

"Hello there," he said, bemused. "You're—"

"Rosamund Wallace, it's lovely to meet you, Lucas," she replied, gripping his hand tightly. "This is my chief of staff, Grady Holt."

The man next to her coughed into his fist without taking his eyes off his phone. He wore the stressed but stoic expression I'd grown used to seeing on the staff of politicians.

"I was a *huge fan* of your father's," the senator added. "I knew him for years even before I was mayor. His death is a massive loss for our community, although you've taken to the role quite nicely, it seems."

Luke clinked the ice in his glass. "It certainly came as a surprise."

"You must be in charge of the Sunrise Village project now, yes?" Rosamund asked. "Lincoln was so excited for it. It's heartbreaking to think he'll never see the finished product. I may no longer be the mayor, but I so love seeing new development come to Cape Avalon."

Luke pressed his lips together. "Well, a bunch of artists have chained themselves to the building, with no intention of leaving. I spoke to the lead organizers a few days ago. The construction is stalled, possibly for good."

The senator's eye twitched—just barely—but her expression stayed agreeable. "I'm sure you'll figure something out. We both know the condos need to be built."

"Do they? Seems to me that a lot of people are angry. And for good reason."

She tipped her head. "I'm afraid I don't follow."

Luke pressed a hand to his chest. "I'm new to all of this, so feel free to call this question rude. But does it *need* to happen? Or do you merely *want* it to happen? Because the residents need a place to live. And TBG evicted all of them."

The senator didn't even blink. "Surely they'll find a new place to live."

"It's not that easy, Senator, and you know it. Especially in a town this expensive," Luke said smoothly. Though his fingers plucked nervously at a loose string dangling from his jacket, making me wonder if he was thinking about what Mía had said to him at the end of their meeting, the power he had to stop the destruction from happening.

His empathy for the protesters was obvious and Luke seemed to openly disdain his father's business. But I didn't believe him when he claimed there was nothing he could do.

"And yet this town takes care of its own," Rosamund said. "Those artists are valuable to our community, and I know they'll land on their feet. It's pointless to contain art to cottages and bungalows when art is simply all around us." Her smile broadened, her body positioned in a way that made it clear she knew she was being filmed. "It's truly so lovely to meet you, Lucas. I'll have Grady set something up for us. I would love to learn more about you. Although there's really no replacing your father, is there? Lincoln was simply a lion among men."

Then she was a blur of motion and armed guards, moving her along to the next person. Luke appeared briefly dazed, a troubled bent to his mouth. Next to me came the sharp sound of glass breaking as a server's platter crashed to the floor. I stopped to help them, scooping up the largest pieces of glass as they ran to get help. When they returned with towels and a broom, I stood and immediately realized Luke was missing.

"Where is he?" I bit out, my pulse spiking.

Kenneth, looking tense, was on a phone call. He waved vaguely toward the back of the house, which faced the shoreline. I saw nothing in the crowd—not Luke's broad shoulders in burgundy nor his crooked grin. I moved as quickly as I was able to without stirring up unwanted attention, pushing past attendees dripping with diamonds and gold watches. I rounded the side of the carriage house just as the last rays of the sun slipped away, plunging the night into a purple twilight. The ocean was an inky black against the shore and the first dusting of stars appeared overhead.

And there, leaning against a gazebo, was Luke. I prowled toward him as my nerves settled and his face was briefly illuminated by the flame of a lighter. His cheeks hollowed, then he exhaled a puff of smoke.

I pinched the bridge of my nose. He was smoking a joint at the Historical Society's garden party.

"Knew you'd come and find me," he said, blowing another stream of smoke to the side. Standing like that, lit like that, the cut of his cheekbones flared in my awareness. His lashes, ridiculously long. The dip of his collarbone and the casual confidence in the way he stretched his long legs out in front of him.

"*Lucas*," I said, in more of a growl than I intended. "How many times—"

He raised a palm in the air. "Before you yell at me, I got Sylvester's permission to come out here." He waved that palm to a point past my shoulders, and when I turned, my colleague gave a quick nod of affirmation before slipping back to the perimeter.

"I wasn't going to yell."

"Yes, you were." His lips curved up slowly. "I think you like putting me in my place, Elijah."

A pause here, thick with tension. His throat bobbed, eyes steady where they met mine. It was too fucking easy to picture this man on his knees for me—and that smart mouth twisting into a taunt, a tease. A plea.

Finally, I said, "I need to know where you are at all times."

"Well, you found me," he said lazily. He took another pull on his joint and said, with smoke flowing from his lips, "It's probably pointless for me to offer this to you, yeah?"

"About as pointless as asking me to bungee jump," I replied. "You want me focused. Not stoned."

He nodded then narrowed his gaze. "How do you wear a suit all the time anyway? I've been in this thing for less than an hour and it makes me want to crawl out of my skin."

I wrapped my right hand around my wrist. "It's the uniform. It's part of the job. We're to appear anonymous to our clients. Nameless and faceless if we have to be."

Luke glanced out toward the dark ocean. "I don't think of you as nameless *or* faceless."

"That makes you extremely unique."

"You own sweatpants, though, right?" he asked. "A hoodie? Basketball shorts that you lounge around in on Sundays?"

My fingers tightened on my wrist. "I don't lounge often."

"You should."

"There's too much to do," I countered.

His answering chuckle had the hair standing up on the back of my neck. "So I've been told. Do you ever, I don't know, get a little too drunk at your local bar? Get high and watch a funny movie?" He pushed off the gazebo and took a few steps closer to me. "Do you ever pretend you're someone else for the night and take a total stranger back to your bed?"

I arched a single eyebrow. "The things I do outside of my time spent protecting you are irrelevant."

"Says who?"

"Says anyone who wants to do this job well. Which requires a focus and diligence honed to its finest point."

His blue eyes traveled the entire length of my body before sweeping back up again. "I see. You're my weapon."

"I'm your *shield*," I corrected. "Nothing gets past me."

"Who's your type then?" he asked, head cocked.

"Excuse me?"

"Your type. The kind of person you like to date. If you like dating." He shrugged. "I'm curious."

I glanced to my left, watching the crowd for any signs of strange movement. "I cannot even begin to tell you how inappropriate this line of questioning is."

"No worries. I'm only making conversation," he said easily. "My type is everyone. You could say I bring a kind of 'disaster bisexual' vibe people can spot from a mile away. My dad always hated when I talked about it. The day I came out to him, he told me he didn't care what I was or who I fucked as long as I married a woman. His words, not mine. I thought coming out might make us closer, because I'm nothing if not pathetic."

I wrenched my gaze back to his. "You're not."

"Not what?"

I swallowed. "Pathetic. Obviously."

His face softened and something squeezed in my chest. "I'd spent the morning watching emotional videos on YouTube of people my age coming out to their parents and it had me believing my father was a completely different person than he was. I wish my mom had been there. *Really* wish my mom had been there. But I'm pretty sure I just said something like 'cool, thanks,' then booked it out of that office before he could say anything worse."

I tugged at my cuff links. "It's...it's normal to have hope. Hope that people can change. Especially when it's a parent."

Luke rubbed a hand through his hair. "I guess you're right. And I was just a kid."

Every rational bone in my body was screaming at me to end this conversation—especially in light of the picture currently sitting in my supervisor's inbox. A supervisor expecting to hand me the keys to his kingdom in a month. *There's only one person I want filling that role, and it's you.*

So close. Everything I'd been working for was *so close.*

But the problem was that I'd been that kid once too.

"Men," I said, as Luke studied me in the dwindling twilight. "Men are my type. I'm gay."

His loose body language went taut, like he was smoothly stringing a bow. "We have at least one thing in common, then."

I rubbed the back of my neck. "Sure. I mean, yes."

"Do you have a boyfriend?"

I shot him a look. "Luke."

"What? Sorry, I'm nosy," he said with a laugh. "You give off a real heartbreaker vibe. I imagine you're slaying men, left and right."

"Nothing could be further from the truth," I said without thinking, and tore my gaze away when Luke brightened like a golden retriever being shown a treat. When I didn't elaborate further—focusing on the horizon instead—Luke leaned over until he could finally catch my eye.

"Whatever boyfriend let you go was an asshole," he said.

"You don't know that."

"Sure, I do," he said cheerfully.

My cheeks burned and I hated it. Every relationship I'd ever been in had ended for similar reasons—work dominated my life. I was too distracted, too ambitious, too unwilling to unwind. I didn't believe that made my past partners terrible people. They were wise, sensing the danger ahead.

They were certainly all wiser than me in this moment.

"Your brother was being shitty to you the other day," I said, the words landing awkwardly in the silence. "I just... wanted you to know that. Part of this job is being in the room when people are having conversations not meant for the ears of total strangers. I don't usually say anything. And I wasn't listening on purpose. But it needed to be said."

Luke eyed me with a wary surprise. When he didn't reply, I continued, "I had a person in my life who took great pleasure in belittling me too, whenever he was in a bad mood. The trick was to keep him in a good mood."

"And how did you do that?"

"Told him what he wanted to hear," I admitted. "Smiled through it. Kept his secrets for him. He had a lot of them."

A pause. Then Luke said, "Was it your dad?"

The scars on my cheekbone itched. "Yes."

"Elijah—"

There was a loud rustling sound to our left and I startled, grabbing his wrist. Heart in my throat, I raised my radio to my mouth and barked, "Any updates?"

"Nothing, sir. Perimeter's been clear," Sylvester replied.

I tipped my head to listen but there came only the safe sounds of the party in the background.

"It was only a bird," Luke said. "We're good. Are you okay?"

I hid a scowl that became a blush the moment I realized I still had Luke by the wrist. Could feel the steady thrum of his pulse beneath my fingers. It beat more rapidly than I expected, his skin there soft and tender. When his focus darted down to the place where our hands touched, I let go and stepped away.

Luke flexed his fingers once, then slid them into his pocket.

"You received another threatening email tonight," I said quickly. "I'm on high alert for a reason. It's why we need to head back to the party."

"I...what? Wait, really?" he asked, slipping out his phone.

"I wouldn't look at—" I started to say, but he had it open before I could get the words out. He was silent as he stared down at it. Another flush crawled up my throat while I wondered if the image meant anything to him other than protection.

"They took this picture of us," he said roughly.

"I know it can be jarring, knowing someone's watching you—"

"Watching *us,*" he said. "Someone is watching us, Elijah."

"They are."

His forehead wrinkled. "The message here... 'you know what I want, give it back.' You think they're talking about the flash drive? The one mentioned in the letter?"

"Most likely. We haven't been able to trace the emails. That's something law enforcement is supposed to be working on. I'd like to assume they're all coming from the same person but I've learned enough on this job to know that these things can also be random and unrelated. Which doesn't mean they're not dangerous. I know you feel compelled to uncover if your father was up to something nefarious, but we have to start accepting that they're openly targeting *you* now. Not Lincoln."

Luke's gaze sharpened. "*Or* they're lashing out because we're getting close."

"You've not gotten close to anything," I said, shaking my head. "The only thing you've succeeded in doing is frightening them into action, which means they'll get more reckless. Be willing to risk more to see you hurt. I can't let that happen."

"No, we had a deal," he argued. "You help me dig up dirt on my dad and in exchange I keep your big, expensive contract. You were with him for five years. I *know* you know more than you're letting on."

"Helping you is one thing. Knowingly putting you in danger is another," I said harshly. "I still have a job to do."

His expression turned smug. "You can't tell me my dad let himself be babysat like this. That man did whatever the *fuck* he wanted to do, whenever he wanted to do it."

"When there were threats against his life, he did. He took it seriously. This isn't a joke, Lucas."

Hurt rippled across his face. "Who said it was? I'm letting you do your job the best that I can. But you're not going to stop me from seeing this through." He brushed past me, stalking back to the glowing lights of the party. "And Ethel and Clarita are coming by tomorrow to meet with us. Thanks for the tip, by the way."

I had no choice but to follow, even as the lengthening shadows threatened to swallow Luke whole, right in front of my eyes.

13

LUKE

The gargoyles had their claws in my chest, no matter how quickly I fended them off.

I pushed and screamed and wailed. Yet in they dug, breaking through my flesh, cracking through bone. And I was somehow back at the adventure park parking lot, seconds before the bomb went off. They'd followed me here. Followed *us* here. And any second, they'd get Elijah too.

"Luke."

Two of the gargoyles had him pinned to the ground. I screamed his name.

"Luke, wake up."

Ran to fight them off, but they were *heavy*. So much heavier than I could manage. One turned its cold gaze toward me and opened its mouth.

"Luke, you're having a—"

I woke with a gasp and promptly fell off the couch. My chest heaved, and sweat dotted my forehead. And there was a big, warm presence crouched down next to me.

Elijah.

One giant hand gripped my shoulder to keep me still

while his eyes roamed frantically from my face to my body. "Luke, it's me. It's only me. You were having a nightmare. I thought I heard screaming from the hallway and ran in here and you were..."

I scrubbed my hands down my face and tried to rein in my breathing. His fingers flexed into my shoulder, inadvertently hitting a tight spot, and I bit back a groan. Memories from the garden party last night filtered in, rapidly replacing the nightmare, and my breathing hitched for an entirely different reason.

I was napping on the couch in my dad's office because I'd barely slept, kept awake by a fantasy I shouldn't have about a man who saw me as nothing more than a job.

And why wouldn't he? I *was* Elijah Knight's job and all I'd done was make it hell for him.

But my fantasies had a mind of their own and not one of them cared much for maintaining the professional boundaries of Elijah's contract. I'd gotten one look at the picture of us in the parking lot—a picture fully intended to be a threat, and it was—and gone fucking haywire.

It was the way he'd been scowling in that moment. Lip curled up, practically a snarl, leaning over me with his bunched muscles and coiled restraint. In every fantasy, I curled my fingers into his collar and yanked him down for a kiss I knew would be hot and bruising.

Dangerous in more ways than one.

"I got you some water," Elijah said, drawing me back to the present moment. I lifted myself until I was sitting with my back to the cushions and took the cup, draining it. Then I counted backward from ten.

There were no gargoyles. No claws. No monstrous beast going after Elijah.

When I opened my eyes and turned my head, he was

still shockingly close, crouched next to me with concern etched into his brow. For a moment I was simply stunned by his beauty. There were crinkled lines around his dark eyes, a divot in his full lower lip. Not a single strand of auburn hair was out of place. And the heat from his body hit me like a wall, as did that crisp scent of his, mixed faintly with what must have been his detergent.

It was Elijah, whom I'd suspected was queer and who confirmed it last night. Who liked men and was potentially single and who wanted me to know he thought my brother was an asshole.

Each word out of his mouth felt earned somehow. Precious, like glimpsing a pod of dolphins at sunrise.

I had a person in my life who took great pleasure in belittling me whenever he was in a bad mood. The trick was to keep him in a good mood.

The surge of violence I'd felt toward his father surprised me. I'd fucked it up afterward, as usual, but I couldn't let myself get distracted by his stern mouth or how badly I wanted to let him keep me safe. He kept reminding me he had a job to do without understanding that getting out of this shit show *was* my job.

"Thank you...thanks, it's..." I mumbled. "I used to get nightmares as a kid. Don't get them much anymore but occasionally they pop up again during a poorly timed nap. I'm sorry I scared you." I attempted a smile. "You probably thought I was being murdered in here."

His throat worked on a swallow. "It's fine. You have nothing to apologize for. You're not my first client to have nightmares like that."

An awkward silence settled between us. We'd barely spoken after our argument last night and he'd been polite and almost entirely silent today. I knew I was being shitty and making his job harder—but I also wasn't willing to budge on what I needed to do.

Neither was he. Yet he stayed next to me on the floor now, his broad body blocking most of my view.

"Do you want to tell me what your nightmare was about?" he asked slowly.

I dropped my head back against the cushion with a sigh. "Gargoyles. Specifically the ones out front. My dad had them installed when Preston and I were little and we always hated them. They show up in my dreams sometimes. I was... *we* were—" His eyebrows raised at that. "We were back in the parking lot with the car bomb and the gargoyles were attacking us both. I couldn't get them off of you. I tried though, I swear."

"That's much appreciated," he said, in a tone that was almost amused.

I cast a glance up at the wall, where there were clear square outlines, indicators of the missing paintings I'd dumped in a hallway closet. "My dad, he...he loved to play these little mind games with us. It's like all the shit with the business, giving me full control while firing Preston at the same time. He enjoyed pitting us against each other to win whatever breadcrumbs of love he could spare that week. He was obsessed with our grades and our performances at school. Whenever I didn't do well, which was all the time in his opinion, he'd withhold things. His attention, mostly." I shrugged. "Food, sometimes. The man definitely believed starvation was a motivator."

Elijah went eerily still next to me. "He starved you?"

"We had to earn that with our grades," I said flatly. "Sometimes I wouldn't earn the right to sleep inside so he'd make me sleep out on that big front porch. Underneath the gargoyles. They always scared me at night."

"That's why you dream about them."

I reluctantly met his gaze, unsure of what I'd find there. And was briefly shocked by something fierce and almost hungry there. "I think that's why, yeah. You ever get bad dreams?"

He hesitated. "Rarely. But yes." He touched the light scarring on his left cheek. "I was in a bad car accident as a kid. Comes back in my dreams."

My stomach knotted as I remembered what he'd said about his dad last night. *Smiled through it. Kept his secrets. He had a lot of them.*

"I'm sorry to hear that, Elijah," I said softly.

He shook his head. "It's nothing." A faint buzzing drew his attention to his watch. "Ethel and Clarita will be here in five minutes."

"Ah, *fuck me*," I swore. "Do I look like a hot mess who just screamed himself awake from a midday nightmare?"

"Not at all. You look..." His eyes traced the shape of my face, calling forth a blush. "You don't look a mess."

Then he extended his hand and I took it, appreciating yet again the firmness in his grip. I wasn't a small man, but Elijah hauled me up like I weighed nothing at all. We made furtive eye contact and my heart stuttered to a complete stop.

I opened my mouth to say something. *Hey, I was kind of a dick last night, right?* Or, *I wasn't joking when I said whoever let you go was an asshole, and maybe I want to find out who it was and hunt him down?*

Which was pointless. I didn't have any skills in the hunting-someone-down department, yet here I was ready to sign right up for the job.

Elijah released me, putting a conspicuous amount of space between our bodies.

"We should, uh... I'm gonna wait for them outside," I said, raking a hand through my hair.

Elijah nodded without comment and followed me, back down the long hallway of photos, the open windows with sweeping coastal views, the antique chandeliers dangling like death traps.

The estate was vast enough that a person could get quite lonely, wandering aimlessly through rooms and buildings that served no other purpose than decoration, like excess baubles on a Christmas tree. Not one, but two libraries. A tennis court, two pools, a guest house. Sitting rooms, sunrooms, an industrial-style kitchen filled with the staff who worked for my dad and Celine.

I hadn't seen her since the will reading but I knew the house hummed with ambient activity partially because of her. Whether that was because she was throwing polite garden parties or moving out, I had no idea.

She really only ever spoke to Preston, and he hadn't graced me with his belligerent presence since before my meeting with the protest organizers. I was secretly grateful that he hadn't mentioned the assistant hiring again. Since I had no intention of staying, there was no reason to find someone who'd only further solidify my role.

I *had* made some attempts at tracking down Adrian, the former assistant. The timing of his quitting was too fortuitous for my liking. Plus Preston hadn't hesitated to hire him on for his new real estate venture, which was two strikes in the negative column for me.

But so far, Adrian had sent my calls to voicemail and ignored my messages.

Per my father's unhinged estate plan, my brother only had another week left working here. The part of me that still remembered sleeping in Preston's room after Mom died wanted to take him out for a drink, commiserate about all that had happened, about all that Lincoln Beaumont had done to us. His lies, his schemes, his manipulations, all in service of his narcissism.

I often wondered if Dad pitted us against each other *because* we were so close. We had been, once. But the tiny flame in my heart that ached for my big brother had been smothered by his obvious disappointment in me, his disdain for my life and what I'd made of it. It was so clearly influenced by working alongside our father for all these years.

I just wasn't sure if the vast distance between us could be crossed.

Once outside, I leaned against the balustrade and slid my hands into my pockets, taking a long inhale of saltwater air. Elijah stood at the ready, with a straight spine and a steady gaze.

"Our contact at the police department has been updated on the threats against you," he said. "Though we've received nothing else of substance. No issues here or at your house. Nothing reported at any other offices."

"No more creepy emails then?" I asked.

"None. And let's hope it stays that way." He shifted on his feet. "Also, I wanted you to know I'll be gone for the next few days. I'm needed back at our New York offices. Once I return, I'll be switching with Ripley and will be on the night shift for a while."

My stomach dipped at the thought of Elijah being close to me after the sun had set.

"You'll be looming over me while I sleep, I assume?"

One brow winged up. "Is that what Ripley does?"

"I *think* he's outside, near the front door? Honestly, I barely know he's there."

"That is the point, generally. You wouldn't know I was

here if you didn't provoke me into conversation as often as you do."

I snorted. "We're working together. There's a difference."

"Technically, you backed me into a corner," he said. "There's a difference."

My face went warm, remembering what he'd said the day I'd signed that contract. *Yes, your father could be ruthless. I didn't think you would be as well.*

"It's worked out for you, hasn't it?" I countered. "It's been a whole week since my last thrill-seeking activity. No bungee jumps, no skydives, no swimming with sharks. You told me that keeping a client alive helps you keep your job too."

His jaw ticked. "I won't have this job much longer. It's why I'm heading back to the office."

"Uh, what?" I sputtered.

"My director is retiring at the end of next month and he's tapped me as his replacement. You're my last client before I leave the field for good. But I'll ensure you're left in excellent hands."

I leaned too far to the left against the balustrade and almost tipped over. I righted myself with as much grace as I could muster and attempted a lazy shrug. "That's not a problem. If I'm still chained to this company by then, something's gone horribly wrong."

"Regardless, you can trust that your safety will remain my priority."

I gave my most charming smile. "And how fortunate, to be ending your illustrious career in the field with your handsomest client. Some might even say...your best and most favorite client."

"This is based on which criteria exactly?" he asked mildly.

I waved a hand through the air. "This blank, stoic stare

of yours. It's *obvious* how much you love being here with me."

"Yes, my liege."

It took a moment to sink in, but when it did, delighted laughter spilled from my lips. "You made a *joke.*"

"Who's to say?"

His lips twitched. I saw it. I *fucking saw it.* I stepped closer, unable to resist him. But then a "Yoo-hoo" echoed across the massive front lawn. We turned toward what looked like two women riding a tandem bicycle up the long, curving driveway. They wore colorful outfits and had a tiny barking dog in the front basket.

"Those are my dad's former real estate partners?" I asked incredulously.

"I believe so," he said with a nod.

"They're your big clue?"

"You wanted clues, Luke," he said, passing a palm down his perfectly straight tie. "You didn't specify whether they had to be good."

14

LUKE

It'd been a long, long time since I last walked the stretch of beach in front of the estate. I'd ditched my shoes back at the house and opted for bare feet, cuffing my pants at midcalf. Elijah was a wall of silence beside me, somehow sand-free in his black suit and aloof behind his sunglasses.

The waving sea grass to our left was a constant, as were the foamy fingers of surf reaching toward us before being sucked back out on the tide. A handful of sailboats dotted the horizon and every fiber of my being yearned to make a break for it. To dive in, swim far out and haul myself onto some kind of watercraft.

The ocean had been my playground, my office, my faithful companion for most of my life, and spending even a week with my feet firmly planted on the ground felt entirely wrong. Like wearing your clothing two sizes too small, just tight enough to make you aware of every stitch and tag.

Ethel Walker and Clarita Reyes-Castillo walked back up from where they'd crouched next to the tiny terrier they'd introduced as Kingston. They were wives in their early sixties, dressed in matching tie-dye and aviator sunglasses, who had somehow worked with my father thirty-five years ago. They were popular local real estate agents, and as soon as Elijah mentioned them, I realized I'd seen their faces in ads all over town.

Ethel was a white woman with gray hair that fell down her back and owlish, wire-rimmed glasses. Clarita had a black bob streaked with white, darkly tanned skin, and chunky rings decorating her fingers.

"It's been, what, thirty years since we were welcome at Lincoln's estate?" Clarita asked her wife. "He invited us around a few times when it was first being built but it was always so obvious that he was showing off."

"Used to be we had a nice thing going with Lincoln," Ethel explained, "the three of us working together to sell houses throughout the South Shore. Clarita and I had a lot of bills to pay back then, so all the money we made with your father at the time made it easier to deal with his ego." She reached forward to touch my arm. "Your mother was too good for him."

My pulse rang in my ears. "You knew...my mom?"

"We loved your mom," Clarita said warmly. "We're so sorry she's gone."

Grief wrapped a hand around my throat. Sometimes it came back to me like this—that stringent medical smell in her room. How the pain seemed to shrink her body. Preston and I sitting at the foot of her bed, trying to make her laugh with stories from school.

"She used to play this game with us as kids, if one of us had to stay home sick," I said. "She called it 'carrot monster,' which meant 'turn every vegetable in the fridge into a terrifying costume.' How she was able to get the zucchinis to look like talons on her fingers, she never told us. Loved to chase us around though, especially out here on the beach. The sea gulls would follow us for stray bits of lettuce."

I avoided looking at the two women in front of me while I spoke. If I did, I had a sneaking suspicion I'd start to cry. My mother came from a small family we weren't close to, and if she had friends in Cape Avalon, I didn't know who they were. I was too young when I lost her to understand the full expanse of her vibrant life.

I often felt like I grieved her alone.

Next to me, Elijah cleared his throat. "Once, my brother and I were home sick with the same head cold. My mom worked the night shift, so she was running on about an hour of sleep when we'd woken her up, coughing. She still ran out to the store and brought us home one of those pizza-sized cookie cakes. She let us eat the whole thing while watching cartoons with her all day on the couch."

"I remember those. The kind with the icing," I said, my smile widening.

He gave a nod, and I couldn't see his eyes, but I felt the solid weight of them. His physical nearness continued to be my undoing, as if my brain knew he'd keep my every childhood secret and tortured memory safe from harm.

Ethel extended a hand, pointing toward the Laurel Lighthouse, at the end of the cape. "Clarita and I got married at the lighthouse. It was the best kind of big gay wedding. Everyone flew in from all over—my family in Maine, Clarita's family in Florida and San Juan. All of our friends from the Shipwreck." She peered back at me with a knowing smile. "Some members of this town like to ignore the deep roots of our queer history here. The drag balls and protests, the ways we've taken care of each other when society refused to. We have to fight to protect our legacy here, our futures."

I tipped my head in agreement. "We do need to fight, every damn day. Is that why you ultimately stopped working with my dad? He wasn't exactly a champion for queer liberation."

"No, he wasn't," Ethel said. "He was only ever a champion for *himself*. But Clarita and I were expert sellers at that time, taking the market here by storm. It was a strategic move for him, partnering with us. Money was what he cared about, everything else was superficial."

"And you know, your father was charming," Clarita said with a sad smile. "Especially in the beginning. A lot of men like him are. They can easily project generosity and charisma, especially when they want something from you. Whether that's your money or your respect or even your jealousy. Ethel and I were just starting to realize he wasn't who we thought he was when your grandfather died, leaving Lincoln an obscene amount of money. He quit the next day to found TBG. It was only afterward that we realized how much he'd manipulated us along the way."

I bit back a sigh. "He did tend to do that."

Ethel squinted into the sun. "Your father never had as much power as he believed he did. Know what I mean?"

I muttered something noncommittal and looked away, very aware that Elijah was studying my profile. Because I didn't know what Ethel meant. I'd spent my entire life resisting my father's manipulation at every turn, so much so that it felt like a twenty-four seven job.

"So why are you calling Lincoln's former business partners out of the blue?" Ethel asked.

Elijah removed his sunglasses. We shared a quick look.

"Someone was threatening my dad before he died," I said. "It started with emails, voicemails. Then a letter arrived, a week ago, demanding that I return some flash drive they believe I have or my dad had? A flash drive I haven't been able to find so far. Oh, also, they tried to kill me and Elijah with a car bomb."

Both women reared back in surprise.

"You mean that bomb at the adventure park was you two?" Ethel said. "Goodness, Luke, how awful."

I raised a shoulder. "I'm out here turning over every rock, seeing what's hiding underneath. You knew him when he was younger. You're local—seems like you've got the pulse on town politics. I'm not foolish enough to think you'd know anything about a random flash drive. But he's clearly angered *someone*."

Ethel and Clarita stared at each other for a moment while the ocean breeze tugged at their hair. Then Clarita said, "Luke, your father owned every secret in the Hamptons, and he wasn't that private about it. He traded in information. Valuable information. The kind worth more than money."

My brow creased. "What do you mean? He blackmailed people?"

"He's certainly not the only powerful person to do so," Ethel said. "Though he would have found the word *blackmail* to be too pedestrian for his tastes."

I glanced at Elijah, who was watching us closely.

"Okay, so..." I blew out a long breath. "He used secrets for...leverage?"

"Your father worked with exceptionally wealthy people. Celebrities, politicians, CEOs. Information becomes highly prized when you have more money than you know what to do with. What's more cash when you have all the cash?" Ethel shrugged. "It's more powerful to say 'I know who you're sleeping with.' And listen, you're right that we can't help you with the specifics of that letter. But you can certainly keep a secret on a flash drive. Photos, files, receipts. *Proof.*"

I scrubbed my hands through my hair, tugging on the ends. "Well, shit. Who knows how many enemies he made doing that. Who hated him the most?"

Clarita chewed on her lip, casting her eyes toward the horizon.

"What is it?" Ethel asked.

"Are you thinking about the tidal wetlands?"

Ethel laughed. "That's a trip back in time. Luke was probably a teenager."

At my questioning look, Ethel waved her hand between us. "Lincoln had this new luxury housing project near the village of Rodanthe Hills, in an area that *used* to be a tidal wetland habitat. It was beloved, it was *beautiful*. Rugged and isolated, completely crucial to the oceanic habitat."

I winced. "Did my dad like…build a mall on top of it or something?"

Clarita tipped her head to the side. "It was more complicated than that. He was granted a permit to build housing there, but on just a small area. Only the most passionate environmental advocates protested it at the time. It barely made the news, mostly because it didn't seem like it would do too much damage. It was within the regulations."

Kingston barked at her feet and she stooped to pick him up. "We have close friends who live near there and they told us about the goings-on at the time. There was a local park ranger who helped manage the wetlands and he fought your father tooth and nail, for *years*, over the project. His name was Clarence Craven."

I caught Elijah's eye. "Clarence Craven? We met him a few days ago. He's co-coordinating the protest at Sunrise Village."

"He mentioned he was only there on a visit," Elijah added. "Usually, he helps virtually from Rodanthe Hills."

"That's where he still lives," Ethel said. "He didn't mention he knew your father?"

"No, no, he didn't," I said slowly. "And he seemed jumpy the whole time." Goosebumps rose on the back of my neck. "What ultimately happened between Clarence and my dad?"

Clarita sighed. "Clarence went to every city hall meeting, started to get bigger crowds to protest at the dig site, was always there himself with a bullhorn. It was alleged that he sabotaged the building equipment, even. But in the end...Lincoln didn't adhere to the permit. The wetlands were razed, homes were built on top of them, and it completely changed the ecological environment, which was delicate to begin with. TBG never got in trouble for it either, but Clarence hasn't given it up. It's personal to him."

"And he didn't say a fucking thing to me about it," I said, cocking an eyebrow toward Elijah. "Does that feel strange to you?"

"Doesn't feel normal," he muttered with a frown.

"Would my dad have cause to blackmail Clarence though?" I asked. "If he did, doesn't seem like it was keeping Clarence quiet."

Ethel scratched behind Kingston's ears. "There are two things to consider, Luke. You wanted to know who publicly hated him the most, and Clarence is high on that list. I can't speak to this flash drive business, but I can speak to a man who feels hostile toward the Beaumont family and what you represent."

Her mouth bunched to the side. "And the other thing? Getting a wetland building permit in the state of New York is a near impossibility. Especially fifteen years ago. So how did your father get one?"

The memory of Senator Wallace at the garden party flashed through my brain. How skillfully she hid her frustration with the Sunrise Village delay, how artfully she redirected my misgivings. I wondered how she would have responded if we'd been alone and not in public. Wondered how long she'd been helping my father by fast-tracking permits he shouldn't have gotten.

And if she had any secrets she didn't want revealed.

A splash in the water drew Ethel's and Clarita's attention and they both brightened when they realized it was a pod of dolphins.

"Oh, Kingston, look," Ethel said, before they set off following him down the beach. "We'll be right back, Luke!" she yelled over her shoulder.

I squeezed the back of my neck. "Turns out they *were* a good clue. Good people too. Wish I'd known them after my mother died." I tossed him a grateful smile. "Thank you, Elijah."

He was eyeing me carefully. "Do you believe what they said?"

"Absolutely. This shit would be easy to hide too. You never saw any evidence he was blackmailing people while you were with him, right?"

"That's..." He dropped his gaze to the sand. "That's not something I would ever have known. Preston, maybe. Kenneth, almost definitely. I'm supposed to blend in with the background, but that didn't mean Lincoln let me see everything. Especially something illegal."

"If Preston knew my dad was blackmailing people, he'd tell me he was doing it for the right reasons. Kenneth would rather eat glass than admit something like that to me, of all people." I tipped my head to the side. "Clarence is suspicious, yeah?"

He nodded. "Agreed."

"And did you think about Senator Wallace when Ethel mentioned the permits?"

He clenched his jaw. "I did. But she's about to announce her run for president. I doubt she'd risk the bad press of being caught arranging for car bombs."

I hummed under my breath, mulling it over. "Possibly. She's not off the hook for me yet, though Clarence is a strong lead, *especially* since he omitted his decades-long feud with my father when we met with him." Then I snapped my fingers as an idea came to me. "We should take a drive out to Rodanthe Hills, try and pin down Clarence. Use the element of surprise to see what he knows."

Elijah stilled. "Luke, I'm not so sure—"

"Have you been before? It's only about a half hour from here and it's beautiful. We could even make a whole weekend out of it. Not that we'd be going just so I could show you beautiful things, but if we're already *there* why wouldn't I show you, right?" I offered up a smile. "We're close to finding out who's doing this. Really close. I can feel it."

His expression slammed shut. "We can't be taking day trips together. It's inappropriate."

"Says who?" I scoffed. "You'd accompany me there if I was traveling for a meeting or going on vacation. You told me when we first met that I was to have round-the-clock protection."

"It's not...that's not what I'm referring to," he said roughly. "It's about blurring boundaries. We talked about this. You signed a contract."

An *oh shit* sensation tightened my chest and sent my

heart flopping to the ground. A pitiful excuse for an organ, really. "The 'we can't be friends' contract. Yeah, I remember. Don't worry, I won't buy you a beer or anything. And I was only joking when I offered you that joint last night, I swear."

Elijah's eyes closed. He slid his sunglasses back on and it felt like a dismissal. "You know what I'm talking about, Luke. Unprofessional behavior leads to distraction, which leads to an increased risk of danger."

His fingers on my wrist. The look of concern after my nightmare. That almost-smile of his, beckoning me close.

"Is sharing personal information about each other unprofessional?" I asked lightly.

"I shouldn't have. Shouldn't have—" He stopped, glaring out at the horizon. "Shouldn't have agreed to any of this."

That tight feeling in my chest cracked, became sharper. "Shouldn't have agreed to help me take down your former client, you mean. Pretty unprofessional of you."

Elijah leaned in close and lowered his voice. "I'm doing what I have to do to keep everyone's jobs because the heir to the Beaumont Group manipulated me into doing his bidding," he snapped. "You're so shocked that your dad was keeping secrets as leverage, but what the hell are you doing to me, Lucas?"

15

ELIJAH

Two days later, I rode the elevator to the fourteenth floor and the East Coast offices for Regent Executive Security Specialists in Manhattan. I checked my posture in the reflective glass and noticed the knot in my tie was off-center by an inch.

Cursing softly, I wrenched it to the side and slid it back where it needed to go. Then I checked one last time for missed wrinkles or stray threads. I was due in a meeting with Foster in a matter of minutes and was running late for the first time in my life.

But I'd missed my subway stop, fretting over the hopeful, happy look in Luke's blue eyes as he said *we could even make a whole weekend out of it.*

The doors opened with a ding and I strode out into the busy environment, pausing to nod at some of the security agents I'd worked with in the past. The offices gleamed in sterling silver—polished, professional. Sleek and anonymous. Foster peeked his head out and brightened when he saw me.

"I'm sorry, sir. I'm late and I—"

He glanced at his watch. "It's thirty seconds past. Relax, Knight."

I peeled open my fingers and felt the ache in my knuckles. "Yes, sir."

"Come in and get the door when you do," he said. "We've got a lot to get to."

Inside, I blinked at the very obvious signs of my boss packing up his office. It was still organized and perfectly clean, but the walls were free of degrees and awards, the top of his filing cabinets oddly empty. He noticed my focus and extended his arm in a semicircle.

"This'll be yours soon," he said. "I'm trying to tie up as many loose ends as I can, but you'll be stepping into a few fires you'll need to put out. Nothing you can't handle, management wise."

I sat in the chair facing his desk. "Thank you, sir. I'm not worried."

"I'm glad you could come in today and tomorrow. I want you in some meetings with upper management and leadership," he said. "It's all the boring stuff, but you know what you signed up for."

A higher salary for my family. A more stable schedule. The kind of position my father dreamed of having but never could. The kind he assumed I'd never have. "I signed up for a reason. I'm ready."

"Shame about the Beaumont situation," he said. "Sounds like our police liaison is doing the best he can with what little evidence he has."

Every muscle in my body tightened as remnants of our conversation with Ethel and Clarita came rushing back in. I'd been more rattled by it than I cared to admit. The blackmail piece was a *huge* complication—and dangerous at that.

Clarence Craven's motivations and jumpy behavior when we met felt like a red flag.

And while I wasn't sure Senator Wallace would orchestrate death threats this close to her presidential campaign, Ethel's warning about *who* was pushing permits through for Lincoln was a fair one.

"Ripley called in before you arrived," Foster continued. "Another email arrived. You're being followed again."

"I'm what?" I asked, surprised.

He turned his screen around to show me and the image there had my stomach plummeting. We'd been tailed. *Again.* This time to the Historical Society's garden party. Someone had captured Luke and me, though the image was grainy and poorly lit in the dark.

In it, I'm close to Luke—much too close.

I knew the exact moment that was being captured. I'd startled at a sound, had grabbed his wrist tightly though we weren't in obvious danger.

I think you like putting me in my place, Elijah.

"That's not possible," I said sharply. "Sylvester was working the perimeter and that party was full of security. A state senator was there. No way some random civilian's able to infiltrate without our knowledge."

Foster pinned me with a level gaze, staying silent for a beat too long. I'd raised my voice, flustered by the new information and the intimacy writ large on his laptop screen.

"Perhaps it's not a civilian in the way you're thinking," he said slowly. "There can be stalkers anywhere. You know that."

"Of course, sir," I said quickly. "I'm sorry. I'm...slightly taken aback by the picture, is all. I'd assumed the first email was a one-off and shouldn't have."

His eyes searched mine. "Understandable. It's uncomfortable. And there's nothing about Lucas Beaumont you'd like to share with me? His behavior? You mentioned before he was impulsive? Reckless?"

Intriguing. Charming. Secretly in pain. Too handsome for his own good.

"We've developed a better working relationship now that he's more accustomed to round-the-clock protection," I replied. "Nothing I can't handle."

He nodded, seemingly pleased with that answer. "I don't doubt it. Not that you'll have to worry about his protection for much longer. It'll be someone else's job to protect him."

The sensation that rippled through me at those words—*it'll be someone else's job to protect him*—had me wanting to claw the chair in two with my bare hands.

"Absolutely, sir. I'm looking forward to it."

Foster shifted a few piles of paper on his desk, accidentally knocking over Sunday's edition of the *Times*. I bent to pick it up and blinked at the face staring back at me: Lincoln Beaumont.

One of his business associates had written a memorial piece about his life in the Opinion section. Scanning it, I picked out phrases like "much adored businessman" and "a fervent believer in giving back." At the bottom, the colleague had asserted that his buildings had changed the landscape of the Hamptons "for the better." There was also mention of the crowds of people who'd gathered at his funeral weeks ago, with lines stretching around the block.

My chest seized up, remembering the look of raw vulnerability on Luke's face after his nightmare. The flat tone in his voice as he said *the man definitely believed starvation was a motivator*.

Sitting up, I set the paper back on the desk. "Regardless

of who's behind these threats, we know...well, I know, that Lincoln Beaumont was...is..."

"He was what?"

"He wasn't...a good man. He wasn't a moral man."

Foster paused, leaning back in his chair and steepling his fingers. "Are you saying that your client did something illegal in your presence?"

"No, sir."

"Then questions of his morality or immorality are of no concern to us," he said. "Our priority is clear—protection from harm. Ensuring high-status individuals with significant wealth and notoriety can move through this world in peace, without fearing for their lives. You're an honorable person, Elijah, and always have been. But my recommendation, especially for taking on this role after me, is to worry less about client ethics and more about client retention."

At the start of all this, I hadn't been overly impressed with Luke's theories about who was behind the threats and what that said about his father's secret actions. Even if I personally found his behavior to be unsavory, that didn't mean he was a criminal.

Except I couldn't really claim to know *what* happened behind Lincoln's closed doors. Even my own father hid his unsavory behavior with an ease and comfort that still boggled my mind.

Foster's phone rang and he picked it up with a clipped, "Yes?"

I heard muffled speaking on the other end, then his eyes darted to mine. "I'll send him down right away."

"Is something wrong?" I asked.

"Your brother is here," he said.

I went still. "Christopher is...*here*?"

"Apparently. He's asking to see you."

My mind raced with a hundred different scenarios, none of them good. Christopher and his family lived in Brooklyn, but I hadn't seen him in almost nine months. We'd come to a tenuous truce on the subject—he stopped complaining that I worked too much while I tried not to feel too guilty about it.

I half rose from the chair and Foster said, "Go, it's fine," before I'd even opened my mouth to ask.

In the elevator, I was so keyed up I should have taken the stairs instead. It was an automated response, developed over the years from Christopher and me being terrified that Dad had returned to skulk around the edges of our family, trying to manipulate his way back in.

As adults, it had taken a few years for us to drop the habit of saying "Don't worry, Dad's not back" whenever one of us called each other unexpectedly.

So it was only normal to want to collapse in relief at the sight of him in the lobby—seemingly safe and unharmed. He brightened when he saw me and then a tiny blur of motion tackled my legs. I bent to scoop up my nephew Skylar immediately, unsure what to do with the starburst of emotion that lodged in my heart when he threw his tiny arms around my neck.

"The prodigal son returns," Christopher boomed, giving me a hug as big as his son's. "I took Sky into Manhattan for the day and he asked if we could walk by your job and surprise you."

He reared back, still squeezing my shoulders. "I told him we had a one in a million shot you'd be here, yet here you are. This is the best day ever."

Before I could respond, he shook his head. "I know what you're gonna say and don't worry. We've got tickets to a movie that starts in twenty minutes, so we won't bother you for long. Though you could come over for dinner if you want. Shana and the twins would love to see you. We could even Skype Mom in from the road. Rumor has it, she adopted *another* dog while in Texas."

Working the night shift all those years had taken their toll on our mother, health-wise, so we were all relieved when she was able to retire with a small pension that allowed her to do what she'd always dreamed of—travel around the country in an old RV, adopting rescue dogs along the way. But her finances were still tight, and every medical bill and health concern sent me spiraling with worry.

"I miss you, Uncle Eli," Skylar said, smiling at me with eyes just like his dad's. He looked so much like Christopher as a kid that it never ceased to provoke a cognitive dissonance. Never ceased to have me listening with one ear for the sounds of our dad waking up. Used to be I could predict his mood based on whether he whistled while making his coffee.

No whistle meant I sent Christopher out to play with his friends all day, with strict instructions not to return until dark.

I ruffled Sky's hair with one hand. "I miss you too, kiddo. Every single day."

"Where have you been?" Christopher said softly. "Mom told me it's been tough to get in touch with you. You're not avoiding your much more attractive younger brother on purpose, are you?"

I shifted uncomfortably on my feet. "Work's been busy."

He wrinkled his nose. "It's been nine months since I last saw you, Eli. You could come around more, you know? I want my big brother back."

I stepped closer, lowered my voice. "I've been busy for a reason. I'm taking over the company. I'll be the youngest director in their history. And the lead-up, the training, it's been a lot. Plus, I'm still in the field with the Beaumont family out in Cape Avalon. But all of this means a much bigger salary. It's for you. For the kids. And for Mom."

His eyes softened. "We didn't ask you to do that. Not if it means we'll see you even less than we do now."

"You don't have to ask," I said. "I'll always take care of you. It's—" I swallowed *because I love you* and said, "I'm your brother and I want to help."

Christopher rubbed the top of his head. We were traipsing through a conversation so well-worn it was frayed at the edges. "I know you do. And I hate sounding like a broken record here but...we want to see you. Please?"

I was never sure how to say it, so I never did. Never sure how to explain what it felt like at fourteen, when Dad finally left for good and I watched my mother sigh in relief. How the relief then turned to a barely concealed panic at the loss of his second income, like ripping the cord for a parachute that only opened halfway.

I'd never told my brother what it was like to step up and take on the responsibility of caring for him. Someone needed to help my mom, because the member of my family who bragged the most about being responsible had fucked off like we were nothing but an afterthought.

Even something as innocuous as having dinner with my family had me itchy and restless, forever trapped in that feeling like I was fifty miles down the highway and realizing I'd left the burner on. *More work, more hours, more money.* There was always more to be done to ensure my family never struggled again.

Skylar reached up and tapped my nose, laughing, while

Christopher eyed me with a tender worry that made me feel like an asshole.

"I want to see you too," I said quickly. "And you're not a broken record. It's on me, anyway. Let's do something soon, okay?"

"You promise?" he asked. "'Cause if not, this kid knows where you work now. He'll stake it out."

I sent my nephew a tiny smile. "Is that true?"

He nodded somberly then clutched at my arms again until I gave him another hug. It was too much and not enough, all at once. The love, the fear, the worry. The cycle I couldn't seem to break.

My phone went off with notifications for a dozen different meeting reminders and emails. With a soft chuckle, Christopher gently extricated Sky from my arms and gave me a salute.

"That's our cue to leave, but I'm so happy we did this. So happy we saw you."

I glanced over my shoulder, nagged by something Luke had said to me. Nagged by the *way* he'd said it, as if each word was a thorn, ripping up his throat.

You know nothing about what it was like growing up with that man, Elijah.

"Can I ask you something before you go? About Dad?"

My brother went rigid. "Did he call you?"

"No, nothing like that. It's a client I have. From what I can understand, his dad was like ours," I said quietly. "Well, not exactly like ours. But the dynamics are similar."

Christopher winced. "I'm sorry to hear that."

"His dad left my client this business when he passed away. A huge business, with a ton of clout and responsibility. And my client wants to give it up. The money, the power, the privilege." I held my brother's gaze. "If something like that happened to you, with the dad we had, what would you do?"

His eyebrows shot up. "With the company?"

"Yeah."

"That's easy." He hefted Sky around his waist and kissed the top of his head. "If Dad gave me his business, I'd burn it to the ground."

16

LUKE

The dim light of the TV in the guest house turned Harriet's darkened living room cave-like. With the windows cracked, the trill of sea birds and the distant crash of the ocean filtered in. We'd muted the Pixar movie my nieces had begged us to watch since they were passed out now—Lizzie with her head in Harriet's lap and Rory on my chest. I kept my breathing slow and even, worried I'd startle her awake. Every so often we could hear the soft crackle of walkie-talkies from the pair of security guards stationed at the front door.

One of the guards was mine, a completely silent woman who was even more stoic than Elijah. And the other was part of the team that now protected Harriet, my nieces, and Harriet's mother, Lois. After I'd seen that picture of me and Elijah post car bomb, I'd asked for my sister to be added to their roster.

If I was being followed even part of the time, then it was likely they knew of Harriet's existence and where she lived. Risking my own life was one thing. I wouldn't put the people I loved the most in danger just so I could get revenge.

Turned out Elijah had been infuriatingly right the other day.

You wouldn't bungee jump with only half a rope. So why take on a job with a giant target on your back and be so cavalier about your own safety?

My scowling babysitter in a bespoke suit had been right about a lot lately. And in these past ninety-six hours without him, I'd missed him so much I'd found myself pacing my father's office like a wild cougar trapped in a zoo.

It used to be that on days like this, I'd spend hours in the ocean, coaching clients how to surf while burning off my own excess energy. Then I'd borrow one of our Jet Skis and jump waves until I scratched as much of the itch as I could, soothed by the combination of fear and euphoria I sought out like a drug.

Instead, I'd spent four days chasing down clues and tearing through my father's office, searching for some fucking flash drive I wasn't even sure *actually* existed. I'd gotten so frustrated I'd moved my search into Dad's library, leaving a tornado swath of mess along the way.

I found no obvious signs of blackmail, although I was pretty sure that was on purpose. Adrian, the former assistant, still hadn't returned my calls. My brother was surly and silent when our paths crossed at the office. The only decent headway I'd made was researching the tidal wetlands near Rodanthe Hills, as well as the properties built there by TBG fifteen years ago.

The houses were massive, garish, completely out of place in what was considered one of the only fishing communities left in the Hamptons. The town itself was small and sleepy, mostly locals who never saw the same surge in tourists the rest of us did. And what Ethel and

Clarita had said was true—the environmental impact on the tidal wetlands had been devastating.

Per the city council meeting minutes I'd scanned, as well as some quick internet research, Clarence Craven was still furious and looking for ways to reverse the damage and restore the delicate ecosystem there.

I could find nothing interesting about the permits. According to records, the permitting process was official and above board. But it would make sense, if my father traded in secrets, for him to have held some kind of leverage over whoever made it happen.

The question being—how would I ever discover who that person was?

Elijah's face flashed through my thoughts—the quiet disgust etched into his features that day on the beach. *You're so shocked that your dad was keeping secrets as leverage, but what the hell are you doing to me, Lucas?*

He'd cut right through my bullshit without batting an eye and I'd fucking deserved it. And my uneasy nerves had been jumpy with guilt ever since.

My sister beamed down at her phone, her face illuminated by the screen in the darkness. Her pink hair was in a long braid, and she wore a faded, crewneck sweatshirt from the South Shore Bookshop.

"I knew you weren't watching *A Bug's Life*," I whispered. "You were texting Kat, weren't you?"

"Maybe," she teased. "I can't help it if she's obsessed with me."

I huffed. "Ignoring your only brother so you can text your girlfriend?"

"She's not my girlfriend. Yet. Though she did have some questions when I showed up to our last date with a bodyguard in tow," she replied, using two fingers to tweeze a potato chip from the open bag between us. "I'd like to think it increases my air of mystery. I appreciate the extra bit of safety though."

Rory shifted on my chest, tucking her tiny fist against her mouth. "I'll double it, triple it, if necessary. Just say the word."

"I'm not worried about us, Luke. I'm worried about *you.*"

"I'm totally fine," I said, scoffing.

"Are you though?" She leaned in closer, pinned me with a look. "The car bomb was bad enough, but now you're being followed? Possibly by some guy named Clarence that Lincoln pissed off years ago? If this man is holding onto a grudge that old, he must have nothing left to lose."

"Neither did Dad," I said. "That's why I'm in this mess, especially now that we know he was operating some kind of...elite *blackmail* operation." I shook my head. "None of this behavior prevented him from amassing money and power to get what he wanted. But there weren't any consequences for his actions."

Harriet's face softened. "He lost you. That's a pretty big one."

"Yeah, well, he lost you too, and that's even worse. You're a much better human than I am. Then you had the gall to go and make even better humans."

Her answering smile was sad at the edges. "I don't know if I'm that great. I fed those better humans hot fudge sundaes for dinner."

I cracked a smile. "That's on me, sis. I brought the supplies over." The TV flickered, highlighting the dark circles under her eyes. When I'd walked in tonight, she'd shoved what looked like a pile of overdue medical bills under a potted plant. I reached over and touched her hand.

"Hey, are you okay?"

"Definitely." She glanced down at Lizzie and kissed the top of her head. "Listen, I know you don't want to hear it again, but I really think you should drop this. All of it. Digging through Lincoln's shit. Chasing down former enemies. All you're doing is drawing attention to yourself, and it's going to get you hurt—or worse— by whoever's threatening you."

The static of radios had us turning to the door. For a brief, foolish moment I hoped that Elijah was back, in which case I could point and say *See? My life's not in danger because Elijah swore he was my shield.*

Instead, the moment passed—although Harriet still wore a look of sisterly concern.

"What about riding it out?" she said. "Just chill, let the board handle most of the job, collect the trust in three years and get out of there alive." She grabbed my wrist and squeezed. "I hate that you have to be there, Luke. I really do. I know how it affects you and I'm not suggesting this lightly. But is it really worth risking your life over?"

I thought about my mom, chasing me and Preston into the waves with zucchinis for talons, laughing as the sun lit her from behind. How big and strong she'd seemed then, untouchable and everlasting. As permanent a fixture on this earth as the ocean that she loved.

How quickly my father decided we'd all pretend she'd never existed after she died.

"Riding it out means no one...no one ever knows the real truth of who my father was," I said, my throat crowded with grief. "Riding it out means I go quietly, like I always have. I let him pay for NYU, let him pay for my apartment there. And sure, I didn't spend my graduation money the way I was supposed to, but I still *took it*. All while keeping my mouth shut about his many sins. Maybe I could have gotten him to help you, to help your mom. I could have done *more*, period."

Harriet sent me a pained look. "Nothing could have made that man behave differently. Not you, not anyone else."

I considered my next words carefully, fighting the urge to fidget. "I saw you hide your mom's bills when I walked in."

She wrinkled her nose, shrugged. "I never wanted a good credit score anyway."

"Harry."

"Luke." She brushed a lock of Rory's hair from her forehead. "Some battles I can fight on my own. You know that, right?"

"Of course," I said with a wince. "Of course I do."

"If the situation becomes dire, you'll be the first to know," she continued. "It's not always about the money. Yes, I need financial support right now and I'm never too proud to ask for it or receive it. But when I contacted you all those years ago, I wasn't looking for some handout. I wanted someone to see what he'd done to us, to affirm that I wasn't completely unhinged for reacting so negatively whenever I saw Lincoln Beaumont in the newspaper looking like a goddamn Kennedy. Completely untouchable."

I nodded eagerly. "That's why I'm doing all of this. You have to believe me."

"I do believe you." She clutched at my hand. "But Luke, what I *really* got from messaging you that day was a *brother*. A best friend. Someone I love to the moon and back. All the other stuff I was feeling I had to work on by myself. Acknowledging pain is just the beginning, because nothing can change how he treated us. Nothing can change the past, and that's the shittiest part of all. All we can do is accept what we can, love who we can, and fight for a better future."

I dropped my gaze and let her words sink in, poking and prodding at every secret part of myself I longed to avoid. Acceptance didn't come easily, especially when it came to my father, but having him reenact one of his psychotic mind games on me and Preston even after he'd died had been too much. Whatever meager healing I'd found over the years had shattered as soon as the lawyers made it clear he'd done all of this on purpose.

I cleared my throat and plucked at a loose thread on the couch cushion. "Elijah and I argued the other day. He, uh... he said I was like Dad."

Her eyebrows flew up. "Who, your bodyguard?"

"He's not *mine*. I mean, he's mine technically but he's not..." I stopped when I realized she was smirking. "Anyway, I fucked up. Elijah was by my dad's side for five years and I thought he'd be able to help me build this case against him, you know? But he didn't want to do that because Elijah lives his life by a strict code of honor and morality the likes of which hasn't been seen since the Middle Ages..."

"Luke," my sister chided, "where is this going?"

I avoided her gaze again. "I kinda...sorta...threatened to fire him and all of his colleagues if he didn't agree to help me dig up dirt on my dad. So when Ethel and Clarita confirmed that he routinely used blackmail to get his way..." I shrugged. "Elijah told me I was no better than he was."

Harriet was silent in response, probably enjoying watching me squirm.

"I definitely fucked up. I know I did. But also...do you think I'm like him? Some manipulative narcissist using people to get his way all the time?"

She laughed softly and handed me a chip from the bag. "I believe that people will do some desperate things for the people that they love. And I believe that you're one of those people, Luke."

I placed my hand on Rory's back and felt her tiny rib cage expanding with each precious breath.

"Which makes you nothing like Lincoln. And yet"—her smile was devilish—"you absolutely fucked up."

My head fell back against the cushion as I sighed. "I knew it. I'm such a dipshit."

"A lovable dipshit. But yes, yes you are."

17

ELIJAH

I trailed behind Luke and a small group of his friends, following at a safe distance as they made their way along the beach to the Shipwreck. The sun was setting, bathing the group in golden light, highlighting their loose limbs, their ease, their laughter.

It'd been five days since I'd last seen him. Four days back at the office, training alongside Foster, then a day to switch my sleep schedule so I could relieve Ripley of the night shift.

The first couple nights on a switched schedule always had a buzzy twilight feel to them, a combination of too much caffeine, not enough sleep, and the sense of innate wrongness that came from being awake when others were in bed.

It made me antsy. Though Ripley had explained that they'd vetted these friends a day earlier, had staked out the walking route and the bar and found nothing to be alarmed by. And it'd been quiet the whole time I was gone. No letters, no emails, no evidence of being followed.

The group paused at a stoplight, with Luke hanging off the post with one arm. His friends talked and laughed around him while he stayed silent. The fading light turned his dark hair bronze, and a curl hung over his forehead. He wore black pants, a white tank top, and a short-sleeved linen shirt patterned in reddish-orange. The ends flapped briefly in the breeze and the tank dipped low on his chest, exposing a swath of smooth skin.

He peered up at me through long lashes. It felt like touching a live wire, all sticky electricity with a neon buzz. He held my gaze for a beat too long before spinning on his heels to amble across the road.

Luke had been polite, if distracted, from the moment I'd checked in with him tonight. But I couldn't blame him. I'd snapped at him the last time we'd really spoken, accused him of being no better than his father. And while it was true that he'd purposefully put me in a shitty situation, comparing him to the man who'd starved and manipulated him felt like a low blow in retrospect.

But that didn't alleviate the gulf of differences between us. Luke would always have the power, the money, the prestige, no matter how fervently he shrugged it off. He'd always be the one holding my contract over my head—my job, my income, my career—and threatening to rip it in two.

But even as I accepted the truth of these things, my gut churned whenever I replayed our conversation on the beach. *We could even make a whole weekend out of it.*

The hurt in his eyes, the slump of his shoulders. It was like watching a light being shut off in a distant room. But what he was suggesting had sounded so much like a date that I'd panicked. Mostly due to my own bodily reaction—a craving so deep it'd taken my breath away.

Why *not* make a whole fucking weekend out of it?

My mind had filled with images much too domestic with a man I was sworn to keep safe above all else. Brunch at some diner along the coast. A charming bed-and-breakfast Luke would get a kick out of. The lock I'd throw on the door so I could drag him back to bed and keep him there for hours.

We were nearing the Shipwreck, where the sounds of a happy crowd and loud dance music could be heard, even this far away. From the outside, it looked like any other dive bar you might see in a small beach town—popular in the summertime and empty in the offseason. A painted mermaid, with long red hair and a beard, held a broken-off helm in her burly, tattooed arms. Twinkle lights flashed around the door, and a few people stood with cigarettes and drinks in their hands.

One of Luke's friends cracked a joke and he laughed, tossing out the charming smile that haunted my dreams. He gave one of the women a half hug. Squeezed the hand of a tall man wearing a beanie. Called out another friend's name when he spied them from down the street, laughing as they jumped into his arms with a squeal.

I ground my molars and fought to stay focused. Assessed every entrance, noted the bouncer at the door, studied the packed bar as soon as we stepped inside. The center of the room held a small stage, and a drag queen in a hot pink wig was performing to a cheering crowd. Next to the dance floor, the long bar stretched the length of the room. A disco ball spun in the center and multicolored lights bounced off every reflective surface.

I flexed my fingers and swallowed against a mounting irritation. Irritation with my team, who'd somehow believed this tiny, tight space, with only two visible exits, was somehow *safe.* Irritation with Lucas, who tested my patience daily like it was a fun game. And irritation with myself, most of all, for crossing boundaries with my client when I fucking knew better.

Luke and his friends made their way to a seating area. I kept some distance toward the back, directly in Luke's line of sight, so I could monitor who was nearby at all times. I'd spoken already with tonight's bartender, informing them of the recent threats. And Luke had agreed to keep his drink choices limited to beer only, each one opened where I could see it.

He sprawled on a low couch now, one long arm slung across the back and his ankle hooked over his knee. His gaze found mine through the crowd, and he sent me a lazy grin that had my face heating in the dark room.

Two hours passed this way. I stood with my feet planted and my hands clasped while the world spun and rotated around a single point of focus.

Luke.

Bathed in multicolored light, his posture relaxed as the music changed. Drag queens performed, people trickled past. He accepted kisses on the cheek from his friends. Let himself get pulled up to dance when a song came on that he liked. Sang along with the performers, winking when they strode by to collect the cash tips he gave them.

But he was watching me too. And it wasn't just a casual perusal. His eyes raked the length of my body with a predator's arrogance, and I felt it like a caress. Gorgeous men and elegant women crowded around him, some spilling into his lap, some dancing nearby to get his attention. He shrugged off his shirt, leaving the rounded muscles of his shoulders exposed.

His forearm flexed each time he raised a bottle to his lips. And he eyed me openly. Brazenly. A dangerous lust coiled in my belly, dangerous because I knew all too well what happened when flirtation gave way to distraction. Even now, I felt the noise around me dim, felt my reflexes dull to a stupor. Luke arched an eyebrow my way—an invitation—and when I matched the gesture, he broke into a smile. Big and dazzling and brilliant. He didn't move, simply traced his lower lip with his thumb and kept his gaze leashed to mine.

Do you ever pretend you're someone else for the night and take a total stranger back to your bed?

I wasn't opposed to the idea, but it generally didn't work for me. Maybe when I was younger, when desperate groping in a darkened room at a party with a man whose name I'd never know had been fine at the time.

Luke made desperation seem appealing again, the kind that thrived in dark corners and furtive meetups. The kind that would thrive in this bar, with its small staff rooms and supply closets. I could drag him into the first private place we found. Kiss that smart mouth of his so hard he'd understand the depths of my unrelenting frustration.

I'd kiss that man until all he could do was pant and shudder. Kiss him until every teasing taunt became a plea, an ache, a craving. I'd kiss Luke Beaumont until he no longer knew his own fucking name—then I'd fall to my knees and worship him further.

I needed his fingers in my hair. Needed him using my name as a chant and a curse. God help me, I'd certainly fantasized about it enough.

Yes, Elijah. Please, Elijah. More, yes, please, more, ye—

The buzzing of my phone shocked me from the lurid images dominating my thoughts. Shocked me so thoroughly that the sounds of the room immediately rose in volume, the dancer's movements back to regular speed, my innate sense of danger suddenly blaring like a foghorn.

The number on my screen was the one we used when something was very, very wrong, calling during a moment when I was so far past the bounds of professionalism it was a goddamn joke. I moved to a quieter corner and kept my focus glued on Luke, who had cocked his head quizzically when I did so.

"What is it?" I barked into the phone.

"Luke's account got another email," Sylvester said. "Another picture, this one of him and his friends outside the Shipwreck."

"As in only two hours ago?" I asked, all the hairs standing up on my arms.

"Yes. And a different message this time," he said. "*If you won't give me what I want, I'm taking it from you.*"

I was already moving, pushing through the sea of people as Luke's eyes widened at my approach.

"Elijah," Sylvester said, "you gotta get him out of there. Now."

18

LUKE

Elijah was barreling toward me through the crowd at the Shipwreck. I had only a second to take in the power radiating off his body before he was dipping his mouth to my ear.

"We were followed here, Luke. We need to go now."

I scoffed, surprised. "What the hell could they do to me here? We're in the middle of a crowded—"

His fingers clamped around my wrist. When I turned my head, startled, the tips of our noses brushed.

"I wasn't asking," he growled. *"Get up."*

I obeyed with an eagerness that should have embarrassed me, but I was three beers deep and the world had taken on that hazy feeling of being pleasantly buzzed. I was growing addicted to what his fingers felt like when they tightened on my skin like this—firm and possessive and competent in a way that made me hard as a fucking rock.

That and something equally as fervent—the urge to apologize for what I'd done, right here in the bar, with someone potentially very dangerous on our heels. But I couldn't stop obsessing over the disgust on his face, the harsh disappointment in his words.

You're so shocked that your dad was keeping secrets as leverage, but what the hell are you doing to me, Lucas?

And that had happened right after I'd suggested we take a weekend trip like some kind of...some kind of *boyfriend.* Like *we* were boyfriends and I was hell-bent on planning the perfect romantic getaway.

Jesus, if I'd suggested we go apple-picking before staking out my father's tormentor it would have been less embarrassing.

"Elijah, I'm so sorry—" I started to say, but it was drowned out by the song being performed on stage. And the fact that Elijah was shoving me through the crowd toward the door, his strong grip on my shoulder just as pleasant as my buzz. I threw my linen shirt back on and tossed a hasty wave to my friends, making a mental note to send them an apologetic explanation some time tomorrow.

Certainly wasn't the first time I'd let myself get dragged out of here by a suited-up smokeshow like Elijah. Though this was the first time it was due to personal security attempting to save my life.

As soon as we reached the door, people burst through it and Elijah reacted immediately, shoving me behind his body. It was nothing, just a rowdy group of locals, but one accidentally knocked into me as they passed, sending me falling against Elijah's broad back.

He remained steady on his feet, with one arm still reaching to keep me behind him. Meanwhile, I was trying not to obsess over the rigid flexing of his shoulders beneath my fingers. But he wasted no time, grabbing my wrist and fixing me to his side as we stepped into the cool night air. We turned to the left, to the direction we would have walked back to my house, when two figures stepped from the shadows and headed toward us.

Nothing gave them away as especially dangerous, except there was an intent to their strides that made the hair rise on the back of my neck.

Elijah turned us to the right, heading toward the well-lit main strip of bars and restaurants.

"We should have driven," he said gruffly.

"But we couldn't," I pointed out. "I wanted to walk."

"Exactly. I shouldn't have let you." A muscle jumped in his jaw. "Follow my lead. We'll try to disappear the first chance we get."

He snapped a phone to his ear and barked out our situation to whomever was on the other line. When the call finished, he slipped us into the crowded street, floating among the Thursday night crowd that was still partially tourists, even this late in the summer season. But it was unseasonably warm, and some of the bars had set up dance floors outside. People spilled onto the street, holding drinks, while others meandered past with takeout containers or handheld snacks from the collection of food trucks at the end of the block.

I craned my neck and Elijah snapped, "Don't look behind you."

"But are they still following us?" I asked, sidestepping past dancing couples.

"Yes."

I shivered, the thought disconcerting while surrounded by laughing people holding red Solo cups.

"I haven't received so much as a threatening *fax* while you've been gone, and as soon as you're back, I've got people following me," I said, casting him a sidelong glance.

He was rapidly scanning every single person we walked past. "Your point?"

"Maybe it's *you* they're after. Ever think of that?"

We cut a sharp left to the other side of the street. White string lights swayed over our heads and Elijah picked up the pace a little.

"You mean, what if I'm paying the price for my father's sins and you're just the one caught in the middle?" he said, with slightly more warmth in his voice this time. Enough warmth to have me turning to face him and almost tripping over a sidewalk dog bowl in the process.

But Elijah caught me, guiding me firmly into a packed cocktail bar. Once inside, he scowled out the window while I feigned nonchalance. The music inside was loud, so I leaned in close until his eyes dropped to my mouth with a look bordering on fury.

And then hunger.

"Stranger things have happened," I drawled.

His eyes rose, boring into mine for one hot second before he refocused on his targets outside. "Your dad had the kind of influence mine could only dream of. He pissed off plenty of people, but he was the kind of man who got his ass kicked in a bar brawl. He's not rich enough to receive a series of threatening emails."

I studied his profile, the thin webbing of scars on his cheekbone. "What secrets did you have to keep for him?"

He blinked, stared at me. "What did you say?"

"The other day," I explained. "You told me you had to keep your father's secrets to keep him in a good mood. What was he doing?"

His throat bobbed. "What your father was doing."

Understanding dawned. "He was cheating on your mom."

Elijah nodded stiffly but said nothing else.

"I'm sorry," I said. "I know...it's awful. And lonely, keeping a secret like that. He was your parent and should have known better."

He briefly looked stunned at my words and I almost raised my hand to reach for him. But then we were on the move again, back into the crowd. He tightened his hand around my shoulder, keeping me close, and I could feel the strength in every finger through the thin material of my linen shirt. Could feel the absolute *sliver* of his skin on mine, where the very edge of his pinkie brushed my collarbone. A centimeter, if that, and I was burning all the way up.

I needed to want this man less. *So much less*, because I'd been a total asshole about everything. He'd be smart to reject my clumsy advances.

He'd be smart to reject me altogether.

He hauled us into a well-lit alley, ducking under fluttering rainbow flags and a series of pop art-inspired murals of surfers and sail boats. He turned his head. Cursed.

"We need to hide for a few minutes until Sylvester gets here," he muttered. "The last thing I ever expected was for these people to approach you in public. That kind of unpredictability is dangerous."

I snapped out of my lust-fueled haze and realized where we were. "Hold up. I know a place. Follow me."

Elijah's definition of *follow me* was to stay glued to my side, his giant hand still grasping my shoulder to keep me near as I moved us through the alley and took a sharp left turn.

"Where?" he whispered urgently.

A moment later we were in front of it—a cozy building painted sky blue with red awnings and daisies in the windowsill. "The bookshop. It closes early on Thursdays."

Elijah blocked my body as I flipped open the keypad and entered in the passcode. The second it beeped, he shoved me inside and slammed the door shut behind us. He threw the locks and checked that all the curtains were drawn. Inside was dark, lit only by the glow of the exit signs and the shimmer of streetlights filtering in past the curtains.

It smelled pleasantly dusty, as usual, and was filled with overstuffed chairs and book recommendations handwritten on index cards. The friendly tabby cat named Calvin spent nights at home with the owner.

Elijah pulled me deeper into the store until we were standing behind the bookcase that housed our poetry collection. I was slightly out of breath, more from adrenaline than exertion. My bodyguard cocked his head, listening for something I couldn't hear. The store was eerily silent. Hushed.

The front door started to shake. Something hit it so hard that I gasped. Elijah's hand shot out and covered my mouth, forcing me back against the wall. His focus was glued to the door, spine rigid. My heart rattled against my rib cage, more from the feel of his hand over my lips than the danger outside. Or maybe *because* of the danger. I shut my eyes against the onslaught of fantasies I couldn't prevent even if I wanted to.

Elijah, dragging me into the bathroom at a party. Shoving me back onto the counter, one hand over my mouth, the other working my cock. Rough and fast, aware of the voices outside, the threat of getting caught, because he knew how much I loved this kind of risk.

The sounds outside stopped, leaving that same eerie silence in its wake. Elijah released a long, quiet breath. His eyes sought mine, barely visible in the darkness and blazing with hunger. Then he dropped his hand from my mouth, looking dazed and contrite.

"Luke...I'm sorry, I shouldn't have—"

"*I'm* the one who's sorry," I whispered. "You were so right the other day. My dad used people to get what he wanted and that's what I did to you. Immediately, as soon as we met. I'm an asshole—"

"Lucas."

"No, Elijah, *please*. I haven't seen you in five days and I can't stop thinking about what you said. There's no excuse for my behavior. Just because I'm trying to expose a monster doesn't mean I have to become one. Definitely doesn't mean I have to threaten your job and your livelihood. If you want to assign someone else to protect me, I'd totally understand."

Elijah closed the gap between us with barely concealed frustration. "*I* protect you, Luke. Not anyone else. I keep you safe."

The sandpaper edge in his voice had me gulping. "O-okay. I still fucked up. Big time. And I'm sorry, truly."

"You're not..." He winced like he was in pain. "Luke, you're nothing like your father. I'm not excusing what you did. It was wrong. But I never should have implied you were like him. You're not, not even close. He was cold and dismissive and cruel. And you're..."

There were no sounds. No partygoers or outdoor revelers. No crashing waves or live music.

"What?" I asked softly. "What am I?"

His throat worked while he slowly flexed his fingers. "Warm. You're warm. And kind. And...charming."

My lips curved up. "Is that so?"

"You're also reckless and irritating and I've already lost years off my life working with you."

I snorted. "You could have left it at charming."

Elijah's lips twitched, eyes crinkling at the sides. It sent me surging up to grab his face. And I got close. So *fucking* close. But Elijah caught both of my wrists, halting my hands half an inch from his cheekbones.

And my mouth...my mouth hovered over his. His breath mingled with mine—hot, ragged.

"What the hell are you doing?" he whispered.

"Kissing you," I said huskily, captivated by his full lower lip. The gray hair at his temples. The ticking of his jaw.

His fingers tightened around me. "Why would you do that?"

"I want you, Elijah."

His breath hitched. He pushed me back against the wall and pinned my wrists down, bringing our faces close again.

Closer.

"And you think I want that too?" he murmured.

I arched an eyebrow. "You're staring at my mouth like you want to bite it."

His gaze flew up. "I'm protecting you."

"Is this how you keep your other clients safe?" I tipped my face to the side, bringing my lips just shy of his. "Pretending won't make it go away. You want me too."

With agonizing slowness, Elijah dropped his nose to the crook of my neck. Inhaled. Shuddered. Inhaled again. I was balanced on a knife's edge, barely breathing even as my pulse roared in my ears. I felt the very tip of his nose travel up the side of my neck, setting off every nerve ending in my body. A hushed groan fell from my lips and Elijah's grip on my wrists squeezed almost to the point of pain.

"What I want doesn't matter," he ground out. "Even if I did want you, I can't have you."

"That can't possibly be true," I said breathlessly as his

mouth caressed my hair. Hot breath, grazing the side of my ear.

"It's the only truth that matters." His lips at my temple. His forehead, pressed to mine. "I break this rule, I lose everything."

Our chests heaved in the darkness, our labored breathing filling the silence.

"What if it wasn't about rules?" I whispered. "What if I was a stranger you took home for a night? Just one night, Elijah. Let me show you how much I want this, how much I want *you*."

A dangerous growl rumbled from the back of his throat. His lips roamed the side of my face—hardly there, barely there—and when he spoke, it was against my skin. "You couldn't handle me, Luke. I'm not sweet. I'm not gentle."

My hips rocked forward of their own volition, colliding with his. He pushed back, trapping me against the wall, and I felt every hard, thick inch of him.

"I'm right about you, aren't I?" I said. "You do like putting me in my place."

I felt his lips at my ear, the barest scrape of teeth. "If I took you home right now, I'd be giving this smart fucking mouth of yours something else to do."

I was flames—pure, incinerating flames. My head tipped back against the wall, my knees already weak.

"How about now?" I gasped. "Give it something else to do right the fuck now."

Elijah released me—and I hoped with every bone in my body it was to shove me to the floor. But he gripped my face instead, his fingers tender, his eyes searching my own as if convinced I couldn't possibly be real.

Beneath the wild rush of lust came the fluttering of my heart in my chest, a dip in my belly. The yearning in his expression took my breath away—he had the look of a man clinging to his last scrap of control.

"Elijah," I whispered. Pleaded. "Elijah, *please*."

A crashing sound reverberated from behind us—someone trying to break in from the back door. Elijah had us moving before I could even blink, out the front and then veering sharply to the left, where a black sedan waited with its lights off. I stumbled and Elijah caught me, but not before I whipped my head around to see who was giving chase.

I caught a glimpse of a tall person in a long black jacket, their face completely hidden in shadow. Elijah yanked open the car door and forced me in. Sylvester took off before I could get my seat belt on, so when he turned to head back toward the shoreline, I fell against Elijah's body with a very unsexy *oooomf* sound.

"We have to go back," I blurted, while trying to belt myself in. "Whoever was following us was right there."

Elijah was having a terse conversation with Sylvester.

"*Elijah*, the guy was right there."

His gaze snapped to mine, informal and businesslike. "We don't risk lives, especially not the lives of our clients. Trust that we've already alerted law enforcement and are providing them with every bit of information that we can."

"Or we can head back to the bookstore and see if they're still there. Once they see that I'm not my dad and I don't know jack shit about some flash drive, maybe they'll tell me what he did—"

He leaned across the seat. "Mr. Beaumont, *sir*, it's not up for discussion."

I reared back, surprised, but noticed the way Sylvester's eyebrows knit together as he watched us in the rearview mirror.

I break this rule, I lose everything.

Gone was the passionate man who'd come *this close* to devouring me behind a bookcase, who'd inhaled my scent like a starved animal. Whatever minuscule shot I might have had with my bodyguard was gone, vanished as soon as the moment had passed.

The ache in the very core of my being hadn't vanished though.

Now I only wanted him more.

But I'd fucked it up again, as usual. I'd let him see my truest self tonight—messy, impulsive, desperate. Not Luke Beaumont, the rich kid with no ambition. Or Lucas Emerson Beaumont, the surprise heir to a tarnished legacy.

But *me*. The kid who'd cried in his brother's bed and slept scared beneath gargoyles and whose childhood nightmares stalked him into the present day.

My gaze drifted to Elijah, who sat ramrod straight and silent next to me.

People never wanted me the way I wanted them.

19

ELIJAH

A nasty storm was rolling into Cape Avalon, turning the sky a gunmetal gray right as the sun was setting. I stood watch beneath the gargoyles at the Beaumont estate as the sea breeze grew angry, rushing past the back of my neck. The waves behind the house were angrier, fuller, more destructive than usual.

A black car sat in the circular driveway while staff loaded up furniture and file boxes. Kenneth stood watch over every piece of paper and sticky note being moved, ensuring that TBG's secrets stayed where they belonged. Per the instructions of the will, yesterday had officially been Preston's last day of work and today his exit was being made official.

A voice came over my earpiece. "Sir...Mr. Beaumont is asking for you again. What should I tell him?"

In the few seconds it took for Sylvester to disengage the call, I heard Luke say, "*I can hear you over there. Tell him that I—*"

My stomach churned with frustration like the cresting

waves. "It's imperative that I'm on duty outside today. I will be with him shortly when I'm ready."

"Yes, sir."

I stretched my neck from side to side and kept a careful eye on the flurry of activity around Preston's car and the several new faces who'd appeared today. Every person had been double- and triple-checked for safety, but we weren't taking any chances.

After the situation at the Shipwreck—and then, later, the South Shore Bookshop—Foster had declared the death threats against Luke to be high priority and officially escalating. We were now cooperating more closely with the police, though two days had passed and nothing had happened.

Two days had passed, and I'd been avoiding Luke ever since. Well, as much as a protection agent could avoid their client. But it was easy to stick the other agents close with him while I surveyed the perimeter and kept my distance.

I just needed some space to get my fucking head on right.

Except my head wasn't getting the message. My thoughts were still a tangled mess of thwarted desires that fractured my focus when I needed to be razor sharp.

And I couldn't stop thinking about how *good* it felt, giving in to something primal and forbidden. To press my nose to the skin beneath Luke's ear and *smell him*—saltwater, sunshine, the sandalwood of his aftershave. To hear Luke gasp in the shadowy darkness and know it was because of *my* touch, *my* breath, *my* hands.

Just one night, Elijah. Let me show you how much I want this, how much I want you.

When I'd finally collapsed into bed later that morning, I fantasized about doing exactly what Luke had suggested—

watching him fall to his knees and take me between his lips, nothing but wet heat and friction, his harsh grunts and my heavy breathing.

All that dark hair of his, twisted between my fingers as I rode his mouth to a reckless pleasure.

None of that could happen now. Not with a client and *never* in the midst of active death threats. The boundaries of this profession were clear and uncomplicated—*no personal relationships with clients.* Not with your active clients. Not even with those you no longer worked for. Our company hadn't developed such a pristine reputation out of nothing. It was our dedication to respect, to safety, to protecting privacy at all costs.

As I'd learned with all things in this life, emotions meant complications and complications meant danger. For *fuck's sake*, I was being promoted to director in less than a month while spending every waking second wondering what Lucas Beaumont tasted like.

And this ache for him was unrelenting, clawing through my chest without sense or sympathy.

When I stayed close, I kept Luke from danger.

When I stayed close, Luke *was* the danger.

The scars on my cheekbone itched and I winced, flexing my fingers into fists to resist scratching. My own father had crashed his car with me in the back, too busy flirting with his pretty coworker in the passenger seat to pay attention to the stop sign he blew through. He and the woman had picked me up from school two hours late that day, a new record.

Before this, he'd talked my ear off about this specific coworker, who he swore was addicted to what he called "the chase."

They all want it like that, he'd said, while slapping aftershave on his ruddy cheeks one morning. *Want you to prove yourself, prove that you deserve them. They won't give it away for free, and if they do, you don't want it. It's all biological, the laws of nature. You can look it up in any book.*

They'd made it out of the accident without a scratch on them, while I hadn't been that lucky.

"Are you avoiding me?"

I went still at the voice, the same low, warm tones that kept haunting my dreams. When I turned, Luke stood behind me, one shoulder propped against the doorframe and his hands in his pockets. He wore a sleek black tuxedo with the bow tie loose and undone around his neck. His black hair was swept off his forehead, drawing attention to the intensity of his blue eyes, the dark lashes.

I felt a corresponding twist in my gut, a knot of need and desire that drew tighter with every passing day.

I cleared my throat. "I am not."

His lips twitched. "You haven't said a single word to me in days."

"Someone's out to kill you. I've been busy."

A spiky hurt flickered through his gaze. But then he dropped it, shrugging one shoulder. "Can you help me tie this thing?"

I hesitated, painfully aware of the various eyes and ears surrounding us—Kenneth, the staff, the wide windows and open doorways. My mouth was already forming the word no when Luke stepped closer, then closer still, and my hands rose to his throat as if he'd commanded it.

Every ounce of my control went to keeping my fingers steady as I looped the fabric. My knuckles grazed the hollow between his collarbones. At the hitch in his breath, my gaze shot to his.

You like putting me in my place.

His cheeks flushed and I wondered if he was reliving the same moment.

Hoped he was.

Hoped he wasn't.

"I know why you're avoiding me," he whispered. "And I don't want you to. In fact, I want the opposite."

I ground my back teeth. "If you're referring to the other night, it won't happen again. Your safety is of the utmost importance to me."

"Elijah, please," he said, in the same urgent whisper from the bookstore. The same urgent, whispered tone that sent my thoughts spiraling into the most dangerous of territories. My hands tightened on his bow tie and for a single terrifying moment I almost gave in and yanked his mouth to mine.

Footsteps echoed near us. I released Luke and stepped back as Sylvester appeared.

I didn't miss the way his eyes narrowed at the sight of us.

"There you are," he said, after a beat of awkward silence. "Is everything all right?"

Luke and I shared a charged glance, just as dangerous as his whispered plea. I shook it away and nodded. "We're fine. I was providing some updates."

"And, on that note, I wanted to talk more about those updates. In the office, if you have a minute?" Luke asked. His expression was pleasant, but I heard the nerves in his voice.

"I do," I said with a nod. "Sylvester, I'll relieve you in half an hour. Why don't you check in with law enforcement? They were supposed to call earlier and haven't yet."

"Sure...yes, sir," he said slowly. "On it."

I turned on my heel and followed Luke through the mansion, past the wide, double staircase and down the gloomy hallway filled with pictures of everyone except Luke, something I'd only noticed recently. Sylvester's concern followed me the whole way, prickling at the back of my neck.

Fifteen years in this job and I'd never, not *once*, been tempted to break the rules I wholeheartedly believed kept our clients safe from harm. And yet days into meeting Luke, and I was storming into his steam-filled bathroom over a minor cut from his razor. Was being kept awake at night, reliving every close call, every mistake I'd made, every charming grin he tossed my way.

I'd hauled him up against a wall with my hand slapped over his mouth, had *smelled* his goddamn *neck* before spilling the filthy fantasies I had no business considering.

Breaking this kind of rule would be the end of all of it. Forget being made director, I'd be lucky to find a job doing low-level security on shitty pay with a dark mark like that on my record. And then what was I going to do? Show up to see my mom and brother, empty-handed, with nothing to show for the promises I'd made when my dad left us?

I'm so sorry I couldn't pay your medical bills and provide food for your table and put my nephews through the best colleges. I was too busy wanting to kiss Luke senseless.

And yet even as I thought it, I remembered the texts from Christopher after he'd surprised me at work. The voicemail from my mother from a week ago, calling to say that she missed me. The many ways I was already failing them, just by putting this job first.

I blinked, and we were suddenly back in the office, which was even more torn apart than last time. Luke was behind the desk, rummaging around for something, and I noticed a worn-looking paperback on the very edge. *Mayhem at Montauk Point* by Nora Jackson.

"I wasn't aware you owned a tuxedo," I said, hooking my hand over my wrist.

He peered out from behind the desk and sent me a crooked grin. "I'm a Beaumont. I was raised in tuxedos, though it was always against my will. But I've got Senator Wallace's black-tie fundraiser tonight in the city and I thought I'd follow the rules for once. Pretty sure I was only invited so she could harangue me about the Sunrise Village protests in an even more elegant location."

"Right, yes." The tuxedo. *Of course.* I hadn't forgotten but I hadn't exactly remembered either. "The...the fundraiser. You'll have three guards with you tonight. We're not taking chances at a new location."

"Three babysitters. Lucky me." He rose to stand and placed a towel-covered plate on the desk. "I'm assuming you're one of them?"

"You assume correctly."

His throat worked on a swallow. "Then I'm even luckier."

I ignored the fluttering in my chest. "What's happening with the protesters?"

"It's definitely the worst media coverage TBG has ever received, and they're getting more and more of it by the day. The size of the protest is growing. Something Kenneth and the rest of the board are strategizing about, mostly by reminding me that I'm a disgrace to the Beaumont name." His grin widened. "I've been ignoring all of it and secretly sending pizzas to the protest at lunchtime."

My eyebrows raised. "I thought you told Nora and Mía that you couldn't help them."

"I'm not, I mean, not really," he said quickly. "But dragging my feet and being openly obtuse around Kenneth is a normal day for me. Seems like the least I can do so they can keep their housing."

I caught his eye. "So you are helping them."

Luke blushed red and the fluttering in my chest increased. "I, uh...well, okay, I'll preface this by saying...this is sort of silly, but I...got you something?"

He pulled the towel from the plate and pushed it toward me. I cocked my head, unsure of what I was seeing at first. But when I stepped closer, I realized it was a giant chocolate chip cookie cake, freshly baked from the smell of it.

The flutters became a flock of wings.

"I baked this here in the kitchen, so it probably tastes like sandpaper. But I...I remembered what you said," he continued, "about your mom making these for you when you stayed home sick. Because I just wanted to say sorry, again, for everything. For pressuring you to help me when it clearly goes against your own personal code and everything in that contract I signed. I know it's important to you and I never should have asked for your help in the first place."

I was still staring down at the cake, wondering when, if ever, anyone had ever done something like this for me before.

"This revenge fantasy is a hundred percent my own shit to deal with," Luke said. "Not yours."

I was so deep in hot fucking water that I was drowning in it.

"Luke," I rasped out, "this is—"

Two sharp raps at the door had me spinning around with my heart in my throat. Preston barged in, looking slightly worse for wear. His jacket was wrinkled and there was stubble on his cheeks.

"I see you never got around to hiring that assistant."

Luke raked a hand through his hair. "Come on in. Wasn't like I was in the middle of anything."

"My apologies, I was only in the middle of being forced out of here," Preston snapped.

Luke winced. "I'm sorry, bro. It sucks. All of it does."

"And how does it suck for you specifically? You won."

"We were raised by the same narcissist," Luke said, pinching the bridge of his nose. "I know how it feels to be passed over. Know how it felt when Dad made me feel less than. But he's gone now and his very last message to us was one more fucked-up mind game, meant to bring about this *exact* situation." He took a tentative step toward his brother, who eyed him warily. "What if we didn't play his games this time?"

"I'm not..." Preston cleared his throat. "I'm not entirely sure what you're talking about."

Luke propped his shoulder against the wall, sending his brother a tentative grin. "Do you remember when Mom used to play carrot monster with us?"

An immense emotional struggle writhed across Preston's face. Finally, he said, "I can't look at a zucchini without assessing its ability to be worn as a costume."

Luke's grin brightened. "And I can't see a head of iceberg lettuce without remembering how you used to fashion them into hats for me."

Preston's lips twitched. "Poorly constructed."

"It was the thought that counts."

Silence hung between them, not as chilly as before. But whatever internal debate was happening within Preston ultimately won. He sniffed, checked his watch. "Anyway. I've passed off everything I could to Kenneth and the team that worked with me." His gaze drifted my way. "Given the increase in threats toward my brother, do I need to be worried?"

"No, sir," I replied. "We've increased security across the board and are monitoring the situation very closely."

Preston nodded and rocked back on his heels.

"Try not to get yourself killed," he said to Luke in a rush. Then he spun around and left, leaving Luke looking so uncharacteristically crestfallen I had to lock my knees to keep from going to him.

Luke was quiet for a bit before flashing me a sheepish smile. "We have a long history of being shitty to each other. But it wasn't always like that. We used to be really close. We used to be *friends*. Dad drove a wedge between us, turned Preston against me. But I can't really blame my brother. There was a time when I would have given anything to get Dad's attention. To have him look at me, to see me, to *hear* me." He shrugged a shoulder. "And how fucked up is that?"

I swallowed hard. "You two were just kids. It's Lincoln's fault, not yours. There's nothing wrong with...with wanting to be loved."

The look of shy astonishment in his eyes had me locking my knees again. He slowly pushed the plate with the cookie cake across the desk with a single finger.

"You can be honest, Elijah. This was a terrible idea, right? Also, I legitimately *cannot bake* so maybe don't even eat it? It could poison you. It could *kill* you. Then I'm definitely getting murdered since you won't be around to stop it. Probably immediately. I'll walk out that door and *boom*, murdered."

I stopped the plate's movement. "Luke. This won't poison me and I'm not letting you get murdered. Immediately or otherwise." Then I took a long, steadying breath. "People always thought my father was charming. He was, in his own way. The way that manipulative people are. And he lied about everything. Broke my mother's heart. Treated my brother and me like rounding errors, just mistakes that cost him money he didn't have. I spent most of my childhood tracking his mood, because if he was in a bad one..." I paused. "You didn't want his attention to land on you."

Luke nodded with understanding. "It's like being under the world's worst microscope."

"Yes, it is." I paused, weighing my next words against all that could go wrong, all that had already gone wrong. "This isn't easy for me to admit. But I wasn't unaware of your father's cruelty. Most people with his power and privilege are cruel in some way. I've seen extreme wealth worsen my clients' worst instincts before, including your father's. If he was hiding something, I understand why you want to find it. Why you want to expose him. And I'll help you do it."

Luke reared back. "Elijah, that's wonderful but...it's not necessary."

"I want to help. I do." Then I reached forward and broke off a piece of the cake, popping it in my mouth. The chocolate was still warm, melting against my tongue. "This is delicious."

Luke broke into a smile—full, dazzling, brilliant.

And I was helpless to resist it.

20

LUKE

Senator Wallace's residence was a sleek mansion in Westchester. The inside was all abstract art and furniture in a dull palette of grays and beige. Lightning flashed through the gauzy curtains, followed by low rumbles of thunder, currently the only evidence of the tropical storm meteorologists were predicting would reach land in a day or two.

The severe weather should have turned this fundraiser into a cozy affair. But the overall vibe remained sterile, although the room was packed with some of the most influential people in the tristate area.

I wondered how many of them had been victims of my father's blackmail schemes.

I'd also been reading up on the senator ever since Ethel and Clarita had suggested Dad had inside help when it came to acquiring permits. I already knew Senator Wallace had helped push through the Sunrise Village project and felt it safe to assume this wasn't the first time. But whether my father was hiding a flash drive full of her secrets was another question entirely—and Elijah's concern that planting car bombs was too risky given her political career was a smart one.

As mayor, she'd originally been beloved in Cape Avalon, promising to bring higher-paying jobs, to invest in affordable housing as well as environmental protections and educational programs. In the end, she'd pursued none of those campaign promises. She did, however, keep climbing the political ladder, next as lieutenant governor and now as state senator.

Her presidential campaign was only in its infancy, but that hadn't stopped the media—as well as early polls—from declaring her a popular front runner.

Elijah and I had taken up a spot in the corner when Grady Holt, her chief of staff, appeared with his eyes glued to his phone.

"The senator would like ten minutes of your time in the drawing room once she's done talking with the governor," he said.

I paused with a drink halfway to my lips. "Am I allowed to say no?"

He frowned. "Why would anyone do that?"

I indicated the shelves behind me. "Because I'm already having a fabulous time trying to figure out if pulling any of these books opens up a secret passageway."

"Find it, and we'll sue you into the fucking stratosphere."

"So there *is* a secret passageway."

Grady gave me a glare that was downright chilling before floating back through the crowd like a ghoul. Sylvester and the other agent had fanned out as soon as we arrived, taking up posts outside while Elijah hovered next to me, impeccable as always in his suit. Not that I'd been able to make eye contact for longer than a second without remembering that he'd agreed to help me uncover Dad's secrets...*of his own fucking volition*.

Then told me my cake was delicious. It was enough to give a man a permanent blush attack. I'd only tried to kiss him, writhed against his body in the dark, begged him to take me home, then baked him an apology cake.

It wasn't like I was totally *head over heels* for the guy or anything.

"Luke."

I startled, almost spilling my champagne. "Hmmm?"

"You're staring at me."

I let out a nervous laugh. "That's only because...because your tie is crooked, which I'm sure breaks one of your job's many rules."

Elijah didn't even look down. "It's not crooked."

"How do you know?"

"This job requires a thoroughness most people could never understand."

I smirked. "Oh yeah? Then prove it."

"I know the middle name of every single person in this room," he said, completely unfazed.

"Well, isn't that convenient," I drawled. "There's no way for me to prove that."

"Then you'll have to trust that your protection agent is better than you could ever imagine." He gave the subtlest arch of his eyebrow. "And the tie is straight."

My stomach dipped. "Unlike you and me, *amirite*?"

One corner of his mouth quirked up, an almost smile. I pointed at his face. "I'll say it again, but feel free to laugh at any or all of my hilarious jokes whenever you see fit. I won't report you to the bodyguard police."

He cocked his head. "Do you mean my boss?"

I shrugged. "Here's the thing about you, Elijah. I don't

think you need a contract to uphold the rules of this position. I think you'd do it out of your own sense of honor."

"Ah, yes. My virtuous honor. And how goes yours? What was it...patience, chastity, and humility?"

I flashed him a wicked grin. "I spent this past week impatient, horny, and arrogant, so you tell me."

This time, he pressed his lips together and sent his focus back out to the room, probably scanning for hidden threats and dangers.

So close.

The tight leash he had on his emotions was so at odds with the man who'd pinned me to the wall of a bookstore with a feral possessiveness. Even in the midst of this party, I yearned to be on the receiving end of that renowned thoroughness. Yearned for his stern gaze to strip me bare and make me beg for it. Beg for anything, really. His kiss, his body, the sweet relief from this attraction that had dominated my every thought from the moment we met.

You couldn't handle me, Luke.

"You can ignore my hilarious jokes all you want," I managed to continue. "But I know your secret now, Elijah Knight."

His dark gaze fell to my mouth and lingered there. "What secret is that?"

"You're a sucker for a chocolate chip cookie cake baked by your best and most favorite client," I said cheerfully. "I'm not just a hot body with charming good looks. I've got marketable skills too. Maybe after I get out of this CEO gig, I'll open up a bakery catered toward rule-following protection agents who never let themselves have any fun."

"And yet those same protection agents keep you alive and safe from murder," he replied. "How interesting."

"I never said I wasn't *grateful*."

His eyes trapped mine. "You don't have to say it, Lucas. Your complete disregard for your own safety is the only thanks I'll ever need."

I laughed into my champagne flute. Then lowered my voice to a whisper. "Speaking of disregarding my own safety, I'd still like to take a drive out to the wetlands, preferably tomorrow as long as the storm holds off. My hope is we catch Clarence off guard. Startle him into spilling what he knows about my dad, if he's the one targeting us right now."

A muscle ticked in Elijah's jaw. But before he could reply, Grady appeared again.

"It's time," he said. "Please come with me."

Elijah and I shared a look as we followed Grady past the jazz trio and the grand piano. And once we entered the senator's drawing room, there was something about the way she sized me up that had me extra-grateful for my bodyguard. Grady pulled the doors shut behind us, closing us into a room that rivaled my father's library in size.

Senator Wallace stood by a large picture window framed on both sides by heavy velvet curtains.

"So lovely to see you again, Lucas," she said warmly, shaking my hand tightly. "Can Grady get you something to drink? Bourbon? Wine? More champagne?"

"I'll never say no to bourbon."

Her eyes darted behind me, passing along a wordless command to her chief of staff. While he busied himself at the small bar, she considered me with a pointed curiosity that sent a shiver down my spine.

"Thank you again for coming tonight," she said. "I could always count on your father for campaign support. I hope to rely on you as well."

I exchanged my empty champagne glass for the highball from Grady and raised it her way. "My father and I were nothing alike. So I can't say what I'll do yet. No offense or anything."

Her polite smile froze in place. "None taken. I understand it's been quite the adjustment for you since his passing. It's why I'm not *too* frustrated about the Sunrise Village delays. Though your father would have squashed those protests within the first few fragile hours. Like stomping out a campfire before you turn in for the night. Can't let any stray embers out that could start trouble."

I rattled the ice in my drink. "That's a weird way to describe people who lost their homes. Aren't they your constituents?"

"I have many constituents. But you can imagine that part of my job is balancing the needs of the few against the needs of the many. As sad as it is, the residents of Sunrise Village are the *few*. That's why TBG needs to break ground as soon as possible. You must understand that every passing day brings worse news coverage, smearing a project I personally put my weight behind."

I raised an eyebrow. "You mean those permits you got my dad through whatever unethical bureaucratic fast-track program you operate on the side?"

Grady was still typing away on his phone with a mildly annoyed expression. But Senator Wallace leaned in with a sympathetic pinch to her mouth that felt *very* fake. "You're new to this, so I say this with kindness. Don't talk about things you don't understand. And it won't hurt you to recall that I fought for people like you. I don't particularly enjoy whatever you think you're cleverly insinuating."

It took me a moment to realize what she was saying. When I did, I scowled into my drink.

"Oh, I get it now," I drawled. "You tossed queer people a few legislative breadcrumbs. So in return I help you bulldoze a community?" I snapped my fingers. "*That's* what queer liberation is all about. Kicking people out of their homes to make way for luxury housing that we don't need. I missed that lesson in my Bisexuality 101 class."

My sarcasm landed with a thud in the middle of her elegant drawing room. Even Grady paused, mid-type, to peer up at me with a darkening expression.

The senator's eyes tightened at the corners, but she kept her cool. "There's a reason why Lincoln left the company to you. You don't see it, but I do."

"Care to enlighten me? I don't have a fucking clue."

She angled her body closer. "I believe that you, Lucas Beaumont, know more than you're letting on."

"Know more about what?"

"Your father and I knew each other for more than forty years," she said smoothly. "He always had my back, and I always had his. There's nothing inherently wrong or *unethical* about partnership. In the end, we both worked for the people of Cape Avalon, for the Hamptons. *We* could continue that tradition, you and me. I'm sure your father spoke to you about our collaboration?"

All the hair on the back of my neck stood up. I heard Elijah shifting on his feet behind me.

"He didn't talk to me about anything," I admitted.

Now I had Grady *and* the senator studying me like a pair of velociraptors, tails twitching and heads cocked.

"You're not a very good liar, Lucas," she said softly. "But until you wise up to what I'm offering, let me be perfectly clear—break ground on Sunrise Village or I'll find a way to make sure your company never builds a damn thing ever again."

I reared back, stunned. So stunned that I blurted out, "It was you, wasn't it? With the car bomb?"

But this time it was the senator's turn to look absolutely stunned. "I beg your pardon?"

Elijah cleared his throat behind me, but I ignored his admonishment. "Did you try and have me killed, Senator Wallace? Or, at the very least, *aggressively intimidate* me with a car bomb at the adventure park?"

Her burst of surprised laughter felt like the most authentic reaction I'd gotten all night. My stomach dropped, especially as I watched Grady go back to frantic emailing on his phone with a barely concealed smirk.

"I've been falsely accused of many things in my time in office, Lucas, but that is by far the most outlandish," she said, brushing a piece of lint from her suit. "No, I did not try to have you killed. And if you won't listen to my first warning, here's a second one." Her smile turned venomous. "Falsely accuse me of *murder* ever again and I'll sue you so fast your head will spin." Then she stepped back, revealing her politician's smile yet again. "Now please do enjoy some light refreshments in the foyer."

It took me so long to react that Elijah had to lead me by the elbow back out into the stilted conversation and soft jazz piano. As soon as we were alone, I said, "Quick question, what the fuck was that?"

"Don't know. Didn't like it though."

"Cool, me neither," I said. "Let's get the hell—"

A tall man with a wiry build slid between the two of us, spinning on his heel when he seemed to recognize me. He appeared to be in his fifties, good-looking in a plastic surgery kind of way, and his whole face lit up when we made eye contact.

"Lucas Beaumont?" he said, taking my hand before I could offer it. "Lincoln's son?"

"Uh...yep. That's me." I pulled back my hand and slipped it into my pocket. "Can I...help you?"

He touched the middle of his forehead. "Right, yes, you wouldn't recognize me. I've had quite a bit of work done since the years when I knew your father so well. I was distraught when I heard of his passing. In fact, we saw each other often at Senator Wallace's events. I'm a significant donor, myself."

I nodded slowly. "Neat."

"We met when he built my second home for me," the man continued. "A beachfront condo near Cape Avalon. Now, it didn't turn out *quite* like I'd hoped but—"

"Hey, I'm not trying to be rude," I said, "but I was just about to leave."

His face brightened again. "Oh, but you can't leave yet. I came here to see *you*."

"Me? Why?"

"Why?" A dangerous gleam appeared in his eyes. "I'm here to kill you."

21

LUKE

The space between the man's words and Elijah's movements lasted a second.

If that.

Yet everything around me slowed to the point of absurdity, becoming painfully obvious.

The wild urge to laugh at the way he'd said *I'm here to kill you,* like he was checking in for a dentist's appointment. How his facial expression never changed, not even when he lunged forward with a knife. How the small plate of mini éclairs he held crashed to the floor first.

How none of those details *really* mattered, because all I cared about was one thing.

Elijah.

He reacted so quickly, so confidently, I was only aware of his body stepping in front as the knife swung my way. Only aware of one big hand shoving me back as he hooked an arm around the man's neck and brought him down to the floor with a quiet fury.

The people around us screamed and a server dropped a plate of champagne flutes.

The man gasped, choking, and then Elijah was flipping his body and pressing him face down into the floor, one knee on his spine. He shouted something into his walkie as other security personnel rushed our way. Someone called 911. Someone else asked if I was okay.

Meanwhile, my brain was stuck in a single loop.

Elijah, knife, Elijah, knife, Elijah, knife.

I frantically searched for blood, for a wound, for any sign he was hurt. I sprang forward, reaching for him, but Elijah stopped me with a hand to the chest. Still kneeling, chest heaving, he twisted at the waist and met my eyes.

"Are you hurt?" he asked, voice eerily calm while anguish burned in his gaze. His fingers flexed where they held my shirt, gripping the fabric.

"Me? No, not at all," I sputtered. "Are you? Did he...?"

"*Your father ruined my life,*" my would-be attacker screamed. "*And you're just like him, you piece of—*"

Elijah gripped the man's hair and yanked up his head.

"Say one more word and I rip your goddamn face off," he said through clenched teeth.

Sylvester was rushing over, followed closely by the police. They shoved Elijah back and took over restraining the man on the ground. I watched Elijah rise slowly and have a short, terse conversation with the other guards. Then he turned on his heel and took me by the elbow.

"I need to speak with you," he growled, "*now.*"

He dragged me through a crowd of people trying to get our attention. Grady pushed toward us, asked where we were going, but I only had eyes for my bodyguard, who radiated a dangerous frustration that tripled my already erratic pulse. The cords in his neck stood out, the muscle in his jaw flexed, and when someone tried to stop him from going down a hallway, he barked *"Move"* so furiously the person audibly gulped.

We passed three doors. At the fourth one, Elijah pushed it open, revealing what looked like a guest bedroom, eerily empty in the moonlight spilling in from the windows. Sirens screamed in the distance as Elijah yanked me inside.

Slammed the door shut.

Locked it.

I was pushed back against the door and Elijah's palms followed, caging me in. It was only then that his distress became clear—the ragged hitch in his breathing, the frantic dart of his eyes across my face.

"Did he stab you?" I asked, lifting his jacket, his shirt, searching for blood. "Elijah, are you hurt? *Please* tell me you did not take a knife for me. I swear I'll beat the living shit out of whoever that was."

But he didn't answer. He was reverently running his fingers up and down my arms, shoving off my jacket, palming my chest, my hips.

"I thought he hurt you," he said gruffly.

"He didn't." I tried to still his hands but to no avail. "He didn't, I swear, I promise. You stopped him. Elijah...*Elijah*."

He fell to his knees, his hands roaming up my calves. His forehead dropped to the center of my thigh and he took a shaky inhale. Gave an even shakier exhale. "I thought he stabbed you."

My fingers sank into his hair, caressing. His back shuddered, and I felt the heat of his breath through the fabric of my tux. "You saved my life. Sweetheart, please look at me."

His head tipped up, and the look of relief carved into his face had my heart in my throat. I couldn't even feel embarrassed by the way *sweetheart* had slipped from my lips like a prayer. Not here, in this silent room, with Elijah on his knees and his fingers trembling where they gripped behind my thighs.

A grip that felt clinical at first but then grew firmer, gliding slowly up the side of my legs until he could hold my hips. My cock was swelling by the second, so close to Elijah's face, his mouth.

He knew it too, because a desperate groan rumbled from the center of his chest. Then he was pressing his open mouth, the tip of his nose, to my cock—now fully erect. His hand joined, cupping me through the fabric with that same urgent reverence.

Lust roared through me, mixed with the adrenaline from the attack, and I was suddenly more turned on than I'd ever been. My fingers twisted in his hair, and he peered up at me. Then a tinny voice on his walkie asked where I was.

Still staring at me, Elijah brought the radio to his lips. "Luke was upset. He's lying down in the dark. Give him twenty minutes."

The person on the other end responded with a quick "yes, sir," and Elijah tossed the radio to the floor. He rose, deliberately dragging his hands up the entire length of my body. He dropped his face into the crook of my neck, same as the other night, and drew in a raspy breath as his mouth moved up the side of my throat.

I went completely still, not entirely convinced this was real. Not entirely convinced I wouldn't wake up from this dream soon, just one of many I'd had starring the man currently holding my face with fingers like steel.

"You should tell me to stop, Luke," he ground out.

I fisted my hands in his jacket and yanked him flush against me. "You know I won't. I've never wanted someone the way I want you."

His thumb traced my lower lip, tugging it down. "If that

man had put even a *scratch* on you, I would have ended him right fucking there. I swore to myself I'd control this, swore that I—"

I kissed him. Felt his whole body freeze up while I was burning alive. For a terrifying moment, I worried that I'd messed up again, pushed him when I should have stepped back, should have listened to his concerns and let him go.

With an agonized growl, Elijah slanted his lips over mine and consumed me. His mouth was a devastation, kissing me so skillfully, with so much goddamn *passion*, I would have collapsed on the carpet if his hips weren't pinning mine to the wall.

I opened for him, moaning with each movement, letting my head tip back as he scraped his teeth across the front of my throat. My fingers dove into his hair while he ran his tongue up the curve of my ear, biting down with a hushed snarl. Then he caught my mouth again. Didn't let up until we were both breathless, until I shuddered against him, already drunk on his taste, his tongue, the smell of his skin.

I opened my eyes to find him staring at me in sheer, glorious wonder.

And then...a miracle in the middle of this moonlit room. Elijah Knight smiled at me. Not just smiled, he *grinned*—one side of his mouth pulling up rakishly, showing off a dimple I never knew was there.

He nudged our noses together. "I've been wanting to do that from the first moment we met."

And if I thought I was gone for this man before, it was no match for the truth of this moment. That I was utterly and completely undone by a single kiss.

There would be no turning back for either of us now.

22

ELIJAH

I could hear the ambient sounds of conversation in the hallway.

Could see the red-and-blue flash of ambulance lights, harsh against the moonlight slanting across the room.

There was an attacker on the ground. Two other guards awaiting my command. A state senator and her chief of staff, probably minutes away from breaking down this door.

And I couldn't stop touching Luke.

Not when I'd been so sure of that knife's trajectory. Not when my own brain had filled in the gaps with the worst images possible—Luke, bleeding on the floor, injured *or worse* because of my own gross incompetence. And if the *worse* had happened?

I'd never have been able to tell him about whatever this was, this all-consuming captivation that had dogged my steps for weeks now. It kept me up at night. Left my thoughts tangled, had me breaking every rule I'd ever sworn by.

Those same rules seemed pitiful and pointless in the face of the violence I'd stopped through sheer luck.

I've never wanted someone the way I want you.

Luke had no fucking *idea* what it was to truly want.

My fingers attacked the bow tie I'd tied back at the house, yanking it clean off before moving deftly down the buttons of his shirt. Our mouths stayed fused together as he shoved the jacket from my shoulders. My palms landed on the bare, warm skin of his chest and we both groaned. I kicked his feet apart and shifted, grinding our cocks together. Luke tore his mouth away as his head fell back.

"You feel amazing, Elijah." He grunted, fingers tangling in my hair again. I flexed my hips and ran my tongue up the length of his throat, turned on to the point of pain by Luke's husky breathing, every harshly whispered *Elijah* that fell from his lips.

There wasn't enough time, there'd never be enough time, but I knew one thing. I needed his body under mine, needed to know what his cock felt like wrapped in my fist, if he'd say *my* name when he came. I hooked my fingers in the top of his pants and hauled him off the wall, walking backward through the room as Luke kept kissing me.

He shucked his shirt while I unbuttoned my own, then I was shoving him backward onto a long couch. He sprawled against the cushions, watching me with heavy-lidded eyes and a swollen mouth, his throat working on a swallow when I finally shed my shirt. His shoulders were rounded with muscle, his chest hair dark, the ridges of his abs flexing with his ragged breathing.

I wiped a hand across my own swollen mouth, tasting him there, and my pulse tripled at the lazy grin that slid up his face.

Luke pushed back his tousled hair and crooked a finger with the boundless confidence of a man who knew just what kind of effect his beauty had on people. The kind of beauty that slams into you like a violent storm.

And who was I to resist such devastation?

I'd fallen to my knees for him once already—did so now on the couch, kissing up his stomach, the planes of his chest, crashing our mouths together as I popped open the button on his black pants.

I nuzzled my mouth into the crook of his neck, grazed the skin with my teeth, felt him arch up in response.

"We don't have a ton of time," I murmured, "or I'd spend an hour on this spot alone."

"There, please, *yes,*" he groaned.

I smiled against his skin, then sucked. Luke cursed, his nails biting into my ribs where he clung to me. I dragged my lips up, to just below his ear. "I'd spend an hour here too."

He whimpered. My hand slipped into the waistband of his briefs and stilled, inches from the head of his cock.

Being short on time didn't stop me from wanting him to beg for it.

"After the bookstore, I went home and fucked my own fist, thinking of you, Luke."

His head fell back, exposing the lines of his throat.

"Thinking of you on your knees in that store for me." My fingers inched down, lightly stroking. Luke jumped. Hissed. "Thinking about how good you'd be. How that smart fucking mouth of yours would look wrapped around my cock."

Another light, teasing stroke. Another kiss, below his ear.

"Elijah, *please,*" he said through gritted teeth. "I'm close and you haven't even touched me yet."

I gripped his length, hard, and tugged it free. We both turned to watch and I lost my mind at the sight of my hand, his gorgeous fucking dick, thick and veined and smooth beneath my fingers. Luke grabbed my face and pulled my mouth down to his, crying out through our kiss as I started to move.

Slow, at first. Teasing, at first. Except Luke was writhing beneath me, bucking his hips up, so I switched to short, rough strokes that had him crying out again.

"Oh, god, you're gonna make me come," he growled, nipping my bottom lip. Tempting me to deepen the kiss, to lick my tongue against his, to sink into the feel of his hot, hard body beneath me. I could hear the slick sounds of my fingers moving, Luke's shaky breath, the roar of my own heart in my ears.

We didn't stop kissing either, even as Luke gasped, "*Elijah...Elijah...yes,*" and climaxed, his come spilling onto my hand.

Something dark and possessive thrummed to life as he said my name, clung to me, took great, gasping breaths with his forehead pressed to mine. I pushed up onto my arms to gaze down at him—a beautiful mess, debauched and disheveled. I grabbed his hand and brushed my lips across the inside of his wrist, his fluttering pulse. His expression softened and something cracked open in my chest.

"Are you..." I cleared my throat. "Was that...okay?"

I bit my tongue. Stopped myself from asking *was I okay*? Because I hadn't held back just now, hadn't controlled my emotions or controlled myself to the point of invisibility.

Luke beamed, chuckling softly. He reared up, holding me still by the chin to kiss me sweetly. "I came so hard I saw through space and time." Another kiss. "I'm more than okay." And another. "I'm ecstatic." Kiss-kiss-kiss. "Euphoric." He nudged his nose against mine. "Happy. Very, very happy."

My cheeks went hot at the compliment. I ducked my

head, hiding the smile that threatened to break across my face.

He caught it, turning me by the chin. "Two smiles from Elijah Knight in one day? I'm one lucky bastard."

"Luke." I scoffed, burying my face in his chest, my brain and body suddenly full of...of too *much*. Too much want and contentment and pride. Emotions I wasn't used to feeling so abundantly.

His lips hovered at my temple. "Do you know how handsome you look when you smile at me like that?" Then I was shoved up to sit with Luke straddling my lap. I groaned at the contact, yanking him against my still-hard cock as he stared down at me. "Do you know what that smile makes me wanna do?"

His lips—hot and firm—descended my neck. My hand fisted in his thick hair, my knees already spreading wide.

"Tell me," I demanded.

He sank his teeth into my chest and I hissed. "It makes me wanna put this smart mouth to work."

"We don't have enough time."

He kissed down my belly with an arrogant smile. "I'm known to be quite skilled in this area, Elijah." He palmed my cock through the fabric and I let out a curse. "I don't need a lot of time."

The walkie crackled to life next to us. "Everything okay with Mr. Beaumont?"

My body was wound so tight I almost cracked the radio in half when I picked it up. Brought it to my lips. Hesitated. The real world was forcing its way back in. But I was too busy having heart palpitations caused by Luke's lopsided grin when he rose on his knees to kiss me again.

What started soft became a surging, reckless desire.

Luke's mouth claimed mine, drank me in until I could only shudder beneath his focused attention.

"Knight?" came the voice on the radio.

Luke trailed a finger across the head of my cock.

"He needs a few more minutes," I grunted, then tossed the thing across the room.

I grabbed Luke by the hair and dragged him close. "Put it to work."

"Yes, *sir*," he said with a wink.

Luke sank gracefully and I raised my hips an inch so he could yank down my pants. When my aching cock sprang free, his eyes went wide. He ran his tongue up the side before taking me into his hot, eager mouth. Everything around me trembled, paused, vanished.

My world narrowed to a single point of focus—the breadth of Luke's muscular shoulders, the hair at the nape of his neck, his fingers on my thigh, sliding up to tangle with my own. My other hand landed in his hair as his head bobbed up and down, obliterating every thought, every fear, every stray worry.

He hollowed his cheeks and sucked me deep. So deep that I growled, "Jesus *fucking* Christ, Luke."

His response was a smug arch of his brow. Then he moaned, redoubling his efforts, and I watched the muscles ripple across his back, watched the pure bliss in his expression.

Pleasure spiked sharply through my body and my head tipped back on another long groan. I was keenly aware of what we looked like, clothing half-off, shirts strewn across the floor, Luke sucking hungrily at my feet. It was too goddamn filthy, too much like my fantasy.

I was on the edge of orgasm almost immediately.

"*God*, it's too good," I hissed, tightening my fingers in his hair.

He gave another moan. Another deep swallow.

"You're perfect," I said, watching his mouth work. "You're so perfect right now."

Those blue eyes flew up to meet mine, singeing me with their heat.

"*Please don't stop,*" I begged—fucking *begged*. "I'm so..."

Footsteps thumped outside the door. Raised voices on my walkie-talkie. Headlights glaring through the closed curtains. I stared down at Luke and couldn't have controlled my reaction for all the willpower in the world. This time it was Luke slapping a hand across my mouth mere seconds before an orgasm ripped through me with a fury, muffling my strangled groans as I came.

"Holy shit," I whispered, my chest heaving. "Holy fucking shit."

Luke wiped a hand across his swollen lips with a decadent, sinful grin. He pressed up onto his knees and whispered in my ear, "Told ya I was good."

I could only kiss him then, a kiss meant to soothe us both as the world outside got closer and closer. But it didn't soothe. It only ignited us again, until I was yanking him against me like I'd never get enough.

"Hello?" came an alarmed voice through the door. The *senator's* voice. "Lucas? Are you unwell?"

My radio squawked. "Uh...Elijah? Where the hell are you guys? The officers need to talk to you."

We froze. Then sprang into rapid action. A host of anxieties surged back into my brain, so quickly I was lightheaded when I stood, shoving myself back into my pants. Luke was hopping on one foot, a shoe on the other, and buttoning his shirt at the same time.

At the mirror, I paled at the sight of my hair, the wrinkles in the sleeves of my jacket. Luke wasn't any better, though he could pull off the slightly rumpled look of the young and wealthy much better than I could.

There were knocks at the door again, louder this time. Luke stepped in front of me with a wry smile and began finger-combing my hair into some sense of order. And I tried my best to ignore how the steady sifting of his fingers in my hair made me feel.

Safe. Appreciated. Seen.

The top few buttons of his white shirt were open, the bow tie hanging loose around his neck. I reached for it, and he batted my hand away.

"Leave it," he whispered playfully. "I need to hide the hickey you gave me."

Alarmed, I pulled back his collar and saw the bruise forming where I'd sucked his skin between my teeth. My fingers tightened, my body's reaction hovering between embarrassment and possessiveness.

"I marked you," I said gruffly.

Luke brushed the remaining lint from my shoulders and checked every button on my shirt, then stepped back to examine me.

"You sure did mark me." He stepped close to breathe in my ear—too dangerous, with the doorknob shaking, the voices rising in volume outside. "I'm gonna get hard every time I see it, Elijah."

I gripped the back of his head, needing him again. But Luke only kissed my cheek and said, "Follow my lead, okay? I got this."

I blinked, stunned by the force of his tenderness. Almost as stunned as I'd been when he called me *sweetheart* earlier, an endearment that had never been used, not *once*, to describe me. Hearing those words from his mouth, in that voice, felt like taking a punch to the sternum.

"Elijah?" he asked. "Are you ready?"

Ready. Yes. *Right.* Luke had been attacked at a party and I was his lead protection agent. The same agent countless people were waiting to hear from just steps outside this room. I marched over to the doorway, remembering at the last second to pick up the radio I'd thrown to the floor. The absolute carelessness would have been astonishing if I wasn't also mentally calculating every damn mistake I'd made since we stepped into this house.

I positioned myself by the door and gave Luke a nod. He rubbed a hand through his hair, messing up the strands again, and shot me a covert wink before he pulled open the door.

"Senator Wallace, hi," he said blearily, rubbing his face. Grady pushed past him into the room, followed by Sylvester. I averted my gaze, keeping it trained on Luke to help my nerves. "I'm so sorry for slipping away like that. Elijah knows that I have a condition."

"You do?" asked Sylvester, confusion evident in his voice.

"After an...an upset like that, my blood pressure always drops," Luke said. "I've fainted before. From shock. Elijah knows to get me to a couch as quickly as possible until the dizziness and the nausea passes. I didn't mean to cause any additional alarm."

The light in the room was switched on. The pillows on the couch were in disarray, but other than that, there were no signs of what had just transpired between the two of us.

Senator Wallace still eyed us with suspicion. Though I hadn't forgotten the threats she'd issued earlier this evening. Different in tone than the knife attack, but no less concerning.

"No apology is necessary," she finally said. "It's chaos out there and you weren't missed at first. But we did want to make sure nothing had happened to you. You've had quite a scare."

"It was my mistake," I said sternly. "I was concerned for Luke and should have updated everyone so they didn't worry. I'm assuming an arrest has already been made?"

Sylvester nodded slowly. "Paramedics are waiting outside to examine you, sir. Are you hurt?"

"I'm fine." I slipped my phone from my pocket and felt a surge of panic at the four missed calls from Foster. "Stay with Lucas while I speak with the director."

I turned to move but Luke's voice stopped me in my tracks.

"Thanks again. For...protecting me. For saving my life." He reached up to his neck, thumb stroking along the tender spot where I'd marked him with my teeth. My blood sizzled, my cock twitched. "I won't forget it, Elijah."

I managed to nod. "Just doing my job, Mr. Beaumont."

His lips tipped up into a half smile, which was my cue to get out of there. I didn't need to be trading flirty inside jokes with my client. I'd officially snapped, lost any semblance of control, which meant one charming grin from Luke would be all I needed to kiss him in front of everyone.

Outside, I raked a hand through my hair as lightning arced across the sky. The cops were still here but they'd have to wait until after I lied to my boss.

You are so in over your fucking head, my brain whispered.

I dialed Foster's number and pressed a hand to my mouth, realizing I still smelled like Luke. His come, his sweat, the salt on his skin. Lust overrode my shame but then Foster barked a greeting into the phone, and it was like a bucket of ice water down the spine.

"Where the hell have you been?" he snapped. "And what the hell happened?"

I pinched the bridge of my nose. "I'm sorry, sir. Luke... Mr. Beaumont was shaken up after the attack and I needed to get him to a couch so he could lie down. He has an issue with his blood pressure, has fainted from stress before. I apologize for not answering. It was only out of concern for the client."

"Sylvester said you were in there with him for almost half an hour."

My eyes rose to the stormy sky as my gut churned with guilt. "Yes, that sounds about right." The silence on the other end was much too heavy. "Foster? Sir?"

"I'm gonna need a full report tomorrow on how Vincent Maura was able to get that close to Lucas *with a knife* given the sheer volume of security involved. Who dropped the ball?"

Me.

"I'm not sure yet, but I'll find out," I hedged. "Sorry, did you say...Vincent *Maura*? That's not possible."

That was the name of the stalker I'd mentioned to Luke when we first met—the B-list celebrity who'd despised Lincoln after he believed he'd ruined his condo. In the end, he'd fled the authorities and was never caught. But his hatred clearly hadn't dissipated with Lincoln's death. I'd seen the look in his eyes when I tackled him to the floor. There was no regret, no equivocation.

He'd intended to kill Luke.

"It is possible. Sylvester gave me that update as soon as the police arrived. So now I'd like to know why I know more about this situation than you do, Knight?"

I winced, rubbing my forehead. "Message received, sir."

More silence from Foster and bile rose in my throat.

Of course, Luke had to swagger into my life and rip it from its moorings *this close* to my promotion to director.

Of course, he had to tempt me away from the rules I held dear, endangering himself and others along the way, when I was right in the middle of securing the position that would ensure my family's stability.

"Do we have a problem, Elijah?" Foster asked softly. "You mentioned Lucas was challenging to work with. Do I need to pull you—"

"No," I said sharply. Too sharply. "What I mean is…the safety of the Beaumont family is very important to me and has been for more than five years now. I'd consider it an honor to protect them until it's time for me to move into the office."

And take on your role when you retire. Those were the words that sat on the back of my tongue, but I was suddenly nervous to voice them aloud. Nervous that I'd somehow be found wanting after years of career perfection.

"Are you sure about that?" Foster asked—and the warning in his tone was clear.

Not that I heeded it. My head was too full of memories. Luke, adorably nervous as he presented me with the cake he'd made. The way he'd shuddered and sighed as I kissed him against that door without mercy.

His lips in my hair, whispering: *do you know how handsome you are when you smile at me like that?*

"Yes, sir. I'm sure," I said firmly.

No one would oversee protecting Luke except me.

23

LUKE

Rain battered the sliding glass door in my bedroom. Through the fog, I could just make out the gray, churning ocean.

It was well past time to give up the ruse of pretending to sleep—almost eleven, and the storm was only getting worse. I dragged myself out of bed and pulled on a crewneck sweatshirt over my board shorts. Scrubbed two hands down my exhausted face. My hair stuck up at every angle, and my pillowcase had left a long imprint down the left side of my cheek.

I looked like I'd been well and truly fucked.

Which wasn't far from the truth.

The night had gone like this: toss, turn, replay every filthy detail of what happened with Elijah, contemplate texting him, toss, turn, draft a text, don't send it, toss, turn.

At dawn, I'd finally kicked away the covers and given in to temptation, jerking off to the memory of Elijah's rough voice when he'd said *you're so fucking perfect right now.*

And then begged me not to stop.

Elijah had *begged* as I sucked his cock, and I would never, not in a million years, forget what it was like to be the cause of his desperate unraveling.

He'd sprawled in front of me like a king, all thick thighs and barrel chest and that massive dick. Throat exposed, fingers in my hair, his husky growls as I took him over the edge with my hand over his mouth.

If this was what it meant to crack that man wide open, I wasn't sure I'd survive much more of it. I'd gotten two real smiles, given one quick blow job, and here I was walking around my bedroom like I'd been whacked upside the head with a frying pan.

I finger-combed my hair into some semblance of order, grabbed my phone and slipped on my sandals. Opening my bedroom door, I found Elijah standing there in a perfectly pressed suit and holding a steaming mug of coffee. He brightened when he saw me, and one side of his mouth tipped up into the subtlest half smile.

I beamed at him.

"Elijah, um...good morning," I sputtered. "What are you doing here? I mean, that came out wrong. I want you here." I coughed into my fist. "In a normal and professional way. Obviously. I just meant—"

He glanced over his shoulder and took a single step into my bedroom. "Ripley and Sylvester are out in the kitchen. We wanted to go over some updates with you about what happened last night."

His eyes fell to the crook of my neck, where I sported a bruise in the shape of his mouth. I touched it, out of instinct, and watched his throat bob as he swallowed.

"Sure thing," I finally said, raking a hand through my hair. "It was...it was an exciting night, that's for sure."

He gave the slightest arch of his eyebrow.

I flushed. "In a bad way. 'Cause of the...knife attack."

Elijah pressed his lips together and passed me the coffee mug. When I took it, he angled his pinkie finger, let it slide along mine before stepping back. My heart flipped twice, and his breathing hitched.

"Thank you," I said, raising the mug. "Did you sleep at all? I thought you were on the night shift now."

"I grabbed a few hours. Wanted to be up for your trip today."

I sipped. "My trip?"

Elijah moved into the hallway and cocked his head toward the kitchen. "You're still planning on heading out to the wetlands, correct?"

I palmed my forehead. "Shit. Yeah. I totally forgot with everything that happened. It was only going to be a day trip, especially with this storm. There's not a lot out in Rodanthe Hills and the roads are pretty narrow. I don't want us to get stuck out there. But I messaged Nora last night and she said the protesters are taking the day off, given the weather. That makes it even more likely that Clarence is home today."

"I'll drive you and we'll make it quick," he said, as I followed him into the kitchen. Ripley had a laptop open on my counter while Sylvester was on the phone. They both gave me a wave and I noted the dark circles under their eyes. In fact, Elijah's were deeper and darker than they'd ever been. "These two are needed here but we obviously don't want you going alone."

My stomach dipped at the realization he meant just the two of us. I could only nod in agreement and sip my coffee like my life depended on it.

"Are you going somewhere today?" Sylvester asked. "That wasn't on the schedule."

I cut a glance at Elijah, whose face was impressively impassive. Sylvester and Ripley couldn't know why I was going out to the wetlands, not without getting Elijah in major trouble for breaking all kinds of rules.

"A quick work thing," I said with a shrug. "The weather could be better, but I'm not too worried. Did everyone end up okay after we got home? No surprise injuries?"

"No, sir," Ripley said. "Elijah followed protocol. Got the assailant to the ground and got you to safety."

I hid a smirk behind my mug, since *got me to safety* was one way to describe what he'd done to me after yanking me into that bedroom.

A memory of Elijah on his knees, the wild look in his eyes, the plea in his voice, came roaring back. *If that man had put even a scratch on you, I would have ended him right fucking there.*

"Excellent," I finally said, with a flutter in my stomach. "Any word on Senator Wallace and if she's prepared to sue me for ruining her party's whole vibe?"

"We've been in contact with her head of security," Elijah said. "Everyone's trying to assess where the mistake was made. Until then, we're on high alert. We've sent extra guards to Harriet's home as well."

"Thank you," I said with a nod. "It's appreciated."

I'd called Harriet late last night to tell her everything, from the thwarted knife attack to the hottest thirty minutes of my life, all thanks to my heroic bodyguard.

When she heard about Elijah, she'd only squealed and yelled *called it*. She was much less thrilled about news of the attack, though she remained less worried for herself and more worried about me. I'd assured her of near-constant updates about both situations—and made her promise three times to stay extra vigilant.

"Do we know who he was? And why he tried to kill me?" I asked.

A muscle ticked in Elijah's jaw. "His name is Vincent Maura, though he's been going by an alias for the past four years. He's the stalker I mentioned to you last week. He was obsessed with your father and ended up being quite dangerous. Until now, he's evaded arrest. Clearly had some plastic surgery done. According to law enforcement, he's spent the past couple months cozying up to Senator Wallace's campaign, making large gifts. Looks like he was hoping he'd get invited to the event last night, and he admitted that the original plan was to kill Lincoln. He wouldn't have been able to enter with a weapon, so he stole one from the kitchen."

Elijah shared a look with his team. "His new identity was a decent enough fake that Senator Wallace's security didn't notice anything when they checked the guest list. And he hadn't been on our radar since he disappeared, which was clearly our mistake."

I blew out a breath. Maybe I didn't need to go out to the wetlands after all today. "Well holy shit. He's the threat, right? The guy following us and sending those emails?"

He shook his head. "Vincent Maura confessed to planting the car bomb."

My eyes widened. "Holy shit, *again*."

"But he denied sending those pictures and the emails and has a solid alibi for the night you and Elijah were chased near the Shipwreck," Sylvester added. "When the cops asked him about a missing flash drive, he had no idea what they were talking about. They believe him."

I set down my mug. "Then what does that mean? We're dealing with two different people?"

Elijah and Ripley shared another look. "Seems likely," Elijah said. "And isn't unheard of. But it does make a certain kind of sense. The car bomb was an escalation that didn't fit with the rest of the threats. Catching Vincent Maura doesn't remove the urgency of whoever's after the missing flash drive. We still consider them to be very dangerous."

I was simultaneously relieved to know who'd planted the bomb and extremely confused about the rest of it. Visiting Clarence today was still a go then, due to his jumpy behavior and long history of hating my father. But Elijah and I hadn't had a chance to talk about Senator Wallace yet and her offer to professionally collaborate. An offer that felt more threatening than friendly. Had Dad been blackmailing the senator?

Or had she been in on it too? What had she said? *He always had my back and I always had his.*

Sylvester cleared his throat. "If mistakes were made last night, please understand that we take full responsibility, Mr. Beaumont."

I waved it away. "Oh, guys, please. I have full faith in your capabilities. Last night changes nothing."

"An attempt was made on your life, Lucas," Elijah said in a voice like steel. "His intent was to kill you in front of all those people. It's a very big deal and we're taking it seriously."

His gaze swept across my face and I was reminded of his frantic hands last night, pulling at my clothing.

I held his stare and said, "I trust you, Elijah."

The silence between us lingered a beat too long. Sylvester coughed awkwardly and said, "Uh, sir? Someone can cover for me at the Beaumont estate today. It's a high alert situation. You shouldn't be going alone."

Elijah didn't even blink. "I'll be fine. Foster is aware of the arrangement."

For a second, it looked like Sylvester was going to argue. But instead he nodded, just as a branch struck the windows next to us.

I winced at the downpour and set down my coffee. "Let me grab a Thermos and an umbrella. We should probably hit the road, yeah?"

Elijah was peering at the sky with a frown. "It's only going to get worse."

And by the time I returned, better dressed for rain and with everything else I needed, Sylvester and Ripley had gone. Elijah was standing in the open doorway, waiting for me, and when I stepped outside and realized we were completely alone, butterflies erupted in my belly like I was a fucking teenager with a crush.

Though I was so far past *crush* at this point it was laughable.

"I'm definitely sitting in the front seat with you this time," I said, cocking a thumb at the car.

His eyes were locked on my mouth. "It's against the rules."

"I think we're well past the rules, don't you?"

He revealed a slow, sexy grin that stole my breath away. "As you wish, my liege."

I was still laughing when he ducked his head and ran to the car, holding open my door as the rain poured down. I darted out and hopped inside, shaking water from my hair as he slid in on his side, looking somehow more immaculate than before. For a moment, there came only the sounds of the rain on the roof and the *whoosh* of the windshield wipers. I noted again the lines around his mouth, the dark thumbprints beneath his lower lashes.

"Did you actually sleep last night?" I asked quietly.

"Some." His hands slid along the steering wheel. "But not much. I had a lot on my mind."

"Anything in particular?"

"You." His gaze lazily traveled the entire length of my body. "I thought about you all night, Luke."

More rain, falling even harder now, almost loud enough to drown out the sound of my heart, roaring in my ears. And I wasn't sure who moved first—him or me—but we collided across the console and our mouths crashed together. My hands clutched at his jacket while his fingers dove into my hair, tipping my face to the side as I opened wider for him.

It was the sweetest relief to feel him again, to taste him again. The intensity of the kiss didn't relent either. I couldn't get enough. Of the strength in his arms, the confidence in his grip, the way being kissed by Elijah was like being savored and devoured in equal measure.

My chest heaved with breath when we finally parted and he gripped the back of my neck, keeping me close.

"I have a dozen drafted text messages I never sent to you last night," I panted. "They started off fairly normal and flirtatious. But by four in the morning, they were severely unhinged. Red flags as far as the eye could see."

His lips twitched. "You should have sent them."

"I should have deleted them. Then never admitted to it. In fact, feel free to toss me out of this moving car as soon as you get a chance."

A husky, melodic sound came from the back of Elijah's throat. Recognition hit a second later. "Was that a...?"

Elijah kissed me again and muttered "Don't push your luck" against my lips.

When he turned to back the car from the driveway, a blush stained his cheeks, and he was clearly fighting a smile.

"That *was* a laugh. I knew it," I said.

"Who can say?"

"Which means you *do* think I'm funny." I held up my

fingers to tick off the rest of the list. "And also warm and kind and charming. Per your own description."

He sent me a sideways glance. "I also described you as reckless, irritating and having taken years off my life."

I settled back in the passenger seat. "Yeah, but I'm funny. And you have a very sexy laugh."

His blush deepened.

And those butterflies floated throughout my entire goddamn body.

24

ELIJAH

We crawled along the back roads, heading toward the wetlands, as raindrops whipped against the windshield. Trees shook and shuddered as we rode past, sending branches hurtling through the air. There'd been conflicting reports of a tropical storm landing on the East Coast later today, but I'd dismissed it as overly cautious.

Now that we were finally on our way, I was adding *ignored dangerous weather reports* to the long list of mistakes I'd made this morning alone.

The most reprehensible being the fact that Foster would never have agreed to send out a high-value client like Luke to another town, the day after being attacked in public, with only a single protection agent.

It was reckless to the point of absurdity.

In fact, every single rule I'd broken for Luke was just as dangerous as the storm outside. Just as dangerous to Luke, to his family. To the career I'd spent a life creating.

That terrifying thought alone should have sent me careening the car in the opposite direction. Back toward safety, back toward the presence of protection agents who still had their wits about them.

My scar itched, and I wondered if I had more in common with my father than I realized. The thought of not being around Luke was enough to have my knuckles in a death grip on the steering wheel. Even though I knew it was irresponsible.

Even though I knew it was wrong.

"You know, what happened last night wasn't your fault, Elijah," Luke said softly. "I can feel you blaming yourself."

I checked the rearview mirror, but we were alone on the road. "It was my fault. I'm the lead agent, and a known threat was allowed into a party. Was allowed to speak with you, to get close enough to cause grave injury. You're my responsibility and I failed you."

A pause, then, "That's not at all how I—"

"It's the job, Luke," I said, speaking over him. "All mistakes are inherently my fault. In my industry, fucking up is fatal. Literally."

Luke was silent, studying me. I hadn't anticipated the intimacy of his close presence. Or how badly I wanted to pull over and haul him into the back seat. Finish the kiss that we'd started until it became more. Until I had Luke's naked body under me, to explore, to tease, to taste. Until all that wit and good-natured charm became raw desperation.

I was already in too deep—there was no reason to pretend I wouldn't happily fuck Luke in this car then drive to the closest bed and do it again.

"I know what that feels like," Luke said. "The mistakes, all the pressure. My father considered my entire existence to be a mistake. He hadn't wanted a second kid, didn't see the need since it was assumed Preston would inherit the company. But my mom got pregnant and...well, here I am.

He loved putting me under that shitty microscope, making me squirm."

"Criticizing your every move," I said, not even a question. I knew the rules of that playbook.

"I did used to think there was a way to breathe wrong," Luke said with a wry grin. "Depending on how many times I'd messed up that day, I used to hold my breath when he was nearby."

My dad whistling. Not whistling. The way his eyes would track Christopher's every sound and movement.

I cleared my throat. "I like the way you breathe." His smile appeared in my peripheral vision while I burned with embarrassment. "I'm sorry. I…I haven't…haven't flirted in a while. That was weird."

"I beg to differ."

"People flirt with you all the time. I'm sure they're experts at it."

"What people?" Luke leaned across the console and every one of my muscles went taut with anticipation. He brushed his lips across my ear. "In case you haven't noticed, I'm only flirting with *you,* Elijah. And I referred to myself as code red in the desperation department not thirty minutes ago. You're much better at this than you realize."

He sat back in his seat and I hated the sudden distance. But his expression remained open, friendly. And there was no one else around. So I said, "My dad left us. When I was fourteen."

Luke's brow creased. "Did he ever come back?"

"No, though Christopher and I worry about it a lot. What it would do to my mom, if he showed up, wanting some bullshit idea of family that he never believed in." My hands tightened on the wheel as rain drenched the road ahead. "My little brother, that's Christopher, he was bullied when he was in middle school. Pretty badly. But he told me once—" I hesitated. "He told me he knew how to deal with them because he grew up with one in the house."

I felt Luke's attention, steady on my profile. "He was charming though, too, right?"

"Very. Could always scam his way into getting what he wanted. Money, status, women. He's probably on his sixth wife somewhere, running some sleazy pyramid scheme."

I swallowed past the knot wedged in the back of my throat. "He was hard on my brother. Mean. Mean to me too, but in different ways. I was older, so he felt like he could confide in me. Teach me all his tricks, you know? How to flirt with women. How to lie to them. How to keep secrets from my mom so he could keep doing what he wanted to do."

"Jesus," Luke muttered. "Did you come out to him?"

"God, no." I scoffed. "He wasn't a safe person to tell. I'm sure he would have told me it wasn't...wasn't manly enough or something equally as horrible."

"Sounds like a complete asshole," Luke said. "Elijah, I'm sorry."

"He's not around anymore."

"Still," he said, "doesn't mean what he did was right. Did anyone help your mom out after he left?"

The knot in my throat grew.

"I did." Lightning flashed in the distance, followed by the low roll of thunder. "I always have. They haven't had it easy. Money's...it's always been tight, plus Christopher has kids. My mom has chronic health issues. The bills pile up." Another flash of lightning. "The director position would afford me much more financial stability."

I saw Luke react to those words out of the corner of my

eye. "The contract. We broke all the rules, Elijah…I didn't even *think*."

"No," I said sternly. "I wanted to, Luke. Wanted you. *Want* you."

He sucked in a breath.

"I will continue to keep you safe. I am keeping you safe," I said.

"I'll go to bat for you, you know," he said. "If anyone says anything about your qualifications, the job. You deserve this."

Warmth flooded my chest. "Thank you."

The storm raged around us, and what was left of the tidal wetlands was already flooding as we drove past, heading for the tiny village of Rodanthe Hills. Fog rolled in off the bay, making it seem like we were the only people around, a single pair of headlights traveling through the downpour. Lightning forked through the sky ahead of us, and Luke jumped in his seat.

"I must have sounded like such a piece of shit when you first met me," Luke said suddenly. "You were right, you know."

"Be specific. I generally am when it comes to you."

He huffed out a laugh, and when I chanced a quick glance, he was tracing his lower lip with his thumb, eyes playful as he stared back. "Wow. Kiss a guy *once* and it's like all bets are off. It's just insults, left and right."

"All due respect, facts aren't insults."

A beat, then, "I like seeing you smile like that."

I hadn't realized I was. I touched my fingers to my lips and cut my gaze to Luke's again. His grin was impish, happy. "What was I right about?"

"Inheriting the company," he said. "It's complicated for me emotionally, but it's also a privilege, one of about a million I've gotten in this life. I shouldn't have been so cavalier about it with you. I must have sounded like a snotty rich kid."

I shook my head. "We grew up totally broke. It was worse, even, after my dad left. So yeah, it's not easy sometimes. Working with clients who treat me like nothing but furniture to move around as they see fit. You're not like that, Luke."

"I'm still sorry about it," he said.

The windshield wipers were starting to struggle against the deluge. I slowed the car down, creeping along a road that felt conspicuously empty. "I saw my brother the other day and asked him what he would do if our dad left him a company."

"What he'd say?"

"That he'd burn it to the ground."

Luke peered out the windshield. "That's relatable."

We were quiet for a minute, surrounded by the sound of the rain hammering against the roof. "Luke..." I started, "why weren't you on speaking terms with Lincoln? You said it'd been six years since you'd seen him?"

He shrugged, kicking his ankle up onto his knee. "I was furious with him. That's why. The expectation as a Beaumont was always that I'd graduate from a top-tier school, be gifted a large sum of money that I would then use to secure an advanced degree to feel vaguely superior over others. Then work with my father at TBG and help him expand his business and probably do a bunch of shady shit that's unethical at best and illegal at worst. But I didn't follow in Preston's footsteps. I took the money, used some to buy my house, and gave the rest to Harriet and my nieces."

I remembered seeing that picture of Luke with his nieces. The obvious comfort, the obvious affection, the tenderness in the way he held them. The sight had stirred something deep within my chest. A yearning for my own family, who I almost never saw. And a yearning for the man sitting next to me, who steadfastly refused to fit neatly into the boxes I wanted to place him in.

"You're close with her," I said, more statement than question.

"She's my best friend," he said with a smile. "She's funny and smart and brave. And my nieces are just like her. When her mom told my dad that she was pregnant, he abandoned her completely. He had more money than he knew what to do with while Harriet said they could barely make rent every month. Her mother had served her purpose as his mistress, and the consequences were of no use to him."

Luke shook his head, his expression darkening. "Anyway, he didn't like how I used the money he gave me, especially because he found out that Harriet was in my life. I went there, to his offices that day, to stand up for her. To make him see how much he'd lost, never having her in his life. To tell him that he was a lying, cheating bastard. To say…" He took a breath. "Well, it doesn't really matter now, because I didn't say a damn thing. Chickened out, completely. Instead, he told me I'd been a disappointment all along. That was the last time I spoke with him."

Five years I'd stood next to Lincoln Beaumont, had protected his life with my own, and here I was wishing I could go back in time and put my fist through his face.

"He never apologized?"

Luke shook his head.

"Do you miss him?"

I watched his throat bob. Saw him wipe quickly at his eyes. We were in a car so I couldn't fall to my knees in front of him again. But the urge thrummed beneath my skin and I would have held him till it passed.

"I miss my mom," Luke finally said. "Every day, I miss her. And I miss the idea of having a living parent who loved me unconditionally. I don't miss him though, and I'm worried that makes me a bad person."

"It's not that black and white," I said—and would have said more. Like, *you said I was right about you but I'm realizing now how wrong I was*. But that was too dangerous, too intimate, and the car was now crawling up toward the gated entrance of TBG's luxury housing community. It stuck out like a sore thumb in the midst of the surrounding nature. Mini mansions with manicured lawns and a fountain in the middle, although it was hard to see much with the weather.

"Wow," Luke said bitterly, staring out the window. "He really went and built all this on top of protected tidal wetlands. What a fucking mess."

I kept driving, heading toward Clarence Craven's home, which was less than three miles from here.

"This was where the money came from," Luke murmured. "The money to buy my house."

"It is," I said. "You could still change that legacy though. The company's yours, isn't it?"

Luke sighed. "I don't know. Feels like the whole thing is composed of just lies and blackmail. It's a lost cause at this point."

That wasn't the first time I'd heard Luke express something like that about TBG. It *was* the first time I heard a tremble of doubt in the words.

"It's up here, I think," Luke said, so I turned to the right and down a long, muddy road. The wind rattled a sign that read Welcome to the South Shore Wetlands Project. Past that was a small cabin with no car out front.

I came to a stop, and we sat, taking in the scene. The windows were dark and grimy, though the garden in front appeared well-cared for.

"No wonder Clarence was so furious, is *still* so furious," Luke said. "My dad came in here and destroyed the place he'd pledged to protect. He's still getting arrested at environmental protests throughout the state. Still shows up at city hall to talk about the ecology of this area. What I don't know is why he didn't identify himself as my father's long-standing nemesis when we met at Sunrise Village."

I shifted in my seat. "Given his rage, I would have thought him a likely candidate for a car bomb. But if that was actually Vincent Maura, then maybe Clarence is mad for more than just the wetlands. Maybe your dad had a flash drive full of *his* secrets that he wants back."

Luke sent me a look. "Maybe not only my dad. Maybe my dad *and* Senator Wallace."

I raised an eyebrow in question. Luke twisted to face me.

"Last night, what she said in the drawing room about working together, about how she and my dad helped each other..." He shook his head. "Made me wonder if they blackmailed together. A local politician and a property developer would both benefit from having leverage over people. Threatening them for votes, for funding, for permits. For all kinds of special access."

A whisper of unease tickled down my spine. "I certainly got a bad feeling from her, even though she didn't initially strike me as violent. But that's the thing about violence. It's unpredictable. It can hide, change shape easily. Look at who attacked you last night. Pleasant smile, polite manners, completely out in the open. A dangerous person like Senator Wallace wouldn't keep to the dark. With all that power, she wouldn't have to."

I reached for my phone, which had no service. "Also, I *really* don't like how isolated we are out here."

I glanced down and saw that I had two missed calls from Foster.

My stomach plummeted, twisting with guilt. I started to say something to Luke, but he was throwing open his door and pulling his raincoat on. He jogged up to Clarence's cabin like he had not a care in the world. As usual.

"God*dammit*, Luke," I muttered, jumping out of the car and doing the same. "*Wait for me*."

He either didn't hear or chose to ignore me. The branches in the nearby trees whipped fast, drawing my attention to the back of the house. It butted up against the ocean, which flowed into the tidal wetlands. The back of my neck started to itch, like we were being watched. Between the roar of the storm and the dim visibility, my heart rate picked up.

I jumped the rickety stairs and landed next to Luke, hooking an arm around his chest and shoving him behind me.

I scowled over my shoulder. "This is what you have a bodyguard for."

"How many times are you gonna save my life?"

"The quantity isn't the issue. Getting hurt on your behalf is part of the job."

He tried to push past me but I stood my ground, turning back and knocking on the door.

"Elijah," he said, exasperated. "I want you to be safe as much as you want me to be safe."

I knocked again. Still no answer. "If that's the case, let's get the hell out of here. I've got a bad feeling again."

Luke slid to the side and cupped his hands around the

window. "No lights. No movement. It's a Sunday and there's a storm. I thought it at least *likely* he'd be here."

The rain dumped down in buckets now, obscuring my field of vision. We were getting soaked to the skin even standing under the roof. Luke checked the other window, then peered around to the back of the house. He shoved the wet hair back from his face, frustration pulling his lips into a frown.

"He's not here. I don't know what I was thinking, having us drive here for no fucking reason."

"You have a reason," I said. "A good one. And the person doing all this is avoiding capture on purpose. They want you agitated and upset. That's the goal."

He tore his gaze away and stared out into the storm. "It's only getting worse. They could hurt Harriet. My nieces. You've been right about so many things, Elijah, and you were right about this too. All I've done is piss them off and make them more reckless."

"No, Luke, I…I don't think that anymore," I started to say, taking a step toward him. And that's when a second set of headlights appeared, barely visible through the rain. It had us both turning on instinct to where the car lingered, to the left of the driveway. It didn't move, though I could hear the engine revving.

That whisper of unease ratcheted up.

"You think that's him?" Luke asked eagerly.

It was impossible to see through the windshield. "I don't know. But we need to get back in the car."

Luke shot me a look. "What's wrong?"

I hooked a hand around his elbow and pulled him close. "It's probably nothing. But get in the car, buckle your seat belt. Do you have service out here?"

"No, why?"

I was almost certainly overreacting. Except I was trained to listen to my instincts and something was screaming *run*.

"I don't like any of this," I said gruffly, then ran us through the rain with every nerve ending on alert. I wrenched open the door and shoved Luke inside before rounding the car and doing the same.

The car still idled. A gust of wind whipped past and I had to muscle the door shut. We were both drenched and shivering, but there wasn't time for comfort.

"Elijah, what's going on?" Luke asked urgently.

I started the car and pulled back onto the narrow road, already starting to flood. All of it was wrong, every fucking thing, and I only had myself to blame.

"Bad feeling," I repeated, eyes on the rearview mirror. "Are you buckled in?"

"Yes."

We winced as headlights bounced off the mirror. And my heart stopped at what I saw—the car was directly behind me, practically on my bumper. So close that I was forced to speed up in dangerous conditions.

Precisely what they wanted me to do.

We came up onto a curve, heavy with fog, and I slowed the car on instinct, not wanting to skid out.

And that's when we were struck hard from behind.

25

LUKE

The car rammed us from behind.

More than a tap, enough to send our wheels skidding slightly on the flooding road. My heart flew into my throat as I was jostled forward, more shocked than injured.

"Are you okay?" Elijah ground out.

"I'm fine, I'm fine," I sputtered. "What the hell's going on?"

I heard revving from behind us and then a sharp crack.

Elijah cursed softly as we were struck again—but I was expecting it this time. I kept my attention glued on him, noting his clenched jaw and focused gaze. His short, fast breaths. The windshield wipers could barely stay on top of the rain, and I was keenly aware of how close to the edge of the road we were. A rural road without guardrails or fences that led straight into the murky waters of the ocean.

Lightning streaked across the sky, followed by a clap of thunder that sounded directly above us. The car was following close behind, and every time it got close it forced Elijah to increase our speed.

I twisted to face him, one hand clenched around the

head rest. He swore again and a bead of sweat glistened on his temple. "We were followed out here and I didn't fucking realize it," he spat out. "And now they want us to know."

Another impact slammed into us. This time it was hard enough to send my shoulder into the side door. I grabbed it with a wince but dropped it when I saw Elijah's intense focus fracture. His knuckles whitened on the steering wheel and he kept darting glances my way.

"It's nothing, really. Elijah, don't worry about me. How can I help?"

"By not getting hurt."

I reached for his wrist and wrapped my fingers around it. His pulse was wild, thready. I stroked my thumb in circles, a paltry attempt to soothe at a moment like this but I couldn't have resisted if I tried.

"I won't get hurt," I said. "How can I help?"

The car flooded with light again and I braced myself. This time they hit our back bumper so hard that Elijah had to spin the wheel in circles to get us back under control.

"Try to get cell service and call 911," he finally said. I reached for our phones, but both had a big *no service* flashing across the screen.

"No dice," I said.

Elijah nodded, throat bobbing as he swallowed.

"Do you want me to keep touching you?" I asked quietly.

Thunder boomed as we hit a pothole, sending us flying. My heart was racing so fast that spots danced at the edges of my vision. But I couldn't tear my eyes away from Elijah. Out of fear. Out of admiration. Out of the deep thrumming in my chest that grew louder and louder with every passing minute I spent with this man.

"Luke," he gasped—and I realized I'd released him in the fray. I reached for his thigh and gripped it. His lashes fluttered and he inhaled long and slow. Then his expression shifted into one of alarm. "Luke, hold—"

They hit us so hard that the car whipped into a tailspin. The world became a jarring blur of lights and bile rose in my throat. A second later we were motionless—but only for a second, because Elijah was driving us forward, tires spinning out, then back onto the narrow road. The other car was still behind us, still flashing their brights with such intensity I thought I might be sick.

Past the road, waves roared and slapped in the churning of the storm and a cold sweat dripped down my spine. I closed my eyes for a few dizzying seconds and tried to remember my emergency safety training—made difficult by the shriek of adrenaline and panic that wouldn't let my thoughts settle.

Just the passing thought that Elijah could be hurt in any way had the panic multiplying, so forcefully that I reached for his leg again. He accelerated, trying to escape the danger stalking us like a pack of howling wolves. But each acceleration had the tires wobbling, spraying water and mud as he wrenched the wheel around turns in the misty darkness.

And it was the final strike—so forceful, so obviously deliberate—that sent us to the very edge of the road. Elijah braked but it was no match for the slick slope. We careened up and over, the car sliding down the bank and another, steeper cliff.

Icy fear had such a grip on my throat I couldn't fucking breathe. Could barely think. But I'd been trained so thoroughly for a reason, a reason our survival teachers had drilled into us over and over again. *If the worst happens, there will be no time for thinking, only doing.*

I pushed to roll my window down and felt for Elijah's hand, squeezing hard as the front of the car struck the water.

A nanosecond after impact, before shock or pain or panic could take hold, I was moving. Shucked my seat belt and immediately released Elijah's. He was holding his side and grimacing, a sheen of sweat on his face.

"We have to go," I said sharply. "Now, before too much water gets in."

His breathing was ragged. "Luke."

I lurched across the seat to examine him, too aware of the rising water outside my lowered window. "What is it... your ribs? Your stomach? Did you hit your head?" My fingers danced across his body, searching for blood, for a wound, for anything that would make this more challenging.

"Ribs...I think," he bit out.

"Okay, okay, okay." I whipped around. Saw the water flowing into the open window now. Waves were sliding up onto the hood, lapping at the windshield. I knew how little time we had left before we sank completely. "I'm climbing out and you'll follow me. And then I'm gonna swim us both to shore."

His forehead creased. Another wince when he tried to move. I touched his chin until his eyes opened, and I flashed him my biggest, cockiest grin. "Aren't you lucky your client is a renowned water sports instructor? I could do this rescue in my sleep."

Water flowed over my feet, and I beat back my own panic as much as I could.

A tiny smile tugged at his lips. "I am lucky to know you. Extremely lucky."

I tossed him a wink. "There's no time for you to be this cute." The car lurched forward and I fought the urge to scream. "Come on, sweetheart. We gotta move."

I moved backward, hooking my legs out the window and

into stormy-cold ocean water. Kicking my legs to stay afloat, I turned and held an arm out, grateful beyond measure when he clasped it, his grip strong. He moved with obvious pain while water rushed past him, rising higher and higher. With a pull, he slid through the window and into my waiting arms.

Rain drenched us and I could hardly see, but I managed to hook an arm around Elijah and start swimming us to shore. A small wave crested over our heads and we were briefly under. Now that we were in the open ocean, my panic subsided. This *one thing* I could do and had been doing for more than a decade now. Still, the cold had my muscles locking up and Elijah's extra weight didn't help. He'd shucked his jacket, but my own sweatshirt hung heavy off my neck.

"You keep...you keep calling me that," Elijah said, teeth chattering. *"Sweetheart."*

We'd just survived our car being forced off a cliff, so my ability to feel embarrassed had disappeared along with my phone and probably my wallet too.

"Well, yeah," I teased. "Who's sweeter than you?"

Elijah coughed out a laugh, then winced. "Not one of my"—he spit out ocean water—"many attributes."

"Bullshit." I scoffed.

"Workaholic," he panted. "Too uptight, probably. Not sweet. Not cute either."

I was out of breath too but could make out the shore. "Look up both words in the dictionary and you'll find your picture next to them."

He gave another weak laugh but at least he was distracted. "You're a strong swimmer," he said.

"Don't I know it. And I'm handsome too."

"Humility. One of your top three virtues."

"You know," I said, "now that we've seen each other naked, I feel like I can be fully honest here." Our feet touched sand, and I felt him sag against me with relief. "I'm not especially virtuous."

"Don't I know it," he echoed. "It's why I like you."

I was amid a heroic rescue in a storm, having just been run off the road by a furious mystery threat, and I still managed to blush at those words.

We staggered onto the beach. Between the rain and the ocean, I'd forgotten what it was like to be dry. Would, in fact, never be dry again. But I didn't want us standing still in this cold, so I kept an arm around Elijah's waist and pointed us back toward the road.

"Is it helpful to point out that we're officially oh-for-two when it comes to cars? I don't think we'll be able to drive that one home."

Elijah sucked in a breath. "And our goddamn phones too." His head shot up and I could feel him scanning for danger around us. "I don't see the other car anymore, do you?"

"No. I don't think a lot of people drive someone off the road into a watery grave and then wait around for a while."

A shudder racked Elijah's body. I clutched him closer and eyed him as we made our way up the beach steps. He caught me staring and tried to pull away, which only made me tighten my grip.

"I can walk, you know."

"I do know. Just as I knew you were gonna say that." I shoved the wet hair off my face. "Do you ever let people help you when you need it?"

He scowled. "I don't."

"But what if you did?"

There was a house in the distance, less than a quarter

mile away. The storm was relentless and there wasn't a single car on the road—no sign of our attacker, but not of anyone else either. I pointed us in that direction and Elijah grunted in response.

"You shouldn't have had to rescue me, Luke," he said. "Shouldn't have...*Christ*, I drove us off the fucking road and you had to pull me from the car. This is what I do for a living and all I've done is fail you."

I would have stopped us in the road to kiss him senseless if we weren't drenched to the skin and freezing. I pressed a kiss to his cheek instead and he turned, eyes full of an emotion too complex for me to name.

"You didn't drive us off the road, we were forced. I know you think you can control everything—"

"Luke—"

"*Elijah...*" I said, drawing his attention again. "I know you think you can control everything down to the very last detail, but it's not possible. And I understand the impulse. Trust me, I do. There were whole years after my mom died where I did the same thing, hoping it would mean I could prevent losing someone again the way that I lost her. I couldn't though, and I can't. Neither can you."

He shoved his own wet hair back. "You told me you trusted me, and this is part of that trust. I keep you safe from harm."

"Well, it just so happens that what *I* do for a living is swim. A lot. In rougher waves than these, hauling much heavier pieces of equipment than you. And years spent thrill-seeking mean I've taken plenty of survival courses and wilderness first aid classes. I can't run a company. I can't get my brother to like me. I *certainly* can't figure out who's trying to hurt us. But contrary to what my entire family thinks, I *do* have actual skills. This is one of them. You need to trust me too."

Elijah didn't respond as we neared the house, though he did go swiftly back into bodyguard mode, approaching like an attack was imminent. We'd gotten lucky—most waterfront properties in the Hamptons had security cameras and high fences. But this little house looked like an old family fishing cabin, with a sign that said Hello Happy Campers and a welcome mat that said "Don't forget to wipe your paws!"

There was no vehicle in the driveway and everything was dark, but I still knocked loudly on the door as we shivered beneath the awning.

After a minute of no response, I kicked over a potted plant and found an extra key.

"We need a place to crash and a phone that works," I said. "This'll do."

He cocked an eyebrow. "We're adding breaking and entering to the list of everything that's gone wrong on this trip?"

I slid the key in the lock and paused to listen. Sent him a grin. "Don't you wanna prove all those people calling you uptight wrong?"

His eyes darted between the door and the horrifying weather. Another racking shiver worked through him and he winced with a hiss. A burst of protectiveness rushed through me. Pushing open the door with my shoulder, I revealed a dim but cozy space, fireplace and all.

"Nope, we're doing this," I said firmly. "You boss me around twenty-four seven so now I'm returning the favor. Get the hell in here. And I'm not askin'."

Exasperation gave way to acceptance...and then a flash of heat burned in his gaze. "As you wish, my liege."

I cocked my head. "Inside, smartass."

26

LUKE

I cast one last look at the raging storm outside before shutting the door and locking us in.

Elijah made his way to the landline on the counter, but based on his worried expression after he picked up the receiver, my guess was that the phone lines had been knocked out, along with the power.

The house was slightly dusty, the air a bit stale, but functional nonetheless. It was essentially one giant room, the style similar to a lot of the older seaside cottages in the area. A large, worn couch sat by the fireplace, which Elijah moved to fill with logs from the stack nearby. As soon as he got it lit, he stood shivering in front of it with his hands out, and the sight of his hunched shoulders had me springing into action.

Still dripping wet, I walked to the tiny kitchen on the left side of the room and began yanking open drawers, until I located emergency lanterns and a few flashlights. After setting them up near the couch, I rummaged around in the shelves and found a bottle of bourbon. With two full glasses hooked with my fingers, I moved across the room and handed him a glass.

He stared down into the pilfered amber liquid, then scowled.

"I know," I said gently. "We're no better than common criminals now. But I'm willing to accept this new lifestyle and go on the run if you are."

Elijah rolled his eyes and knocked back the bourbon with more skill than I was expecting. I followed suit with my own shot, shuddering as a bright burst of heat worked its way into my chest.

"If it makes you feel any better, I have every intention of leaving them a note and then sending them money as soon as I recover my wallet. It'll be like...like an Airbnb stay they didn't realize they'd booked for us."

A hint of a smile appeared on his face. "I'm not *that* uptight. I'm capable of having fun."

I tipped my head to the side. "Name three things you've done for fun in the past year that aren't being the very best protection agent the world has ever seen."

He glanced to the side with an exasperated sigh. "I...I was on vacation when Foster called about your dad. The first one in five years."

"And did you enjoy yourself?"

"There was...the sun," he said. "And also...lounge chairs."

I placed my hands gently on his shoulders and turned him around, back to an armchair that sat by the fire. "Good god, we need to get some fucking whimsy in your life, Elijah." He sat when I pushed him down, albeit reluctantly. "As soon as we're past this, I'm taking you to a field of wildflowers and we're gonna lay in it and watch the clouds pass us by. Maybe have a picnic. Get our faces painted. Find an old, rickety rollercoaster and ride it just for kicks. Eat too many candy bars. I'll even drag you into a store and make you watch me have a wacky trying-on-clothes montage."

I twisted around, poured him a bit more whiskey, then pressed the glass into his hand. "Drink this and try to warm back up. I shall return with towels and dry clothes."

Elijah fisted a hand in my damp clothing, preventing me from sidling away. He pulled me close, until I could see the drops of water in his eyelashes. "What are you doing?"

I swallowed thickly. "Taking care of you."

"Why?"

I brushed a lock of hair from his forehead. His arm banded around my waist, keeping me close. "Because I want to. Because you deserve everything that's good. We're not going anywhere in this storm, but it's safe here, and there's a fire going and all of our problems and worries will still be there in the morning. Which means it's okay if we don't worry about them till then."

His eyes searched mine and then he tipped his face up and pulled my mouth down to his. His lips were red-hot against the chill, parting as he licked his tongue inside. His hand came around to grip my face, and a low, satisfied groan rumbled from the center of his chest. I melted at his obvious pleasure, at how he deepened the kiss slowly. Thoroughly. When he pulled back, he had to steady my weak knees.

"You're the last time I had fun, Luke," he said, nipping the side of my neck with his teeth.

Soft laughter shivered from me. "Is this the kind of fun you like? Getting rescued from a submerged car after being run off the road?" His lips moved firmly up my neck, hovering at my ear, breath hot. "I'm free..." I sighed. "I'm free next weekend if you wanna do it again."

"That's not the kind of fun I was referring to." His teeth

closed around my ear, and I had to fight to remain standing. "I'm talking about you coming with my hand wrapped around your cock at that party. How fucking sexy you were, how fucking perfect. I haven't known a moment of peace since." Another kiss below my ear. "I can't stop thinking about the sounds you made."

His big hands curved around my hips and landed on my ass, where he grabbed with a hushed snarl that had me cursing. "How desperate you were. How eager." His lips brushed across my cheek before landing on my own again. This kiss shattered me from the inside out, a deep, searching caress that had my fingers twisting in his wet shirt. "I wanted to spend days with you on that couch, Luke. Not minutes. Never minutes when it comes to you."

Another kiss, this one darker. Harsher. He hauled me flush against him.

And then winced in obvious pain.

I reared back and caught him by the chin. "I'm going to commence taking care of you now."

"Luke, I'm fine," he said with a smile. Reached for my face again, and that's when I noticed the knuckles on his right hand, torn open and bleeding.

I shot him a look, then dipped to examine them closer. "I need to bandage these, put some ice on those ribs. But first, strip out of these wet clothes. I'm on a mission for something clean and dry."

He gave a grumpy growl that I ignored. Instead, I pressed a smiling kiss to his temple and strode to the small bedroom in the back, one of the lanterns lighting my way. I returned after a few minutes with fluffy, dry towels and some clothing for Elijah. I'd thrown my own soaked ones into the tub and pulled on sweats that were short in the leg but too loose at the waist, so I yanked them as tightly as I could and tossed on a shirt.

Back in the main room, I found ice, a dish towel, and a newish first aid kit. When I turned around, Elijah was stepping out of his clothing. I stopped at the sight of him, bathed in golden firelight, my heart in my throat.

Flickering light danced across his broad, powerful back and the chest hair spreading to his strong belly. He caught me looking, sent me a glower as he shucked his wet pants, revealing thighs so thick I wanted to bite them.

I moved closer, tracking the bruising on the right side of his ribs already starting to turn purple. His swelling knuckles. I nodded at the chair again and he sat. Took the ice I offered, sucking in a breath when he pressed it to his skin. I rubbed a towel down his arms, his burly chest. Our eyes stayed locked, a pleased half smile playing on his lips.

"You really learned all this from doing all those extreme sports?"

"Do you mean my obvious expertise in the medical arts?" I asked with a grin.

"You're very good at it," he said softly.

I moved to stand behind him, drying the damp strands of his hair, working my fingers along his scalp.

"You have to be, if you're gonna fling yourself out of an airplane with a parachute on. Need to be able to save yourself in a hundred different ways if the worst happens." I toweled off his rippling back, the nape of his neck. "My job is pretty easy and go-with-the-flow. But that's what the customers pay us for—skilled competence out on the water and the ability to save their life if need be."

I ran the towel down his flexing thigh muscles. Watched the thick length of him harden in his borrowed shorts.

Kissed the top of his knee with a coy smile. "Let me see your hand now."

He set it gently on his leg while I settled on my knees in front of him. "I think I hit it on the car when I was swimming out."

I found butterfly bandages and antibiotic ointment in the first aid kit. When I applied the ointment to the open skin, he didn't flinch. I felt the heavy weight of his attention, tracking my every movement.

"How many times have you jumped out of an airplane with a parachute on?"

I laid the first bandage on his skin. "I've skydived more times than I can count. More than I bungee jump."

"And what else?"

Another bandage. More ointment. "I love to kite surf. Regular surf. Rock climb. Whitewater raft when I can make it out west." I peered up at him through my lashes. "There was a time in my early twenties when I got obsessed with cage-diving with sharks. Great whites, mostly."

Elijah eyed me with something like wonder. The soft warmth from the fireplace surrounded us, even as the wind howled past, rattling the panes. And I contemplated staying right here, trapped in this moment, for as long as the outside world would let me.

"Do you ever get scared?" he asked.

I nodded and went back to my bandaging. "Always. It's too dangerous otherwise. You need that voice inside that urges caution. Fear is part of it, but it also"—my mouth pulled into a grin—"feels so fucking good. Makes me feel alive, completely present in the moment. The first time I ever skydived was because my mom had it on her bucket list. She never got to do it. There was so much she never got to do."

I sat back on my knees. "She was really sick at the end. But she made a bucket list, showed it to me and Preston. It was silly—I think she drew the whole thing in crayon. But he and I tried to cross some things off the list for her."

"Like what?" Elijah asked.

I shoved a hand into my hair, slowly drying. "She wanted one last Christmas, but she ended up dying during the summer. Preston and I got her a tree. Hauled out all of our ornaments. Wrapped presents that we made ourselves. We played Christmas music for a week straight, watched all of her favorite movies. She loved it."

Elijah's fingers brushed a lock of hair off my forehead. "And you don't worry about the risk? Swimming with sharks and jumping off bridges?"

"Being alive is risky." I turned, pressed a kiss to his palm. "My mom lived a year after her diagnosis. It was random. Violent. Shocking. Horrible in every way imaginable. And it took away the person I loved most in the world."

I met Elijah's gaze again and was stunned at the reverence there.

He swallowed hard, multiple times. "I'm so sorry she was taken from you."

"She would have liked you a lot, Elijah." I busied myself with setting aside the first aid kit, rolling up the towels and shoving them away. "I...I like you a lot."

Silence lingered between us, and I fought the urge to fidget. There was no reason to hide. I wasn't shy about how I felt. Hadn't been shy from the moment we met. But there was something about this sweet slice of time, in this house we didn't own, as a storm devastated the landscape outside.

It felt beyond boundaries, beyond reality.

"Do you know how beautiful you are?" Elijah asked, his voice rougher than normal.

A blush stained my cheeks. "Wanna tell me in extremely specific detail?"

Another husky laugh. "Come here."

I pressed up onto my knees until we were face-to-face. His strong thighs bracketed my waist, his body heat warmer than the fire. I reached for him, but he stopped me, grabbing my wrist like he had the night at the bookstore. He pressed his nose to my pulse point, inhaled like a starving man.

"I was an asshole to you earlier."

I blinked. "Really? When?"

He dragged his nose up and down the delicate skin there. "After the car. After you rescued me. You're more than what your family thinks of you, and I'm sorry I ever made you feel that same way. The truth is, I was so fucking scared when we went over that cliff. We're trained to stay calm in those situations and all I could do was panic."

He kissed my wrist. Lingered there. Kissed my palm. Every fingertip.

I stopped breathing altogether.

"No one told me it would feel this way," he murmured. "Caring for someone. Wanting someone. The fear is debilitating, Luke. I keep having nightmares that I'm messing up, that you'll get hurt, that every mistake I've ever made will stack up against me and you'll pay the price."

Elijah dragged his open mouth across my palm. The tip of his tongue caressed my inner wrist. I was frozen on my knees, incinerated from the inside out.

"I wasn't supposed to want you, Lucas. I wasn't supposed to give in," he said, in the cadence of a confession. As if I had the ability to absolve him, when my desire for this man burned hot enough to engulf the sun.

There's a moment when skydiving, before you step out

of the plane, when your brain can't comprehend how high up you are. It's the combination of some ancient fear mixed with the desire to leap into clouds that look like marshmallows. It's the most dizzying sensation, the euphoria paired with icy panic.

That was what it was like, watching Elijah Knight inhale the scent of my skin like it was sacred to him.

My heart thrashed with a wild and unruly hope—while my brain screamed at me to run. I knew what it was like to have every vulnerability wielded against me. To be left, abandoned and betrayed by the people who were supposed to protect me.

"Why did you give in?" I asked.

His eyes lingered on my mouth before traveling up to find mine. "Because I'm completely undone by you."

Then Elijah's lips claimed my own in a bruising kiss.

And I was gone.

27

ELIJAH

I was drunk on Luke Beaumont.

Drunk on taking what I was pretty sure I didn't fucking deserve. But Pandora's box was wide open now. And I couldn't stop—hoping for him, dreaming of him, needing him.

I'd sat as still as I was able while Luke tended to the cuts on my hand with fingers that trembled. Such worship, such focus, only pausing occasionally to send me one of those roguish grins—the one he used to flirt, to tease, to seduce.

To break me wide open.

I'd never been more terrified, more out of control. There were moments at *every step of the way* when I could have pulled back. Admitted to Foster that things had grown personally complicated with Luke and then crawled back to the offices, prepared to eat shit about it for however long it took.

But the glaring, painfully obvious truth was that I didn't want to.

I grabbed Luke by the arms and hauled him up until he could straddle my lap. Gripped his face, a few inches from mine, and watched the way the dancing firelight highlighted his cheekbones. His full, defined lips. The dark blue of his eyes, the color of the ocean after a hurricane.

"Beautiful," I whispered and licked my tongue against his lips. Felt him open for me, groan for me, felt his fingers slide into the back of my hair and yank. I splayed my hands under the ridiculous T-shirt he'd found, hissing in a breath as I stroked his feverish skin. Shoved the material up and over, and then Luke was naked from the waist up.

Glorious and strong. Sinful, every single bit of him. His smooth, defined chest. The flexing ridges of his abdomen. The taste of sweat and seawater in the hollow of his collarbone. I roamed my hands up the expanse of his back, felt each muscle twitch beneath my fingers.

We didn't stop kissing. Our mouths moved hungrily, furiously. Luke's ragged moans vibrated against my lips, had me opening wider. Kissing him harder. I grabbed his ass and yanked him closer, until the slick hardness of his cock pressed to mine through the fabric.

His head fell back and I didn't hesitate to send my mouth to that spot he'd liked so much—the crook where his neck met his shoulder. I traced my tongue around the still-sensitive bruise and Luke hissed. I grinned against his skin and kept my tongue working, my teeth scraping.

He cursed and started to rock against me, his upper body writhing as my mouth sucked along his skin. He gave another rock, but this time I grabbed his ass with more force, stilling him.

"I don't remember saying you could move," I growled into his neck.

His thighs tightened against me. Every muscle went taut. "I can't help it," he panted. "It's your mouth, it's too good, it's...yes, *right there*."

I'd switched to the other side of his throat. Licking. Sucking. I let my palm drift up his side until I could circle my thumb around his nipple. Luke cursed again. His nails bit into the tops of my shoulders, sending sparks of pleasure down my spine. I tightened my grip on his ass and set my own pace, grinding him down on top of me. Slow. Lazy. Luke retaliated by wrenching my face to his and kissing me with a fury.

"Don't tease me tonight, Elijah," he whispered.

"You can take it." I kissed his throat. Nuzzled his ear. Thrust my hips up and bounced him against my cock. "You'll do anything I say, won't you?"

A smirk appeared. "Depends on what you say."

I pushed up from the chair and had us moving backward in the next instant—moving until Luke's back collided with the wall. I pinned his wrists by his head and caged him in. Gave a deliberate thrust of my cock against his. Again and again and again until our kisses turned sloppy, more groans than connection. Pure need and raw desire.

The friction from each thrust drove me wild, had me dropping his hands to grip his hips instead. Driving between his legs. Wrenching moan after moan from the back of his throat.

Luke's fingers dove back into my hair, and I dropped my face to his neck, biting him on my next thrust. He shuddered, huffed out a laugh. "God, I could...I could come like this."

I hummed under my breath. "That's not how you're coming."

I kissed along his collarbone, felt the goosebumps shivering across his skin. Bent further so I could flatten my tongue against his nipple. Lapped at him there until his nails were clawing down my back.

"I love that," he sighed.

My mouth moved lower, tongue tracing every flexing ridge of muscle. "How about this?"

"Please."

My hands bracketed his hips while I teased him—inch by inch. I nuzzled down the patch of hair leading to his belly button. Scraped my teeth along his hipbone. I dropped to my knees and tucked my fingers into the top of his sweat-pants. Tugged down slowly. Slower still. I flicked my gaze up to find Luke staring down at me with an expression of pure hunger. Pupils blown out, chest heaving. I yanked his pants to his ankles, grinning when his cock bobbed in front of my face. I'd been aiming for patience but couldn't help myself. I dragged my tongue up the side of him and groaned at the taste.

"Your cock is so fucking pretty, Luke," I growled. "You like me down here on my knees for you?"

He had both hands in my hair. "I like everything you do to me."

I reached up, pressed two fingers to his lips until he opened and took them inside. He moaned, getting them wet with his tongue, sucking with the same intense suction he'd used on me the other night. When he released my fingers, I lifted an eyebrow. He was already smiling before he gave me a nod.

Something primal tore through my chest, growing when he spread his legs wider and whispered, "I need this."

He needed me. And I needed *him*, with such ferocity my body trembled. I propped my chin on his thigh and watched —watched this confident, gorgeous man turn desperate as soon as I reached between his legs. Cupped his balls, squeezing while he cursed. Kept exploring, slipping between his ass cheeks until I landed on the tight ring of muscle. His spine arched from the wall. Head back, throat exposed, Adam's apple bobbing as I circled and circled and then pushed a wet finger inside.

Luke hissed in a breath. "Shit, *fuck*."

I stilled, letting him adjust. When he nodded again, I added a second finger. Crooked them, then took his cock between my lips.

Luke's head thrashed, breath heavy. "Yes, oh yes, oh *yes*."

He twisted his fingers and pulled on my hair, making me moan as I took him deeper. He hit the back of my throat and my eyes closed in pure pleasure. It was the heady, salty taste of him, the way his hips punched forward, his anguished sighs with every stroke of my fingers. He was already shaking, cock pulsing with every swipe of my tongue along the underside.

"I love this so much," he said through clenched teeth. "Why are you so good at this, *goddammit*, Elijah."

I moved faster. Worked my fingers in his ass. Groaned along with his every jagged, keening cry. I wanted to see what we looked like right now—Luke naked and perfect, every muscle standing out as he fucked my mouth. The snarl in his lips, the flush creeping up his neck. If I'd had anything to grind myself against I would have been—shamelessly—because my cock was so hard it hurt.

"Elijah...Elijah, sweetheart...."

I took him to the very back of my throat again. Hollowed my cheeks and stroked my fingers deep. Luke roared his climax, chanting my name. When I finally released him, it was to press my cheek to his stomach, chasing my breath. My heart jerked against my rib cage, and when I sat back to look at Luke, it skipped several beats, until I was dizzy from desire. He shoved his hair back and pulled me by the chin to stand. His kiss was an explosion, a giant ray of light shattering through us both. I held him by the face and drank him in.

When we parted, he whispered, "You're incredible, you know that?"

I nudged his nose with mine. "I've been thinking about that for two weeks now."

"Oh, yeah?" A teasing half smile appeared on his face. "Care to share any more of your dirty thoughts, Mr. Knight?"

I gave his ass a light smack and growled, "Get in that damn bedroom."

He moved to the side and gave a tiny salute. "Yes, sir."

I smacked him again and he laughed. Then I marveled at Luke's back as he walked into the small bedroom—the strength in his shoulders, his trim waist, and a round, muscular ass that had me wiping a hand across my mouth.

In the bathroom, I pulled open drawers, moving quickly to get past how awkward I felt being here without the owners knowing about it. But a dark lust snapped beneath my skin, growing in strength when I opened the last drawer to find an array of condoms and a few unopened packets of lube.

I let out a surprised laugh and scooped up what I needed. Walked back into the bedroom and propped a shoulder against the door frame, condoms and lube between my two fingers. Luke's eyes widened.

"Some Airbnb you broke us into," I said, dropping them onto the nightstand.

"I'll be sure to leave them an extra big tip for that," Luke said. "You got any specific plans for those?"

I stood at the end of the bed and let my shorts fall to my ankles. Stepped out of them and enjoyed the way Luke's hands clenched in the bedsheets. I dropped to the bed and prowled his naked body, kissing up his stomach. Strumming both nipples with my thumbs. Leaving a trail of bites and kisses along his throat.

When I reached his face, I licked deeply into his mouth and dropped my hips down, sliding my cock against his, already hardening again. When I pulled back, I tugged his lower lip down with my thumb.

"I might have some plans. If you're good."

Luke bucked his hips and flipped me, pinning my arms to the bed. I reared up, tried to catch his mouth, but he kept away with a taunting smile. "That's a shame, because I'm never good."

I returned the smile—part flirting, part pure wonder that I was here, naked in bed, with the most beautiful man I'd ever seen. When he finally dipped down, hovering his lips over mine, I whispered, "Don't I know it."

28

LUKE

It should have been a crime for Elijah to smile like that.

He'd been distractingly handsome before in a stern and stoic way. But now smiles appeared on his face with an ease that shocked me, transforming his beauty from stern to *breathtaking.*

Knowing that I was the reason was enough to have my heart leaping from my chest. It was beating so loudly I was sure he'd hear it in this small, quiet bedroom with only the light from the hallway filtering in. I had him pinned to the bed now, my thighs straddling his hips, and his dark eyes roamed my face like he was memorizing every detail.

"Hmmm," I said, stroking a finger down the center of his chest. "Maybe there's one way I can be good."

I followed the path of my finger, sliding my face through his soft chest hair, rubbing my cheek against it. I licked lightly at his nipple and watched him seize up and curse, his hand flying to the back of my head.

"Yeah, right there," he groaned.

Captivated, I did it again. There was nothing more

addictive than this—bringing a man like Elijah Knight to his fucking knees. Feeling his muscles shiver with every kiss, every touch, every circle of my tongue. I dragged a palm down his stomach as my mouth moved lower. He was so big, so strong, but the hands cradling my head were gentle.

I eyed the bruise blossoming on his rib cage and brushed my lips across it. "Does it hurt, sweetheart?"

"A little."

Another kiss, this one over his heart. "Do you want me to stop? Take a break?"

"No, never...Luke, *please*."

So I took his cock between my lips, and his breath grew rough, ragged. One hand fisted in my hair, the other in the sheets. Like the other night, the taste of him, the smell of him, had me hard in an instant.

"That's it," he grunted. "You're so good at this."

I relaxed my throat and took him deeper, holding him there as a string of colorful curses fell from his mouth. I took my time on the way up and met his eyes, saw the wild arousal there, the affection, the desperation. A second later he yanked my head up and said, "Get on your stomach."

I sucked in a breath and did as I was told, crawling alongside him on the bed. He watched me with a predatory gleam, rubbing a hand across his mouth. I pillowed my cheek on my hands and said, "You promised to share your dirty thoughts about me."

He reached for my ass. Palmed it roughly, hefted each cheek. I purred and rocked against the bed. He gave me a slap and my hips shot up immediately, begging for more, and his answering chuckle was dark and dangerous.

"I have some thoughts about you," he ground out. Spanked me again. "A lot of thoughts. Too many. But I don't know what you like."

"Then ask me."

He dipped his fingers along my crease and circled my hole. "I want my mouth here. And then I'll fuck you through this goddamn bed."

"Yes, please," I said, dropping my face into the blanket. "I'll lose it, Elijah."

The mattress dipped as he moved down my body. Then I felt his teeth nipping at the back of my thigh. "Is that a promise?"

"Please," I begged again. And was treated to another slap. My breath hitched, every muscle tight in heady anticipation. His hot breath skated across my tender skin. His hands pushed my thighs open and spread my ass cheeks. I couldn't see his face, but I heard his rumbled groan. When his mouth landed on me, I cried out into the pillow.

His tongue circled and circled before wiggling inside me, setting off every single nerve ending. I couldn't even talk, could only cry and moan at the invasion. I tried to hump the bed but Elijah wouldn't let me. His arm kept my lower body still while his tongue and fingers stretched me, worked me open, hit every sensitive spot until I was close to sobbing.

"ElijahElijahElijah," I cried.

He snarled and spanked me. "You are so fucking sexy like this, Luke."

Then he wiggled his tongue again and the edges of my vision went dim. I kept saying *please*, kept saying *more*, though I was unaware of conscious thought. Only Elijah's hungry moans as he buried his face in my ass and made me see every one of the stars. When his head finally lifted, he left a finger teasing my entrance, keeping me ready.

His mouth roamed up my spine, reached the back of my neck. He cautiously lowered himself on top of me and his weight pressed me down into the mattress. It was decadent, it was delicious. He was so warm. He slid his cock between my ass cheeks while licking my ear.

All I could do was whine and cry. And his voice was so rough I knew he was barely hanging on.

"Can I fuck you now?" he asked softly.

"God, yes, please," I begged.

He nipped at my neck and then I felt him move off me. I turned my head and watched him rip open the condom wrapper and slide it on. Watched him oil his hand with lube and work it up and down his cock, all while staring at me like the meal he was about to devour. My hips rocked back until I was on my hands and knees—cock heavy, aching, my fingers curling around the metal headboard. Then he was behind me, the tops of his thighs lining up against the back of mine. Hips strong. Powerful. Cock nudging at the spot where I felt the emptiest.

My heart beat so fast I was legitimately worried it might stop working.

His hands curved around my ass, massaging. He nudged my knees a little wider. I felt a lubed-up finger dip inside me and stretch and stroke. My face dropped to the mattress as I cried out, pushing back against him. I was balanced on a razor-thin wire. Pure sensation, all euphoria, a growing wave cresting and cresting.

"Yes?" he said again.

I nodded furiously and bucked into his hand. "Yes, yes."

The tip of his cock breached me and I felt the first bite of pain. I breathed hard through my nose and shuddered under Elijah's palm, stroking soothingly up my spine.

"I wanted you from the first moment we met," he whispered into the darkness. He slid in another inch and I started to relax. Then another few inches, lighting me up like fireworks bursting in the sky.

"Oh my god," I moaned. "Me too, me too. I wanted you so much."

He rocked out gently. Rocked back in. My thoughts evaporated in the rush of pleasure. I chanced a glance over my shoulder and bit my lip. Sweat shone on Elijah's broad chest as he yanked my hips back onto his cock.

I growled out *"You're so big"* and was treated to a flash of arrogance in his eyes.

"You like my cock, Lucas?" he asked.

I dropped my head back into the covers and grunted. "Shut the fuck up—you know I do."

He smacked my ass and I laughed. Moaned. Tore at the sheets until I was sure I'd shred them. He was moving steadily now—bruised ribs be damned—and I was barely hanging on. Not when his cock stretched me so fully it felt like I was floating through space. Not when I could hear the slap of his legs thrusting into me. His husky breathing, every gruff curse and sigh. I let myself get taken away on it all, every indulgent sound and detail. Elijah reached around my hip and grabbed my cock in a tight grip.

"So perfect," he panted. "I'll never get enough of this, Luke." His hand worked my cock as he fucked me faster. "Never get enough of you. I can't stop now that I have you."

I bit my lip so hard I broke the skin. Pushed back on his cock until he grunted his approval. "Elijah, I'm gonna..."

"You're goddamn right you are," he swore. "Don't hold back."

I didn't. Couldn't. Wouldn't have been able to if someone had offered me a million dollars right here to stay quiet. Sensation tore through me relentlessly. I bucked and writhed and chanted his name, over and over, finally coming in his fist. My knees collapsed, but I found the strength to turn my head and catch sight of the image I wanted to burn into my memory.

Elijah, kneeling forward and driving against me, gripping my hips with white knuckles and a look of drunken ecstasy on his face. He tipped his head back on a long, anguished groan as he climaxed. Dragged a hand down his face then pinned me with a look that had me wanting to squirm. It was a look of pure devastation, like I was personally responsible for his unraveling.

I'm completely undone by you.

The fear crept in past my bone-deep satisfaction—and I knew why. This was no longer a flirtation with my cute bodyguard. Not some fun crush or distracting fantasy. My feelings for Elijah steamrolled me into the damn ground. There was no going back. It hadn't been an option for me since that first kiss at Senator Wallace's mansion.

I was falling for Elijah—and that gave him all the power to hurt me. To examine every flaw and mistake, then toss me aside. The words crowded at the back of my throat...but what was I gonna say? *That was the most intense sexual experience of my life, so thank you, but also please don't hurt me ever?*

Asking him to keep that promise was neither fair to him nor realistic.

Elijah stood up slowly from the bed...then pressed his forehead to the wall, catching his breath. When he left, I could see his legs trembling, and my worries threatened to wash me away. Memories of my father cleaved their way in —his impassive expression every time he let Preston but not me eat dinner, pointing at my report card to demonstrate my lack of value. Preston's imperious tone—*I so love hearing all the ways you've squandered your responsibilities.* My mother's smile, weaker and weaker at the end.

From the bathroom I heard running water, the soft gurgling of mouthwash. Then Elijah returned with a washcloth and a giant throw blanket. Brow furrowed, he used the warm cloth to clean my stomach before draping the blanket over my naked limbs. I had already started to shiver.

He climbed in under the blanket and turned on his side. He must have sensed my wariness, because he tugged me close until we lay chest to chest, with his leg hooked casually over my own. His arm looped around until his palm could press into the center of my back.

His nose nudged mine. His lips hovered, like he was just as uncertain as I was, in the cool, dark aftermath of such an incendiary experience. We inhaled. Exhaled.

I brushed my lips over his and thought about skydiving again. How the sensations of fear and love were so delicately intertwined. If Elijah was standing next to me with a parachute on and a lifetime's amount of fear, I'd tell him to embrace it and jump anyway.

The options were either jump or return to earth without ever experiencing the freedom of flight.

I kissed Elijah. Wrapped my arms around his back and pulled him close. His fingers brushed my hair away, curled around my ear. He smelled like peppermint and the crisp air outside, sweat and the ocean, smoky fire and starlight.

"I like you so much it scares me," I whispered against his mouth.

He reared back, a crease between his brows. "I thought it was just me."

That had me laughing softly in the darkness. "No, sweetheart. It's not just you. We're officially in trouble now."

One side of his mouth hitched up, flashing his adorable dimple. "I knew you were trouble from the start, actually."

"That's my whole vibe. You could have asked on Day One if I was gonna tempt you into a night of tawdry passion in a cabin we sorta-kinda broke into—"

He snorted. "You mean definitely broke into."

"Semantics." I kissed him again. "Anyway…I would have said *of course*."

He tangled his fingers in my hair. Stole a kiss he had no business giving after fucking me into the next universe. His body was warm and relaxed pressed to mine, and we were cozy under the blanket. Outside, the storm still raged, unabated, and I winced, picturing the car sinking deeper into the ocean.

That's tomorrow's problem, I reminded myself, and kissed Elijah harder. When we broke apart, he dragged his thumb along my lower lip until I bit it. Another shadow of a smile flickered across his face, sending my heart spinning.

"Tonight, it's…" he started, then paused. "It's been a little while, for me, since I've been with someone. I'm out of practice. Was it okay?"

It was the same worry he'd had the first night. The same light blush on his cheeks, the same vulnerability. It made me want to find whoever dumped this man and say *thank you* but also *you're a fucking fool.*

I cupped his face. "Two things. First, I'm not sure my body is prepared for whenever you're *in* practice. Because I no longer know my name or what year it is after two of the best orgasms of my life, and that is one hundred percent because of you."

He gave me a quick peck with eyes full of gratitude.

"And secondly, everything you do to me is more than okay. In practice, out of practice. We could have fumbled our way through the most awkward sexual experience ever, and I would have had fun with you. Because I like *you* just the way you are."

Elijah ducked his head. "Luke..."

"Has an ex ever told you differently? If so, I'd like to punch them in the face."

He pressed a palm over my heart. "Your threats of violence are quite romantic."

"Oh yeah?" I laughed. "You're the first person I've ever been with who's made me feel that strongly."

He rolled his lips together, studying me. "My exes are fine, really. They were nice, and well-intentioned, and their only crime was wanting a partner who paid attention to them. Something I didn't do well."

"Workaholic," I said, repeating him from earlier.

He nodded. "I work too much. I'm too serious. I never... never lighten up." His fingers flexed against my skin. "It hasn't been easy, letting others in. You're...a force of nature, Luke. I've never felt more out of control then when I'm with you."

I let my fingers trace a path along his cheekbones, the sharp line of his jaw. "Good way or bad way?"

"A new way," he whispered. "It's why I'm so nervous."

I let those words settle over me as I traced the white lines of his scarring. The day I'd had that gargoyle nightmare, he'd told me this scar was from a car accident. One he still dreamed about.

I stroked it gently and said, "Was your dad driving the car when you got this?"

He flinched. I pulled back, startled, but then he grabbed my hand and pressed it to the scar again. Nuzzled into it. "Sorry. I don't talk about it a lot."

"You don't have to tell me anything."

"I want to." Elijah kissed my fingers. "He had a new woman in his life. A coworker he was sleeping with, and they were late to pick me up that day from school. Christopher was at soccer practice, so it was only me. Mostly I was just so mad at him when they finally arrived, two hours late. I had to wait in the principal's office. It...it was embarrassing. So I was ignoring them for most of the ride home. Plus, it made me uncomfortable, the way he'd flirt when I was there, when I could hear what he was saying."

I hooked my leg through his, pulling him closer.

"She was younger than him and he was going all out," he continued. "I should have known he wasn't paying attention, should have said something. But I didn't. And I remember looking up and seeing him smile at her, trying to get her to laugh at one of his jokes. His eyes weren't even on the road, so he blew through a stop sign and a car T-boned us, hitting the back passenger side."

I sucked in a breath. "Where you were sitting?"

"Yeah." He reached for the scar, tangled our fingers together. "It was turning to see the car barreling toward me that still gives me nightmares. There was no stopping it. No hiding. It struck me going forty-five miles an hour. I remember the metallic sound it made when it collided with us, but that's about it. I woke up in the hospital with a concussion and broken ribs. Dislocated collarbone and a smashed elbow."

He flinched at the memory. "The window had shattered in my face on impact—that's where the scars come from. My mom and Christopher were there. I remember her face being white as a sheet. And that was the beginning of the end of their relationship. She didn't know the extent of it all. Her job was the one that paid all the bills, and she worked nights, slept during the day, was so exhausted she began to look like a zombie. Whatever my dad told her, she believed. Besides, we were so young and he was our dad and the violence he enacted, it wasn't clear-cut. It was thoughtlessness...carelessness...manipulation. A hair-trigger temper he made sure to hide when the right people were in the room."

I stroked my fingers through his hair. "That kind of deprivation is another kind of violence. Easy to conceal. Harder to understand, especially for two kids."

His gaze sharpened. "I carry so much guilt with me. I should have told her what he was doing behind her back. I was old enough to know better."

"He was old enough to know better," I said firmly. "You were a child."

Elijah studied me closely. "Making your kids sleep outside when they got bad grades is also violence."

"It is," I murmured.

"Does Preston remember it fully? What your father did to you both?"

I rolled over onto my back and blew out a breath. "Who the hell knows. We don't talk about it. Until recently, we rarely spoke. I think our brains protect us from this stuff, so if he doesn't fully remember, I don't blame him. We were young; it was confusing. Mom died, our world ended, then Dad shuffled us around like pieces on a chessboard. We only wanted love. His love."

I turned to look at Elijah. "When he bestowed his fucked-up love on Preston, I'm sure it felt good, you know? I'm sure it felt safe."

Elijah stroked circles through my chest hair. "What makes you feel safe now?"

My smile was easy. "You, Elijah Knight. My handsome shield."

He pulled me toward him until I was curled against his

body with my head pillowed on his chest. His heart was strong and steady against my ear, lulling me into relaxation as soundly as the rain outside. He brushed his lips along the crown of my head, so tenderly that tears threatened.

"Go to sleep, my liege," he whispered. "We're safe here."

And so I did.

29

LUKE

I woke with the stunning realization that Elijah was the little spoon.

We'd managed to switch positions in the middle of the night and I was now curved around his back with my face pressed to his neck. His limbs were relaxed, though he gripped my hand tightly, keeping me close as he slumbered. A surge of affection shot through me for this man who knew the singular pain of having a parent treat them like love was conditional. A thing to be bartered and sold—for secrets or loyalty or good grades.

It infuriated me, to realize the pain we had in common. To think of a tiny Elijah in a hospital bed with a face full of glass and a father who couldn't have cared less.

I gently kissed the back of his neck and breathed in the scent of his skin. Based on the murky light outside, it was just before dawn. Not having a phone only added to the dazed, twilight feeling in the cabin, as did waking up in a bed where we most definitely did not belong.

Through the thin curtains, I could see the effects of the storm—the ravaged trees, the broken branches. Waves were higher than usual, still frothy with rainwater. Elijah stirred and I kissed his neck again, the curve of his shoulder. Freckles dusted the skin there, as did more visible scars I hadn't noticed last night. I wondered if they were from his childhood car accident or from his job—both dangerous in their own right.

I dragged my nose through his hair and he stirred again, arching slightly against me. His breathing shifted, eyes fluttering open. And then a sleepy, almost feline smile appeared on his handsome face.

I was stunned—as usual.

Humming softly, I gave him an open mouth kiss on the side of his throat. A satisfied rumble came from the center of his chest.

"You're the little spoon," I said.

He gave a raspy grunt and pulled me flush against him. "As you wish, my liege."

I laughed into his hair. "Oh, he's got jokes in the morning now."

"I had to do this to stay warm. You hogged the blanket."

I pushed up onto my elbow in mock outrage. "I did no such thing."

Elijah half turned, blinking up at me. His hair was mussed and stubble shadowed his jaw. "I dreamed about you last night," he said, voice still rough from sleep. "We were back in the car again. It kept sinking. We couldn't get out."

I caressed my lips against his and said, "We made it out. We're safe."

He speared his fingers into my hair and closed the remaining distance. He parted his lips and moaned as I kissed him. We moved sweetly against one another, exploring, tasting. It was a sultry discovery, tongues meeting, teeth grazing. I was rock-hard, grinding against his thigh, and then he took my hand and dragged it down his stomach. He hardened as I gripped him, and I moaned at the contact.

"Like this?" I whispered, tugging him gently.

He nodded and captured my mouth again, kissing me eagerly. I stroked him slowly, an indulgent tease, as he grew more and more desperate beside me. All that harnessed control, all those tight expressions and flexing muscles, unraveled before my eyes.

He kept whispering my name, low and gruff, and I watched my hand squeeze up and down his thick cock. He was beautiful like this. Completely at my mercy, willing and open, needing me within seconds of waking. And I was fully prepared to stay like this—possibly forever—when his eyes flew open. He wrapped his fingers around mine and we jerked him together, which only had me thrusting more urgently against his thigh.

"Can I ask you something?" he panted.

"Anything." I kissed him. "You want the whole world? Done. I'll bring it to you on a silver platter."

He gave a half smile. "Will you fuck me?"

My hand faltered out of surprise. "I'll do anything you ask."

He swallowed. "I want it...I want you...but I'm"—a slightly sheepish look—"also a little out of practice."

I grinned and tugged his earlobe between my teeth. "We can go slow, sweetheart. So very, *very* slow."

He groaned. "Not too slow."

I swung my leg across his body and pinned his arms down. "I'll hardly move at all."

"Lucas."

I winked at him, then reached across the bed and found the lube. Coated my fingers and was grateful they weren't shaking. I stretched out alongside his body and used my leg to press open his knee, sliding my finger along the underside of his balls, his taint, and then the puckered muscle.

Elijah pulled me in for a kiss and I obliged, licking my tongue between his lips. I circled my finger lightly without penetrating, letting him get used to the feel of it. Within seconds, he was shuddering against my mouth. Gasping. He grabbed his cock and squeezed.

I pushed my finger inside. There was a brief clench of resistance and then he relaxed with a long sigh as I moved a little deeper.

"How does it feel?" I asked, forehead pressed to his.

"Good," he gasped out. "Intense. Amazing. I forgot"—a shaky laugh—"how much I love it."

"Yeah? I love it too." I gently—very gently—worked my finger in and out, addicted to the ecstasy already blossoming on his face. "How do you like it? More?"

He nodded, biting his lip. I obliged, working a second finger inside of him while his muscles stretched around me. Elijah exhaled shakily and started stroking his cock in earnest.

"Yeah, that's...that's it. *Fuck*, I love it."

His chest heaved with every jagged breath, and sweat dotted his temples. I kept my movements leisurely, not wanting to hurt him. But his hips were already writhing, and his harsh groans grew louder and louder in the quiet room. I was captivated, glued to my front row seat for Elijah's euphoria, the way it seemed to roll through his body until even his toes were curling in the sheets.

He yanked me down for a bruising kiss. His fingers fisted in my hair and when we parted, he growled, "I need you now."

I was so turned on by him I was practically vibrating.

Could barely keep my movements restrained when this sharp need clawed through me. I managed to sit back and gently remove my fingers, keeping an eye on Elijah's body language.

"You're sure?" I asked, rolling a condom down, then coating my cock with lube. "We can stop at any time, okay?"

He pinned me with a pleading look. "Never been more sure of anything in my life."

Everything between us was different now, and it had me as elated as it did nervous. But there was no denying how I felt, crawling up Elijah's body and dropping my hips down between his legs. Like I wanted to possess this man, mark him, make him want me as desperately as I wanted him.

He hitched his knees high until they brushed against my elbows, and I nudged my cock to his hole. He held my face and whispered, "Yes," so I surged forward as carefully as I could.

He hissed through his teeth at the first inch and I waited, suspended, while he exhaled through his nose. Another nod from Elijah, and I pushed in farther, grinding my molars at the intensity of his grip. An electrifying heat set fire to my nerve endings and I groaned his name into our kiss, already lacking in finesse.

Another inch, another, until I was fully seated and rocking in and out. A bead of sweat rolled down his throat and I lapped it up with my tongue. Elijah's nails dragged down my back until his hands came to my ass. He squeezed hard, urging me on. Gave me a single ringing slap that had me grunting and speeding up.

I let out a half laugh, half moan. "Topping from the bottom, I see."

His smile was wicked. "Tell me you don't love it."

He squeezed my ass roughly again, possessively, like he

owned me. And god help me, in this very moment, it felt like he did. And I would willingly hand over mind, body and soul to keep feeling this way.

"You feel so amazing, so beautiful, so perfect," I whispered at his ear. "Tell me how it feels for you, sweetheart."

He turned his head and kissed me while my hips drove between his legs. "So intense and more...more of everything. I can feel you...feel you everywhere, Luke."

"Touch yourself," I said. And he did, letting me watch as he fucked his fist while I rode him, which was when I officially lost my mind. We became one heaving, grinding mess of limbs, rocking on the bed. Elijah kept our mouths close, so I could hear every harsh growl, every curse, every time he begged. He kept squeezing me tightly, and the vulnerability on his face gave me that skydiving sensation again.

Weightless, free, falling and falling and falling.

"Come with me, please," he begged. "I'm so close."

I managed a nod, a few more rough thrusts. Elijah arched off the bed and groaned my name, and I climaxed so furiously that the room went black. I collapsed on his chest and buried my face in his neck. His arms came around to hold me, and I swore I could hear our hearts beating in time, a steady metronome that sounded something like *home-home-home-home.*

"That rearranged every atom in my body," I panted, still out of breath.

Elijah's soft laughter pulled a smile to my face. I nuzzled into his neck, inhaling this out-of-space-and-time moment. Trying to grab hold of something that already felt tenuous at the edges.

"You are phenomenal," he said. He turned me by the chin and stole a kiss. "That was everything I wanted."

A tiny sliver of sun peeked through the gauzy curtains.

Elijah was backlit and I was astonished by his beauty—the lines around his eyes, the cut of that jaw, how adorable his auburn hair looked, messy from sleep.

I knew what I wanted to ask him next and didn't anticipate how nervous I'd feel. Butterflies the size of Montana suddenly decided to take root in my belly, so much so I was worried my voice would shake.

"Are you gonna let me take you out for some whimsy when we finally get home?" I asked lightly. "I wasn't joking about laying down in a field of wildflowers with you so we can watch some clouds."

I saw the way Elijah's face opened, the way his eyes warmed, like he was reaching for something he'd always wanted.

And then he shut those eyes, like he was in severe physical pain. "When we get back home, we can't...be together like that. At least not out in the open."

I scoffed. "What, you actually care about that contract you had me sign? Those are words on a page, Elijah. I don't care about that. I care about *you*."

The pain on his face deepened. "I care about you too. But those words on a page are legally binding. They directly affect my job."

"Then I'll ask for a new bodyguard," I said. The smile on my face was starting to fade and a sickly heat was rising up my neck.

Elijah pushed to sit on the edge of the bed. I noted the tight line of his shoulders, hunching toward his ears. He stood and yanked on the pair of sweatpants I'd found for him. "Luke, it's more complicated than that. I can't have a relationship with anyone that I've worked for. Past or present. It's against every bylaw and code of conduct that we have. Clients know they can trust us with their lives because we're not distracted by our emotions."

He pinched the bridge of his nose. "It's especially impossible since I'm about to become the director of the whole agency. Foster will have my fucking head *and* my fucking job if this ever gets out."

My stomach pitched to the ground. "Oh. Okay. Then, uh..." I faltered. "What was everything that just happened?"

Elijah looked at me. *Really* looked at me. Even already naked, it stripped me bare. "This was...this was something I wanted, badly. I want *you*, badly. Want to be with you, I swear to god. But I don't know what to *do* about it—"

A pair of headlights swept through the room and we both jumped. It was the first sign of human life since the car that rammed us into the ocean, and it had Elijah moving panther-like through the house. I heard him check the locks again. I stood, quickly disposed of the condom, then yanked on my own pants, following him into the small main room.

He stalked over to the landline and said, "I need to call the office. *Jesus*, they probably think we're dead."

"Blame it on me," I said, aiming for carefree. "Whatever your boss thinks...tell him I made you do it, let me take the fall. I was the one who made us drive all the way out here in a tropical storm."

He gave me a nod and dialed, then drilled his gaze into the floor. I blew out a frustrated breath and rubbed a hand through my hair. I felt shitty about all of it—I didn't want Elijah losing his job because of something we *both* did. But there was also a mild panic rising in my body, a sensation that I was about to lose something precious and beautiful that I'd just been lucky enough to find.

"Sir, it's Knight," Elijah said in the clipped tones he'd used when we first met. He winced, then hid it, rattling off our location. "I'm aware. ... No, we're both okay. We ended up sheltering in a nearby house. ... I was injured, not thinking—"

He stopped talking. Set his focus on the ceiling while he listened to whatever his boss was saying on the other end. Finally he said, "I take full responsibility. It was shortsighted and dangerous. ... Yes, I know. ... Yes, sir, we'll be waiting."

Elijah ended the call with a stricken expression. He dragged both hands down his face and when his eyes met mine, they were filled with a grim determination. "Ripley and Sylvester are on their way, along with police to deal with the car. And we'll need to figure out how to contact the owners here. Apparently the team was out all night, searching for us. They saw the tire tracks, thought we'd been run off the road."

"We *were* run off the road," I said. "That's why we ended up here in the first place. You didn't do anything wrong."

"I have done every single possible thing wrong in this scenario," he said quietly. "Starting with lying to my team about why I was the only one escorting you on this trip."

"Why did you do that?" I asked, my heart leaping a little.

He crossed the room to stand in front of me, though we didn't touch. "I did it because I wanted to be with you, just the two of us. What happened at the senator's mansion..." He rubbed his forehead, turning slightly away from me. "What happened there shouldn't have, but I couldn't convince myself otherwise. Years of rigorous training, thousands of hours in the field, three weeks from a promotion and I stopped caring about all of it. For fuck's sake, our car ended up in the water, Luke. We could have drowned out there and it would have been my fault."

"That's bullshit," I snapped. "We're being stalked by someone who clearly isn't gonna stop until they get what they want. You can't possibly think you can control every outcome that perfectly. Violence is random, Elijah—how many times have you told me that? We can't blame ourselves for being victims. We can't blame ourselves for...for developing feelings for each other." I stepped closer to him. "This was real to me. All of it. I thought you felt the same."

Elijah dropped my gaze. Two spots of red appeared on his cheeks. "I'm not in the same position that you're in here. You're the client. You can hire and fire me."

"But I'd never do that," I said quickly.

"Really? You spent the first two weeks we knew each other threatening me with exactly that action."

I passed a hand over my eyes, felt bile rise in my throat. "I know, I know. I never should have done that and I'm still so sorry."

"No, you shouldn't have," he said, "and that's exactly why I wasn't supposed to fall for you."

I blinked, stunned by his admission. At the blazing heat in his tone, half passion and half frustration. Like he'd said last night, *I wasn't supposed to want you. I wasn't supposed to give in.*

"This could mean the end of my career," he added. "I don't have a billion-dollar company to fall back on or a trust fund coming my way. It's just me, and my family has relied on me ever since my piece-of-shit father walked out the door. If I don't have this in my life, I have nothing."

An awkward silence lingered after those words. And my voice sounded much too pitiful when I finally said, "You'd have me though, right? I'm not nothing."

His features drew tight. "Luke...that wasn't what I meant."

I stepped back. Dropped my hands into my hair. "This isn't a life, Elijah."

"Excuse me?" he asked, tone icy.

"It's *not*," I said. "It's a half life, at best. All you do is...is parcel out bits of happiness from time to time, only after you think you deserve it. You won't even let yourself smile. *Obviously* I don't want you to get fired. But please don't run from this. We could be together—we could figure something out—if only you'd let yourself live a little."

"Run?" He shook his head. "Luke, you've done nothing but run your entire goddamn life. You were handed an entire company, a company that could actually do some good for this place you claim to love so much, and yet you refuse to take even an iota of responsibility for it. That's running."

His words struck all the chords I'd been trying to ignore these past weeks. Harriet's gentle questions. Mía pushing back on my own hesitations—*you have power too, Luke.* Ethel, Clarita, my community at the Shipwreck, all of them reminding me of Cape Avalon's other history.

Deep down, I knew Elijah was right and the responsibility was real. But instead of admitting that out loud, I pushed past him and stalked toward the door.

"Luke," he called out. "You can't leave right now."

I yanked open the door. "I just...I need a second, okay?"

It slammed behind me as I stepped out onto the small patio, dropping my hands to the railing and lowering my head. Every word out of my mouth right now was wrong. Clunky and sharp and pitiful and selfish. When what I really wanted to say was *to hell with your job, at least we'd have each other.*

And how insulting and brutally naive was that? Elijah was right. I was the one with the trust fund, the generational job security, the total freedom to follow every wish and whim. I'd endangered his career twice—how could he trust me after this?

I'd bared my soul, my secrets, my vulnerabilities, and all that had done was guarantee he'd see the worst version of me.

The churning worries ricocheting through my thoughts were almost certainly why I didn't hear anyone approach. But then a board creaked. And a bag was jammed over my head before I could even scream Elijah's name.

30

ELIJAH

It was like trying to communicate from deep within the ocean.

I was aware of a question being asked by the young police officer. Was aware of Foster, peering at me from behind his desk like I was a total stranger and not the person he'd trained all these years. And I knew what the facts technically were—we were back in the Manhattan offices, and for the first time in my entire career, I wore joggers, a sweatshirt and a day's worth of scruff on my jaw. And my coworkers, milling about in the hallway, had all stared at me like I'd committed a grave personal offense against each of them when I walked in.

It wasn't true. There was only one person I'd let down. And I wasn't sure if I'd ever get the chance to apologize to him.

"Mr. Knight?" the officer asked. "Mr. Knight, do you need to take a break?"

I turned to him the way a scuba diver turns in the water. Slow, ungainly, bewildered.

"I'm sorry?"

The officer exchanged a glance with Foster. "Do you need some extra time?"

"He doesn't," Foster said sharply.

A pause, then, "What happened when you went outside to look for Mr. Beaumont?"

"Luke," I said quickly. "His name is Luke."

The glare that Foster sent me could have stripped paint from the walls. But I was still miles beneath the waves and unable to give a shit.

"What happened when you went outside to look for Luke?"

"I shouldn't have let him go out there," I replied. "That was my mistake."

"Do you know why he stepped outside?" the officer asked.

Guilt invaded my every thought and emotion. I couldn't share the real reason why. *He went outside because we'd argued after spending an incredibly passionate night together. Then I accused him of running away from his responsibilities and he accused me of living half a life, of parceling out bits of happiness only when I thought I deserved it.*

And I should have said, "You are so right. Whenever I'm around you, I can't seem to parcel it out. I only want to take big greedy handfuls of happiness for myself. Want to take risks and throw myself straight into the fire and stop looking over my shoulder, terrified to see a father who's never coming back."

Instead of saying *I want to take a big leap with you*, I implied that he was nothing to me.

"It'd been a hard night," I said. "We'd been run off the road. Had to swim to safety. I was injured and he was—" *Luke, on top of me. Luke, moving inside me, holding me while I slept.* "He was still pretty shaken up."

The officer cleared his throat again and scribbled some notes. "And how long do you believe he was out there by himself?"

I pinched my nose. "No more than five minutes."

That was all it had taken for me to regret everything I'd said. But that regret was nothing compared to the feelings that ripped through my body once I realized he'd been taken from me. The agony was like a living thing, driving me to a swift madness as I stalked the road surrounding the cabin. Stalked all the way back to Clarence Craven's house, which remained infuriatingly empty. I prowled the beach with a single-minded intensity, so furious that when Ripley and Sylvester finally pulled up, I almost yanked the rear door from its hinges hoping he'd be in the back seat.

"And you didn't hear anything? See anything?" the officer asked.

"No, uh... I was in the back of the house, the bedroom, trying to put everything back in order. I believe he was taken from the front patio. I didn't hear or see a thing."

The officer peeked at his notes. "And that's where you and Mister...Luke, uh, slept last night?"

Feverish images flickered in from last night. Luke, naked and face down on the bed, writhing as I worked him over with my tongue. The way he whispered *I like you so much it scares me* and my heart stopped. His fingers, tracing my scar. His hungry mouth on mine as he fucked me, the ecstasy so intense I forgot how to breathe.

You want the whole world? Done. I'll bring it to you on a silver platter.

"As I mentioned earlier, we were in shock," I said roughly. "We were injured. We'd both lost our phones and our belongings in the ocean. The tropical storm was bearing down on us. I'm not saying it was my best decision, but I did what I could with the resources I had."

I didn't have to look at Foster to know what his question was. *Who slept where*?

"Once I confirmed that Luke wasn't nearby or had just taken a walk somewhere, that's when I realized that he had most likely been kidnapped by whoever ran us off the road the night before. Probably the same person or persons who's been sending him death threats for the past two weeks. The very same who was sending threats to his father before he died."

I clenched one hand around the other, forming a fist to keep my fingers from shaking. I hadn't heard him call out for me when he was kidnapped. Hadn't heard a fucking thing.

So what did they do to him to make him stay quiet?

"All right, well, that's all I've got for now. We'll keep looking through all the other pieces of evidence you've given us," the officer said. "Unless there's anything else you'd like to tell me?"

This is all my fault.

"Nothing comes to mind," I replied.

As soon as the officer stepped back outside, Foster shut the door behind him and pulled the blinds closed. I felt his eyes, heavy on my profile, but I kept mine glued to the floor. This was our first moment together entirely alone since the disastrous call I'd made to him early this morning.

He perched on the edge of his desk. "They found the car. Should be easy to drag out, though I doubt anything can be recovered from it."

"Yes, sir."

"And I personally spoke to the couple whose house you

broke into last night. Explained the situation, and they expressed their sympathies, won't be pressing charges."

I nodded through the guilt carving a path inside my brain. Every single mistake, stacking up higher and higher. "What do we do now?"

"We don't do anything," he said simply. "We've had clients kidnapped and harmed before. In every other situation, we've cooperated with the investigation, provided evidence and then hoped for the best. We've not lost a client yet, Elijah. And we won't this time either."

I bit back a burst of rage. "With all due respect, that's foolish, sir. Luke could be anywhere, Luke could be in *danger*. Just because we haven't lost people yet doesn't mean we won't."

Foster arched a single eyebrow. "What did you say to me?"

I rubbed the middle of my forehead. "I'm...I'm sorry, sir."

He was quiet for an excruciating few seconds before saying, "Ripley and Sylvester informed me that I signed off on Luke's spontaneous trip to Rodanthe in the middle of a tropical storm warning. And that I approved him traveling with only a single escort mere hours after a physical attack was attempted on his person. All of that was a lie, correct?"

I finally raised my eyes to his. "Correct."

"Why did Lucas Beaumont feel the need to travel to the wetlands in the middle of a storm?"

My right knee started to shake. "He...Luke...he wanted to catch the person who was sending him threats and demanding back a flash drive, which Luke inferred was most likely being used to blackmail someone. His hope was that if he discovered who it was, he could stop the threats, clear the air. There's a person who lives out there, Clarence Craven. Lincoln Beaumont was a well-known enemy of his."

Foster's nostrils flared. "You didn't think to inform us of this? Nor did you think it best to convince our client of the dangers of that kind of vigilante investigation?"

"I did, I…he couldn't be deterred."

Foster's gaze darted back and forth, studying my face. "I asked you multiple times if you were having trouble with Lucas. And each time you told me no."

I didn't respond. My body's responses were swinging wildly between *cry* and *vomit.*

Foster leaned forward. I already knew what he was going to ask. Knew it from the moment he'd shut the blinds.

"What is the nature of your relationship with this client?" he asked.

I bounced my knee. Squeezed my hands together. "Personal."

His face went dark. "In what way?"

I pictured Luke's smile when I asked him what made him feel safe. *You, Elijah Knight. My handsome shield.* Felt torn anew when I tried to imagine how terrified he must be.

"Romantic, sir."

"Jesus *fucking* Christ," he snapped, spinning off the desk and crossing the room. "Please, for the love of god, tell me you're joking."

I shook my head.

"So you…you and Lucas Beaumont are…what, together?"

I nodded, even though it wasn't entirely true. But we were something to each other. Something that mattered, even if I'd been terrified to say the words out loud.

Foster's head tipped back and he stared at the ceiling. "Three weeks before my retirement and you're telling me you went and violated the single most important rule we adhere to? Elijah, you're in a romantic relationship with a high-profile client who was kidnapped after a series of massive mistakes that you personally made due to being emotionally compromised. Everything that's happened has been your fault. Do you understand that?"

"More than you know," I said softly.

"Good. I hope you do know. After this is through, you'll be lucky to find any job in this field, let alone assume the director position." He slammed his hand down onto his desk and I jumped. "Just...listen. Go home. Keep your head down. Do not come back into this office until I tell you to. When Lucas Beaumont is found, there is a slim possibility this will not get out. Which means there's a slim possibility I can keep you on a desk somewhere."

"Sir..." My throat felt too tight to swallow. "I can't go home and do nothing."

"You can and you will."

"Would you? If it was someone you cared for?"

Foster stared at me like every word out of my mouth was absolutely fucking madness. Who knows, maybe it was. But a switch had been flipped somewhere, deep in my chest, and I couldn't have shut it off if I tried.

"Go. Home. Now," he repeated, then pointed at his office door like I was a pet who'd misbehaved.

I walked back through the offices, avoiding every questioning look, and wandered the streets of Manhattan. Too stunned to do much of anything except panic and worry.

Which was how I ended up at the last place I would have expected.

31

ELIJAH

My brother opened the door and looked just as shocked to see me as I was to be there.

I blinked, rubbing my forehead as he stepped forward and grabbed both my elbows. "Eli? What are you doing here? What happened?"

I blinked again. "Christopher?"

He ducked to catch my eye. "Are you hurt?"

"No, no… It's…my client. Luke. Luke's hurt. Missing. He was kidnapped early this morning." I swallowed past the lump in my throat. "I, uh, I messed up."

My voice cracked at the end. Christopher didn't hesitate to hustle me inside the Brooklyn apartment, where I could smell dinner cooking, hear the TV playing cartoons. Then there was Sky, barreling down the hallway and hitting me knee-level with a hug. I'd just managed to scoop up my nephew before I was being pressed into the living room, then down onto the couch. Christopher spoke softly to Skylar, who gave me a sweet smile before running back into the kitchen.

"Where's Shana and the twins?" I asked.

"At book club with her sister," he said. "Sky and I were making macaroni and cheese with hot dogs. When was the last time you've eaten?"

Sky returned with a children's plate shaped like a tiger and loaded up with noodles and sliced pieces of hot dog slathered in Dijon mustard. Like I used to eat as a kid. My chest cracked in half—Christopher had remembered, was being so nice to me when I hadn't returned any of his calls. I hadn't eaten since yesterday and wanted this macaroni and cheese so badly I could weep.

"Thank you," I said gratefully. He passed me a fork and then he and Sky busied themselves in the kitchen for a bit, letting me inhale my food in peace. I fixed myself a second plate, followed by a third. Christopher joined me on the couch with two beers and I wanted to cry again.

"Tell me what happened," he said, settling in next to me. "I haven't seen you this upset since we were kids."

Because I'd stopped letting myself be anything other than in control the day Dad left.

This isn't a life, Elijah. It's half a life.

I scrubbed a hand down my face. "I have this client. Lucas Beaumont. I was his dad's bodyguard for five years, but his dad just died. His dad was getting death threats. Garden variety stuff. But they increased in intensity when Luke took over. I didn't take them seriously enough at the beginning, didn't...didn't take him seriously. Except we..."

You know how handsome you are when you smile at me like that, Elijah?

"You what?" Christopher prodded.

I inhaled, met his gaze. "I'm falling in love with him."

His eyes went wide.

"Which is against every rule in the book, for obvious

reasons. And we got stuck last night, in the storm, near Sag Harbor in the Hamptons. Just me and him. And we..."

I shrugged a shoulder and Christopher reared back. "That's probably against the rules too, yeah?"

I nodded. "He was taken this morning. From that location. I wasn't with him, didn't hear anything. And they don't know where he is or who has him."

"Holy shit, Eli," he whispered.

I sniffed. Squeezed the beer bottle too hard.

He rubbed a hand across my back, his face pinched in sympathy. "This is awful."

I nodded again. "I'm gonna lose that promotion I told you about. My boss knows. He knows everything. Believes my behavior to be abhorrent, which it was. At every single step of the way, I knew the right thing to do and I couldn't stop myself." I sniffed again. "He's hurt because of me, and I keep thinking...what if I'm like Dad?"

My brother pulled a face. "Don't say that."

"Isn't this what he did?" I said bitterly. "Act selfishly out of, what...his lust? His ego? His need to be wanted? He used to tell me that he couldn't stop. That he would, that he'd treat Mom right if he could, but it wasn't in his DNA."

Christopher sagged, falling back against the cushions. "First of all, I wasn't saying what you *did* was awful. I was saying this *situation* is awful. The guy you love just got kidnapped and you don't know who took him. That is categorically fucked up, and I don't care how many rules you broke. Who cares? This is devastating news."

Hot tears threatened. I swiped at my eyes, fast, before my brother could notice.

"Secondly." He paused to stand up, starting to pace. "Please don't *ever* say you're like Dad again. I'm serious, it's gross."

I opened my mouth to argue, but he held up a palm.

"Eli, cut yourself a little slack. You fell in love with someone you weren't supposed to at what sounds like the worst possible time. It happens. Pretty often, in fact. You're a human being and you met someone you're falling for. In my experience, this stuff doesn't really happen on some agreed-upon timeline."

I jabbed my thumb into the center of my chest. "But I'm the one that fucked up. Big time."

"People do. No one's perfect. Not even you, and I know how much you try."

His words sat uncomfortably in the pit of my stomach. There was a reason why I'd been drawn to this career, beyond the job stability. There were rules to follow, hierarchies in place, strict codes of conduct and very little gray area. We had a singular goal—keep the client safe. Anything else was extraneous.

There were very few ways in which you could make a mistake—and yet I'd somehow smashed through all of them. I'd lied to my supervisors. Knowingly placed my client in excessively dangerous situations. Shoved my client up against a wall mere minutes after an attempted attack and kissed him senseless.

Christopher sat down next to me again. "Do you know what I remember most about you when we were growing up? You were always my protector. You took care of me and Mom, even when it seemed hard. You were my own personal superhero."

He reached forward and squeezed my knee.

"But look around. We're doing fine. Better than fine. Mom has her RV and all those dogs she rescued. She called me from the Grand Canyon this week, actually. She's still having a blast."

Another uncomfortable twist in my gut. She'd called me too, left cheerful voicemails about watching the sunrise from her campsite.

"Shana and I are doing great. The twins are healthy. Sky's happy. Is money tight? Sure. Does Mom's health worry me sometimes? Absolutely. But that kind of stuff is just normal, Eli. That's life." He caught my gaze and held it. "You don't have to save us. After Dad left, we saved ourselves. You included."

The great knot that had resided permanently in my chest for as long as I could remember started to loosen ever so slightly.

I released a long breath. "I don't want you to struggle the way we did growing up."

"We aren't struggling," he said easily. "My kids eat every day and they never have to worry. Shana and I don't have to work the night shift. We're home at night, to spend time with them. Most importantly, Dad isn't here, making everything worse. Isn't it nice to realize we don't have to tiptoe around him anymore? Don't have to listen to his bullshit or keep his secrets?"

The knot tugged open a little more.

"Sometimes I..." I cleared my throat. "Sometimes I forget. I act like he's still hovering nearby, watching. Criticizing."

"He's not," Christopher said softly. "But whenever you feel that way, you could come over here and talk to me about it."

I stared at the floor.

"Dad abandoned us, but honestly good riddance. We're better off without him. I don't want you to do that too."

My gaze snapped back to his. "I'd never do that."

"Except"—he reached forward and poked me in the arm

—"you never come around, never return our calls, never text us back. I know your job is intense and demanding, but I think you're afraid to let go. You can be a responsible person, you can protect your family, and still have fun. Still be happy. We love you, Eli. Not out of some sense of obligation but because it's *you*. And I wanna have more fun with you."

My eyebrows flew up as the tight spot over my heart kept shifting and loosening. "You do?"

He laughed. "Hell yeah, I do."

I sent him a tentative smile, a gesture that had felt impossible from the moment I realized Luke was gone. "Luke told me I needed more whimsy in my life."

He clinked his beer against mine. "Luke's right."

Skylar came running back into the room and clambered onto my lap, displaying a coloring book about giraffes and a small pack of crayons. I dropped my nose onto the crown of his head and felt those tears again, threatening to spill over. A wave of emotion washed over me—grief, love, so much regret. Christopher was right, as painful as it was to admit it. It was easier to hold my family at arm's length and exhaust myself with work as an excuse. Loving people was messy by nature. Emotions were messy by nature, and at some point after my dad left, I'd locked them all away to focus on being a caregiver for my brother.

I took the blue crayon Sky offered to me and started coloring in a cloud. "The promotion is off the table. My boss thinks there's only a slim chance I can stay in this industry, but only if I stay away from Luke's kidnapping case and keep my head down."

Christopher finished the rest of his beer. "What does your gut say?"

My hand paused. I glanced up at my brother. "That

every second counts. That Luke's out there somewhere. Scared or hurt or cold...and hoping I'll find him. But if I do that, it's over. The career I've trained my whole life for."

He shrugged one shoulder. "Good thing you're thirty-seven and not a hundred then. Plenty of time for a restart."

I remembered what Luke looked like that first day we were together, playfully tossing me a wink before falling backward off that bridge and into nothing but thin air.

What would it be like to go after the things I wanted like that?

Sky's fingers slipped, sending a large orange streak across an illustration of baby giraffes. "Uh-oh, didn't mean to do that," he said softly. He turned the page and started fresh. "When we mess up, we just try again. That's what Dad says."

I trained my attention on Christopher. "Your dad's very wise."

He raised his glass my way. "Guess who I learned it from first though."

My heart squeezed in my chest. A moment later, the front door opened and I heard the cheerful sounds of Shana and her sister, then the happy squeals of my two-year-old nephews.

"Eli's surprised us with a visit," Christopher called into the kitchen. All four of them popped into the room, happily surprised and immediately telling me a story about their book club. Then relating another story that had me laughing, and then somehow I'd had a second beer and the twins had fallen asleep on the floor and Sky still quietly colored on my lap.

Christopher sent me a warm smile through the chaos. "Welcome home, Elijah. We missed you."

32

ELIJAH

I was up early the next morning, having barely slept. Each time I drifted off, I was tortured by nightmares, of Luke being dragged off, alone in some dark room in handcuffs. So when a message from Ripley came through on my back-up phone around six a.m., I bolted upright in bed and listened with my heart jammed in my throat.

"The police don't have a lot of leads so far," he said, "except for some tire tracks and a couple witnesses at a nearby gas station. No ransom note, but if they were going to send one it'd be within the first forty-eight hours."

A ransom note would be something at least. Some indicator that he was alive and hadn't vanished in the five minutes he was out of my sight.

After a quick shower and a few sips of coffee, I pulled on a sweatshirt and a pair of basketball shorts. I got on the road, out of the city and heading back to the Hamptons. I wasn't unaware that I was dressed in the exact outfit Luke had teased me about by the gazebo at the garden party.

But thoughts of Luke only evoked a rising anxiety, so I

calmed myself by following the threads of every single piece of information he'd gathered in the last two weeks.

There was Clarence Craven, the environmental activist, who'd hated Lincoln and TBG for three decades. And the angry protesters at Sunrise Village. Plus, per Ethel and Clarita, there were Lincoln's abundance of secrets, the ones he used to blackmail influential people to make his job easier and more prosperous.

Vincent Maura, the stalker, had been responsible for at least two of the threats since Lincoln had died, but he was still in police custody and couldn't have kidnapped Luke yesterday.

Of course, there was Senator Wallace, who'd clearly been helping Lincoln to grease the bureaucratic wheels for who knew how long. Luke's working theory was that she and Lincoln worked *together* as a team to blackmail people throughout Cape Avalon.

But who of these people would have cause to actually *kidnap* Luke? And why? If this was still all related to some missing flash drive, then what the hell was on that thing?

When I finally reached my destination, I triple-checked that I had the right address. The parking lot was nearly empty, though a moving truck was being unloaded. A new sign on the side of the building read Preston Beaumont Real Estate and the website described the business as focusing on luxury properties throughout New York and Connecticut.

I was here to finally speak with Lincoln's hard-to-pin-down assistant, Adrian.

But there was one person I wanted to see first.

I found Preston in the largest office, palms on the desk, wearing a slightly rumpled suit with stubble dotting his jaw.

When he noticed my approach, all the blood drained from his face.

"Did...did something else happen to Luke?" he asked.

I stopped midway into the room. "No. Unless you've heard something I haven't."

He straightened and rubbed his temples with his thumbs. "The authorities were here till late last night." He rounded the desk. "I knew he was being threatened, I just never..." He gave a shrug. "We come from a high-profile family. Security risks come with the territory, but I never thought he'd actually get *kidnapped*, for Christ's sake."

I was quiet, studying him, as a cold fury rose up my spine. I understood Luke wanting to mend the burned bridge between them, now that their father was dead. But I'd also watched Preston belittle Luke in front of me like he was a meddlesome child.

"Do you have siblings, Elijah?" he asked.

"One. A little brother."

His eyes darted across my face. "Luke...Luke was my hero, when I was younger. Before I stopped being allowed to think things like that. When I suddenly *mattered* to our father. It was like I'd spent my entire life in darkness and then finally saw the sun. I didn't know what it would do to me—I'd never *seen* the sun. All I had to do was turn on my brother, my hero, and Dad would make life easier for me. Pure sunlight, every hour of the day. But that was his thing, you know? Lincoln Beaumont made everything easy for people until he no longer had use for them. And all I could think about when the cops called, when they told me that Luke..."

He blinked rapidly, clearing his throat. "All I could think about was that my whole life has been a lie up until this point."

I stayed completely still, unsure of what Preston might admit to next, letting him fill in the silence. Wanting to rip open a theory I'd had about exactly how far a brother might go to regain the company he'd been raised to lead.

"Luke never let things get to him," Preston continued. "He was always so calm, so relaxed. Dad could say all kinds of shit to him, and Luke would go out with his surfboard, catch a few waves, then return like nothing had happened." He scratched the top of his head. "I knew what Dad was doing. Not letting him eat. Making him sleep outside. I tried to help him. To sneak him food, to pull him back inside. But Dad's fucking bodyguards always stopped me."

My jaw clenched. "I didn't know that."

"It's why Luke hated them when we were kids. They were only eager to follow orders. But I could have tried harder, *should* have tried harder." Preston moved to brush past me, but I stopped him with a hard palm to the chest. He stared down at my hand, startled. "Excuse me?"

"Your brother is missing," I said harshly. "He could be hurt. He could be"—a silent scream kicked up in my brain—"worse than that. Tell me now if you did something to him. It's not too late to stop whatever it is."

Preston's nostrils flared. "Why would I do something to him?"

"He inherited a billion-dollar company and you didn't," I said with a scowl. "People have done worse things for much, much less."

He shoved off my hand with a growl of frustration. "No, I didn't do anything. I wouldn't. I *could never.* And also *fuck you* for thinking it."

He stormed out of the office, leaving me still shaking with restraint. It was exhausting, projecting an air of nonchalance when I wanted to tear this town to shreds until

I found Luke. Which was when Adrian found me. He was young, probably in his midtwenties, white with boxy glasses and tattoos peeking out from the sleeves of his button-down.

"So *you're* the one who sent my boss huffing out to his car in a terrible mood," he said, crossing his arms over his chest. "I know you, don't I?"

I nodded. "Elijah Knight. I was Lincoln's protection agent."

"I knew it." He tipped his head to the side. "Are you here about his son?"

I moved to shut the door. "I'm here about your former boss. Whoever kidnapped Luke was pissed at his dad. You were his assistant. I know you saw the messages, heard the voicemails."

Adrian raised a shoulder. "Nature of the job. They get a lot of death threats. Weird shit too. A woman once mailed a former boss of mine a paper bag full of her own hair."

"Did you have any suspicions about who was doing it?"

"Not a damn clue," he said with a frown. "I'm an executive assistant. I'm paid for speed and discretion. Whatever I see or hear goes in one ear, out the other."

I bit back a sigh and switched tactics. "You quit a few days before Lincoln died and have been avoiding Luke's calls and emails ever since. It's an interesting coincidence, don't you think?"

"*Wow*. I didn't anticipate this line of questioning. Are you insinuating that I'm at fault?"

When I didn't respond, he sighed and said, "It was *just* a coincidence. I quit that Thursday, left with my things. He died that Sunday, I think. I had nothing to do with it. And I just started a new, extremely stressful job. I'm avoiding everyone's calls right now."

He cocked his head to the side again. "Who is Luke Beaumont to you?"

"What do you mean?"

"You're not in your uniform and you look about a hundred different kinds of fucked-up. He's more than your client, right?"

I gnawed on the inside of my cheek. Dropped my gaze.

"If it helps, I'd burn this town to the ground to find my partner if they'd been kidnapped. So I get it."

"Is it that obvious?"

He gave me a warm smile. "It is when it matters."

We could be together—we could figure something out—if only you'd let yourself live a little.

Emotion clawed at the back of my throat. But I shook it off before I broke down in front of a complete fucking stranger.

"It does matter. He matters," I finally said. "Is there anything else you can give me? The first letter Luke received mentioned a flash drive they were coming for, a flash drive Luke—or probably Lincoln—*owed* to them."

His tipped his head to the side. "Kenneth and Gregory finally convinced Lincoln to digitize everything, right before I started. One of my jobs was offloading every stray flash drive lying around that place. And I checked *everything* in those files. It was all above board and perfectly legal. Last I knew, there wasn't a flash drive left. I tossed them all."

I cursed, raking a hand through my hair.

"But you know..." He lowered his voice. "Lincoln hid stuff like a little pack rat in there."

I reared back. "He...what?"

"There's a loose board under his desk where he would hide all the trinkets he bought for his mistresses. In liability terms, the man was a walking disaster. But like every other narcissist I've worked for, his arrogance was his downfall. Lincoln never thought he'd get caught. If you're looking for some secret flash drive or whatever, I'd tear that office apart."

The small clue energized me so much, I was halfway out the door before I said, "Thank you. Your help is appreciated."

"Don't mention it," he said, sending me a playful wink that made me think of Luke. "Now go get your man back."

33

ELIJAH

I drove to the Beaumont estate as soon as I left Adrian, stopping first to pick up a few supplies and tools. There'd been no updates on Luke from Ripley, and the only other message I had was an extremely terse voicemail from Foster, reminding me to stay home and keep my head down.

I deleted it.

Outside the estate, I triple-checked the calendar we used to keep track of everyone's whereabouts. Confirmed that Celine, Luke's stepmother, was off on a trip somewhere and her security team was with her. The rest of the team had been rotated off the estate for the time being. I was able to slip in through the back, thanks to one of the estate staff, who brightened when she saw me and let me in immediately.

All of it was a stroke of luck I couldn't take for granted. I was about to turn Lincoln Beaumont's office inside out, an act that wouldn't go unnoticed for long.

Once inside, I pushed back my body's immediate reaction to Luke's lingering scent in the air. The sweatshirt he'd tossed over an armchair. An extra pair of sandals. Nora's book, *Mayhem at Montauk Point,* open face down on the page he'd left off.

Even the couch still bore the imprint of his body.

I shut the curtains and flipped on all the lights. Stripped away the emotion brimming over in this room and tried to examine it from a fresh perspective. It was true I often stood outside in the hallway when Lincoln worked in here, but I still spent more time here than almost anywhere else in the world. Except Luke had already spent countless hours doing exactly what I was about to do—evidenced by the overturned chairs, the piles of paper on the floor, the flipped-over shelves.

Which meant I had to go even deeper.

I tried to picture Luke's dad here—where did he stand? What parts of the room did he favor? My eyes roamed over to the empty spots on the wall where the hunting paintings had hung, the ones Luke had dispatched to a closet. I hauled them back out, then removed every painting in the room. Checked the backs of the canvases. Tapped on the walls in the spots where they hung, listening for hollow sounds. Found the loose floorboard under the desk and discovered Lincoln's collection of illicit gifts for various mistresses.

I searched the fireplace. Tested the bricks in the mantel. Pulled out books on the bookcase and opened them. After three hours, the office looked like a tornado had ripped through it, which didn't help my mounting panic. So when the office door creaked open, I was so focused that I dropped the ashtray I'd been holding. It broke cleanly in half.

Nora Jackson stepped through—palms out. "Elijah? Luke's bodyguard, right? I'm so sorry. I didn't mean to startle you."

She walked over to pick up the broken ashtray, but I waved her away. “It’s fine. It’s not important.”

She gave a sheepish smile, then raised the stack of books in her hand. “If it helps, I come bearing gifts. Is Luke around? I found some first editions of *Death on the Dunes* and a few other of my novels, thought he might appreciate them.”

My stomach hollowed with grief. “He’s...Luke’s not here. He was kidnapped yesterday morning. No leads or ransom note so far.”

“Oh my god,” she said, her hand rising to her throat. “Elijah, that’s *horrifying*. Someone *took* him?”

I nodded, my chest aching with emotion. Nora set the books down on the desk and leaned against it, a dazed expression on her face. “I’m so sorry to hear this. You must be worried sick.”

I waited a beat, then said, “Did you know Clarence Craven had been feuding with Lincoln Beaumont for three decades? He didn’t mention it when he met Luke at the protest.”

She blinked. “Clarence? He was no fan of Lincoln’s, that’s for sure. I had no idea he personally knew him.” When she noticed the look on my face, she said, “You can’t possibly think *Clarence* is responsible?”

“Can’t rule it out.”

She pursed her lips. “If it helps, Clarence has been gone the past few days, down in Philly visiting some activist friends of his. He left on Sunday, got out of here right before the storm hit.”

I sagged back against the wall. The timeline did fit—his house had been empty the day before Luke was kidnapped *and* the day after.

“And besides, Clarence’s focus from an activist standpoint these days has been on the *systems* of inequality in this country, not on the individual. Kidnapping Lincoln's son doesn't help the cause from that standpoint," Nora continued. "It's why he wanted to help with the Sunrise Village protests. Prioritizing luxury housing over affordable housing is a choice we make, whether that's from our elected leaders or from men like Lincoln, whose wealth and influence means they can change the landscape of a community whether we like it or not. Deciding which of our neighborhoods have well-lit streets is a choice. Deciding who goes hungry and who doesn't is a choice. Who has rights and who doesn't, who feels safe and who feels fear, who thrives and who struggles."

I sighed again, rubbing my hand across the back of my neck. "Like you told Luke that day. He has a choice too, a responsibility." I nodded at the stack of books she'd brought. "That was nice of you to do, given that Luke is technically your enemy right now."

"Luke's been sending us pizza every day and blocking TBG's construction. He's not our enemy, not really, especially once he gets out of his own way and sees the good he can do."

Nora placed her hand on top of Luke's copy of *Mayhem at Montauk Point* with a fond expression, like bumping into an old friend she hadn't seen in a while.

"That's the one where the villain was loosely based off of Lincoln?" I asked.

Her smile was playful. "Indeed. Though the character itself wasn't a greedy property developer but something much worse. A corrupt politician."

Sparks danced through my thoughts, like small threads connecting. "What's your opinion on Senator Rosamund Wallace?"

Her entire body rippled with anger. “Violence is a choice too. Some of it obvious, bloody. Some of it much more subtle. It dresses up in fancy clothes and pretends to be on your side, pretends to care about your concerns when it’s really only out for itself. Senator Wallace never cared about this town, never cared about the South Shore. We were a means to an end for her.”

“You’re talking about when she first ran for mayor?”

She drummed her nails on the spine of her book. “Funny thing about Rosamund. She won in a tight race, narrowly defeating a popular grassroots candidate, when a slew of public endorsements for her came through, from elected officials on both sides of the aisle. A whole bunch of positive media from the local papers sprang up too, articles that positioned Rosamund as someone who’d fight for our schools, our workers, every inch of this precious, beautiful land. It worked. She won in the end, but I’m not the only Cape Avalon resident who found her last-minute popularity suspect.”

Clarita’s words about Lincoln came back to me from that day on the beach. *Your father owned every secret in the Hamptons, and he wasn’t that private about it. He traded in information. Valuable information. The kind worth more than money.*

I stiffened as a new theory blazed through my brain. Luke had wondered if Lincoln and the senator had worked together to blackmail influential people.

Now I was wondering if the senator was *being* blackmailed…by Lincoln.

Nora must have noticed the expression on my face, because she chuckled softly, then pressed *Mayhem at Montauk Point* into my hand. “If you need anything, call on us down at Sunrise Village. Regardless of who his father is, there are a lot of people who love Luke. More than he probably realizes."

My throat tightened. "What if I can't save him?"

"You'll bring him home, Elijah," she said, patting my hand. "Take it from a mystery author. The only good thing about villains is they can't stay hidden forever."

After she left, I stood in the middle of the torn-up office and tried to figure out what I'd missed. That's when I caught the flash of something sparkling in the middle of the rug. When I bent to pick it up, it nicked my skin.

It was a tiny shard of glass, the same color as the glass from the chandelier that had lurched from the ceiling, narrowly missing Luke, and shattered across the floor. The contractor had carted everything away after, claiming it was just an unlucky accident. *An undetected leak*, he'd said, causing the wood to weaken.

The panel where the chandelier hung was still there. I grabbed a screwdriver and dragged over a chair, feeling my heart race with every twist of the tool. The panel popped open and then I was staring into a bunch of disconnected wires. Tentatively, I turned on my phone flashlight and slipped my hand inside, splaying my fingers forward.

They closed around something small and rectangular.

When I brought it out into the light, it was a flash drive.

34

LUKE

When I finally woke—groggy, with a splitting headache—my first thought was *I'm going to die.*

I'm going to die and I'll never have the chance to tell Elijah how sorry I am for being such an *asshole*. Never get to tell him how I really feel—that I'm falling in love with him, that I've never felt this way before in my life. That his concerns were valid and I was wrong to push them away.

My second thought was *Why the hell am I handcuffed in some random bathroom?* Specifically, my hands were looped and chained around a sink pipe. I was sitting upright, propped against a wall, and the only window was narrow, high up near the ceiling and shut tight.

I didn't remember much after the bag was placed over my head. Whoever had taken me had knocked me out somehow, possibly with a choke hold, because my neck felt tender and bruised and I had the vaguest recollection of a forearm against my throat. Turning, I pressed my ear to the wall and tried to listen. I thought I could hear the faintest sounds of the ocean, but that was probably wishful thinking. The light coming in through the window was golden and dreamlike, the way the sky got in Cape Avalon when the sun set.

It felt foolish to hope that we were still somewhere in the Hamptons, to hope that I'd awoken just this morning curled around Elijah's sleeping form. But it was there, a tiny spark of a thing.

Maybe, if not too much time had passed, if I hadn't been taken far from my home, someone would find me.

Maybe, even, Elijah would find me.

Though who I was kidding? I was falling for a man who should run in the *opposite fucking direction* if he ever saw me again. I'd forced him to risk his job for me, drawn him into my shady revenge plan, dismissed him for calling me out on something I'd been avoiding for years.

You've done nothing but run your entire goddamn life.

He wasn't the one living half a life. I was.

Suddenly, I heard the crunch of wheels on gravel from outside the tiny window. Car doors, slamming shut. If the window faced the parking lot of wherever we were, the people might hear me if I...

"Hey!" I screamed. *"Hey, help me! Help! Someone locked me in this bathroom! Hel—"*

The door to the bathroom flew open, and a person wearing a black ski mask crouched down and backhanded me across the face before I even realized what was happening.

"Shut the *fuck up*," he hissed.

My ears rang like a church bell and when I spat on the floor, there was blood. My thoughts moved cartoonishly slow, either from the shock or the pain. The man in front of me pushed to his feet, and something about his abnormally tall height, the shape of him, made me wonder if he'd been one of the people who chased me and Elijah into the South Shore Bookshop.

Through the wedge of open door, I caught what looked like threadbare carpet and two double beds. A budget motel, maybe? I rattled my cuffs against the pipe and said, "So is this the kidnapper suite at the Holiday Inn? You guys couldn't have sprung for the honeymoon penthouse?"

I was expecting the blow this time. It didn't lessen the agony that shrieked through my temples though. I spat more blood onto the tile as the man left, slamming the door.

With a ragged sigh, I let my head fall back against the wall and released a pitiful groan of a laugh. The pain of being smacked upside the head was preferable to thinking about my final moments with Elijah, the last words we'd said to each other, how I'd never hold him in his sleep again. Never be on the receiving end of his brilliant smiles, never say *I love you so much*, never kiss him awake or make him laugh.

I wasn't going to see Rory graduate from kindergarten. Wouldn't make chocolate chip pancakes with Lizzie on Saturday mornings or watch bad horror movies with Harriet.

Harriet. *Harriet.*

A ferocious regret tore through me, unrelenting in its furious clarity. I would probably lose my life in this dingy bathroom and for *what*? To dig up secrets on a man who was already dead? To let him control me *yet again,* to let him become the dominating source of my pain years after I left that house?

My sister had seen the inadequacy of my shoddy plan from the beginning, and I suddenly ached to be back on that couch with her again, with the soft flickering of the TV, the sweetness of Rory asleep on my chest, her impossibly small fingers curled above my heart.

Acknowledging pain is just the beginning, because nothing can change how he treated us. Nothing can change the past, and that's the shittiest part of all. All we can do is accept what we can, love who we can, and fight for a better future.

Elijah was right. Mía was right. Harriet was right. All I'd done so far was fight a ghost. All I'd done was prepare to battle a past that had nearly destroyed me the first time.

I thought letting my father's reputation remain untarnished was letting him win.

The opposite was true. He was winning *right now*.

And I was letting him.

An hour passed, maybe two. The light from the window shifted from golden to indigo to inky black. The man who'd struck me pushed open the door at one point and unceremoniously dropped a sandwich in my lap and a bottle of water at my feet. Even with a jaw that still throbbed, I wrangled my awkwardly cuffed hands onto the sandwich, tearing open the packaging and wolfing it down. The last time I'd eaten had been breakfast the day before.

After that, I dozed fitfully, waking every so often drenched in cold sweat. And during those bleary, in-between moments, I let myself bask in the memory of Elijah, sitting shirtless and wounded by the fireplace. His open mouth on my palm, his ardent longing. His gravelly voice saying *Do you know how beautiful you are?*

I wasn't supposed to want you. I wasn't supposed to give in.

I'm undone by you.

Later, though it could have been an hour or only five minutes, I perked up at the sound of new voices outside, a hushed conversation that ended with two sets of feet leaving the motel and one set coming toward the bathroom door.

Terror gripped every cell in my body. The doorknob turned slowly. I wanted Elijah. I wanted Harriet.

I wanted my mom.

Whoever walked through switched on the harsh overhead light, and in the glare, it took me a moment to realize who was standing in front of me. Slightly rumpled suit, an expression that was somehow bored and stressed at the same time, a clawlike hand gripping his cell phone.

Grady Holt, Senator Wallace's chief of staff.

The man had his head down, fingers flying as he typed out some message or email or memo. "Nice to see you again, Lucas, though under less-than-desirable circumstances."

I blinked, stunned. *"Grady?"*

That same icy terror tore through me again. I'd read too many of Nora Jackson's mysteries. Villains didn't fear showing their faces if their victims weren't meant to survive.

Grady finally looked up. "Where's the flash drive? Your father told us that in the event of his death, you'd have it. So where is it?"

"Oh my *god*, enough about the fucking flash drive," I snapped. "News flash, Grady. My dad's always been a huge liar. I don't know what you're talking about and I certainly don't know where it is. Don't you think I would have given it back to you by now?"

He was silent. Calm. "Where is it?"

"I don't know."

"Where is it, Lucas?"

I clenched my jaw. "Ever since you sent that letter, I've torn the office apart looking for it. You're delusional if you think my father would have trusted me with something that's clearly this important. You've got the wrong son."

"Lincoln Beaumont was an exceptionally smart man," Grady said. "An innovator, a genius. Which is how I know you're lying. He left you the company for a reason. He left you the flash drive for a reason. You played it way too cool at the fundraiser to be sitting there not knowing what I'm talking about."

"Played it *too cool*?" I yelled. "I don't know what the hell is going on here. I don't even know what's *on it*."

"Don't be an asshole. You know what he did to her, what he's *doing* to her."

A million loose threads began tying themselves to each other in my frazzled brain. Rosamund and my father hadn't been blackmailing people together...

"He was blackmailing her, wasn't he?"

Grady sniffed. "We're not the first political campaign to do what has to be done to ensure victory."

"Even if it's illegal?" I said, hazarding a guess.

"It might be illegal, but that doesn't make it wrong. It was the right thing to do for the right candidate."

At my flabbergasted expression, he narrowed his eyes. "This is all your father's fault. I'm the middleman here. He's held that information over her head for *years* and when we finally got him to name his price, he took her money and kept the drive. And then he up and *died* so what were we supposed to do? We've come too far to risk exposure like this."

My thoughts were tumbling around like rocks in a landslide. The flash drive was some kind of...blackmail deal gone *wrong*? And my dad told them he'd give it to *me* if he died?

"Grady," I said slowly. "Does...does the senator know you're here?"

He went back to emailing. "She's got enough on her plate right now. Rosamund told me to handle this. So I'm handling it."

I rattled my cuffs against the pipe. "Oh, is this *handling it* to you?"

His gaze snapped to mine. "She tried to get the information back her way, but you can't blame her for being much too soft and much, *much* too slow. She has a reputation to maintain. She can't be tailing people all over town or driving them off the road."

Understanding dawned on my face. "Right. That was... that was all *you*."

"Please, I hired people," he chided. "Senator Wallace is about to announce her presidential candidacy at any moment. We're cleaning house, destroying every skeleton in her closet before opposition research does it for her."

"I think kidnapping and murdering me is a pretty big skeleton, don't you?"

"Don't be dramatic," he drawled. "I'm not going to murder you. Though I can't say the same for that bodyguard of yours. He's got a dangerous job, wouldn't be that hard for him to have an accident."

I lunged across the tiled floor so fiercely that the cuffs sliced into my wrists, drawing blood. "Touch a hair on Elijah's head and I will fucking *end you*, Grady," I snarled. "I'll end you, then bring you back to life just to *end you again*."

His answering smile was smug. My hands clenched into fists. "I knew you loved him. Word of advice—don't be so obvious with your feelings. The night of the fundraiser you looked like some dopey teenager with a crush. It's nothing but a weakness. Look at how easily I can bend you to my will."

"What do you call what's going on between you and Rosamund then? Aren't you secretly in love with her or something?"

His face turned cold. "She took pity on me when I was nothing but a bumbling, twenty-year-old intern. She saw something in me, gave me a chance to be someone *important*. What I feel for her isn't romantic love. She's power incarnate, same as your father." He turned back to the door and pulled it open again. "I'll be back tomorrow. My advice? You should rethink every single lie you've told me tonight."

Then he was gone, leaving nothing but a ringing silence in his wake. I heard the lock engage, a mumbled conversation in the bedroom. Small trickles of blood still ran down my hands, and I shivered against the cool tile at my back.

Power incarnate. I'd once believed that to be true about Lincoln Beaumont. But nothing was more clarifying in this moment than being chained to a sink in a bathroom growing darker by the second, held hostage by a man so clearly swayed by yet another narcissist who cared only for themself.

People like Rosamund Wallace, people like my father, weren't actually powerful. They manipulated power, forced it to do their bidding, wielded it for selfish reasons motivated by money or greed or delusions of grandeur.

I had that same opportunity, but I'd been squandering it. The truth was, I could honor the worst, most painful moments of my childhood *and* fight for a better future, just like Harriet had said. A better future for her, for my nieces, for people like Ethel and Clarita, for my friends and community, for every artist living at Sunrise Village and every queer person at the Shipwreck. For my mother's memory and the vast ocean she loved so much, for the delicate tidal wetlands and ancient shorelines.

For every person who loved Cape Avalon, who loved this island, for all that it was and all that it could be.

And I could fight for a better future for Elijah. For every

kid who'd been through what he and I had and had survived. Because we hadn't survived those things alone. We'd survived them together.

Nothing was more powerful than that—hope, community, *love.*

From the very moment I'd been told I had inherited TBG, I'd gone about *every single thing* wrong. With the business, with its impact, of course.

With Elijah, most of all.

I had to believe there was time to fix it.

I just had to get myself unkidnapped first.

35

ELIJAH

Grady Holt was on the move.

He and Senator Wallace were currently at a pancake breakfast at a community center in Manhattan. The state senate had gone on recess a few days before, so it wasn't hard to follow the senator's social media pages to see the campaign events she was scheduled to attend. But this was the first one where Grady appeared, flanking her right side while she greeted attendees on the steps outside the building. She then gave a short speech to the press and had what appeared to be a terse meeting with a few of her advisers.

It was probably wishful thinking on my part that Grady didn't look quite right. His suit was wrinkled. There were heavy bags under his eyes, and the fingers of his left hand fidgeted when they weren't tapping away on his phone.

I watched all of this from a café across the street, wearing dark sweats and a hat pulled low, hiding my face behind one of Nora Jackson's books. Grady spoke briefly with the senator and then peeled away from her entourage, heading toward the parking garage one block away. I threw cash on the table for my coffee, collected my book, and then followed him.

Based on my conversation with Nora the day before, I wasn't wholly surprised when I plugged in that flash drive and found what appeared to be years of blackmail evidence on Rosamund Wallace. I *was* surprised at the sheer depth of it, at how much leverage Lincoln had on a woman who'd described him as "always having her back."

The flash drive held evidence from a journalist threatening to expose the Wallace mayoral campaign for election fraud. Their sources claimed that Rosamund, then a newbie city council member, had paid for her political colleagues to endorse her. Had even paid off staff at the local Cape Avalon paper to write favorable opinion pieces about her campaign. Local business owners who had been waffling on their endorsements suddenly came through in grand, public fashion…but only after sizable gifts appeared in their bank accounts.

All the last-minute support allowed her to eke out a win against the more popular grassroots candidate.

If Lincoln was leveraging this information he had over her to fast-track his projects while bypassing the red tape, then the friendship that existed between him and Rosamund was an uneasy détente at best. She knew Lincoln was using blackmail to drive up his company's profits… because *Rosamund* was the person being blackmailed.

Neither could expose the other without exposing themself.

What I didn't understand was why they thought Luke would have this flash drive full of incriminating evidence when it was all clearly orchestrated by Lincoln himself. But maybe they weren't aware of the strained father-son dynamic. Or maybe they were just plain desperate. Their reason for coming so hard for Luke now certainly made sense. The senator was savvy and ambitious and well-liked. She was rapidly climbing the political ladder, and a secret like this could end her career for good. Not to mention it was all *very* illegal.

As soon as I'd read through the information, I did the exact opposite of what Foster had instructed me to do. I drove right to the police station, leaving them copies of everything on the flash drive and imploring them to focus on the senator's team as the potential kidnappers. Then I'd spent the night researching, learning everything I could about Rosamund's life and the people she surrounded herself with.

My options were throwing myself into learning all that I could about this woman in a single evening. Or spending that same evening haunted by the memory of Luke whispering *I like you so much it scares me* before tracing the scars on my cheek with an intoxicating reverence.

Which was how, sometime around midnight, I'd landed on Grady as my target. There was an amateurish violence to the threats Luke had received that didn't feel like the work of a polished political official obsessed with maintaining her reputation. But she'd have given the task to someone she trusted implicitly.

Like the chief of staff who'd been by her side since he was just a college intern...and she was a newly elected city council member.

Now I sat low in my own parked car, grateful for the tinted windows, waiting for Grady to exit the parking garage. When he did, I kept as many vehicles between us as possible as we left Manhattan, drove through Queens, then hopped on Sunrise Highway heading toward the Hamptons.

Traffic kept our cars gridlocked, so by the time we were veering off Hill Street in the village of Southampton, my hands were clammy where they gripped the steering wheel. Grady finally pulled into a grimy Motel 6, and I forced myself to keep driving, hoping it would throw off any suspicion if he'd noticed me.

With every muscle taut, I drove a few blocks away, parked, then walked back to the motel with every nerve ending on hyper alert. I was tempted to storm the building and tear every door off its hinges but knew I needed some kind of plan. I stopped and made a hasty call to the police officer I'd spoken to last night, letting him know my location and what I was expecting to find. Midway through the officer instructing me to stay put in my car and out of harm's way, I hung up, then tossed a bag over my shoulders with supplies I hoped I wouldn't need.

When I was within eyesight of the parking lot, I took a right turn, keeping to the shaded parts of the sidewalk, then ducking behind the back entrance. Creeping low, light on my feet, I rounded the side of the motel and crouched behind the ice machines. The lot was empty except for two cars, the surrounding streets so quiet they were practically deserted.

I could just make out Grady, talking to a tall, broad man smoking a cigarette. Bile rose in my throat at the thought of Luke somewhere inside one of those rooms, at the mercy of those people, hurt and hungry and alone.

Grady left, striding toward a room I couldn't see from my vantage point. The man still smoked, messing around on his phone as he took long drags on his cigarette. When I felt like enough time had passed, I moved as quickly and quietly as I could, behind a short row of bushes, until I was close. I carefully, silently, retrieved the Taser from my bag. Then I was on my feet, wrapping an arm around the man's neck and pressing the device to the hollow of his throat.

"Don't say a fucking word," I hissed. I felt him go rigid and prepare to fight back. "And don't move. I'm guessing you know as well as I do what will happen if I activate this thing."

He grunted, looking furious.

"Now, which room did Grady Holt walk into?"

When he didn't answer, I wrenched his arms behind his back and pushed him forward, with the Taser now lodged against his nape.

"Tell me, or you're getting fifty thousand volts to the back of your goddamn skull," I said, seething.

The man released an angry breath. *"Five."*

I kicked him toward the door with my heart jackhammering in my chest. The room key was sticking out of his back pocket. I retrieved it with the hand holding the Taser, then shoved open the door and pushed my poorly-bound captive into the dim room.

But my plan fell apart as soon as I stepped inside and saw the bathroom door cracked open. Grady was crouched on the floor, speaking to someone in a voice dripping with condescension. And there were Luke's bare feet, the bunched material of the borrowed sweatpants he'd been wearing the morning he was taken.

You'd have me though, right? I'm not nothing.

My grip loosened with shock, dropping the Taser, and the man took advantage, darting back out the door in a full sprint. But I hardly noticed, every cell in my body flaring to life as I realized Luke was *right there.* Grady's gaze flew to a scratched-up coffee table, where a tiny circle of handcuff keys lay in the center. We both made a break for them at the same time.

And I was faster.

I snatched up the keys with one hand—with the other, I grabbed a fistful of Grady's shirt and hauled him back into the bathroom, slamming him up against the first wall we came to. It was too dangerous to look, too dangerous to look, *too dangerous to look...*

I turned my head and saw Luke, sitting on the floor with his hands cuffed to a sink pipe. He'd been gone for two and a half days at this point, less than sixty hours, and yet I stared at him like we'd spent decades apart. There was stubble on his cheeks, bruising around his lips, a hollow exhaustion in the lines around his eyes, which were wide with surprise.

"Elijah?" he asked hoarsely.

Before I could respond, Grady started to flail against me. One look at the clammy cowardice on his face had a fiery rage rising in me like a swarm of bees.

"You're the bodyguard, right?" he sputtered, seconds before I lodged my forearm against his throat, pinning him. "It's not," he wheezed, "not what it looks like."

I dipped my head until he could see the extent of my fury. "You kidnapped the man I love and chained him to a fucking *sink*."

His nails bit into my arm. "Just give me what I want, okay? Give me the drive and I'll pretend"—I pressed harder and he winced in pain—"I'll swear this never happened."

"Who put those bruises on his mouth?"

"Oh, stop being so *pathetic*, both of you," Grady spat out. His feet kicked at my shins as he struggled, but the movement barely registered. "You think any of this *matters*? You think having a little *boyfriend* matters in the end—"

I released my hold on his throat and punched him square in the face. He dropped to the tile, blood spurting from his nose, as the motel door burst open and police officers filled the small space. In the chaos, I forced my way to Luke and dropped to a crouch in front of him, reaching for his cuffs with hands that wouldn't stop shaking. The whole ordeal was made harder by the fact that I couldn't wrench my gaze away from his.

Wanted to stare forever at the person I feared I'd never see again.

I dropped the keys. Cursed. Picked them up and tried again, with even less luck.

"My handsome shield," Luke whispered, eyes filled with tears. "You rescued me."

I swallowed past the lump in my throat. "Anything for you, my liege."

"Elijah," he started, as I finally got the key in the lock. "Elijah, I'm so sorry. About our argument, what I said, I'm such an *asshole*."

My gaze snapped back to Luke. "Don't you dare say that. *I'm* the asshole."

"No, that's ridiculous. We can't *both* be—"

The cuffs fell open and clattered to the floor. And then I was pulling him toward me, wrapping my arms around his body. He hugged me back so tightly the air was knocked from my lungs, not that I could even conceive of breathing.

My only concern was Luke, with his face buried against my neck, his trembling shoulders, my hand cupping the back of his head. After a minute or ten or a hundred, he turned and kissed me. Bruised and probably sore, right there in the bathroom, surrounded by strangers and his kidnappers. The world around us vanished, like it always did, and I kissed him back with every bit of yearning I'd once locked away.

When we finally parted, he was wearing the same lopsided grin from the day we met.

"You're not nothing, Luke," I whispered. "You're everything."

36

ELIJAH

I stood in the parking lot of the local police station and watched Luke be examined by the paramedics. He wore one of those Mylar emergency blankets wrapped around his shoulders, and whatever he was saying to the medical crew had them laughing while they checked his vitals. In the end, he'd been extremely lucky—walking out of there tired, sore, a little hungry.

But he was alive and that was all that mattered.

I'd fired off a series of texts to Foster, Ripley and Sylvester. Sent an urgent message to Preston and personally called Luke's sister, Harriet, who burst into tears when she heard the news. Grady Holt had been carted away, as had the man who'd run off. They'd found him a mile down the road. We still had plenty of questions to answer, most importantly—how much did Senator Wallace know about his actions and had she signed off on any of this?

Even if she hadn't, Nora's words still rang in my head. *Violence is a choice too. Some of it obvious, bloody. Some of it much more subtle. It dresses up in fancy clothes and pretends to be on your side, pretends to care about your concerns when it's really only out for itself.*

Every piece of this—Lincoln's blackmail practices, Rosamund's election fraud, Grady's dogged pursuit—exposed Cape Avalon's dark underbelly in a way that sent an uneasy shiver down my spine. But something told me Luke was going to be changing that.

My phone rang in my hand. Foster, of course. I thought about Christopher, the earnest look on his face while he comforted me on his couch only a few days ago.

You don't have to save us. After Dad left, we saved ourselves.

In so many ways, turning my back on the career that had brought me much needed stability was the hardest thing I'd ever done. Scarier, probably, than bungee jumping the way Luke loved to do. I wasn't naive enough to think this next part would be easy or free of regrets.

Luke's head turned and his eyes sought mine from across the parking lot. He beamed a charming smile my way that warmed me from the inside out.

No, this next part wouldn't be easy. But being with Luke would make it a hell of a lot more fun.

"Hello, sir," I said. "I'm looking at Lucas Beaumont right now, upright and mostly okay aside from a few bumps and bruises. Grady Holt, Senator Wallace's chief of staff, was taken into custody. Law enforcement has everything I discovered so I'm sure they'll fill you in on the whole story."

There was a long pause on Foster's end. "Yes, they've... they've been in touch. Of course, we're happy to hear the client is safe and you are as well. I just got off the phone with Preston and Kenneth, who will be alerting the media."

I didn't reply. Merely kept my gaze trained on Luke, who was strolling my way with an expression of pure delight on his handsome face.

"You did good work, Knight," Foster grumbled. "I know you know that. Just like you also know that I have to fire you."

The words sliced through my chest. But then Luke reached me, tangling our fingers together and softening the blow.

"Yes, sir. I understand."

"Unless..." There was another long pause. "Unless you've ended that romantic relationship you told me about?"

Luke brought my hand to his lips. Kissed every knuckle.

"That's not an option for me," I said, starting to smile.

He cleared his throat. "Then I hope it was all worth it."

"He is," I said, and hung up the phone, pulling Luke against me as we stood beneath the golden sunlight. "Let's go get you some food. I've got a place in mind."

One eyebrow winged up. "Like a *date*?"

"If you're good," I said, brushing a lock of hair from his forehead.

"But I'm never good."

I chuckled, twisting at the waist to reach inside the open window of my car. "This was an act of delusional hope at the time, but I brought you a change of clothes. They'll be a little big on you, but..."

Luke opened the bag and gasped. "So you *do* own basketball shorts."

I tugged him even closer, pressing my nose to the crook of his neck and inhaling. "I never said I didn't. You assumed, Lucas."

Laughter rumbled from the center of his chest. "I'm sorry, but your exact words were 'I don't own a single comfortable item of clothing. Relaxation is an impossibility when your name is Elijah "Fun Should Be Illegal" Knight.'"

I gave a playful growl and bit down on his ear. He laughed and tried to squirm away, but I only locked my arms tighter. "Such a fucking *smartass*. I just rescued you and I'm still getting that mouth of yours."

His response was to kiss me, for longer and harder than his bruised lips could probably allow. He pulled back with a wince. I caught his chin with my fingers, tipping it so I could examine his wounds up close.

"Was it Grady who did this to you?" I asked softly.

"No, but that didn't mean it was any less satisfying to watch you punch his fucking lights out," he said. "It was one of the guys he hired. I'm not positive, but sounds like the people who followed us outside of the Shipwreck and the people who ran us off the road, took our pictures, sent those emails... It was likely those same guys. I got the impression Grady thought they'd done a sloppy job."

Sloppy or not, the knowledge that someone had put their hands on Luke was enough to send me into a frenzy. It must have been obvious, because he reached up and slid his palm against mine where I cupped his face.

"I'm okay, Elijah," he said. "More than okay. I'm relieved, I'm overjoyed, I'm *euphoric* and so damn grateful I could cry. I thought I was gonna die in there."

All the air left my lungs. "Luke," I whispered. "That's..." I noticed the bandages around both wrists. "Wait, what happened here?"

"It turns out, I didn't have to worry about Grady ending my life over that flash drive full of Rosamund's secrets. But he did threaten to kill you if I didn't cooperate and I...I didn't handle it very well. Tried to lunge for him and ended up cutting myself on the metal cuffs."

I pulled him back into me for another hug, full of empathy for what he'd been through. "When I walked outside that morning, when you were gone, when I realized..."

My throat closed up and I couldn't finish.

"No one ever told me it would be this way," he murmured, repeating my words from our night together. "I'll never forget the moment you walked into that bathroom to rescue me. No matter what Grady said, I didn't think I would ever see you again, Elijah."

We held each other in a comfortable silence for another minute, the joy coursing through my body so different from the despair I'd felt the morning he was taken, when I prowled up and down the shoreline in search of him.

"Hey, how did you find me anyway?" he asked.

"I found the flash drive. Remember the chandelier that almost fell on you the first day? It was hidden in that ceiling panel."

Luke reared back to look at me. "Holy shit. You never believed that was an unlucky accident, did you?"

I raised a shoulder. "We'll never know for sure, but my guess is that after Lincoln stored the drive there, he didn't rehang the chandelier properly. Once I saw the files on there and put together what they meant, Grady seemed like the person Rosamund would trust the most with a secret as career-ending as fraud. It was definitely a risk, tailing him, but he led me right to you."

Luke nodded. "Grady spent most of his time in there trying to get me to disclose the location of the drive. Because, according to him, he and Rosamund had paid my father off for it. And then he didn't return it. Or maybe he returned a fake or decoy—who knows. Sounds like once they started with the threats, he implied it would go to the heir of TBG if anything bad happened to him."

"So that's why they were threatening you." I rubbed a

hand along my jaw. "They genuinely believed you had it. Why would your dad tell them that?"

"No clue. Maybe the same mystery reason he left the company to me and not Preston."

Luke yawned suddenly, his shoulders slumping.

"Come on," I said, "let me get you some food. Then I'm taking you home, because Harriet's already planning a giant party at your house. Your sister cried when I called her and told her the good news."

"Thank you for doing that."

"No thanks necessary," I said, giving him a kiss on the cheek. "Now get in the car so I can take you on a date."

Before he did, he quickly shucked the clothes he'd been kidnapped in. He yanked on the sweatshirt and shorts I brought, as well as the barely worn pair of flip-flops I dug out of my closet. The drive over was less than twenty minutes, but Luke was asleep, curled against the passenger door, before we were halfway down the road. He'd taken my hand and placed it in his lap. He gripped it tightly, even as he slept.

Meanwhile, I was fairly calm given I'd just lost my job, my career and the promotion that had been the focus of my life for the past six months. But Luke was safe. The threats against him had been extinguished and his sister was filling his house with the people he loved.

I understood now, even more, Christopher's message to me. There was no perfect way to survive in this world. I would never control every outcome, correct every mistake. Perfection wouldn't prevent the people I loved from getting hurt. It was loving them and being loved by them—the big, giant mess of it—more than being perfect that gave life meaning.

We pulled up at a roadside café and ate facing the ocean,

sitting on top of a picnic table with our shoes kicked off and our feet warming in the early October sun. I had a lobster roll, dripping with warm butter, on crusty, crumbling bread. Luke inhaled not one but two grilled cheese sandwiches, then placed the paper basket of french fries in his lap.

He curled against my side, dropping his cheek to my shoulder. I cleaned my fingers with a napkin, then scratched the top of his head, feeling more alive in this moment of autumn sunlight and greasy food and cool ocean breeze than I had in years.

The beach in front of us was mostly empty, although a few happy dogs chased Frisbees and a couple of kids built sandcastles near the burned-out logs of an old bonfire.

"I spent five years at your father's side, most of that time here." I paused to press a kiss to the top of Luke's head. "I'm just now realizing that I've never really *looked* at the ocean before. When the sun hits it like that, it's like glitter on top of the waves."

Luke hummed under his breath. "After my mother died and was cremated, Preston and I tossed her ashes into the sea so she could be returned to us again and again, floating in the water that she loved so much. She believed the ocean to be the greatest gift the planet had given us, vast and full of uncharted mysteries. But also, comfortingly cyclical. The tides rise and fall, the waves curl then dissipate. It's endless. Persistent. It continued long before we got here and will continue long after we're gone."

He sat up, turning to face me fully on the picnic table. "Based on how I felt about my family, a lot of my friends thought that after I graduated and got that money, I was gonna fuck off as far away as I could. But that would have meant leaving Harriet and my nieces, which I'd never do." He smiled out at the ocean, face tinged with sadness. "And

I'd never leave these waves. They were her home and they're mine too."

When he looked back at me, his body was loose, relaxed. "I hoped that you would come and rescue me, Elijah. But I wasn't sure if I deserved it."

I opened my mouth to argue, but he held up a palm.

"I woke up in that bathroom, scared and alone and fully convinced I was going to die without ever getting to say these words to you. It made me realize how *wrong* I'd been, about so much. I'm so sorry, Elijah. I risked your job, your integrity, your *life*. You were right about everything: my ill-conceived revenge plan, the very real danger we were in. You were right about *me*."

He hooked his fingers through mine and squeezed. "I've spent most of my life running from the privileges of my family because I thought it would heal me, thought it would make the pain easier or erase the horrible memories. Showing the world that my dad was a monster will *never* change the past. He's gone, but I'm still here, and that means I should be doing more for this community that I love. *That's* the real revenge. It's..."

Luke paused, eyes searching while my heart lodged in my throat.

"It's what?" I asked.

He leaned in close and kissed me. "I heard what you said back there, to Grady," he whispered.

I blushed, my entire face going hot. *You kidnapped the man I loved*. "I meant"—I swallowed—"I meant every word."

His answering smile was so bright it reflected off the waves. "I love you too, Elijah Knight."

My heart cracked open, overwhelmed with the beauty of it all. I dropped my forehead against his with a long exhale. *"Luke."* I dragged my lips through his hair, along his temple, kissed a path along his jawline. "I love you," I whispered back. Kissed along the side of his throat. "I love you so much. Please...please don't ever get kidnapped again. I won't survive it."

He laughed softly. "I think that's one risky activity I can safely say I'll never do again. But I'm gonna need some bungee jump therapy, preferably soon, if you wanna join me."

"Can I say maybe?"

He leaned back, bewildered. "That wasn't an *absolutely not*."

I shook my head. "It wasn't, because I need to tell you something too. My boss fired me, just now, over the phone."

"Oh my god, *really?* Even after you rescued my ass?"

I grinned, scrubbing a hand down my face. "Yes. Even after I rescued your ass. As soon as I went after you, my job was over. I was told to stand down, let the professionals work. I refused." I sobered, held Luke's gaze. "Sitting in my apartment, doing nothing while you were in danger, when you'd been *taken* from me, was impossible. I couldn't do that, Luke. I wouldn't ever do that to you."

He blinked back tears. "But you'd still have a job if it wasn't for me. Let me talk to your boss. You, of all people, don't deserve this."

I grabbed his hand and kissed his palm. "I also told Foster we were together."

A giant grin sprang across Luke's face.

"I choose you. I choose us." I watched pure happiness ripple across his features. "I choose *myself*. And it's for the best, Luke. You were right about me too. I *am* living half a life. It's infuriating, realizing how much of my adulthood I've spent trying to prove to a father who *isn't even here* that

I'm a good person. That I'm worthy, that I have value, that I'm *better*."

Luke grabbed my face, held it tenderly. "You're the worthiest person that I know. No one deserves to live a full, joyful life more than you."

"I might have to...get some whimsy."

He laughed and kissed me. "That can be arranged, sweetheart."

37

LUKE

As soon as I stepped out of the car, Harriet launched herself into my arms.

"I thought I'd lost you for good," she said, her voice thick with tears.

"I thought I was never coming home," I replied, every fear and every regret I'd had in that tiny bathroom roaring back. Reminding me how close I'd come to losing everything because of my father.

She leaned back, and we laughed at the sight of our soggy faces.

"Please don't ever get kidnapped again," she said, laughing through her sobs.

I kissed her forehead and pulled her in for another hug. "Never, ever, ever again."

I watched Elijah sink to a crouch in front of my nieces, playing in the grass. They were smiling and presenting him with wildflowers they'd picked from my garden. He let Lizzie tuck a wild daisy behind his ear and my heart tried to catapult from my chest to the sky.

Harriet turned and followed my gaze. "They must have

noticed you pulled up," she said with a sniff. "I've been trying to keep it together for them, but they could tell I was worried sick about you."

"Oh, it's fine," I said as we started to walk over. "I'm just their uncle who was kidnapped. Elijah's a *new* person and new people always win."

"Good lord, that man is *handsome*," Harriet muttered. "Only you could go through something so traumatizing and end up with a boyfriend at the end of it."

Elijah glanced up from where he'd been charming my nieces. He now wore a crown of daisies and an easy smile. "Am I your boyfriend?"

I flashed him a grin. "If you'll have me."

"I'd be honored, my liege," he replied, eyes dancing with mischief.

My nieces dragged me toward the house before I could swoop down and kiss Elijah—my *boyfriend*—square on the mouth in front of everyone. Inside, the kitchen was full of people. Friends, coworkers, most of my neighbors. The music was upbeat, there was cold beer, tons of food and my nieces had drawn a sign that read, "Please don't get kidnapped again, Uncle Luke!"

For the first hour of the party, I took Elijah by the hand and beamed as guests exclaimed over his heroism. He kept our fingers entwined and blushed adorably with every compliment he received. I was going to remember the moment Elijah burst through that bathroom door to save me for the rest of my life. I'd been so sure he was a feverish hallucination, standing there like an avenging angel, coldly competent in his fury. Then tender and delicate as he pulled me toward him with so much love it took my breath away.

I did eventually let Harriet drag me off to the hammock, with the girls playing on the sand directly behind my house.

I filled her in on everything that had happened from the last time we'd spoken, from the car going off the road to Elijah saying *I love you so much* in the parking lot.

By the time I finished, tears fell freely down my cheeks. "I couldn't stop thinking about how I might never see you again," I said. "Wouldn't see Lizzie or Rory. This big, beautiful life that I'd miss because I was stuck getting revenge on a man who was truly incapable of love. I don't want to be stuck in that past anymore, Harriet. I want to do what you said. Fight for a better future."

She handed me another tissue before reaching up and curling her hair into a bun. "So what does that mean for TBG? Are you gonna sell it or keep it?"

"I had a lot of time in that bathroom to think about this," I said slowly. "And if I sell the company, I lose my trust, and we're gonna need it. But not only for you and the girls. I want to start a foundation, a way to direct my father's money back into the community. To give every penny of it away for as long as it lasts. If we invest it right, that could be for a long time."

Harriet's smile was watery. "Oh, Luke. I love that idea."

"We could have a great board too," I said, getting more excited. "With people like Clarence Craven and Nora and Mía. Ethel and Clarita, people who believe in Cape Avalon. I'll still sell off the company in three years, but until then I'll talk to Gregory, our lawyer, about the rules and bylaws, what I can realistically change. I want to bring in affordable housing experts, see what good my dad's company can do before we sell it. In the meantime, I'm putting a permanent stop to the construction planned at Sunrise Village. All the artists will be able to stay."

Harriet threw her arms around me. I laughed so hard we almost fell out of the hammock.

"What was that for?" I asked.

"There's the big brother I know and love. Knew you had it in you."

I tossed her a wide smile. "Luckily I've got people in my life who will tell me when I'm being an obtuse asshole."

"Luke, you survived a childhood of grief and abuse and deprivation," she said softly. "Survived a father who openly declared you worthless at every opportunity. That anger you carry, that need to turn your back on your family, there's nothing wrong with it. There's no shame in being a human with feelings that will ebb and flow as you change."

She cast a glance at her daughters, playing in the sand. "I never met your mother, but I'm a mother now too, so I think I can speak from experience when I say she'd want you to feel anger when you feel it. And she'd want you to know that *none of it was your fault.* But she'd also want you to have a life full of things to hope for, to fight for, to believe in. To balance out the days when you feel sad or stuck in the past. There's no single way to survive what you and Preston went through. But we get through it together."

I was quiet for a while, too overcome with emotion to say much of anything. When I could finally speak, my voice trembled. "You know, I had the same thought when I was stuck in that bathroom, thinking I was gonna die."

She wiped a tear from my cheek and pulled me in for another hug. "It's almost as if we're siblings."

"I love you, Harry," I said. "More than hot coffee on freezing winter mornings."

"I love you too. More than ice cold lemonade on hot summer evenings."

And just when I was about to call Elijah over to tell him I had exciting ideas to share, a shiny town car parked in front of my house and out stepped Kenneth and Preston.

When I caught Kenneth's eye, he jerked his chin toward where he and Preston were standing, with the same demeanor of a dog owner calling over his pet. Irritation zipped up my spine as I carefully disengaged from the hammock.

"Do you want a buddy?" she asked, following my gaze.

I almost said yes, but then caught sight of Elijah, making his way toward the two of them. I shook my head and said, "My boyfriend's still in bodyguard mode, so I'm well and truly protected for the time being."

After I strolled over, I shot Elijah a grateful look before taking his hand. If Preston was surprised to see the two of us together, he didn't show it. Though Kenneth's lips thinned when he noticed.

"Luke, I'm..." Preston started, voice cracking slightly. "I was so relieved when Elijah told me you'd been found."

The unexpected emotion on my brother's face had me smiling—just a little. "I'm relieved to be back. I don't recommend getting kidnapped. Wasn't my favorite."

Kenneth sniffed. "And you're welcome for keeping things running while you were gone. Which I've been doing these past two weeks on your behalf without an ounce of recognition."

Elijah went rigid next to me. But before he could say anything, Preston pinned Kenneth with a glare.

"Frankly, you don't really have a leg to stand on," he snapped. "Tell Luke what you told me on the ride over here."

Stunned, I looked over at TBG's board president, whose ruddy face was growing ruddier. "Are you here to tell me that Dad's prosperous career relied on his long-standing blackmail practices, holding leverage over rich and influential people to ensure his properties were successful?"

"Wait, *what*?" Preston said. "Did you know about this too?" he asked Kenneth, who was starting to fidget.

"As if I'd be foolish enough to answer that question without my lawyer present." Kenneth scoffed.

My brother raked his hands through his hair. "Tell him, Kenneth. Luke deserves to know."

In the frustrating silence Preston rolled his eyes, looking so like his fourteen-year-old self that my stomach hollowed out at the memory. Of sitting at the table during one of Kenneth's pompous lectures, both of us trying to find the funniest way to piss him off.

"Tell me what?" I finally demanded.

Kenneth blew out a noisy breath. "I knew your father was planning on changing the terms of his will. He told me a few months before he died, late one night after one too many drinks. Which was rare, for him. I talked him out of it, of course. Leaving a company as prestigious as TBG to you would have been a disaster. Clearly, I was right."

"Watch it," Elijah growled.

Kenneth looked appropriately miffed. "Like I said, I talked him out of it. Then things with Sunrise Village got worse and I forgot to confirm that he actually *did* change it. No one was expecting him to die. I was just as surprised as you were to learn that the last-minute change he'd made out of fear and paranoia had stayed in there."

I took a step closer. "Fear and paranoia? What does that mean?"

"Your father's life was being threatened by a local politician."

"Yeah, Senator Wallace," I said. "We already know that. Her chief of staff is the one who kidnapped me."

"From a liability standpoint, the less I say the better,"

Kenneth said through clenched teeth. "He was being threatened by an unnamed local politician."

Elijah cocked a brow. "That he was actively blackmailing."

"I can neither confirm nor deny that. Except your father did refer to a successful payoff, but then he didn't return the"—he seemed to consider his words—"the material, and the politician was upset."

I glanced at my brother. "Grady told me that Dad held proof of Rosamund Wallace's election fraud over her head for years. Now that she's running for president, they wanted it back. Paid him off and everything but he never actually returned it and they don't know why."

"If your father had his reasons, I would trust them," Kenneth said.

"Cut the shit, Kenneth," Preston said, hands on his hips. "Over the last few years, Dad was getting more paranoid, hoarding everything. It didn't matter that he had all the money in the world. If he could get paid off for blackmail secrets and keep the leverage, he would have done it even if they threatened his life. That's who he was at the end, who he was becoming. We all saw it. You saw it."

"I saw no such thing," Kenneth replied.

I snorted. "Yet according to you, Dad was also getting drunk and changing his will erratically, so maybe there's some truth to what Preston's saying?"

When Kenneth avoided my gaze again, I bent my head to catch his eye. "Why did Dad leave it to me?"

He sighed dramatically. "They were threatening his life on more than one occasion, and he told me he'd threatened them back. Told them that if anything ever happened to him, his heir would take ownership of the flash drive and make sure that they never got their hands on it. He thought it was a brilliant insurance policy."

"Arrogant," Preston muttered, shaking his head.

A sick feeling was starting to unfurl in my stomach. "Dad...Dad assumed that if he died and the senator took that opportunity to make a play for the flash drive, whichever son took over the company would be the one in danger. He wasn't only transferring a company, he was putting a bull's-eye on the back of one of his sons."

But it wasn't Kenneth who answered. It was Preston.

"That's correct," he said, his voice even more anguished than before. "That's what Kenneth just told me. Forcing me to quit was Dad's twisted way of keeping me safe, out of the senator's line of sight. He was too greedy to give the flash drive back and too selfish to give the company away."

I was going to be sick right here on the lawn. Elijah's palm was stroking up and down my back in long, soothing lines.

"I was always the spare," I said. "The kid he didn't want, the disappointment. He got the best of both worlds—his legacy stayed in the hands of his family and he got to put the son he never loved directly in harm's way."

"It wasn't his most well-thought-out or rational plan now, was it?" Kenneth chided. "The errors are obvious now, but he wasn't...he wasn't thinking *clearly*. It's why I was so angry the night he told me. But I also don't think he presumed that he'd die of a heart attack at the age of sixty-three either. It's a tragedy, one that you never took seriously, Lucas. Yes, he was a complicated man, but he was still your *father*."

"And you're a fucking coward and always have been," Preston shot back.

Kenneth looked about as stunned as I was. Which was

when Elijah stepped forward and put a hand on Kenneth's shoulder, turning him toward the car. "Time for you to go, Mr. Bromley."

"Pretty unethical of you to date your bodyguard," he sniped.

"I'm not his bodyguard. I'm his boyfriend," Elijah said—and even in the midst of this terrible conversation, I didn't miss the thrill that shot down my spine at his words.

Elijah had a quick conversation with the driver, then all but shoved Kenneth back into the town car. When he returned, Preston said, "Can I have a moment alone with my brother?"

Elijah nodded and bent to kiss me on the cheek before walking back to the house.

Preston looked carved up and wrung out, with dark circles under his eyes.

I shrugged a shoulder. "I'll have to ask Gregory first, but I'm pretty sure I can fire Kenneth from the board immediately."

"I always hated him," Preston muttered.

I sent him a questioning look. "Really? 'Cause two weeks ago you were reminiscing about how helpful his *mentorship and guidance* was to us as teenagers."

My brother paled further. Shook his head. "That's because...that's because I'm finally waking up to...everything that happened." He blinked rapidly. "Luke, listen. I don't expect you to ever forgive me for the things I've done, the things I've said. But ever since you were taken, I started to realize that my life with Dad was a complete fucking lie. And then Kenneth revealed that nightmare scenario to me in the car. And I—I'm sorry from the bottom of my heart. I'm so, so sorry and so happy that you came home safely."

I looked back toward the shoreline, at the way the sun

shimmered on top of the waves like glitter, just like Elijah had pointed out earlier. I watched the water for a moment and remembered what it was like between me and my brother before Mom died.

We were once so close people thought we were twins.

"I know you tried to sneak me food, Preston," I said, "when Dad would punish me. I know you tried sneaking me blankets and pillows too, when I was sleeping outside."

"But it never worked. I told Elijah that I should have tried harder."

"We were children." I lightly touched his arm. "I don't say this easily, because I don't think rebuilding our relationship *will* be easy. It'll probably take a long time and be super hard. Because of all the ways you were, like, a huge dick to me."

I watched and waited for his reaction. When his lips twitched into a half smile, I felt a tiny glimmer of hope. It was small, practically minuscule, but it would do for now.

"I've spent so much of my life feeling angry at Dad for what he did to both of us," I continued. "Spent so much of my life wanting to rail at the injustice of it all. Spent so much of my life wishing that Mom was here, because I think she'd know what to do."

"What do you think she would say?" he asked, blinking back tears. I realized now that at Dad's funeral—a hazy day for me at best—I hadn't seen my brother cry once.

"She'd want us to be brothers again," I said.

He blew out a ragged breath. "Christ, I'm gonna need to talk this through in therapy."

I let out a laugh. "Me too. Maybe we could go together sometime."

We were quiet for a moment. Then my brother cocked

his head in Elijah's direction and said, "I like him for you. You complement each other."

"I'd like to think I bring a bit of fun and whimsy his way."

"And what does he do for you?"

I relaxed into a smile. "Reminds me to take some things a bit more seriously."

I suddenly realized how alone and awkward Preston looked, younger even. I cleared my throat and indicated our sister. "I can't promise she'd be open to it, but you know that's Harriet, right?"

Preston nodded. I'd told him about her after we first met but he'd never been interested in getting to know her, already too caught up in Dad's bullshit.

"We've even got nieces too. And they're extraordinary," I continued. "We obviously don't share a biological mom, but Harriet reminds me of the best parts of her."

Harriet glanced over at us and gave a tentative wave.

"Wanna go say hi?" I asked.

"Sure, I'm... Yeah. Let's do it. And Luke?"

I turned, felt a genuine shift in the energy between us.

"You remind me of the best parts of her too."

38

LUKE

A few hours later—after my brother and sister had had their first slightly awkward, but still nice, conversation and my nieces had fallen asleep on the living room floor and pizzas were ordered and snacks depleted—Elijah found me curled up in the armchair, exhausted yet full of the most sublime gratitude.

I dozed lightly as Elijah cleaned up the kitchen, took care of the empty pizza boxes, took out trash bags full of plastic cups and paper plates. He shut off the music so only the peaceful sounds of the ocean outside could be heard. And when I blearily opened my eyes, he was crouched down in front of me, cupping my face with his hand.

"What do you need?" he asked.

"I need a shower. Then I need you to take me to bed and lie on top of me like the world's sexiest weighted blanket."

"Happy to be of service," he said with a grin. His thumb traced my cheekbone, and his expression turned somber. "I can't stop thinking about what Kenneth said, about what your father did to you. Luke, I'm so sorry."

I shifted in the chair, placing a palm on my chest where

the news of my father's betrayal sat heavy and jagged. It would be tender for a while, a newly forming bruise, but it didn't scare me the way others had in the past.

I smiled down at the gorgeous man in front of me. Smiled at the remnants of the warm welcome party full of friends and family. I finally understood why the betrayal felt sore but survivable.

"I'm furious," I said. "I really am. Deep down, I always figured the reasons behind the will were shitty and fucked-up. Hearing it only confirmed my suspicions. Am I hurt? Yes, very. Am I surprised?"

I brushed a lock of hair from his forehead. "No, not really. The man used to make me sleep outside when I got bad grades. He wasn't a good person. He wasn't capable of love. We're so much luckier than he was, Elijah. We love and are loved. That's the only thing I care about right now. Loving you."

He kissed my fingers. "I love you too. Let's get you into that shower."

I would have collapsed, zombielike, if he hadn't forcibly pushed me down the hallway. Sat me on the lid of the toilet while the room filled with steam and gently undressed me. Off came his sweatshirt, a little big on me and smelling like his detergent. Off came the rest and then he was tossing away his shirt too, his grin just shy of wicked when he caught me staring at the rippling muscles of his torso. He took my hand and tugged me under the hot spray, where I moaned so loudly that Elijah chuckled against my hair.

"What are you gonna do now? Now that you can't be a protection agent anymore?" I asked.

His hands were strong and slick on my skin, working out the knots in my back, my neck, my shoulders. "I don't know yet. My brother helpfully reminded me that I'm thirty-seven, not a hundred, meaning a career change is totally possible."

I hummed. "Christopher is smart."

With my eyes closed against the spray, I heard him pop open the shampoo. Then his fingers were working through my hair. "That he is. I've never, ever…taken a real break. Never thought about anything other than my clients and their safety." He kissed the nape of my neck. "I'm terrified but in a good way."

"I know the feeling."

He tipped my head back to rinse. I was on the verge of becoming pure liquid beneath his magic hands.

"Would you go on vacation with me, Luke?"

I turned in his arms, surprised, slicking my wet hair back. "Didn't you just go on your first one in five years?"

His lips twitched. "I didn't actually enjoy myself."

"Yeah, no shit," I said with a grin. "You're a doer, Elijah Knight. I'm not saying you wouldn't enjoy a relaxing beach environment for part of the time. But you might need a bit more excitement on your vacations."

His gaze fell to my mouth. "You might be right."

"Good thing your boyfriend is the adventurous type." I stole a kiss. "Count me in. We can leave this weekend if you want. Given what we went through, I don't think anyone would blame us for sneaking away."

He smiled at me—slow, languid, lines crinkling around his eyes. "You'll really come with me?"

"I'd love nothing more, sweetheart."

He brushed his lips across my forehead. "When I was on that vacation, I remember seeing this couple. Two men, romantic, affectionate. So at ease with each other, with their love. I wanted"—he swallowed—"I wasn't sure that would ever happen for me. Wasn't sure I deserved it."

I gripped his face, rose up on my toes, and kissed him. Long and sweet beneath the hot water, the steam surrounding us as our mouths met again and again. "I meant what I said, that night in the cabin," I said softly. "You deserve the world, and I'll do everything in my power to give it to you."

On any other night, the possessive sound that rumbled from Elijah's chest just then would have had me falling to my knees—and gladly. But he must have sensed my bone-deep exhaustion because he merely kissed the top of my head and then gently toweled me dry. I was half asleep by the time he pulled the covers up to my chin. And the second he curled his big body around mine, I was out.

So it could have been hours or days later when I finally surfaced from my well-deep sleep. I wiggled back against the wall of solid, muscular heat still wrapped around me and was rewarded with Elijah's husky laughter against my ear. That was all it took for me to turn and reach for him, my need for this man suddenly as urgent as my next fucking breath. He crashed his mouth against mine but then yanked back, eyeing the bruising near my lips with obvious concern.

I shook my head, bringing his face back down. "I'm fine. Really. Please don't stop."

His jaw flexed. "Are you sure?"

"Elijah, *please*."

His next kiss was pure devastation—soft and dreamy, and then demanding. He kissed me like he never planned to stop, like we could share a single breath for all of eternity. His mouth moved down my body, taking my cock between his lips as my head tipped back on a gasp. I gripped his hair with both hands while he slowly, expertly, pulled my world apart.

By the time he'd driven me to the point of babbling madness, I was more than ready to take every inch of him. With lubed-up fingers, he slipped inside my ass, mouth at my ear as he stroked.

"That's it," he kept whispering. "Show me how good you feel, Luke. Give it to me."

"Elijah," I gasped. "I need you."

Intensity blazed in his gaze. He sat back on his heels and pressed my knees wide open. Crawled back up my body and worked his cock inside me, so deliberately that my head fell back again as I begged.

"Who do you need?" he asked, thrusting hard now.

"You," I panted. "The man that I love."

Elijah swore and kissed me. "I love you," he said. "I need this, need *you*."

I grabbed his ass and he growled against my mouth. Took me in long, thorough strokes that had both of us out of breath, kissing as we rose higher and higher. When he reached down to grip my cock, I came in seconds, awash in pure ecstasy. Elijah climaxed with his mouth on mine, groaning low and rough and sending an indulgent shiver down my spine.

We laughed together—still panting, Elijah's shoulders shaking as he kissed my cheek.

"Does that...does that count as whimsy?" he asked, breathless.

I yawned happily and pulled him against my chest, wrapping my arms and legs around him. "I'll allow it. If you allow me to go back to sleep for another four hours."

He popped his head up and pushed the hair off my forehead. "I'll allow it if you teach me how to do something fun out on the ocean today. Something that'll make me forget that I have to figure out what I'm doing with the rest of my life."

I arched an eyebrow. "You ever been on a Jet Ski before, sweetheart?"

He grinned. "I'm in."

I nudged my nose to his. "My handsome shield. What would you do without me?"

"Get in less trouble, that's for sure."

"Secretly...you love it," I teased.

"I love *you*," he said with a kiss. "Not so secretly."

Outside, the sun danced along the ocean waves like glitter, while inside Elijah placed his ear on my chest, directly above my heart. It fluttered and preened at his nearness, and I whispered "I love you" into the crown of his head. The future stretched long ahead of us—all the hope, all the community, all that we'd do together. Filled with moments like this one, when the world was alive and beautiful, suspended on a honey-gold morning in October.

I was ready for it now.

EPILOGUE
ELIJAH

One year later

I gazed up at the platform and finally felt ready.

Luke, to his credit, hadn't pushed the bungee jump issue once in the past year. Had even been surprised when I woke up this morning and suggested it. True, since meeting Luke, I'd been happy to learn that I enjoyed some of the same thrill-seeking activities that he did. I rode Jet Skis regularly now. Enjoyed parasailing when he was up for it.

At Christmas, I surprised him with a trip to Moab and he took me whitewater rafting for the first time, surrounded by red rocks and warm sun. I'd had so much fucking fun I made him book us a second trip immediately.

I wasn't a surfer, though I liked watching Luke do it. Didn't want to cage-dive with sharks. Rock climbing held no interest to me.

But in the back of my mind, I'd never stopped thinking about Luke winking at me before falling backward off that bridge. Totally free and completely alive.

"What do you think, sweetheart?" Luke asked, stepping up behind me and wrapping his arms around my waist. "You still feel like today is the day?"

I raised an eyebrow. "It's higher than I remember."

"Yeah, that never changes," he said with a laugh. "It's always higher than you remember."

I turned to face him and kissed the tip of his nose. "That was nice of you to invite a cheering section."

As if on cue, the family and friends that Luke had invited to witness my first bungee jump let out a raucous cheer from the guest viewing section. Harriet's bright pink hair was obvious, and I could see our nieces standing next to her girlfriend, Kat. My brother, Christopher, was there with Shana, and our nephews held a sign that read, "Good Luck Uncle Eli!"

The sight of them hollowed my stomach with affectionate appreciation. I'd spent the year spending as much time with my family as I possibly could. And discovering just how much I'd missed by chaining myself to a job that never allowed me to enjoy the world beyond my clients' minute-by-minute schedules. We did weekly movie nights now. And Christopher and I met up for diner breakfasts or runs on the beach, catching up on all that we'd missed.

Luke's brother, Preston, stood in the middle of the throng, looking much more comfortable and at ease than he had when he first started coming around. Luke described their progress as "slow but steady," a careful mending of childhood wounds and adulthood hurts.

It helped that Preston was so involved with the foundation that Luke was setting up to give his father's money back to the Cape Avalon community. Preston was even preparing to sign away a significant portion of his trust fund to be the seed money. And I'd seen the emotion on their faces when Luke proposed that they call it the Stella Rush Foundation —named for their mother, the queen of the carrot monsters.

Luke was busy now and very happy. Like his mother, he started his mornings with a brisk swim in the ocean before heading off to oversee the creation of the foundation and the dissolution of TBG. Sunrise Village remained open and full of artists. And Luke had been delighted when Clarence, Mía and Nora joined the new foundation board. The trio had tons of ideas for where to start directing the funding, from the tidal wetlands to more affordable housing.

The details of Luke's kidnapping had sent shockwaves through the Hamptons. Senator Wallace had postponed her presidential run, and her campaign team was currently under investigation for fraud. Grady was awaiting trial on kidnapping charges. From what had been shared in the paper, Grady had been solely responsible for the threats against Luke's life, taking increasingly reckless risks without Rosamund's full knowledge. The people Grady had hired had been responsible for the majority of the threats, although Grady had masterminded the kidnapping scheme on his own. They'd broken into Lincoln's office. Left voicemails and emails. Had Luke and me followed, took pictures, then sent them to us.

Though Vincent Maura had planted the car bomb in this very parking lot, Grady's men had already been following us. So while the picture they caught of Luke and me post-explosion had been mere coincidence, Grady later confessed that seeing it had given him the inspiration to take things in a darker, more dangerous direction.

Luke placed his hands on my shoulders and gently pushed me forward. "To be clear, you can join the cheering section at any second and not jump at all. The platform will still be here. And as you know, I'd follow you to the ends of the earth. Say the word and we can come back and try again."

"But I might lose my nerve, my liege. I'm ready now."

He cracked a giant smile. "Then let's do it."

He tugged me inside the elevator, which delivered us to the platform. Luke squeezed my hand, sensing my nerves. He'd done the same thing when I sat at the table in his house—our house now—and applied for an online program to get my degree in social work.

I was only a few weeks into classes, but as I'd tried to figure out what I wanted to do next in my life, I hadn't been able to stop thinking about what had happened to me and Luke and Preston and Christopher when we were kids. And I knew that there were schools and community centers and colleges where social workers could help kids like us.

I had known it was right because applying had been scary the way that whitewater rafting had been scary. Scary as in *exhilarating*. Scary as in *unknown* but not necessarily *wrong*.

Something told me bungee jumping might feel the same.

Luke offered to go first, and just like the first time, my stomach lurched violently as the love of my fucking life fell backward off a bridge with a flirty wink in my direction.

I didn't have time to worry too much because the team was prepping me to go next. The music blared as they expertly locked my harness and bound my feet. We were close to the edge, much too close, and our cheering section of friends and family appeared ant-sized from this vantage point.

"First time, right?" one of the crew asked.

I nodded, heart in my throat. But I whipped my head around at the sound of them pulling Luke back up to safety from the other side. As soon as he opened his eyes, he brightened at the sight of me trussed up and ready to jump.

He mouthed *I love you so much* and blew me a kiss.

Within seconds of my first jump, I understood exactly why Luke loved it.

There were the first terrifying moments of free fall and then the sharp yank of the cord, tossing me back up into the bright blue sky. *Exhilaration* couldn't begin to describe the sensation of flying, the way my body was suffused with ecstasy. Exactly how I'd seen Luke appear that first time.

It wasn't sexual, but something more primitive than that. A thirst for life, for experience, for adventure.

When I was dragged back onto that platform, the crew had barely gotten me out of the harness before I was prowling toward Luke, bending him backward for a dramatic kiss.

He laughed against my lips. I whispered, "I love you, I love you, I love you."

It was true—no one told me it would feel this way. That living a full life would be so rich with emotion. More than that, that I was *allowed* to feel this way. But I was here now and present for all of it—the mistakes and failures, the lust and the affection, the lazy mornings and busy weekends, all the boring moments and the thrilling ones.

I was there to bandage up my nephew when he skinned his knee. To laugh with Luke's sister while he cooked us dinner. To walk the beach with Luke at night, our pant legs rolled up and the surf crisp against our feet.

It was impossible to parcel out tiny bits of happiness

anymore. It was all there, mine for the taking, messy and complicated and real. I was greedy for it now, eager to reach for the joy we all deserved.

Eager to live this full life with Luke by my side.

THE END

BONUS EPILOGUE
LUKE

Two years after the epilogue

The Laurel Lighthouse rose in front of us like some kind of coastal candy cane.

Elijah and I stood at its base, surrounded by the open ocean on all sides. I was suddenly deeply fucking grateful for the surging surf.

Maybe it would drown out the sound of my heart, currently thrashing around at a volume he *had* to be able to hear.

I'd hovered in a cage in icy waters while a Great White shark clamped its teeth around the bars. Had dangled from the sides of mountains and been tossed overboard more times than I could count. Absolutely none of it compared to what I was about to do.

I was scared *shitless*.

My phone buzzed in my pocket, and I hoped it was text messages confirming what would happen next. Gulping, I raked a hand through my hair and nodded up at the lighthouse.

"She's a beauty, isn't she?" I said, aiming for casual.

Elijah stepped behind me, surrounding me with his solid warmth. His big hands wrapped around my waist, his nose landing in the crook of my neck. "You're the beauty," he rumbled. "Much as I love it here, is there a reason why you dragged us from bed?" His nose traced my ear. "I had plans for you."

I smirked. Turned my head to give him a quick kiss. "You already executed those plans this morning, sweetheart. *Quite* well, as you'll recall."

"I had more."

"Did you now?" My grin widened as he caught my chin and turned me for another kiss. "Not sure I would have survived it."

His answer was a pleased growl from the center of his chest. His lips roamed the side of my neck, which was exactly how he'd woken me this morning—unknowingly disrupting *my* plans.

Which had been to worship and tease him until he begged me for release.

Those moments between us felt like the best kind of secret—his knuckles white as he gripped the headboard. Every jagged groan, the hushed vowels of *god, Luke, please, Luke*. This man owned me—mind, body and soul—so I appreciated every chance I had to turn the tables a little.

In true Elijah Knight fashion, he'd spent the morning making me come so hard I'm pretty sure I saw the rings of fucking Saturn. The tables were officially *turned*. So I was hoping what happened next might do the trick.

"Come on," I said, tugging him toward the shoreline. "I've got something to show you."

His lips twitched. "You look like you're about to cause some trouble."

"That's my natural state."

A smile flashed. "Don't I know it."

We ditched our sandals and waded into the soft foam, both of us quiet as crabs scuttled past. A trio of seagulls squawked overhead, and Elijah's hand tightened around mine.

"You look nervous," he said softly.

My heart lodged in the back of my throat. "And you know me too well."

He chuckled. Squeezed my hand again. "You've never been good at hiding your emotions, Lucas. It's one of the reasons why I love you so much."

Three years in, and I still blushed every time he said *I love you*. "All this time, I thought I was cultivating a sexy and enigmatic air of mystery."

He shook his head, eyes sparkling. "Never. You're a wide-open window."

I dropped my gaze to the water swirling around our feet, feeling stripped bare by Elijah's sweet attention. This also still happened three years in—feeling endlessly undone by him *seeing* me, the way no one else had seen me before. It made the words I'd practiced for this moment scramble around in my brain, turning haphazard and chaotic.

"I always..." I stopped, cleared my throat. "I always knew that when I finally did this, I'd do it in the ocean." I cast my gaze up to meet his, watched his brow furrow as he listened. "I thought it'd be romantic, to have a reminder right outside our window every morning. To feel it every time I surfed, every time we strolled the beach like this."

He swallowed hard. "When you did what?"

Every word I'd ruthlessly memorized these past few weeks went up like a puff of smoke. I stopped. Pressed up onto my toes and kissed Elijah, a soft, lingering kiss that made everything I wanted to say seem paltry in comparison.

I dropped to one knee in the wet sand. Took Elijah's hand and looked up to find him visibly stunned.

"Luke," he said hoarsely. "What are you..."

"I have spent every single moment we've been together being so in love with you I can hardly see straight," I said, voice already shaky. "I dreamed of finding someone like you, of finding a love like this, but didn't expect it to happen. Didn't think I *deserved* it, Elijah. And yet, against all odds, we've spent the past three years together and I've somehow managed not to annoy you to death."

And—oh god—tears were already spilling over and my throat was closing up. But there was Elijah, with shining eyes and a face filled with so much devotion I forgot how to breathe.

"You could never...never annoy me to death," he said roughly. "All I want is you, Luke. You're all I've *ever* wanted, from the first moment we met. Sometimes I don't..."

"What?" I asked, tears tracking down my cheeks.

He blew out a breath, like he was trying to steady himself. "I love you so much I don't know where to put it. It feels so *big*. I'm worried you'll think I'm obsessed."

I laughed. Swiped a hand across my eyes. "Right back atcha, sweetheart."

I reached into my pocket, and my fingers closed around the ring. Bringing it into the light, I heard Elijah's sharp intake of breath. Watched his chest shudder and felt his hand start to tremble. "I wouldn't be the person I am today without you, Elijah. You're my handsome shield, my sweetest heart, the person I would follow to the ends of the earth."

Elijah fell to his knees in front of me, the water

splashing around us both. But I didn't feel cold or damp, didn't feel the sand biting into my knee. I did feel the warmth of Elijah's lips as they caressed my knuckles. Did feel his calloused palm, cupping my cheek.

And when our eyes met, I said, "I want nothing more than to spend the rest of my life with you. Would you marry me, Elijah Knight?"

"*Yes,*" he choked out. "Yes, and *please*."

I didn't even get a chance to slide the ring on before he was yanking me to his chest and crashing our lips together. It was hot and rough, our lips salty from tears, both of us smiling so broadly it was hard to keep our mouths connected.

"Wait, wait. I have to put the ring on your finger," I said, laughing, and grabbed his hand.

"I love you," he said. "Luke, I love you so fucking much."

The ring slid on perfectly. I looked up as peace and relief washed over me, staring at the man who'd turned my life upside down in the best way possible.

"I love you"—I kissed him—"so much." Another kiss. "More than anything in this world. And now you have someplace to put all that extra love."

One eyebrow raised. "Into seducing my husband?"

I hummed as I nuzzled his cheek. "*Husband.* I like the sound of that."

He traced his fingers along my face, like he was memorizing its shape. "If I could marry you tomorrow, I would."

I opened my mouth to respond when there came a shriek from the beach. Elijah turned, eyes narrowed in confusion.

"Who is that?" he asked.

I smiled. Shrugged. Slowly pulled us both to stand and

raised a hand to wave. "Hmmm, I'm not sure. What say we go investigate?"

With much less trepidation—and a lot more relief—I tugged Elijah back toward the lighthouse. A small head poked around the side and yelled, "Did you say yes, Uncle Eli?"

Elijah looked stunned for a second time. His nephew, Sky, came barreling toward him holding a bouquet of balloons. Behind him ran Christopher and Shana, holding the twins, as well as Harriet, Rory, Lizzie and Preston. And after that, more friends, more family, every person who'd loved us and showered us with support whenever we'd needed it. They brought flowers and streamers, food and music, hammocks and beach chairs.

A surprise party, for a surprise engagement, for the man who deserved to feel loved by his community most of all.

Elijah laughed as he knelt to pick up Sky. "I did say yes."

The crowd cheered, and I was vaguely aware of my loved ones crowding around us, hugging and squeezing us both.

We had eyes only for each other though. I winked at my former bodyguard turned boyfriend—now *fiancé!*—and watched him smile like he'd just won the lottery.

"There's no turning back now," I said. "You're stuck with me."

Elijah leaned in for a kiss. "Anything for you, my liege."

THE END (again!)

(ANOTHER) NOTE FROM THE AUTHOR

Hiya, readers!

Thank you *so very much* for reading FREE FALL. Readers who follow me online got a front row seat to my deep and horny devotion to Luke Beaumont and Elijah Knight while writing their story. These two hooked into my heart and dragged me to their happily-ever-after with so much fierce tenderness. They taught me so much about craft, about the balance between suspense and romance, while letting me have fun with my favorite elements of the bodyguard trope: the stern and stoic protector who's secretly *soft* and just wants to be held. The flirty, reckless client who pretends he *doesn't* want to be safe when really all he's ever *wanted* is for someone to keep him safe!!

And they taught me so much about myself, for which I am forever grateful.

I've got a few special folks to thank for this one. I owe a debt to Sarah MacLean's "Mastering the Art of Conflict" class, which helped me keep Luke and Elijah balanced on the knifepoint of delicious tension while allowing them to stretch, grow, poke and prod each other. It truly rewired my brain, craft-wise, and I've got this story to show for it.

A huge thank you to my dear friend Jodi, who is actually from Long Island, and was *so beautifully patient* in walking me through the best ways to create a fictional Hamptons that was playful and flexible while also honoring some of its truest parts. I mentioned it up at the top, but Cape Avalon is an entirely fictional village in the town of (real) East Hampton and the majority of the town/village names and landmarks were similarly invented so that the location and plot could work together more effectively.

I was consuming a lot of media about queer and trans history while writing this book—specifically the *Making Gay History* podcast, which is so tender and beautiful. I put in a little nod to bisexual pioneer Stella Rush and named Luke and Preston's foundation after her. From the podcast: "Stella Rush (aka Sten Russel) was ahead of her time, defying the binaries (gay/straight/butch/femme) that defined the lives of women in the mid-twentieth century and resisting society's expectations—marriage, kids. She took a huge risk by writing for *ONE* magazine while working as a civil servant at the peak of the Lavender Scare. (If discovered, she would almost certainly have been fired.)"

My favorite moments in this book are *many*: when Elijah *smiles at Luke for the first time!!!!*; "my liege" and "sweetheart"; Elijah inhaling Luke's neck in the bookstore; Luke's flirty, semi-himbo, disaster bisexual energy that is also 100% my personality; when Luke rescues Elijah in the ocean and then tenderly cares for his wounds by the fire (!!!!!!!!!); when Elijah rescues Luke and says "you have the man that I love chained to a bathroom sink"; Luke baking Elijah a cookie cake!!!; Luke's "dark night of the soul" realizations while he was kidnapped; Elijah being like "I'm gonna John Wick this town to find my man!"...

And that kiss when Elijah rescues Luke in the bathroom. That kiss! THAT KISS!! Romance authors live and *breathe* for a scene like that, and I certainly did.

I had a *lot* of fun telling this story—and I hope you had equally as much fun reading it. My wish for all of you is a little extra whimsy in your big, full life. Enjoy the mess *and* the miracles.

With love from Cape Avalon,
Kathryn

ACKNOWLEDGMENTS

I'm incredibly grateful to be surrounded by some of the best human beings in the world. So I'm sending all of my messy and whimsical love to the following people who made FREE FALL possible:

To Faith, my best friend, editor and soul bro—your absolute excitement over Luke and Elijah made drafting this story so much more fun. You're the queen of my heart and I'd find you in any timeline, dude! (affectionate)

To Jessica Snyder, my story editor and details genius! You push me every time to make my stories bigger, better and more nuanced. FREE FALL wouldn't be the same without you.

To Julia, Jodi and Bronwyn, my incredible beta readers—thank you so much for reading this story early and helping Luke and Elijah shine. Working with you on these projects is such a privilege and I treasure it every single time.

To Joyce and Tammy, for making me smile and laugh every day. You are both absolute *gems*. To Tracey and Laura—your sweet love and kindness makes this world a better place (and you always keep me afloat when I'm struggling). I truly couldn't do it without you. The same goes for Avery, my favorite person to float with in big water while brainstorming and daydreaming! Our happy hours always make me feel so loved and affirmed.

To the incomparable Score sisters, Lucy and Madison—

you two are such bright lights in this community (and my life), and writing wouldn't be nearly as much fun if I didn't have you around, making us all laugh. As always, to the whole team at TWSS, for running so many behind-the-scenes tasks I can't even list them all. Y'all are just the best.

And to the Hippie Chicks—you've held me close and supported me so much this year. I can never say *thank you* enough.

Always, always, always for Rob—you've taught me so much about reaching for joy and living our lives like happy dogs running down a beach. I'm down to chase sunsets together forever if you are.

HANG OUT WITH KATHRYN!

Sign up for my newsletter and receive exclusive content, bonus scenes and more!
I've got a reader group on Facebook called **Kathryn Nolan's Hippie Chicks**. We're all about motivation, girl power, sexy short stories and empowerment! Come join us.

Let's be friends on
Website: authorkathrynnolan.com
Instagram at: kathrynnolanromance
Facebook at: KatNolanRomance
Follow me on BookBub
Follow me on Amazon

ABOUT KATHRYN

Kathryn Nolan (she/they) is an Amazon Top 25 bestselling author. Her steamy romance novels are known for their slow-burn sexual tension, memorable characters, and big, hopeful feelings.

Kathryn is a bisexual bookworm and femme cutie with big Leo energy. They love to spend their free time hiking, camping and traveling. When not on the road, they live in their hometown of Philly with their cute husband and giant-eared rescue pup, Walter.

Sign up for Kathryn's weekly newsletter to see what she's writing, what she's reading/watching and get all her travel stories (plus an abundance of Walter photos!):

https://www.authorkathrynnolan.com/join-my-newsletter

BOOKS BY KATHRYN

BOHEMIAN

LANDSLIDE

RIPTIDE

STRICTLY PROFESSIONAL

NOT THE MARRYING KIND

SEXY SHORTS

BEHIND THE VEIL

UNDER THE ROSE

IN THE CLEAR

WILD OPEN HEARTS

ON THE ROPES

OUT OF THE BLUE

RIVAL RADIO

OFF THE MARK

KEEP YOU BOTH

FREE FALL

Made in the USA
Middletown, DE
08 January 2025

68982120R00224